I Got a Story to Tell, Tale, Tail

Some Lies, Some Truths, Some Make Believe

Short Stories & Poems

I Got a Story to Tell, Tale, Tail

SHORT STORIES & POEMS

All the stories will end in trauma, murder, or triumph.

———

*Everyone Has a Story
The Lies They Tell, Tale, Tail
What's Your Story???*

———

A. Lee

Published by Creative Love Network Press
CreativeLoveNetwork.com

I Got a Story to Tell, Tale, Tail
© 2025 A. Lee
ISBN: 978-1-961523-07-4 (paperback)
ISBN: 978-1-961523-11-1 (ebook)

First Edition, 2025

To request permissions, you may contact the Publisher at
Info@CreativeLoveNetwork.com

Printed in the United States of America.

Cover design by A. Lee & Emily Anne Evans
Layout design by Emily Anne Evans
Edited by Maria Duarte

*To the storytellers who dare to embrace
vulnerability, to the dreamers who transform
pain into purpose, and to every soul yearning
to be heard—may your words find their way
to the page and inspire the world. This is for
those who carry untold stories in their hearts,
waiting for the courage to speak, and for those
who have faced life's storms yet still choose
to create. Let this book be a light of hope,
a reminder that your voice matters, and a
testament to the power of sharing your truth.
May you find the strength to uncover your
passion, the bravery to write your journey, and
the freedom to let your soul shine through
every word you create. This dedication is for the
resilient, the bold, and the hopeful—your story
is waiting, and the world is ready to listen.*

Contents
Italic title indicates poetry

3   *3 Part Stories*

PART ONE: **I Got a Story to Tell**

7   **The First Whisper**

8   *Knowing the First Whisper*

10   **The Ripple Effect**

11   *The Ripple Effect*

13   **Mysterious Discovery Unearthed at Former Home of Broken Engagement**

19   *Betrayal and Trust*

21   **Curiosity Leads to Silence**

25   *Curiosity Leads to Silence*

27   **The Gathering Storm**

34   *Premonition*

39   **Suppressed feelings**

42   *Suppressed Feelings*

44   **Embracing the Past**

48   *Embracing the Past*

49   **Shedding Skin**

52   *The Weight of Her Tears*

PART TWO: **I Got a Story to Tale**

57   **Fairy Tale**

60   *Fairytale's*

62   **Forgiveness of Self**

68   *Forgiveness of self*

70 **Lost**

73 *Lost Child*

74 **Finding My Voice**

77 *Finding My Voice*

79 **"She Used to Love it Here"**

83 *She used to Love it here*

85 **By Design**

87 *By design*

89 **Broken pieces of a shattered heart**

91 *Broken pieces of a shattered heart*

93 **Inside Out**

97 *Looking outside of myself*

99 **What separates us as people?**

103 *Divided*

105 **Trigger Warning**

108 *Trigger Warning*

110 **Natural Women**

113 *Natural Women*

115 **Unexpressive**

120 *Unexpressive*

122 **The Power of Connection**

126 *The Power of Connection*

128 **Journey to Self-Love**

130 *Journey to Self-Love*

132 **Exploring Connections**

134 *Exploring Connections*

136 **Second Chance**

138 *The electric symmetry of the ocean waves clear sky's great times it was all a blur*

140 **The Great Divide**

145 *The great divide*

146 *Ancestors*

PART THREE: **I Got a Story to Tail**

151 **In the Dark**

153 *In the Dark*

155 **Kinda Sorta**

157 *Kinda Sorta Wrong v. Right*

159 **Don't**

161 *Don't*

162 **Journey**

165 *A Feast of Creation*

166 **Hard Life**

168 *Rock Bottom*

170 **Precipitating Factors**

172 *Precipitating Factors*

174 **Blame**

178 *1977*

181 **Happy**

183 *Happy*

185 **Hurt**

187 *Hurt*

189 **Unbreakable**

190 *Unbreakable*

191 **Misplaced rage**

192 *The Weight of Misplaced Rage*

194 **Turning Pain into Purpose**

197 *Turning Pain into Purpose*

199 **The great pretender**

202 *The great pretender*

204 **After the Pain**

207 *After the Pain*

208 **Consumed by Remorse**

211 *Consumed by remorse*

213 **Pressure**

216 *Pressure*

217 **Over**

221 *Over*

223 **Trauma bond**

229 *Trauma bond*

231 **Eye's Wide Shut**

236 *Eye's Wide Shut*

238 **36 Weeks**

242 *36 Weeks*

244 **Facing Reality**

248 *Facing Reality*

250 **Broken pieces of a shattered heart**

256 *Pick Up the Pieces*

258 **Glamorous Life**

261 *Glamorous Life*

263 **Breaking the Silence: Rising from Pain to Purpose**

266 *Rising from Pain to Purpose*

267 **Flash Backs of the Past**

271 *Flash Backs*

273 **Where I'm From**

276 *Where I'm From*

278 *History*

281 **Never Compromised**

287 *Never Compromised*

289 **Never comparing**

293 *Intoxicating*

294 **Hidden Truths**

300 *Elucidate*

302 **Intoxicating Soul**

309 *Intoxicating Soul Elixir*

311 **Self-Doubt**

314 *Words Unspoken*

316 **Twin**

321 *Twin Whispers: A Journey to Balance*

323 **Tailspin**

330 *Holiness*

333 ENDING OF **I Got a Story to Tell, Tale, Tail**

335 *Your Story Awaits*

I Got a Story to Tell, Tale, Tail

Some Lies, Some Truths, Some Make Believe

Short Stories & Poems

3 Part Stories

In words, we craft a three-part tale,
A journey through time, we all set sail.

With tails of wonder and wisdom's grace,
These stories we tell, a wondrous embrace.

The first part, "tell," is where we begin,
With voices and words,
we let our tale's spin.

In language's dance,
we shape the thought,
In sentences and paragraphs,
it's carefully wrought.

But "tail" as a verb, a twist in our song,
Like a fox's sly move,
it doesn't take long.

It weaves through the narrative,
in subtle display,
Adding layers of meaning
in its own special way.

Now, the third part, a tale within this rhyme,
In the ever-shifting sands of linguistic time.

So, remember well, as these words twirl and swirl,
The nuances of "tell" and "tail" in their intricate twirl.

In the vast canvases of our shared tongue,
These words find their place,
where they've always belonged.
In stories we tell, in tails we unveil,

A play on words, a linguistic trail.
A Play on Words
I Got A Story To Tell, Tale, tale

PART ONE

I Got a Story to Tell

The First Whisper

A small voice inside me urged me to share my story with the world. At first, I hesitated, feeling the weight of vulnerability and the fear of judgment. But the whisper grew louder and more insistent. Soon, it was a cacophony of memories, lessons, and experiences that refused to remain silent.

It all started with a single whisper, a soft and delicate sound that echoed through the depths of my mind. At first, I barely noticed it, too preoccupied with the noise and chaos of everyday life. But as the days passed, the whisper grew louder and more persistent, like a gentle tug at my heartstrings.

I didn't know what to make of it at first, but as I listened more closely, I realized that the whisper was trying to tell me something. It was urging me to share my story with the world, to break the silence and speak out about the things that had happened to me directly and indirectly. The things I witness or have heard that happened to people in my life as well.

At first, I resisted the urge. The thought of opening up about my deepest fears and insecurities was terrifying, and I worried that people would judge me or think less of me because of my past. But as the whisper grew stronger, I began to realize that staying silent was no longer an option.

And so, tentatively at first, I began to share my story. I started small, talking to close friends and family members about the things that had happened to me. It wasn't easy, and there were times when I felt like giving up. But every time I spoke out, the whisper grew louder and more powerful, pushing me to keep going.

Over time, I began to see the impact that my words were having on others. People would come up to me after I spoke and tell me how much my story had inspired them, how it had given them the courage to speak out about their own experiences. And every time I heard those words, the whisper grew even louder.

Now, I realize that the whisper was never meant to be silenced. It was a call to action, a reminder that our stories have the power to change lives. And so, I will continue to speak out, to share my story with anyone who will listen. Because in the end, the whisper was not just my own – it was the voice of all those who have been silenced, urging us to break free from the chains of shame and fear and stand tall in our truth.

Knowing the First Whisper

It began as a feather, a soundless breath,
A whisper weaving through silence and depth.
Barely a murmur, a thought undefined,
Yet it lingered, persistent, within my mind.

The world roared loud with its chaos and din,
But the whisper insisted, its song from within.
"Speak," it implored, "for your voice is the key,
To unshackle the silenced, to set truth free."

I turned away, afraid to expose,
The fractures, the shadows, the scars I'd composed.
Yet the whisper grew fierce, no longer so small,
A tempest of purpose, a clarion call.

Tentative words became steady streams,
Carrying the weight of my fears and dreams.
I spoke of wounds, of battles endured,
Of pain once hidden, now finally cured.

And in the speaking, I saw the spark,
In others' eyes, once lost in the dark.
The ripple began, from one to the next,
A shared understanding, unspoken text.

Each voice added strength, each whisper a song,
A symphony rising where we all belong.
The stories we carried, once buried, concealed,
Became the foundation of wounds being healed.

Knowing the first whisper was never just mine,
It was woven from threads of the human design.
A history shared, both fragile and strong,
Each thread a note in a resounding song.

Now the whisper is thunder, unyielding, profound,
Breaking the chains where silence was bound.
For every voice lifted, another will find,
The courage to speak and leave fear behind.

So, listen closely, to the whisper's start,
It carries the weight of a million hearts.
And know as you share, your voice will ignite,
A inspiration of hope, piercing the night.

The Ripple Effect

As I continued to share my story, the ripple effect became apparent. It was like dropping a pebble into a calm pond, and the ripples of my words spread far and wide, touching the lives of people I had never met.

One evening, as I stood in front of a small audience, recounting my experiences and the lessons I had learned, I noticed a woman in the crowd. Her eyes were filled with tears, and her face was a mixture of pain and hope. After I finished speaking, she approached me with a trembling smile. "Thank you," she said softly, her voice quivering. "Your story... it's so similar to mine. I thought I was alone, that no one would understand. But hearing you speak, it's like you were telling my story too."

In that moment, I realized the true power of sharing our stories. It wasn't just about catharsis for ourselves; it was about connecting with others who had experienced similar pain, struggle, and triumph. It was about creating a community of survivors, a network of support that extended beyond the boundaries of our individual lives.

As weeks turned into months, I received messages from people all over who had been touched by my story. Some shared their own experiences, while others simply expressed their gratitude for shedding light on the dark corners of life. It was humbling and awe-inspiring to see how the whisper that had started within me had resonated with so many.

But with this newfound connection came a responsibility. The whisper had grown into a chorus, and it was no longer just about my story; it was about the collective stories of resilience, courage, and healing. I felt a deep sense of duty to continue speaking out, to be a voice for those who were still struggling to find theirs.

The ripple effect continued to spread, and the small voice that had once been a whisper was now a symphony of voices, echoing in unison. Together, we were breaking down the walls of silence and shame, replacing them with a choir of shared experiences and empathy.

And so, I journeyed onward, carrying the stories of others with me, amplifying their voices alongside mine. The first whisper had ignited a fire within me, a burning determination to make a difference in the lives of those who had been silenced for far too long. Each chapter of my story became a steppingstone on this path of healing and empowerment, as we all learned that our voices, no matter how soft they may start, have the power to change the world.

The Ripple Effect

I dropped a pebble into a pond, A quiet act,
a trembling hand.
The water stirred, a gentle wave,
Its reach unknown, its course unplanned.

My story poured, a whispered plea,
A tale of pain, of breaking free.
The ripples danced, they stretched and grew,
Until they touched my heart.

In a crowd, her eyes found mine,
A mirror of her wounds a glimpse of time.
She spoke in tones both soft and shy,
"Your story's aligned with mine."

And there it was—the truth revealed,
Our shared despair, a bond that healed.
What once was silence now was sound,
A harmony of lives unbound.

The waves kept moving, far and wide,
From soul to soul, from tide to tide.
Each tear, each word, a sacred spark,
A light that glimmered in the dark.

The chorus rose, no longer lone,
Each voice a note, a stronger tone.
Together breaking shame's tight hold,
A harmony both fierce and bold.

I carried stories not just mine,
A whirlwind of pain connected.
The ripples turned to roaring seas,
Of empathy, of love's decrees.

So cast your pebbles, soft or small,
For even whispers can captivate a memory.
A single story, shared and true,
Can change the world for me, for you.

Mysterious Discovery Unearthed at Former Home of Broken Engagement

Terry and Alex's journey towards a perfect life together takes an unexpected turn when Alex's estranged daughter, Vanessa, and her young son, Jacob, suddenly reappear in their lives. As they prepare for their upcoming wedding, Terry finds herself questioning everything she thought she knew about her fiancé.

Vanessa and Jacob move into their new home, and Terry attempts to maintain peace in the household. However, a growing sense of unease creeps over her.

Vanessa's flirtatious behavior with Alex raises red flags, leaving Terry to wonder if there's more to their relationship than meets the eye. The dream of a harmonious family life is overshadowed by the mysterious presence of Alex's newfound family.

As Terry embarks on a quest for answers, she stumbles upon hidden truths that could shatter her world. With her trust in Alex wavering, Terry must confront the uncomfortable reality or continue living a lie. As the wedding date approaches, tensions escalate, and the strength of their relationships is put to the test. Can Terry and Alex overcome the obstacles threatening their happily ever after, or will the truth tear them apart?

As the weeks passed and the wedding date drew nearer, tensions in the household continued to rise. Terry couldn't shake the feeling that something was off about Vanessa and Jacob's sudden reappearance in their lives. Late one evening, after putting Jacob to bed, Terry decided it was time to confront Alex about her suspicions.

She couldn't help but wonder about the dynamics in her own home. One evening, as the wedding preparations continued, Terry decided it was time to have a candid conversation with Alex about her concerns. She found him in the study, going through old photo albums. "Alex," she began tentatively, "we need to talk."

Alex looked up from the album, concern in his eyes. "Of course, Terry. What's on your mind?"

Terry hesitated for a moment before speaking her thoughts aloud. "It's about Vanessa and Jacob. I understand they're your family, but it feels like they're taking over our lives. The wedding is just around the corner, and they've been living here for three months now. I'm having doubts, Alex, and it's making me question whether we should go through with this."

Alex sighed, putting the album aside. "Terry, I know this situation is difficult, and I should have been more transparent from the beginning. I never meant to hide them from you. But I also can't just kick Vanessa and Jacob out of our lives now. They're family, and they need our support."

Terry nodded, her expression softening. "I understand that, Alex, but it's not just about them being here. It's about the way they behave around you. Jacob always calling you 'pop pop,' and Vanessa's flirtatious behavior, it's unnerving. Can you see why I'm concerned?"

Alex looked thoughtful for a moment before speaking. "I see your point, Terry, and I promise I'll talk to Vanessa about her behavior. As for Jacob, he's just a toddler; that's how he's been raised. But I'll make an effort to set boundaries."

Relieved that Alex was willing to address her concerns, Terry gave him a small smile. "Thank you, Alex. I appreciate your understanding."

In the days that followed, Alex had a heartfelt conversation with Vanessa, explaining that her behavior was causing strain in their relationship. Vanessa, although initially defensive, eventually understood and promised to respect their boundaries.

As the wedding day drew closer, the atmosphere at home worsted. Terry felt reassured that Alex hadn't taken her concerns seriously, but she hoped that their love would prevail over the challenges they'd faced. She was willing to give their relationship a chance.

Terry walked into the living room and witnessed a scene that would shatter her trust completely. She saw Alex and Vanessa in an intimate embrace, their lips locked in a passionate kiss. The sight left Terry stunned, her heart pounding with betrayal. Terry snapped backed to reality and yelled it's just days before the wedding.

Terry quickly backed away, her mind racing. She couldn't believe what she had just seen. Her doubts and suspicions had finally been confirmed, and she was faced with an impossible decision. She confronted Alex and Vanessa immediately, the truth had been unveiled, and Terry's world was now in turmoil.

Terry confronted them with a mix of anger, hurt, and disbelief. "What the hell is going on here?!" she yelled, her voice trembling. Alex and Vanessa pulled apart, their faces pale with guilt. Vanessa stammered, "Terry, I... we didn't mean for you to see that." Alex, too, looked ashamed as he said, "Terry, I can explain."

Terry's hands were shaking, but she demanded an explanation. "Explain? Explain what, Alex? Are you two... having an affair? Is that what's been going on all this time?" Alex looked down, unable to meet Terry's eyes. "It's not that simple, Terry. Vanessa and I have a history, a complicated one. I never told you because I thought it was all in the past."

Terry couldn't believe what she was hearing. "A history? What kind of history?" Vanessa stepped in; her voice filled with remorse. "Terry, I'm Alex's ex-wife. We divorced years ago, and I left with Jacob. But recently, we reconnected, and things got complicated. I didn't want to come between you two, but I couldn't stay away from Alex."

Terry's world was crumbling around her. The man she was about to marry had been keeping such a significant secret from her, and the woman who was supposed to be her stepdaughter had betrayed her trust in the worst way possible. Tears welled up in Terry's eyes as she whispered, "I can't believe this, Alex. You lied to me."

Alex reached out to Terry; his voice filled with desperation. "Terry, I love you, and I never wanted any of this to happen. I should have been honest with you from the beginning, and I'm so sorry."

Terry pulled away from his touch. "Sorry isn't enough, Alex. You've broken my trust, and I don't know if I can ever forgive you for this."

Vanessa chimed in, her voice trembling. "Terry, please understand that I never wanted to hurt you. I still love Alex, but I never meant for things to go this far."

Terry felt a whirlwind of emotions, but she knew she needed time to process everything. "I need some space, both of you. This wedding is off, at least for now."

As Terry retreated to her room, she was left with a shattered heart and a future that felt uncertain. The truth had torn her perfect life apart, and she had to decide whether to try and salvage her relationship with Alex or walk away from it all.

Terry went back and forth on if she should continue the relationship and marry Alex. Terry replayed the many conversations she had with Alex regrading the situation giving Alex plenty of chances to tell her the truth.

• • •

The day of the wedding arrived, with a mixture of nerves and excitement in the air. Terry had flashbacks of the incident when she went upstairs to talk with Vanessa and witnessed Alex kissing Vanessa Terry flashed back to her unease that had been growing ever since the day Vanessa and Jacob had arrived unannounced. Her initial shock at discovering that Alex had a daughter and grandson he'd never mentioned had turned into a constant feeling of uncertainty.

Terry thought to herself I was such a fool he told me the same lie each time and I choose to believe him. Terry yelled I'm done the wedding is off. Terry asked to speak with Alex and Vanessa and informed both of them that the wedding was off, and they both had 30 days to leave her house which they both agreed to do. Terry resided in the house for a few months after they left but found herself in tears from all the memories and decided to put the house on the market. Terry found a great family to purchase the house and they accepted all of her demands. Terry instructed the new buyers not to change anything about the property and they agreed. 5 years later the family kids went off to college and they decided to sell to a real-estate investor. The house went under construction for a remodel and when the contractors dug-up the pool the immediately called the local police department helicopters were ever where the local new stations. Breaking news spread like wildfire: "Mysterious Discovery Unearthed." The entire neighborhood buzzed with speculation, and Terry's heart sank as she watched the events unfold on the news from her new apartment.

• • •

The police had cordoned off the area around the house, and forensic experts were brought in to investigate. The news anchors talked excitedly about the possibility of a long-lost treasure or even a buried body, but no one knew for sure what had been uncovered. Terry couldn't help but be curious, so she decided to visit the scene in a disguise. As she approached the house, she saw a crowd of onlookers and reporters gathered outside the police tape. A detective flashed her ID to the officer on duty, who allowed her through. Terry felt a strange mix of emotions as she looked onto the property she had once called home.

The construction workers were still gathered around the uncovered pool, nervously chatting amongst themselves. The detective approached the foreman, a burly man with a puzzled expression on his face. "What did you find?" she asked anxiously. The foreman turned to the detective and said, "You won't believe it, but we found a chest buried at the bottom of the pool." He pointed to the hole in the ground where the chest had been lifted out by a crane. It was a beautifully crafted wooden chest, covered in ornate carvings and with a heavy padlock securing it shut.

The detective heart raced as she stared at the chest. She couldn't help but wonder what secrets it might hold. Terry remembered the years she had spent in that house and the lies that had torn her life apart. Could this chest hold the key to the truth she had been searching for?

$$\cdots$$

The police had taken the chest into custody, and an onlooker spent hours at the station answering questions about her time in the house. She told them everything she knew about Alex and Vanessa, the previous owners, and her own experiences there. She couldn't help but hope that the chest might contain evidence of their deception.

Days turned into weeks as forensic experts carefully examined both chest and its contents. The media frenzy continued, with speculation about the chest's origins and its potential historical significance. Terry grew anxious, unable to concentrate on anything else. She knew she had to wait for the experts to reveal their findings.

Finally, after what felt like an eternity, the police held a press conference to announce the contents of the chest. The detective along with reporters and curious onlookers, gathered to hear the revelation. The lead investigator stepped up to the podium and cleared his throat. "Inside the chest," he began, "we found a collection of old letters, photographs, and journals. It appears to be a time capsule of sorts, documenting the lives of the previous owners, Alex and Vanessa." The second chest contained two unidentified bodies buried.

Terry's heart sank. She had hoped for evidence of their lies, but it seemed that the chest contained only memories. The investigator continued, "These documents shed light on the couple's history and their love story, but there is also an indication of any foul play and deception." Terry's disappointment was palpable, but she couldn't help feeling a strange sense of closure. The truth may not have been what she expected, but at least she had some answers about the mysterious chest.

As the media frenzy did not die down and the house became a crime scene, Terry realized that she needed to let go of the past completely. She had spent enough time dwelling on what could have been. It was time to move forward and focus on building a new life for herself, free from the weight of broken promises and buried secrets.

With a heavy heart, she turned away from the house that had once been her home and walked towards a brighter future, ready to embrace whatever adventures lay ahead. She went back to her apartment collected her passport and took a plane to a country far away and was never heard from again. The investigation still remains open.

Betrayal and Trust

In the love's triangle,
lies a thread of secrets,
a heart to deceive.
words unspoken,
shadows that shift,
a bond once sturdy begins to rip.

Terry's voice, trembling yet strong,
unearthed a tale hidden too long.
Vanessa, Jacob—what's their place?
Why does guilt linger upon your face?"

Alex, weary, burdened by shame,
spoke of a past life in a different name.
Vanessa, not daughter of his blood,
Jacob, a grandson, not quite understood.

"Oh, Alex," she cried, her trust torn in two,
why keep from me what is simply true?
Love demands more than lies and disguise.
It craves a foundation, not riddled with lies."

His eyes held sorrow, his hands reached out,
"I feared the truth, plagued by doubt.
But now I see; to mend this divide,
we must face the storm, side by side."

In the days of reckoning, wounds laid bare,
they rebuilt a love with tender care.
Forgiveness was thorny, the path unclears,
yet they chose to walk it, shedding fear.

For betrayal and trust are twin flames that burn,
from ashes of sorrow, to lessons we learn.
The road to honesty is never smooth,
But hearts that endure find love to soothe.

So let this tale be a lesson through shadows of wrong,
to the dawn of right. For even in brokenness,
love can heal, when truth becomes the bond, we seal.

Terry tried to endure the pain, love was lost
Fear of betrayal clouded her mind
She snapped & broken by all the lies
A plan was constructed in her mind
The only why to heal is if they all die

Lives were lost because of lies
Never allow truth to hide
No one wins when hurt feelings are involved
Tell your truth and let them decide

Curiosity Leads to Silence

Monique was known throughout the neighborhood as the go-to person for all the latest gossip and juicy tidbits about everyone's lives. She had an uncanny ability to always be in someone's business and to know exactly what was going on at any given moment. Monique's friends often joked that she had a sixth sense for neighborhood drama.

Monique's daily routine always started the same way. She would pick up her phone, dial a friend's number, and as soon as they answered, she'd excitedly proclaim, "I got something to tell you!" or "You won't believe what I heard!" Her tales of neighborhood intrigue were filled with details that no one else seemed to know, and her laughter was contagious.

Monique's knack for gathering and sharing information made her the life of the neighborhood. She was always invited to parties and gatherings, and her presence ensured that there was never a dull moment. People loved her stories and couldn't wait to hear what she would uncover next.

Her talent for uncovering secrets and her insatiable curiosity were deeply rooted in her personality and upbringing. She had always been an inquisitive soul, even as a child. Growing up, she had a knack for observing the world around her, always asking questions, and seeking answers. As a teenager, Monique's natural curiosity evolved into a passion for understanding the lives and stories of those around her. She found herself drawn to the drama and intrigue that unfolded within her neighborhood. It wasn't just about gossip for Monique; it was a way of connecting with people and feeling like she belonged. She genuinely cared about her neighbors and wanted to know what was happening in their lives.

Monique's daily routine of sharing the latest gossip was not born out of malice or a desire to harm others but rather a genuine enthusiasm for life's twists and turns. She reveled in the excitement of being the one who brought news to her friends, often feeling like the neighborhood's storyteller, weaving narratives that made everyday life more captivating.

Her friends appreciated her for knowing the neighborhood drama they appreciated her for it. Monique's laughter and animated storytelling brought joy to gatherings, turning mundane moments into unforgettable experiences. People loved to have her around because they knew she would always make them laugh and keep them entertained.

Yet, beneath Monique's vivacious exterior, there was a vulnerability. She was aware that her obsession with gathering and sharing information had its downsides. She sometimes felt like an outsider, observing life from the sidelines rather than fully participating. There were moments when she wondered if her friends valued her for who she was or just for the stories she brought.

However, one sunny afternoon, Monique's curiosity got the best of her. She had heard whispers about a secret meeting happening in the woods behind Mr. Johnson's house. Monique couldn't resist the temptation to find out what it was all about. She quietly made her way through the dense trees, careful not to be seen.

As she reached a clearing, Monique peered through the bushes and witnessed something she had never expected. It was Mr. Johnson, along with several other neighbors, gathered in a circle. They were all wearing cloaks and holding candles, and there was an eerie silence in the air. Monique's heart pounded in her chest as she watched in shock.

Suddenly, they began to chant in a language she couldn't understand, and the ground beneath them seemed to tremble. Monique couldn't believe her eyes. She had stumbled upon some sort of secret ritual, and it sent shivers down her spine. She knew she shouldn't have been snooping around, but it was too late now.

Terrified and unsure of what to do, Monique accidentally stepped on a twig, causing it to snap loudly. The neighbors turned towards the noise, their faces contorted with anger and surprise. Monique's heart raced as she realized she had been caught.

Without a moment's hesitation, she turned and sprinted back through the woods, leaves and branches whipping at her as she ran. She didn't stop until she reached her own house, breathless and shaken. Her days of prying into others' business were over.

Monique realized that some things were best left undiscovered, and that her insatiable curiosity had led her into a situation she could never have imagined. From that day forward, she never shared another neighborhood secret or tried to uncover someone else's business. She had learned the hard way that there were things in the world better left unspoken, and she was content to live a quieter, more peaceful life, far away from the world of gossip and intrigue.

In the days that followed her harrowing encounter in the woods, Monique found herself in a peculiar situation. The very thing that had made her so popular, her ability to uncover secrets and gossip, had become a burden she couldn't bear. She felt a heavy weight on her shoulders, knowing she had witnessed something she couldn't explain, and she couldn't share it with anyone for fear of what might happen.

Monique's once cheerful demeanor began to fade. She withdrew from social gatherings, no longer excitedly dialing her friends' numbers with the latest scoop. Her friends noticed her change in behavior and wondered what had happened to their lively, gossip-loving friend.

One evening, as the sun set behind the houses, Monique sat alone on her porch, lost in thought. She couldn't shake the images of the secret ritual from her mind. What did it all mean? Why were her neighbors involved in something so mysterious? Her curiosity gnawed at her, but the fear of being caught again held her back.

As days turned into weeks, Monique became a recluse, spending most of her time at home. She focused on her studies, immersed herself in books, and avoided any talk of neighborhood gossip. Her friends tried to reach out, but she kept her distance, unwilling to involve them in the strange world she had stumbled upon.

One evening, a knock at her door brought her out of her self-imposed isolation. It was Sarah, her closest friend, standing on her doorstep with a concerned expression. "Monique, what's going on with you?" Sarah asked, her eyes filled with worry. "You've been so distant lately. We miss you."

Monique hesitated for a moment, then finally decided to confide in Sandra. She invited her inside, and with a heavy heart, she recounted the entire story of what she had witnessed in the woods that fateful day. Sandra listened intently, her eyes widening with each revelation. When Monique finished her tale, there was a silence that hung in the air, heavy with the weight of the secret they now shared. "I can't believe you went through all of that alone," Sandra said softly. "But now that you've told me, we need to figure out what to do. We can't just ignore something so strange happening in our neighborhood." Together, they decided to discreetly gather more information, trying to uncover the truth behind their neighbors' mysterious activities. They did research, dug through public records, and cautiously questioned other residents. As they pieced together the puzzle, they discovered that the ritual Monique had witnessed was part of an ancient neighborhood tradition meant to bring unity and prosperity. Armed with this newfound knowledge, Sandra and Monique decided to approach their neighbors and express their concerns. The neighbors, surprised that their secret had been uncovered, explained the meaning behind the ritual and assured them that it was harmless.

Over time, Monique's reputation in the neighborhood began to change. She was no longer known as the neighborhood gossip, but as the brave and resourceful young woman who had uncovered a long-held secret and brought the community closer together. People admired her courage and determination.

Monique had learned a valuable lesson about the consequences of prying into others' business, but she had also discovered the importance of standing up for what was right. Her life had taken an unexpected turn, and as she looked back on her journey, she realized that sometimes, it was better to be a seeker of truth than a spreader of gossip.

• • •

Monique's encounter in the woods that fateful day shook her to her core. It made her realize that her curiosity could lead her into dangerous territory, not just in terms of the secrets she might uncover but also in jeopardizing her relationships and trust within the community. It was a turning point in her life, prompting her to reevaluate the way she approached the world around her.

In the end, Monique's journey was one of self-discovery and growth. She learned that while it was natural to be curious about others, there were boundaries to respect and lines not to cross. Her transformation from the neighborhood's gossip queen to a seeker of truth who stood up for what was right was a testament to her character and the resilience of the human spirit.

Curiosity Leads to Silence

Beneath the sunlit days of cheer,
Where laughter echoes far and near,
Monique once thrived, a voice so loud,
A flare of stories, drawing a crowd.

Her gift, her curse—a restless ear,
The whispers of lives, both far and near.
She spun the threads of others' tales,
Painting lives in vibrant details.

Yet one fateful day, her steps were led,
To woods where whispers softly tread.
A clearing cloaked in shadowed air,
A ritual—secrets laid bare.

Candles flickered, chants arose,
The earth beneath them subtly froze.
A snap, a twig—her cover blown,
Curiosity chilled her to the bone.

She fled, her laughter now subdued,
The weight of silence in her mood.
The stories once her claim to fame,
Now carried risk, now carried shame.

No longer the queen of gossip's court,
She sought the truth of a deeper sort.
With Sarah's help, she faced her fear,
The veil of mystery growing clear.

What seemed so strange, so dark, so dire,
Held unity's spark, tradition's fire.
Neighbors' secrets, misunderstood,
Were symbols of hope, a bond for good.

From spreader of tales to truth's embrace,
Monique had found her rightful place.
No longer a watcher on the fringe,
Her soul, once restless, began to singe.

Curiosity still stirred her heart,
But now with wisdom played its part.
Respect for boundaries, trust anew,
Her voice, a whisper, strong and true.

For in the woods, she learned to see,
That life's great stories, when set free,
Are better shared with love, not strife—
A seeker of truth, she found her life.

The Gathering Storm

As the symphony of voices continued to grow, we realized that there was more we could do together than as isolated individuals. We began to organize gatherings, support groups, and events to bring survivors and allies together. It was during one such event, a community healing circle, that I witnessed the profound impact of our collective strength.

People from diverse backgrounds and experiences sat in a circle, their faces reflecting a myriad of emotions—pain, resilience, hope. Each person took their turn, sharing their story, their pain, and their triumphs. There were tears shed, but there were also tears of solidarity and understanding.

In that circle, I met Sarah, a survivor of a different kind of struggle. Her battle was with a debilitating illness that had taken away her ability to walk. As she shared her journey, it became clear that the challenges we faced were different, but the emotions we felt were strikingly similar. We both knew what it was like to confront adversity head-on and find the strength to persevere.

Sarah's story resonated with me, as did the stories of countless others in the circle. It was in that moment that I realized the true power of the collective. We were not just a ripple; we were a force of nature, a gathering storm of resilience and hope.

Inspired by our shared experiences, we decided to embark on a new mission—to create a platform where people from all walks of life could share their stories and find support. We called it "The Gathering Storm Project," a fitting name for our growing movement.

The project started small, with a website where people could submit their stories anonymously or openly. It was a space where voices that had been silenced for too long could finally find an audience, where pain could be transformed into healing, and where isolation could turn into a sense of belonging.

As the project gained momentum, we expanded our reach. We hosted workshops and seminars on storytelling and healing, empowering others to share their narratives. We partnered with organizations dedicated to supporting survivors and advocating for change.

The whisper that had begun with a single voice was now a

symphony of stories, a chorus of resilience that could no longer be ignored.

The Gathering Storm Project became a light of hope for those who had felt lost in the darkness of their own experiences. It wasn't just about sharing stories anymore; it was about creating a movement, a force for change that could challenge the systems that perpetuated silence and suffering.

Our journey had evolved from a single whisper to a gathering storm, and there was no turning back. Together, we would continue to amplify our voices, break down the barriers of shame and fear, and pave the way for a future where no one felt alone in their struggle.

Uniting the Voices

As "The Gathering Storm Project" continued to grow, it became clear that our collective strength was making a profound impact. Stories poured in from all corners of the world, and the platform we had created became a sanctuary for survivors and allies alike. We were no longer just a gathering storm; we were a powerful force of change.

One of the most remarkable aspects of our journey was the sense of unity that emerged from the diversity of voices. We realized that stories of pain, resilience, and hope transcended cultural, geographic, and social boundaries. We began to collaborate with storytellers from different backgrounds, encouraging them to share their unique perspectives.

Through these collaborations, we discovered the universal themes that connected us all—strength in vulnerability, courage in adversity, and the power of community. We held storytelling festivals that featured voices from various walks of life, showcasing the richness of human experiences.

The impact of our work extended beyond our online platform and events. We actively engaged in advocacy and awareness campaigns, aiming to challenge the stigma surrounding issues such as mental health, trauma, and discrimination. Our voices became a force for change, demanding social reform and justice for those who had been marginalized and silenced for far too long.

As we united our voices, we saw tangible results. Life changes were implemented, support systems were strengthened, and survivors found the courage to seek help and support. The ripple effect had transformed into a tidal wave of transformation.

One day, Sarah, the woman I had met in that first healing circle, shared a remarkable idea. She suggested that we create a documentary film, weaving together the stories of resilience we had collected through "The Gathering Storm Project." It would be a testament to the power of storytelling and the strength of survivors.

The idea resonated with all of us, and we embarked on this ambitious project. We reached out to filmmakers, artists, and activists who shared our vision. The process of creating the documentary was challenging, emotionally charged, and deeply rewarding. It became a labor of love, a testament to our collective journey.

When the documentary was completed, we organized a premiere event that brought together survivors, supporters, and allies from around the world. As the film unfolded on the screen, there was not a dry eye in the room. It was a powerful reminder that our stories, once whispered in isolation, had now become a source of inspiration for countless others.

Our journey, which had begun with a single whisper, had evolved into a movement that transcended borders and barriers. We had shown the world that when voices unite, they have the power to break down walls, bring about change, and inspire hope. The gathering storm we had become was a force of transformation, and there was no limit to what we could achieve together.

A World Transformed

The premiere of our documentary marked a pivotal moment in the history of "The Gathering Storm Project." It was an emotional evening filled with tears, laughter, and a profound sense of unity. As the credits rolled and the audience erupted into applause, I couldn't help but reflect on how far we had come.

The documentary, titled "Voices Unite: Stories of Resilience," resonated with audiences around the world. It wasn't just a collection of stories; it was a testament to the human spirit's ability to overcome adversity and find strength in vulnerability. Viewers were inspired to share their own stories, and our platform saw an influx of submissions from people eager to join our community.

As the project continued to evolve, we expanded our reach and impact. We collaborated with schools and universities to introduce storytelling and empathy-building programs, nurturing the next generation to be more compassionate and understanding. We partnered with mental health organizations to provide resources and support for those in need.

Our advocacy work led to changes in legislation and policies that better protected survivors and marginalized communities. The collective voice of "The Gathering Storm Project" was now a force that politicians and policymakers couldn't ignore. It was a testament to the power of storytelling as a catalyst for change.

But perhaps the most heartwarming aspect of our journey was the connections we forged. Survivors from different parts of the world reached out to one another, finding solace in the fact that they were not alone. Bonds were formed, friendships blossomed, and our global community grew stronger every day.

Sarah, whose idea had sparked the creation of the documentary, had become a symbol of resilience within our project. She not only regained her ability to walk through intense therapy and determination but also found her calling as a motivational speaker, inspiring countless others to overcome their own challenges.

As the years passed, our movement continued to gain momentum. The gathering storm had transformed into a beacon of hope and change, illuminating the darkest corners of society with the light of shared experiences and unwavering support. Our voices had united to create a world where stories were no longer whispered in shame but shared with pride.

It was clear that the small voice that had urged me to share my story with the world had set in motion a series of events that had touched countless lives. What had started as a whisper had become a roar, a symphony, and a movement for positive change.

Our journey was far from over. The world was still a place where countless voices remained unheard, and there were battles left to fight. But as long as we stood together, united in our mission to empower, inspire, and heal, there was no doubt that we could continue to transform lives and make the world a better place—one story at a time.

The Ever-Evolving Symphony

With each passing year, "The Gathering Storm Project" continued to evolve and expand. Our movement had become a powerful force for positive change, and we were determined to reach even greater heights. Our mission was clear: to ensure that every voice had the opportunity to be heard and that every survivor knew they were not alone.

One of our most significant achievements was the establishment of "The Gathering Storm Foundation." This nonprofit organization aimed to provide direct support to survivors in need, offering counseling, legal assistance, and resources to help them on their journey to healing. We also collaborated with other organizations to create safe spaces and shelters for those facing abuse and discrimination.

Our annual "Voice of Resilience" awards ceremony became a prestigious event, honoring individuals and organizations that had made significant contributions to the fields of advocacy, mental health support, and survivor empowerment. The awards not only celebrated their efforts but also served as a reminder of the progress we had made as a collective.

Our storytelling festivals had grown into international events, drawing participants and audiences from all corners of the globe. These gatherings allowed survivors and allies to connect in person, share their stories, and form lasting bonds. It was a testament to the power of human connection and the healing potential of storytelling.

But perhaps the most profound impact was the change within individuals themselves. Many survivors who had initially hesitated to share their stories found the courage to do so through the support of our community. They discovered the therapeutic value of opening up, not just for themselves but for others who could relate to their experiences.

Sarah continued to be a source of inspiration for us all. Her journey from adversity to empowerment had not only transformed her life but had also touched the lives of countless others. She had become a bestselling author, sharing her story of resilience and determination with the world. Her message was clear: no challenge was insurmountable, and every setback could be a steppingstone to greater heights.

As I looked around at the thriving community we had built, I couldn't help but feel a deep sense of gratitude. The small voice that had once whispered to me had initiated a chain reaction of healing, empowerment, and transformation that had rippled across the world.

Our journey was far from over, and new challenges awaited us. There were still voices to be heard, stories to be shared, and battles to be fought. But we faced the future with unwavering determination, knowing that as long as we stood together, our symphony of voices would continue to inspire, heal, and change the world—one story at a time.

And so, "The Gathering Storm Project" remained an ever-evolving symphony, a testament to the resilience of the human spirit and the power of unity. Our movement was a reminder that even in the face of adversity, our voices could create harmony and hope, transforming the world into a place where every story mattered.

Epilogue: A World Transformed

In the years that followed, "The Gathering Storm Project" continued to thrive and evolve, leaving an indelible mark on the world. The impact of our movement reverberated far and wide, reaching individuals and communities in every corner of the globe. Our symphony of voices had become a powerful force for change, and the world had been transformed in ways we could have only dreamed of.

The Gathering Storm Foundation expanded its reach, offering support and resources to survivors in need on a global scale. Counseling centers, hotlines, and safe spaces became more accessible, ensuring that those who had suffered in silence could find the help they deserved.

Our annual "Voice of Resilience" awards continued to honor those who had made significant contributions to the cause of survivor empowerment and advocacy. These awards not only celebrated their achievements but also served as a reminder that positive change was possible, even in the face of adversity.

The storytelling festivals grew larger and more impactful, drawing participants from diverse backgrounds and experiences. These events became a celebration of human resilience, a testament to the healing power of storytelling, and a source of inspiration for all who attended.

Through advocacy and education, we continued to challenge the stigma surrounding issues such as mental health, trauma, and discrimination. Laws were reformed, policies were changed, and society became more inclusive and understanding.

Sarah's journey, from her own struggles to becoming a bestselling author and motivational speaker, continued to inspire countless individuals. Her story served as a beacon of hope, a reminder that resilience and determination could overcome even the most daunting challenges.

As I looked back on our remarkable journey, I couldn't help but be filled with a profound sense of pride and gratitude. The small voice that had whispered to me had set in motion a series of events that had touched countless lives, creating a world where stories were celebrated, and survivors were supported.

Our movement had transformed the world into a place where every voice mattered, where shared experiences brought about healing and hope, and where the power of unity had shattered the chains of silence and shame.

Though our journey had faced its share of challenges, we had always stood together, united by our mission to empower, inspire, and heal. Our symphony of voices had indeed changed the world—one story at a time.

Our movement was a reminder that, even in the face of adversity, our voices could create harmony and hope, transforming the world into a place where every story mattered, and where healing was possible for all.

Premonition

On our first introduction he greeted me by shaking my hand. "I think I could be your man." I giggled at first, I felt a strange, feeling like lightning shot through my veins. It seems like forever when I finally got a hold of myself, I kind of snatched my hand away, in those few seconds I could see life flash before my eyes, and I decided to walk away. "No, thank you. Nice meeting you, have a good day."

When Love Turns Lethal

The tug-of-war goes on for years
appearances change
new faces every day
strangers in a crowd
You can't come back from death

My mind plays the same picture on reply
Fast forward past all the hurt and pain
Getting to the good parts of me and of course you

But how could I forget what led us here
Trauma, stress, lies, and tears
I was broken down to my lowest point
And brought back to life twice

I have a calling I'm meant to be
Be here in this present moment
To save me once again
I can't relive this no not again

Life on replay
Different faces of the same story line
You would have thought I learned after the first time I died

I stayed of course because I loved him but what is love really? He said he love me each and every time he hit me, and I end up in cardiac arrest. This time I was on life support, and they took my children again, but

I loved him I chose him over everything, I was literally and figuratively his ride or die.

I turned tricks, hit licks, I would do anything for him. He found out I was pregnant again and tried to beat the baby out of me, blood everywhere, my face is unrecognizable, I was unresponsive.

He dragged my body across the pavement. At least 11 blocks to the local hospital in our neighborhood and left me at the emergency room door. At least he didn't let me die and he tried to get me help. All I saw was this bright light, it was time for me to go, my body took its last beating, I had lost hope.

As I drifted towards the light, I couldn't help but feel a sense of relief washing over me. The pain and suffering that had been my life was finally coming to an end. But then, a strange feeling came over me. I was being pulled back, away from the light and back into my body.

I woke up in the hospital, confused and disoriented. The doctors told me that I had been in a coma for weeks and that I had suffered extensive injuries. But despite everything, I was alive.

As I lay in the hospital bed, recovering from my injuries, I couldn't help but wonder what had happened. How had I survived yet another brutal attack? And why had I been given a second chance at life? It wasn't until I had a vivid dream that I finally understood. In the dream, I saw my grandmother, who had passed away years ago. She told me that she had been watching over me all these years, and that she had been the one to give me the premonition that had saved my life.

She told me that I had a purpose, that I was meant to do great things in this world. She also said I could never give up hope, no matter how difficult things may seem.

With those words ringing in my ears, I made a vow to myself. I would never again allow myself to be a victim. I would take control of my life and use my experiences to help others who had suffered as I had.

And as I left the hospital and stepped out into the world, I felt a sense of strength and determination that I had never felt before. The premonition had saved my life, but it was my own strength and resilience that had allowed me to survive. And from that day forward, I knew that I would always be a survivor.

I began the long journey of healing, both physically and emotionally. The scars on my body served as a constant reminder of the horrors I had endured, but they also became symbols of my resilience. Each day, I worked with therapists and support groups to rebuild my shattered self-esteem and regain my sense of self-worth.

One of the most difficult steps was breaking away from the toxic relationship that had nearly cost me my life. It was a challenging and dangerous process, but with the help of a network of friends and professionals, I managed to escape the clutches of my abuser. It was a liberating moment, one that allowed me to start fresh and regain my independence.

As I rebuilt my life, I found a new purpose. I decided to dedicate myself to helping others who had experienced similar traumas. I joined support groups, became an advocate for domestic violence survivors, and started speaking at events to raise awareness about the issue. I used my own story as a beacon of hope for those who were still trapped in abusive relationships.

Over time, I also reconnected with my children, who had been taken away from me during my darkest days. It was a difficult and emotional process, but with therapy and support, we began to rebuild our relationship. I was determined to be the loving and stable mother they deserved.

The premonition that had initially saved my life had given me a second chance, and I was determined to make the most of it. I pursued education and training in counseling and therapy to better support survivors of abuse. I founded a nonprofit organization dedicated to helping survivors rebuild their lives, providing shelter, counseling, and legal support.

As the years passed, my organization grew, and I saw countless survivors find their strength and break free from the cycle of abuse. My grandmother's words continued to guide me, reminding me that I had a purpose to fulfill in this world. I had become a symbol of hope and resilience, not just for myself but for countless others.

Through all the pain and darkness, I had emerged as a survivor, an advocate, and a beacon of hope. My premonition had led me down a path of healing and purpose, and I was determined to shine a light for others who had lost their way. In helping them find their own strength, I found my own redemption and a life filled with meaning and purpose.

As the years went by, my nonprofit organization continued to grow, expanding its reach and impact. We opened more shelters, hired dedicated staff, and partnered with law enforcement agencies to ensure the safety of survivors. Together, we provided not only shelter and legal support but also counseling and therapy to help survivors heal from the deep emotional wounds that abuse had inflicted upon them.

I was often invited to share my story at conferences and events focused on domestic violence awareness. Each time I stood on that stage and shared the painful journey that had led me to where I was, I could see the impact it had on the audience. People came forward, sharing their own stories, seeking help, and breaking their silence. It was a powerful reminder that my experiences, painful as they were, had a purpose.

Reconnecting with my children had been a bittersweet journey, but it was one filled with love and growth. We built a new life together, filled with laughter, support, and understanding. I was determined to be the mother they needed, to break the cycle of abuse that had plagued our family for generations.

One day, as I was working at my organization's headquarters, a young woman walked through the door. Her face was bruised, and her eyes were filled with fear. She had just escaped an abusive relationship and had nowhere to go. Our staff welcomed her with open arms, providing her with a safe space and the support she needed.

I sat down with her, and as we talked, I shared my own story, letting her know that she wasn't alone. I saw a spark of hope ignite in her eyes, the same spark that had once flickered within me. It was a turning point in her life, just as it had been in mine.

Over time, she became an integral part of our organization, using her own experiences to help other survivors. Together, we expanded our outreach, reaching even more people who needed our support.

As I looked back on my journey, I couldn't help but marvel at the twists and turns my life had taken. The premonition that had saved my life had set me on a path of healing and purpose. I had not only survived but thrived, and in doing so, I had become a beacon of hope for others. My story was a testament to the strength of the human spirit, the power of resilience, and the capacity for love and compassion. And as I continued to work alongside other survivors, I knew that together, we could break the cycle of abuse and create a world where everyone had the opportunity to heal, grow, and thrive.

Our organization's impact continued to ripple outward, touching the lives of countless survivors. We had become a lifeline for those in desperate need, providing not just physical safety but also a community of understanding and empowerment. Each success story, each survivor who walked away from abuse and towards a brighter future, fueled our determination to keep pushing forward.

One of our most significant achievements was the establishment of educational programs in schools and communities. We firmly believed that prevention was as crucial as intervention. By educating young people about healthy relationships, warning signs of abuse, and the importance of seeking help, we hoped to break the cycle of violence before it even started.

As I stood in front of classrooms filled with eager students, I could see the curiosity in their eyes and the willingness to learn. I knew that our efforts were making a difference when a student would approach me after a session, sharing their concerns about a friend or family member who might be in an abusive situation. These conversations were the first steps towards breaking the silence and seeking help.

Our organization's reputation also caught the attention of lawmakers and policymakers. We began collaborating with local and state governments to improve the legal protections for survivors of domestic violence. Our advocacy efforts resulted in stronger legislation, increased funding for support services, and more comprehensive training for law enforcement and healthcare professionals.

Reconnecting with my children had been a constant source of joy and motivation for me. Seeing them grow into resilient, compassionate young adults filled my heart with pride. Together, we had broken the cycle of abuse that had plagued our family for generations, and it was a testament to the power of healing and love.

The young woman who had walked through our organization's doors that fateful day had not only found safety but had also discovered her own strength. She had become a powerful advocate, sharing her story, and providing support to others in need. Our paths had crossed for a reason, and together, we had turned pain into purpose.

Now, I realized that the premonition that had once saved my life had set me on a remarkable path. It had guided me to become a voice for the voiceless, a beacon of hope for those trapped in the darkness of abuse. The scars on my body were no longer just reminders of pain; they were symbols of resilience and transformation.

And so, I continued to stand alongside survivors, offering my support, my story, and my unwavering belief that healing and happiness were possible. Together, we were breaking the cycle of abuse, one survivor at a time, and creating a world where love, compassion, and empowerment prevailed.

Suppressed feelings

Growing up in disfunction caused him to question love in everyone. With suppressed feelings he walked away from every relationship that felt real. Tyler was a very successful. He was in a monogamist relationship with Drina, to his surprise, for over 5 years. He seemed content and happy for once in his life. Tyler has never introduced a woman to his family and friends and after five years he made the decision to invite Drina to a family get together.

Drina was ecstatic and couldn't wait to meet Tyler's family and friends. The big day had arrived, and Tyler was so excited. Drina and Tyler arrived at his family childhood home and was greeted by his best friend Paul. Paul introduced himself to Drina and stared at her and said, "you look very familiar" and walked away.

Drina was spooked by Paul's statement and begin to panic. Tyler asked Drina if everything was alright, she said "yes" and asked where the bathroom was. Tyler pointed to the front door and Drina went. In the restroom she shook it off by splashing her face with water and putting a smile on her face.

As the night progressed, Drina couldn't shake off the feeling that something was off. Tyler's family and friends were warm and welcoming, but Paul's words still lingered in her mind. She tried to brush it off and enjoy the evening, but the feeling of uneasiness remained.

As the night came to an end, Tyler's family and friends said their goodbyes and left. Drina and Tyler were left alone with Paul, who had stayed behind to help with the clean-up. Drina couldn't help but feel uncomfortable around him and decided to stay close to Tyler.

As they were saying their goodbyes, Paul pulled Tyler aside and whispered something in his ear. Tyler's expression changed, and he looked at Drina with a mix of confusion and sadness. Drina asked Tyler what was wrong, but he didn't answer. They said their goodbyes to Paul and left.

On the ride home, Tyler finally opened up to Drina. He told her that Paul was an old flame of his and that they had a complicated history. He also revealed that Paul had recognized Drina from a dating app that they had both used in the past.

Drina was shocked and hurt by Tyler's revelation. She felt like she had been deceived and couldn't understand why Tyler had kept this from her. Tyler explained that he had been afraid of losing her and that he didn't want to risk their relationship by revealing his past.

Drina didn't know what to do. She loved Tyler, but she couldn't shake off the feeling of betrayal. They spent the rest of the night in silence, both lost in their own thoughts.

The next day, Drina decided to confront Tyler about his past. They had a long and difficult conversation, but in the end, they were able to work through their issues. Tyler apologized for keeping his past from her, and Drina forgave him.

In the end, their relationship became stronger because of their honesty and openness with each other. Tyler learned that love requires trust and honesty, and Drina learned that forgiveness and understanding can overcome even the most difficult of challenges. Together, they faced their fears and grew even closer as a couple.

Over the following months, Tyler and Drina continued to build their relationship on a foundation of trust and honesty. They made a pact to share their pasts, no matter how complicated or uncomfortable, so that there would be no more hidden secrets between them.

As they got to know each other more deeply, they discovered shared dreams and aspirations. They talked about their future together, their desires, and the life they wanted to build as a couple. They decided to move in together, combining their lives in a small but cozy apartment that quickly filled with laughter, love, and shared memories.

Tyler also decided to confront his past with Paul. He reached out to him and asked for a meeting to clear the air and resolve any lingering issues. It was a difficult conversation, but ultimately, they both understood that they had moved on in their lives and that their paths had diverged. They agreed to let go of any lingering feelings and wished each other well.

Drina, on her part, decided to be more open about her own past, sharing her experiences, both good and bad, with Tyler. This vulnerability brought them even closer together, as they realized that their love was strong enough to withstand the weight of their past mistakes and insecurities.

Over time, Tyler introduced Drina to his family and friends again, this time without any secrets or hidden agendas. Drina was welcomed into the fold with open arms, and she felt like a true part of Tyler's life. She finally understood why Tyler had kept her hidden for so long – he wanted to be absolutely sure that their love was real and that they were both ready for the challenges that come with blending their lives together.

As their relationship deepened and grew, Tyler and Drina found themselves more in love than ever before. They realized that suppressing their feelings and past experiences had only held them back, and that true love could only flourish in an environment of trust, communication, and openness.

Their journey was not without its challenges, but they faced them together, knowing that their love was worth the effort. With each passing day, they became stronger as a couple, building a future together that was free from the weight of suppressed feelings and filled with the promise of a love that could weather any storm.

One sunny afternoon, while Tyler and Drina were sitting on their apartment balcony, sipping on cups of coffee, they found themselves reminiscing about the past. It was no longer a painful topic but rather a chance to reflect on how far they had come as a couple.

Tyler looked into Drina's eyes and said, "You know, Drina, I used to be so afraid of love and vulnerability. I suppressed my feelings for so long because I didn't want to get hurt. But meeting you changed everything. You showed me that love is worth the risk, and I'm so grateful for that." Drina smiled warmly, squeezing Tyler's hand. "I used to have my own walls up too, Tyler. I was scared to let someone in, to truly open up. But you taught me that real love is about being your authentic self with someone who accepts you for who you are. I love you for that."

Their love story was a testament to the power of honesty and vulnerability. They had learned that love wasn't about being perfect or without flaws; it was about accepting each other's imperfections and growing together.

As time went on, Tyler and Drina continued to build their life together. They pursued their shared dreams and aspirations, supporting each other every step of the way. Their cozy apartment became a sanctuary filled with love, laughter, and cherished memories.

Their journey wasn't always easy, but they faced every challenge together, knowing that their love could overcome anything. They had learned that suppressed feelings could only hold them back, but when they allowed themselves to be truly open and vulnerable with each other, their love flourished.

And so, Tyler and Drina's love story continued, a beautiful testament to the transformative power of trust, communication, and the courage to face their pasts and build a future together.

Suppressed Feelings

Silent storms raged within his chest,
A tempest bound by an iron vest.
Love knocked gently, yet he withdrew,
Fearing its fire might burn him too.

Childhood shadows, whispers of pain,
Wove a tale of loss, of disdain.
He built walls brick by brick,
no one could break
Burying truths he dared not hide.

Years of success, a life refined,
Yet echoes haunted his restless mind.
memories appeared, a light, a spark,
Illuminating his long-caged heart.

Five years passed in a blissful blur,
 A quiet life he thought secure.
But secrets lingered, buried deep,
Threatening peace he'd longed to keep.

The gathering came, a chance to share,
A life built on love, free from despair.
Yet one small phrase, a fleeting glance,
Sent the evening into a fragile dance.

Paul's words struck like a phantom blow,
A past reviled, a truth to know.
Secrets faltered, her trust undone,
Two souls wrestled with what was begun.

In silence, their fears found room to grow,
But love demanded they face the woe.
Truth unfolded, like pages turned,
Through pain and fire,
their bond was earned.

Suppressed feelings, like vines, uncurled,
Binding two hearts in a fragile world.
Honesty bloomed where fear once stood,
A love reshaped, misunderstood.

Together they built a life anew,
Where trust and courage carried them through.
For love, they learned, is a fearless art—
A mirror held to the human heart.

In Tyler's eyes, everyone could see,
A man reborn, yearning to be free.
And in her touch, Tyler found peace,
A tender strength, a sweet release.

No more secrets, no shadows remain,
Love's light shone through their shared pain.
Two hearts now one, a lesson clear:
To love is to face what we most fear.

Embracing the Past

Before I could share my story, I needed to confront my past. I revisited the chapters of my life, both the joyous and the sorrowful, and embraced every experience that had shaped me. From the innocence of childhood to the turbulence of adolescence and the journey into adulthood, I discovered the moments that had made me who I am today.

As I delved deeper into my memories, I realized that some of the most profound moments of growth had come from the times I had struggled the most. It was in these moments of darkness that I had learned the most about myself and had found the resilience to keep going.

I began to see my past as a tapestry of experiences, both positive and negative, that had come together to create a unique and complex individual. I learned to embrace my failures and mistakes as opportunities for growth and to forgive myself for any regrets.

Through this process of introspection and acceptance, I found a newfound appreciation for my past. The difficulties and struggles I had faced were not something to be ashamed of or hidden away but instead were important parts of my journey.

Embracing my past also allowed me to understand and empathize with others more deeply. As I came to terms with my own experiences, I recognized the universality of struggle and the importance of empathy and compassion.

This newfound perspective allowed me to connect with others on a deeper level and to appreciate the beauty and complexity of the human experience.

As I continued my journey, I found that embracing my past had given me a newfound sense of freedom. No longer burdened by shame or regret, I was able to move forward with a renewed sense of purpose and clarity.

I also found that my past had given me a unique set of skills and strengths that I could draw upon to navigate the challenges of the present. By embracing my past, I had found a deep reservoir of resilience, determination, and empathy that I could tap into whenever I needed it.

In the end, I realized that the past is not something to be feared or avoided but instead is a valuable resource that we can draw upon to create a better future. By embracing the complexities and challenges of our past, we can develop a greater sense of self-awareness, empathy, and purpose that will serve us well in all areas of our lives.

With my newfound sense of self-acceptance and appreciation for my past, I felt a profound transformation taking place within me. It was as though I had unlocked a door to a hidden chamber of my heart and mind, revealing treasures I had never before recognized.

As I continued to reflect on my life's journey, I decided to reach out to those who had played significant roles in my past. I wanted to reconnect with old friends, mentors, and even some family members with whom I had lost touch over the years. Revisiting these relationships was a way to not only heal any lingering wounds but also to express gratitude for the positive influences they had been in my life.

One by one, I sent heartfelt letters, made phone calls, and scheduled meetups. These interactions were sometimes joyful reunions and, at other times, conversations that needed to happen in order to find closure. Regardless of the outcome, each interaction contributed to my sense of wholeness and understanding.

One day, I received a letter from my high school English teacher, Mr. Anderson. He had been a mentor to me during a particularly difficult time in my teenage years, helping me discover my love for writing and literature. In his letter, he expressed how proud he was of my growth and how much he believed in my potential.

Touched by his words, I decided to visit him in person. Sitting in his cozy study filled with books, we shared stories of the past and the present. He told me how my determination to overcome adversity had left a lasting impression on him and that he had always believed in my ability to succeed.

· · ·

Our meeting was a reminder of the impact we can have on one another's lives. It also reinforced the idea that embracing our past is not just about personal growth but also about acknowledging the people who have shaped us along the way.

In the months that followed, I continued my journey of self-discovery and reconnection. I started a journal to document my thoughts and reflections, which allowed me to track my progress and gain even more insight into my evolving self. The act of writing became a therapeutic exercise, helping me process my emotions and experiences more deeply.

As I embraced my past and connected with the people who had been part of it, I felt an increasing sense of inner peace and purpose. My newfound resilience allowed me to face the challenges of the present with greater confidence, and my empathy for others deepened my connections with those around me.

With each passing day, I became more convinced that our past is not something to escape or forget but a rich tapestry of experiences that make us who we are. By acknowledging and embracing this tapestry, we can harness its power to create a brighter and more fulfilling future.

The more I delved into my past and rekindled relationships, the clearer it became that my journey was far from over. I realized that there were unresolved chapters in my life that needed closure, and there were bridges that needed to be rebuilt.

One such bridge was with my estranged sister, Sarah. We had grown apart over the years, fueled by misunderstandings and disagreements that had never been properly addressed. My newfound perspective on the importance of embracing the past led me to reach out to her.

I wrote her a heartfelt letter, expressing my desire to reconnect and heal the wounds that had separated us for so long. In the letter, I acknowledged my role in our strained relationship and expressed my willingness to work together to rebuild our bond.

Sarah's response was cautious but hopeful. She agreed to meet me for coffee, and as we sat across from each other in a quiet café, the weight of our shared history hung in the air. It was a vulnerable moment, but it was also a necessary one.

We began by discussing our childhood, the shared memories that had once bound us together. As we talked, I realized that we had both carried the scars of our past, but we had also shared moments of joy and love that were worth preserving.

Over time, our meetings became more frequent, and our conversations deepened. We tackled the difficult topics we had avoided for so long, addressing the hurt and misunderstandings that had driven us apart. It wasn't easy, and there were tears shed along the way, but it was a cathartic process that allowed us to move forward.

Rebuilding my relationship with Sarah was a significant milestone on my journey of embracing the past. It taught me that sometimes the most challenging relationships in our lives are the ones that can bring the greatest growth and healing.

As I continued to reconnect with people from my past and heal old wounds, I also began to explore new opportunities in the present. My renewed sense of purpose and self-assuredness led me to pursue a career change that I had long dreamed of but had hesitated to pursue.

I enrolled in writing courses and started submitting my work to publications. My passion for storytelling, nurtured by Mr. Anderson all those years ago, had never faded, and now it was time to fully embrace it. The process was not without its challenges and rejections, but I persevered, drawing on the resilience I had discovered within myself.

With each byline and publication, I felt a sense of accomplishment and fulfillment that I had never experienced in my previous career. Embracing my true calling was a testament to the power of embracing my past. It was a reminder that our past experiences, both the triumphs and the tribulations, shape our journey and prepare us for the future.

In the end, my journey of embracing the past had not only led to personal growth and healing but also to a newfound sense of purpose and passion. It had shown me that the key to a brighter and more fulfilling future lies in acknowledging and learning from our past, and that the treasures we discover along the way are worth the journey.

Embracing the Past

The whispers of yesterday linger still,
Echoes of laughter, and shadows that chill.
Memories etched in the sands of time,
Each one a verse in life's tender rhyme.

The past, a canvas of lessons and scars,
Guides us like constellations, the brightest of stars.
It's there we find roots, the start of our story,
In triumph and trials, in heartbreak and glory.

To embrace it is not to cling or regret,
But to honor the moments we cannot forget.
The smiles, the tears, the paths we've crossed,
A love woven of found and lost.

For every mistake, a wisdom unfolds,
In every wound, a healing soul molds.
The past is a mirror, a teacher, a guide,
A compass that points to the strength inside.

So let us not run from the shadows it casts,
But dance with the light that shines from the past.
For within its depths lies the key to today,
A reminder of how far we've come on our way.

Shedding Skin

A tear dropped from her face and rolled down the left side of her cheek. It landed in between her bosom as she snapped out of her trans and realized that the wetness hit the exact scar that healed from the first attempt on her life by the hands of her father.

She shed so many tears over the years falling in and out of destructive relationships trying to hold on to the unrealistic fantasy of what one should or even could be.

Waking up to nightmare after nightmare screams of terror irrupt in her small one-bedroom apartment as the lights flickered. Flashbacks of the miscarriages after he beat her and dragged her across the pavement because he didn't want a child well not by her. She cursed the day he was born. This just could not be happening again.

She gathered her strength and slowly got out of bed, her body aching from the memories that haunted her. She made her way to the bathroom and looked at herself in the mirror. The reflection staring back at her was a shell of the woman she used to be. The bruises on her face were still visible, and her eyes were filled with fear and sadness.

She knew she had to leave, but where would she go? She had no family, no friends, no one to turn to. She had cut herself off from everyone who cared about her believing that she deserved the abuse she received. But now, she knew she needed to break free from this cycle of violence and pain.

With trembling hands, she dialed the number of a domestic abuse hotline she had seen advertised on TV. A kind voice answered, and she found herself pouring out her story to a stranger on the other end of the line. The woman on the phone listened patiently and offered her resources and advice.

It wasn't going to be easy, but for the first time in a long time, she felt a glimmer of hope. She wiped away the tear that had fallen on her scar, took a deep breath, and decided. She was going to leave and start a new life, one where she was free from the abuse and pain.

As she packed her bags, she felt a sense of empowerment she had never felt before. She was taking back control of her life, and nothing would ever make her feel weak and helpless again. She left her old life behind and stepped into a new world, one full of possibilities and hope. She would never forget the tears she had shed, but she would never let them control her again.

With a determination burning inside her, she left her small one-bedroom apartment behind, leaving the painful memories that haunted her for years. She followed the advice from the domestic abuse hotline, deciding to escape her abuser and start fresh.

She found refuge in a women's shelter where she met others who had endured similar horrors. They shared stories of resilience and survival, forming a sisterhood built on support and understanding. For the first time, she realized she wasn't alone in her struggles.

During her time at the shelter, she attended therapy sessions and support groups that helped her heal both physically and emotionally. She slowly regained her self-esteem and began to rebuild her life. With the help of social workers, she secured a job and found a small but safe apartment of her own.

As she settled into her new life, she reconnected with the hobbies and interests she had abandoned during her abusive relationship. She found solace in painting, a skill she had once cherished but had been forced to abandon. Her art became an outlet for her emotions, and she poured her heart into each stroke of the brush, creating beautiful works of art that spoke of her resilience and newfound strength.

Over time, she began to make new friends who supported and encouraged her. She learned to trust again and opened her heart to the possibility of love. She met a kind, compassionate partner who treated her with the love and respect she deserved. Their relationship was built on trust and mutual understanding, a stark contrast to the destructive relationships of her past.

As the years passed, she continued to thrive. She became an advocate for survivors of domestic abuse, sharing her story to inspire others and raise awareness about the importance of seeking help and breaking free from toxic relationships. She became a symbol of hope and resilience in her community, proof that it was possible to shed the skin of a painful past and emerge stronger and wiser.

The tear that had fallen on her scar all those years ago was a reminder of the pain she had endured, but it no longer held power over her. She had shed not only her tears but also the skin of her old self, emerging as a survivor, a fighter, and a beacon of hope for others who needed to find their own strength. Her life had transformed from one of darkness to one filled with light, love, and endless possibilities.

With her newfound strength, she continued to pursue her passion for art. Her paintings began to gain recognition in her community, and she was invited to showcase her work at local galleries. The themes of her art reflected her journey – vibrant colors symbolizing resilience, intricate brushwork representing the complexity of her emotions, and powerful imagery conveying the strength she had discovered within herself.

Her art exhibitions not only showcased her talent but also served as a platform to raise awareness about domestic abuse. She used her voice and her creations to advocate for survivors and to educate the public about the signs and consequences of abusive relationships. People who attended her exhibitions were deeply moved by her story and the courage she displayed in sharing it.

As her art career flourished, she also became involved in community organizations dedicated to supporting survivors of domestic violence. She volunteered her time and resources to help those in need, providing them with a safe space to share their experiences and offering guidance on how to break free from their own cycles of abuse.

Her advocacy work extended to lobbying for changes in laws and policies aimed at protecting victims and holding abusers accountable. She tirelessly worked with local legislators and organizations to ensure that victims of domestic abuse received the support and resources they needed to rebuild their lives.

Over time, her efforts began to make a significant impact on her community, and her story reached a broader audience through media coverage and interviews. She became a symbol of resilience not just in her hometown but across the country, inspiring countless individuals to seek help and escape from the clutches of abuse.

Her life had transformed from one of pain and suffering to one of purpose and fulfillment. She had not only shed the skin of her past but had emerged as a beacon of hope, a powerful force for change, and a testament to the indomitable strength of the human spirit.

In her quiet moments, as she stood in front of her canvas, her scar – once a painful reminder – now served as a symbol of her triumph over adversity. Each stroke of her brush was a declaration of her resilience, and each painting was a testament to the healing power of art and the unbreakable spirit within her. She had not only survived; she had thrived, and in doing so, she had become an inspiration to all who had the privilege of knowing her story.

The Weight of Her Tears

A tear drops from her face rolled down
the left side of her cheek
landed in between her bosom
she snapped out of her trans and realized
that the wetness hit the exact scar that healed
from the first attempt on her life
 by the hands of her father

She shed so many tears over the years
falling in and out of destructive relationships
trying to hold on to the unrealistic
fantasy of what one should or even could be

A teardrop traced the path of her pain,
A silent witness to wounds that remain.
It landed softly, where scars now lie,
A mark of survival, her muted cry.

The memory burned like an ember's glow,
Of the first betrayal, the lowest of lows.
Her father's hands, meant to protect,
Had left her shattered, broken, wrecked.

Years passed like shadows, fleeting yet deep,
Her heart on a journey, yearning for peace.
She wandered through love, both toxic and cold,
Clutching at fantasies that promised to hold.

But the fairy tales faded, their edges sharp,
Each lover's touch left a jagged mark.
She chased perfection in imperfect men,
Falling and rising, then falling again.

Her tears, like rivers, carved through stone,
Echoing whispers of being alone.
Yet beneath the surface, a strength took root,
A voice emerging, a resolute truth.

"Love," she thought, "is not made of pain,
Not bound by scars, nor tethered to shame.
It's a light that heals, a balm that restores,
Not the chain that binds, nor the wound that sores."

With that thought, she wiped her eyes,
Looked at her reflection, no longer disguised.
She saw not the victim, but the survivor within,
A woman reborn, ready to begin.

Her scars became stories, her tears became streams,
Washing away the remnants of dreams.
For now she knew, love starts with the self,
Not in the arms of someone else.

And as she stood, the past faded behind,
Her heart now open, her spirit aligned.
The teardrop that fell had carved its place,
Not as a symbol of loss, but of grace.

PART TWO

I Got a Story to Tale

Fairy Tale

They were groomed as young children to be a bride. Fed fairy tales of a lifestyle; a grand knight in shining armor that will make all of their dreams come true and a lot of you believe in this, too.

Once upon a time, in a quaint little village, there lived a mother named Emily and her young daughter, Lily. Emily had always believed in the romantic tales of love that had been passed down through generations, tales of knights in shining armor and fairy tale endings. She cherished these stories and saw them as a source of hope and inspiration for her daughter.

From a very young age, Emily began to groom Lily with these unrealistic notions of love. She would read her bedtime stories filled with damsels in distress, waiting for their brave knights to come and rescue them. Emily would tell Lily that one day, she would meet a prince charming who would sweep her off her feet, and they would live happily ever after in a grand castle.

As Lily grew older, these stories became deeply ingrained in her mind. She started to believe that in a perfect and flawless love, like the ones she had heard in those tales, was the only way to find happiness and fulfillment. Her mother's well-intentioned teachings had planted unrealistic expectations of love deep within her heart.

Years passed, and Lily grew into a young woman. She became obsessed with finding her own fairy tale romance, convinced that it was the only path to true happiness. She turned away potential suitors who didn't meet the impossibly high standards set by the romantic tales her mother had ingrained in her. She believed that unless her partner was a knight in shining armor, her life would never be complete.

But as time went on, Lily's unrealistic expectations of love began to take a toll on her. She felt lonely and isolated, constantly searching for a love that simply didn't exist in the real world. Her pursuit of the perfect fairy tale romance caused her immense frustration and heartache.

Emily, witnessing her daughter's struggles, realized the error of her ways. She had unintentionally instilled harmful and unrealistic beliefs about love in Lily. She had failed to teach her daughter the importance of realistic expectations, communication, and the complexities of real-world relationships.

Realizing her mistake, Emily decided it was time to have an honest conversation with Lily. She explained that while fairy tales could be enchanting and inspiring, they were not a blueprint for real-life love. Emily shared the importance of accepting imperfections, building healthy relationships based on trust and communication, and setting realistic expectations in matters of the heart.

Lily, although initially resistant to change, slowly began to understand the wisdom in her mother's words. She realized that real love wasn't about finding a perfect partner who would solve all her problems but about building a strong and mutually supportive partnership with someone who shared her values and goals.

Over time, Lily let go of her unrealistic notions of love and began to focus on nurturing real connections with the people she met. She learned that true happiness could be found in the journey of self-discovery and in the bonds, she forged with those who truly cared for her.

As mother and daughter embraced a more realistic perspective on love and relationships, they realized that the most meaningful love stories were not those found in fairy tales but the ones they were living each day, where they supported and cared for one another, accepting imperfections, and growing together in the process.

In the real world, outside the confines of fairy tales, Lily faced the challenge of adjusting her sails. Her mother's well-intentioned tales of love had led her to expect a love from above. But life was complex, not a scripted play, and real relationships had their own way. She'd turned away those who didn't fit the mold, searching for perfection, leaving her heart cold.

Loneliness crept in as the years went by, her standards impossibly high in the sky. The quest for a fairy tale left her torn, in the world of reality, love had to be born.

Emily, watching her daughter's pain unfold, knew it was time for truths to be told. She sat Lily down, their hearts open wide, to discuss the realities of love, side by side. "Fairy tales are lovely, my dear," she began, "But love in the real world has its own plan. It's not about perfection or a flawless knight, but finding someone whose love feels just right."

Emily spoke of trust and communication's role, how love wasn't perfect, but it made them whole. She shared stories of life's ups and downs, and the strength in love that knows no bounds. Lily felt free. She learned that love's journey was worth the ride, embracing real connections with hearts open wide.

Over time, they let go of the fairy tale dreams, and reality's beauty began to gleam. In the messiness of life, they found their way, growing together, come what may. No longer obsessed with a knight in the night, Lily found love that felt just right. Her heart no longer bound by a fairy tale's sway, in the real world, she found her way.

As Lily opened her heart to a new way of thinking, life's complexities and joys she began embracing. Her mother's wisdom, though once met with resistance, had shattered the illusions, offering her a chance.

In the real world, her journey took flight, no longer searching for the impossible knight. She realized that love, in all its forms, could weather life's storms and reshape norms.

She met someone whose love felt just right, not a fairy tale, but a comforting light. Their bond grew strong with trust and care, a partnership built on the love they would share. The imperfections of life, they'd both embrace, in the messiness, they found their own grace. They communicated openly, hearts intertwined, in the real world's love, they both defined.

No longer imprisoned by fairy tale lore, Lily discovered something worth so much more. A love that was genuine, authentic, and real. A love that could conquer, a love that could heal.

Emily, watching her daughter's blossoming smile, knew they'd navigated life's trials, mile by mile. Together they'd learned, grown, and found their way, in the real world of love, where hearts had the final say.

And so, in the end, their story was rewritten, from fairy tales to reality, they were smitten. For love, though not perfect, could be a beautiful song. In the real world, where they both truly belong.

Fairytale's

Groomed from youth to be a bride so fair,
In fairy tales, a grand life they'd declare.
A knight in shining armor, dreams anew,
A storybook love, forever tried and true.

But tales spun from dreams, oh, how they deceive,
For life's not a script, no make-believe.
Reality unfolds in shades of gray,
With battles fought, in the light of day.

The armor may tarnish, the dreams may fray,
As life takes its toll along the way.
But in the midst of trials, strength they find,
Resilience, courage, hearts intertwined.

For love is not perfect, it's a journey, you see,
With its highs and lows, its complexity.
No fairy tale ending, but a tale of real,
Where bonds are forged, and hearts truly feel.

So let go of the myths, the grand charade,
Embrace the love that in real life is made.
In the messiness of it all, you'll find the clue,
That love, though imperfect, can still be true.

In fairy tales they were raised to be a bride, with notions grand, in stories they'd confide. A knight in shining armor, a dream so high, they believed in this love, reaching for the sky. But life's not a tale, it's not make-believe, in shades of gray, it's the truth we receive. Battles to fight in the light of the day, The armor tarnishes, dreams may sway. Yet amidst the trials, strength they'll discover, in love's embrace, they'll both recover. Imperfections embraced, in real life's dance, hearts intertwined, taking a chance. Love's not a fairy tale, but a journey, you'll see, with highs and lows, a complex decree. No storybook ending, but love that is real, where hearts truly feel, and emotions reveal. So let go of myths, the grand charade, embrace love's truth, don't let it fade. In the messiness of life's grand view, love's imperfect beauty will shine through.

Forgiveness of Self

Over time, Lauren physical wounds began to heal, but the emotional scars were deep and would take much longer to mend. She started attending therapy sessions to address the trauma she had endured, and slowly but steadily, she began to rebuild her sense of self-worth and self-esteem.

One of the turning points in her recovery was joining a support group for survivors of sexual assault. There, she found a community of people who understood what she had been through, people who didn't judge or blame her. The stories she heard from other survivors gave her strength, and she no longer felt alone in her journey towards healing.

As Lauren continued her therapy and advocacy work, the woman also became involved in local organizations and initiatives aimed at preventing sexual violence and supporting survivors. She shared her story openly, hoping that by speaking out, she could empower others to seek help and justice.

During the trial of her attacker, she faced the difficult task of testifying against him. It was emotionally draining, but Lauren held her ground, determined to ensure that he faced the consequences of his actions. Her bravery in the courtroom helped secure a conviction, and her attacker was sentenced to a lengthy prison term.

Over the years, the woman's advocacy work expanded. Lauren worked with lawmakers to push for changes in legislation that would better protect survivors and hold perpetrators accountable. She also became involved in educational programs, speaking at schools and universities to raise awareness about consent, boundaries, and the importance of supporting survivors.

Through her journey of healing and advocacy, the woman found a renewed sense of purpose. While she could never erase the pain of what had happened to her, she had transformed her trauma into a force for positive change. Her experiences had shaped her into a fierce advocate for justice and a beacon of hope for survivors everywhere.

The path to recovery was still challenging, and there were days when the memories haunted her, but she had learned to manage her pain and channel it into her mission. She had released the burden of guilt and shame that had once weighed her down, and in its place, she had found strength, resilience, and a determination to make the world a safer and more compassionate place for all survivors of sexual assault.

As the days turned into weeks, the woman's recovery continued. She underwent therapy to address the emotional scars left by the traumatic event. It was during these therapy sessions that she truly began to understand that she was not at fault for what had happened to her. The support from her therapist helped her recognize that she was a survivor and not a victim.

Her family and friends rallied around her, providing a strong support network that she could lean on during her most challenging moments. They listened to her, believed in her, and offered unconditional love. It was through their unwavering support that she found the strength to keep moving forward.

In the midst of her healing journey, the woman discovered a newfound passion for advocacy. She started volunteering at a local organization that provided support and resources for survivors of sexual assault. She met other survivors and heard their stories, which only strengthened her resolve to make a difference.

With time, the woman's advocacy work expanded beyond her local community. She began speaking at conferences, sharing her story on national platforms, and collaborating with organizations dedicated to preventing sexual violence. Her courage and determination to speak out inspired others to do the same.

One day, she received a call from a survivor who had read about her story online. This survivor had never spoken to anyone about her own experience, but after reading about the woman's journey, she felt compelled to reach out. The two of them formed a deep connection, offering each other support and understanding as they navigated their healing paths together.

As the years passed, the woman's advocacy efforts had a tangible impact. She lobbied for changes in legislation that improved the rights and support systems for survivors of sexual assault. She helped establish support groups in communities across the country and played a vital role in changing the conversation surrounding sexual violence.

Though the memory of the rape would always be a part of her life, it no longer defined her. Instead, she had transformed her pain into a powerful force for change. She was a survivor, a fighter, and a voice for those who had been silenced.

Through her advocacy work, she not only helped others find their strength and heal but also contributed to a world where survivors were believed, supported, and empowered to stand up against their perpetrators. The woman had turned her darkest moment into a beacon of hope, proving that even in the face of unimaginable pain, the human spirit could prevail.

As the woman's journey of healing and advocacy continued, she found herself making a profound impact on the lives of others. Her advocacy work expanded beyond her local community and even beyond her country's borders. She became a global advocate for survivors of sexual assault, sharing her story with a wider audience and working with international organizations to address this pervasive issue.

One of her most significant accomplishments was the creation of a foundation dedicated to supporting survivors and preventing sexual violence. The foundation provided resources, counseling, and legal assistance to survivors, ensuring they had the support they needed to rebuild their lives. It also funded research into the causes and prevention of sexual violence, contributing valuable insights to the field.

Her advocacy work also extended to the digital realm. She became an influential voice on social media, using her platform to raise awareness, challenge stereotypes, and engage with a diverse audience. Her online presence allowed her to connect with survivors and supporters worldwide, fostering a sense of community and solidarity.

In addition to her advocacy efforts, the woman continued to work closely with lawmakers and policymakers. She played a pivotal role in the development of legislation aimed at improving the rights and protection of survivors, and she was a tireless advocate for the enforcement of these laws. Her commitment to holding perpetrators accountable remained unwavering.

Despite her busy schedule and the emotional toll of her work, the woman made sure to prioritize self-care. She understood the importance of taking breaks, seeking support when needed, and continuing her therapy sessions. Her journey of healing was ongoing, and she recognized that healing was not linear; there would be good days and challenging days, but she had learned to navigate them with resilience.

As the years passed, the woman's story became a symbol of hope and resilience for countless survivors. She received numerous awards and honors for her advocacy work, but the most rewarding part was seeing the positive change she had helped create in the world. Survivors who had once felt alone and silenced now had a network of support and resources thanks to her efforts.

While the memory of the traumatic event would always be a part of her life, the woman had found a way to transform her pain into a powerful force for good. She was no longer defined by her past but by her unwavering dedication to creating a safer and more compassionate world for all survivors of sexual assault. Her journey of healing and advocacy was a testament to the strength of the human spirit and the enduring power of hope.

In the quiet corners of her mind, Lauren carried a heavy burden, a secret she had kept locked away for years. It was a weight that had grown heavier with time, a pain that had festered and gnawed at her soul. She knew that the only way to find peace was to confront the past and forgive herself.

The memory was etched in Lauren's mind like a permanent scar. She had been young, too young, when she found herself in a situation that she was ill-prepared to handle. The choices before her seemed impossible, and the weight of judgment from those around her loomed like a dark cloud. "I can't bear to ever hold your hand," Lauren had said, referencing her child she gave up. Laurens voice trembling with fear and uncertainty. It was a decision made out of desperation, a decision that had haunted her ever since. She had carried the guilt and shame of that choice like a heavy chain around her heart.

• • •

But now, standing at the edge of the river, Lauren realized that forgiveness was the only way to set herself free. The river flowed before her, its gentle current a metaphor for the healing power of forgiveness. She took a deep breath and began to speak, her words a whispered prayer to the universe.

"Forgiveness is a river that flows, from a heart that's willing to let go," she murmured, tears welling up in her eyes. She closed her eyes and allowed the memories to flood back, the pain and regret washing over her like a tidal wave.

Life, she thought, was a precious gift, a connection that bound us all together. She had made a choice, a difficult choice, but it was time to forgive herself for that choice. She needed to release the hurt and pain that she had been holding onto, to let go of the stories that had defined her for so long.

As she stood there, tears streaming down her face, Lauren realized that forgiveness was not just for herself, but also for the one she had made that painful choice with. She whispered words of forgiveness to her abuser too, understanding that he, like her, had been caught in the web of circumstances and choices. The river continued to flow, its gentle murmur a soothing backdrop to her catharsis. She forgave herself and him, and in that moment, she felt a weight lift from her shoulders. The burden she had carried for so long began to dissipate, and she could finally see a future unburdened by regret and shame. Lauren knew that the road ahead would not be easy, but she was ready to face it with a heart full of forgiveness and a spirit renewed. She would share her story, not as a tale of pain and regret, but as a testament to the power of forgiveness and the capacity of the human heart to heal.

As she walked away from the river, she knew that the journey towards self-forgiveness was a lifelong one. But she was no longer weighed down by her past, and for the first time in a long time, she felt a glimmer of hope and the promise of a brighter future.

Lauren's path to self-forgiveness was a transformative journey that would reshape her life in profound ways. The burden of her secret had been lifted, and with each step she took, she felt lighter, as if the weight of her past was gradually evaporating into the ether. With newfound determination, Lauren began to seek ways to heal and grow. She reached out to a therapist, someone who could help her navigate the complex emotions and memories that had held her captive for so long. Through their sessions, she learned coping strategies and gained a deeper understanding of herself.

Over time, she also confided in a few close friends who had stood by her through thick and thin. Their unwavering support and compassion further reinforced her belief that she was not defined by her past actions, but by her capacity to change and grow.

Lauren's journey toward self-forgiveness was not without its challenges. There were moments when doubt and guilt would resurface, threatening to pull her back into the darkness of her past. But each time, she reminded herself of the river of forgiveness and the promise of a brighter future. She had made a choice to release the hurt and pain, and she was committed to living a life free from the chains of regret and shame.

As time passed, Lauren found herself drawn to new opportunities and experiences. She pursued hobbies she had long neglected, rekindling her passion for art and music. She also volunteered at a local community center, using her own experiences to support others who were facing difficult decisions and seeking solace.

One day, while volunteering, she met a young woman who seemed lost and burdened by her own secret. The woman's eyes reflected the same pain and fear that had once consumed Lauren. Without hesitation, Lauren reached out and offered a compassionate ear. She shared her own journey of forgiveness, giving the young woman hope that healing and transformation were possible.

Months turned into years, and Lauren continued to evolve. She found love, a deep and nurturing love that she had never believed possible. Her partner embraced her for who she was, scars and all, and together they built a life filled with understanding, empathy, and love.

Lauren's journey toward self-forgiveness had not only transformed her own life but had also become a source of inspiration and hope for others. She realized that her story was not just her own; it was a testament to the resilience of the human spirit and the power of forgiveness.

As she stood by the same river where her journey had begun, Lauren looked back on her path with gratitude. The river still flowed, a symbol of the constant movement of life, and she knew that her journey was far from over. But she was no longer defined by her past; she was defined by her ability to forgive and her capacity to love herself and others.

Forgiveness of self

Forgiveness is a river that flows
From a heart that's willing to let go
Of the hurt and the pain that we hold
And the stories that we've been told.

Life is a connection, a bond we share
Breathing inside us, a heartbeat we bear
Yours and mine, intertwined in time
A gift to cherish, a love divine.

But I'm too young to carry you full term
It's time to let go I hope you understand
I can't bear to ever hold your hand
My innocence was taken used and abused.

If I choose to carry you for 36 weeks
I must live with the turmoil and the grief
Regret, shame, and pain will be my lot
Disappointment, sadness, and anger will haunt.

But either way I choose, I know I've sinned
Lost and confused, judged by those who've not been
Through the how, the when, the what, the why of
my life story, of my silent cry.

I wasn't built for pain, but I endured
The hurt and the wounds, the scars that lured
Me into a world of shame and pain
But now I'm ready to release and gain.

To be free, to share my story, to heal
The hidden parts of me, to feel
The glory of a life without shame or pain
To walk tall, to rise again.

Forgiveness is the key to it all
To let go of the past, to stand tall
And face the future with hope and love
To cherish the bond, we might have shared
yours and mine, above.

So, I forgive myself, and I forgive him too
For the pain and the hurt, the things we couldn't do,
and I choose to disconnect you with love and grace in
my heart, in my soul, in this sacred space.

Lost

The weight of the past hung heavy on her shoulders as she walked the lonely path of grief and guilt. Each step seemed to echo with the haunting memories of that fateful decision, one that had left her with an ache that seemed impossible to heal. As she navigated the maze of her emotions, she grappled with the question of whether she would ever find forgiveness, both from herself and from a higher power.

For too long, she had carried the burden of her secret, afraid of the judgment and condemnation that she believed awaited her. The world seemed to be divided into those who saw her as a sinner and those who urged her to repent for her actions. But the truth was far more complex than anyone could understand. Her heart was a battlefield of conflicting emotions, where love for the child she could never hold warred with the pain of the past.

She sought solace in prayer, kneeling in the quiet sanctuary of a church. With tears streaming down her face, she beseeched for answers, for a glimmer of hope, for a path to redemption. The divine response remained elusive, shrouded in silence, leaving her to wrestle with her own conscience.

As she walked through the town, she couldn't escape the whispers and stares of judgmental onlookers, each word and gaze another reminder of the choices she had made. But amidst the condemnation, there were also voices of compassion and understanding. Some offered their support, recognizing the pain she carried, even if they couldn't fully comprehend it.

In the midst of her turmoil, she discovered a support group for women who had experienced similar loss and difficult decisions. In that circle of understanding, she finally found a space where she could share her story without fear of judgment. The women who had walked a similar path embraced her, offering comfort, empathy, and the reassurance that she was not alone.

Over time, as she continued to confront her past, she began to understand that healing was not about erasing the past but learning to live with it. Forgiveness, she realized, started with forgiving herself, acknowledging that she had made the best choice she could under the circumstances.

Her lost child would forever remain a part of her heart, a silent presence that had shaped her in ways she could never have foreseen.

She had learned that the complexities of life could not be easily judged or condemned, and that true compassion and understanding required a willingness to listen without prejudice.

With each step along the path of self-discovery, she found a measure of peace. The child she could never hold would always be a part of her, and while the scars of the past would never fully fade, they served as a reminder of her resilience and the capacity of the human spirit to endure, heal, and find hope amidst the darkest of journeys.

As the seasons changed and time continued to pass, the woman's journey of healing and self-discovery deepened. She had come to accept that her past was a part of her, and she couldn't change the choices she had made. Instead, she had chosen to focus on the lessons she had learned and the strength she had gained from her experiences.

One day, as she walked through the town, she noticed a flyer for a local charity organization that provided support and resources to women facing difficult decisions during pregnancy. The sight of the flyer stirred something within her. She realized that she could use her own story to help other women who might be facing similar challenges.

With determination and a newfound sense of purpose, she reached out to the organization and offered to share her experiences with other women who were grappling with difficult choices. Her story became a source of inspiration and comfort for those who felt lost and alone. She shared not only the pain and guilt she had experienced but also the resilience and self-compassion she had discovered on her journey.

Over time, she became a trusted mentor for women in need, offering them a listening ear, guidance, and support as they navigated their own paths. She helped them understand that they were not defined by their choices, and that forgiveness, both from within and from a higher power, was possible.

• • •

The judgmental voices in the town began to fade as more people saw the positive impact of her work. Compassion and understanding replaced condemnation, and the community became more open to discussions about the complexities of life.

The woman's journey had become a catalyst for change, challenging the rigid beliefs that had once kept her in the shadows.

As she continued her advocacy, she found moments of solace in the quiet sanctuary of the church. She no longer prayed for answers but for strength and guidance to continue her mission of compassion and healing. She understood that the divine response she had once sought had been within her all along, in the form of her own capacity to love, forgive, and make a difference in the lives of others.

The woman's path was no longer lonely or filled with guilt. It was a path of purpose, compassion, and resilience. Her lost child would forever hold a place in her heart, a reminder of her journey of healing and transformation. She had learned that healing was not about erasing the past but about finding meaning, growth, and hope amid the shadows of regret.

Lost Child

A child lost before it had the chance,
A decision made, but now a haunting dance,
Memories that continue to run their course,
A pain so deep, with no clear source.

Should I suffer in silence and hide in shame?
Blaming myself for a decision made in vain,
The scars of life, a hurried deed,
Still not given up, but still in need.

I can't bring you into this world, they say,
It's a sin, and I'll pay the price one day,
Some say if I repent, I'll be forgiven,
But which one is it? My heart is still driven.

I'll pray for the answer as I walk the line of shame,
People shouting, "You're a sinner!" with jars of life to claim,
My heart in turmoil, I want to disappear,
The tears won't stop, I can't face this pain and fear.

A child lost before it had the chance,
But in my heart, it will always dance,
A love so strong, yet forever out of reach,
My lost child, my soul will always beseech

Finding My Voice

With my past acknowledged, I sought to find my voice. I experimented with various forms of expression, from writing and speaking to painting and music. Each medium revealed a different aspect of my story, allowing me to grow in confidence and self-awareness.

As I sat down to write, I felt a knot in my stomach. For years, I had bottled up my feelings and experiences, afraid to share them with anyone. But something inside me had shifted, and I knew it was time to find my voice.

At first, my writing was hesitant and disjointed. I struggled to put my thoughts into words, afraid of what others might think if they read them. But as I continued to write, I began to feel a sense of release, as if each word I put on paper was a weight lifted from my shoulders.

Through writing, I discovered that I had a lot to say. I had stories to tell, feelings to express, and opinions to share. It was as if the act of writing gave me permission to speak my truth, without fear of judgment or rejection.

As my writing improved, I started to share it with others. At first, it was nerve-wracking to let others read my innermost thoughts and feelings. But the more I shared, the more I realized that my words resonated with others. People thanked me for putting into words what they had been feeling but had not been able to articulate themselves.

Encouraged by the positive feedback, I started to explore other forms of expression. I took up painting, using colors and shapes to express emotions that I could not put into words. I learned to play guitar, using music to convey the depth of my feelings.

Each medium revealed a different aspect of my story, allowing me to grow in confidence and self-awareness. I found that I had a talent for expressing myself through various art forms, and that by doing so, I could connect with others on a deeper level.

As I continued to experiment with different forms of expression, I began to see myself in a new light. I was no longer the scared, silent person I had been before. Instead, I was someone with a unique perspective, a story to tell, and a voice that deserved to be heard.

Through finding my voice, I learned that there is power in vulnerability. By sharing my experiences and emotions, I gave others permission to do the same. I realized that we all have stories to tell, and that by speaking our truth, we can create connections and understanding that transcend our differences.

Finding my voice was not an easy process, and there were times when I wanted to give up. But the more I expressed myself, the more I realized that my voice was worth fighting for. It was the key to my self-discovery, my healing, and my growth.

In finding my voice, I found myself. And for that, I am forever grateful.

As I continued to explore and refine my various forms of expression, I couldn't help but notice the impact it was having on those around me. It was as if my newfound voice had a ripple effect, touching the lives of people I had never even met.

One day, I received an email from a reader who had come across one of my written pieces. They shared their own struggles and how my words had provided them with comfort and hope during a challenging time in their life. It was a humbling experience to realize that my vulnerability and willingness to share had made a difference in someone else's life.

Encouraged by these interactions, I decided to take a step further. I started a blog where I regularly posted my writings, artwork, and even recorded some of the music I had composed. The response was overwhelming. People from all walks of life reached out to me, sharing their own stories, and expressing how my journey had inspired them to find their voices too.

In the local community, I began to participate in art exhibitions, sharing my paintings and their accompanying stories. It was at one of these exhibitions that I met Sarah, a fellow artist who had been grappling with her own demons. She told me how my paintings had resonated with her, how they had mirrored her own experiences, and how they had given her the courage to start expressing herself through her art.

Sarah and I became fast friends, and together, we organized a series of community events aimed at promoting self-expression and healing through the arts. We invited people to share their stories, their poems, their paintings, and their music. What started as a small gathering grew into a movement that helped countless individuals find their voices and heal their wounds.

As I continued to connect with people through my art and writing, I realized that finding my voice had not only been about personal growth but also about creating a supportive and empathetic community. Together, we were breaking down the barriers of silence and shame, encouraging one another to speak up and share our truths.

Over the years, I received messages and letters from people who had been inspired by my journey. Some had started writing their own books, others had embraced their artistic talents, and many had found the strength to confront their past traumas. It was heartwarming to witness the transformation that could occur when one person's willingness to be vulnerable sparked a chain reaction of empowerment and healing.

Finding my voice had not only been a journey of self-discovery but also a mission to empower others to do the same. It became clear to me that our stories, no matter how painful or difficult, had the power to connect us, heal us, and help us grow.

As I looked back on my journey from that hesitant writer to a catalyst for change in my community, I realized that finding my voice had not only given me a sense of purpose but had also allowed me to create a positive impact on the world. It was a reminder that our voices are not just for ourselves; they can be a beacon of hope for others who are searching for their own path to self-expression and healing.

And so, I continued to write, paint, and make music, not only for my own healing but for the healing of all those who crossed my path. Through the power of expression and vulnerability, I had found my voice, and in doing so, I had found a deeper connection to humanity and a profound sense of fulfillment.

Finding My Voice

It began as a nudge, subtle yet strong,
A quiet rhythm pulling me along.
Years of silence dulled my song,
Fears and doubts told me I was wrong.

With shaking hands, I wrote the first line,
Letting my truth take shape, define.
Each word I placed became a key,
Unlocking the parts I longed to see.

Colors came alive, bold and bright,
Brushstrokes painting my soul's fight.
Shapes and patterns spoke untold,
Stories hidden, now uncontrolled.

Music followed, steady and clear,
A melody rising, silencing fear.
Each note carried emotions deep,
Awakening dreams I thought asleep.

Sharing my story was the next step,
A leap of faith where courage crept.
At first, the fear was hard to bear,
But soon I found connection there.

"You put my thoughts into words," they'd say,
"Helped me find light on the darkest day."
Their gratitude strengthened my resolve,
To let my voice continue to evolve.

Through art and words, I came to see,
A new reflection staring back at me.
No longer silenced, no longer small,
I embraced the fullness of it all.

Now I write, I paint, I play, I sing,
With every form, my spirit takes wing.
For finding my voice was never just mine,
It's a gift for others, a bridge to align.

"She Used to Love it Here"

He spent a lifetime searching for his equal, chasing dreams and seeking the one who could complete him. He thought he had found her once, but she slipped in and out of his life like a phantom, leaving him with a sense of longing and emptiness. She was nowhere to be found when he needed her the most.

He found himself chasing a love that didn't know how to love him back, just as he had once chased his own desires without considering the consequences. It was a painful realization, a mirror reflecting his past actions.

"I guess that's how she felt when I was running the streets," he mused, recognizing the irony of his situation. He had been reckless and indifferent to her feelings, and now he understood the loneliness she must have felt during those times.

Now, the tables had turned. He was ready to commit and be there for her, but she had moved on. It was a cruel twist of fate. He never realized the value of what he had until it was gone, a lesson learned too late.

He decided to visit their old apartment, a place that held so many cherished memories. As he walked in, he was greeted by an overwhelming sense of nostalgia. The rooms were empty, devoid of the life they once shared.

He remembered the joy they had experienced here, the laughter and happiness that used to fill these walls. They had danced in the living room, carefree and in love, believing that their bond was unbreakable.

But time had changed everything. Now, he stood alone in the same space, wishing he could turn back time and rewrite the story. He longed for a chance to make amends, to tell her how deeply sorry he was for his past mistakes.

Yet, he knew it was a futile wish. She had moved forward with her life, found someone else to love, and he couldn't blame her. He wondered if she ever thought about the moments they had shared, the love that had once flourished between them.

As he prepared to leave, the weight of his regret bore down on him. He walked out of the door, feeling the emptiness of the apartment echoing in his heart. In a soft, remorseful whisper, he muttered to himself, "She used to love it here." The words hung in the air, a poignant reminder of the love he had lost and the price he had paid for his past actions.

Days turned into weeks, and the echoing refrain of "She used to love it here" remained etched in his mind. It had become a haunting mantra, a testament to the love he had lost due to his own mistakes.

With time, he found himself reflecting on the past, replaying the moments they had shared in their beloved apartment. He couldn't escape the memories, and each one was a painful reminder of what could have been. The laughter, the love, the stolen kisses in the kitchen—all of it seemed like a distant dream now.

One evening, he stumbled upon an old photo album tucked away in a dusty corner of his closet. It was a treasure trove of moments frozen in time; memories preserved in faded photographs. As he flipped through the pages, he couldn't help but smile at the images of their happier days.

He saw snapshots of them at their favorite park, their faces beaming with joy as they sat on a swing set, lost in each other's company. There were pictures of them cooking dinner together in the cozy kitchen of their apartment, captured in candid moments of shared laughter and whispered secrets.

One particular photo stopped him in his tracks. It was a candid shot of her, caught in the midst of her infectious laughter, her eyes crinkled with mirth. He remembered the way her laughter used to fill the room, how it could banish any trace of sadness or doubt.

• • •

Tears welled up in his eyes as he continued to flip through the album, realizing that he had lost not just a love, but his best friend. She had been the one who knew him better than anyone else, the one who could make him laugh even when he didn't want to.

In the quiet solitude of his apartment, he decided he couldn't change the past, but he could try to make amends. He wanted to reach out to her, not to win her back, but to apologize for the hurt he had caused. He owed her that much.

He spent hours crafting a heartfelt letter, pouring his soul into every word. He acknowledged his mistakes, expressed his deepest regrets, and told her that he would always cherish the beautiful memories they had created together.

With trembling hands, he sealed the letter in an envelope and addressed it to her. The next day, he walked to the post office, the weight of his past actions heavy on his shoulders. He mailed the letter, hoping that somehow, it would find its way to her and offer a glimpse of the remorse and love he felt.

As he returned to their old apartment, he realized that even though she had moved on, the love they once shared would forever linger in the walls, the echoes of their laughter and the whispers of their dreams. He couldn't change the past, but he could honor the memories by becoming a better person, one who learned from his mistakes and carried the lessons forward.

In the quiet solitude of their former home, he whispered softly to the empty room, "She used to love it here." But this time, the words were filled with a promise to never forget, to cherish the past, and to build a future that honored the love they once had.

Weeks turned into months, and he continued to wait, his heart heavy with hope and regret. The letter he had sent remained unanswered, and he couldn't help but wonder if it had reached her at all. Doubt crept into his mind, and he questioned whether she would ever forgive him for the pain he had caused.

He tried to fill the void in his life with work, hobbies, and new friends, but nothing could truly replace what he had lost. The apartment, once a place of love and happiness, had become a constant reminder of his mistakes. He contemplated moving away, starting fresh in a new city, but he couldn't bring himself to leave behind the memories they had created together.

As the seasons changed, he noticed subtle signs that someone had been in their old apartment. The mail he hadn't collected started to disappear, and occasionally, he would find fresh flowers in a vase on the windowsill. It gave him a glimmer of hope that perhaps she had received his letter and was reaching out in her own way.

One crisp autumn afternoon, he heard a knock at the door. His heart skipped a beat as he rushed to answer it, hoping beyond hope that it was her. To his surprise, he found an envelope lying on the doormat. It was addressed to him, in her familiar handwriting.

With trembling hands, he opened the envelope and read her words. In her heartfelt letter, she acknowledged his apology and the pain they had both endured. She shared her own regrets and mistakes, admitting that she had never stopped loving him.

Tears welled up in his eyes as he read her words, and he realized that the love they had once shared had not vanished entirely. It had survived the trials and tribulations, the mistakes, and misunderstandings. They had both grown, and in their time apart, they had learned valuable lessons about themselves and each other.

Determined to make amends, he reached out to her, and they agreed to meet in their old apartment—the place where they had first fallen in love and the place where they had once danced, laughed, and dreamed together.

As they stood face to face, years of separation melted away, and the love they had shared rekindled like a long-lost flame. They talked for hours, sharing their stories, their dreams, and their newfound wisdom.

In the end, they decided to start anew, building a future that honored their shared past. They knew that it wouldn't be easy, that there would be challenges ahead, but they were willing to face them together.

Their old apartment, once a place of sorrow and longing, was now a symbol of their love's resilience. As they held each other close, they whispered softly to the empty room, "She used to love it here." But this time, the words were filled with hope, forgiveness, and a renewed commitment to cherish the present and build a future that honored the love they had once shared.

She used to Love it here

He spent a lifetime searching for his equal
Chasing his dreams, he thought he found her
no sequel she ran in and out of his life
he searched for her nowhere in sight

He found himself chasing a love
that didn't know how to love him.
I guess that's how she felt when
I was running the streets

Now the tables have turned I'm ready
and she moved on. You never realize
what you had to it's gone

She used to love it here
She used to love it here

He walked into their old apartment,
the place where they once shared so many memories.
It was now barren and empty, a shell of its former self.
He remembered how happy they were here,
how they used to dance around the living room,
laughing and joking as if they were the only
two people in the world.

But that was a long time ago. Now, he was alone,
standing in the middle of the empty space,
wishing he could turn back the clock and make things right.
He remembered how much she used to love it here,
but now all he could hear was the echo of his own footsteps.

He closed his eyes and took a deep breath,
trying to will away the memories.
It was too painful to think about what he had lost.
He wished he could see her again, even just for a moment,
to tell her how sorry he was for everything he had done.

But he knew it was too late.
She had moved on, found someone else to love.
He wondered if she ever thought about him,
if she remembered the good times they had shared.
He hoped she did, but he knew it was unlikely.

He turned to leave,
feeling the weight of his regret heavy on his shoulders.
As he walked out the door, he whispered to himself,
"She used to love it here."
The words echoed through the empty apartment,
a haunting reminder of what he had lost.

She used to love it here

By Design

The tragic story of this young girl is a painful reminder of the dark side of our society. It's a story of how a human life can be undervalued, used, and abused by a system that exploits people's vulnerabilities and dreams. It's a story of how a young girl's beauty and body became her curse rather than her blessing. It's a story of how a girl's family and social structure failed to protect her and instead, pushed her into a life of prostitution and violence.

It's hard to imagine how anyone could sell a human life and sleep well at night. But unfortunately, this is not an uncommon phenomenon. There are people who prey on vulnerable individuals, who lure them with false promises, who exploit their bodies and minds, and who discard them when they are no longer useful. There are people who profit from human trafficking, forced labor, and prostitution, who treat human beings as commodities to be bought and sold. These people may not see their victims as human beings, but rather as objects to be used and disposed of.

The story of this young girl reminds us that we need to do more to protect vulnerable individuals, to empower them with education and skills, to provide them with a safe and nurturing environment, and to hold those who exploit them accountable. We need to challenge the narratives and stereotypes that reduce people to their looks, gender, or social status, and recognize the inherent dignity and worth of every human being. We need to work together to create a world where every individual can thrive, not just survive, and where human life is valued and respected above all else.

In the wake of the tragic story of the young girl, there emerged a groundswell of compassion and determination within the community. People from all walks of life began to rally together, determined to make a difference, and ensure that such a heartbreaking tale would never be repeated.

First and foremost, they recognized the need for education and skills to empower vulnerable individuals. They launched initiatives aimed at providing accessible education and vocational training for those who had been marginalized and left behind. These programs focused on not only academic education but also life skills and emotional well-being. It was a step toward breaking the cycle of poverty and despair that had ensnared so many like the young girl.

A safe and nurturing environment became a cornerstone of their efforts. Shelters were established to offer refuge and support to those seeking to escape exploitative situations. These shelters provided not only physical safety but also counseling and emotional healing, allowing survivors to rebuild their lives with dignity.

At the heart of their mission was holding those who exploited others accountable for their actions. Advocacy groups and legal organizations joined forces to strengthen the legal framework against human trafficking, forced labor, and prostitution. They worked tirelessly to ensure that the perpetrators faced severe consequences for their crimes.

The community also embarked on a campaign to challenge harmful narratives and stereotypes. They sought to redefine beauty, gender roles, and social status, emphasizing that every individual had intrinsic worth and unique qualities that extended far beyond their outward appearances or circumstances. They encouraged media outlets, schools, and influential figures to promote inclusivity and respect for diversity.

As these efforts gained momentum, they began to see the transformative power of unity and collective action. The tragic story of the young girl served as a catalyst for change, inspiring individuals to come together and address the systemic issues that allowed such tragedies to occur.

Over time, stories emerged of survivors who had not only rebuilt their lives but had also become advocates for change themselves. They shared their experiences, shedding light on the harsh realities they had faced and inspiring others to break free from the cycle of exploitation.

The young girl's story, while undeniably tragic, had ignited a movement that was determined to create a world where every individual could not only survive but also thrive. It was a testament to the resilience of the human spirit and the capacity for compassion and change within society.

In the end, her legacy was not one of despair but of hope—a reminder that even in the darkest of times, there could be a path toward a brighter future for all.

By design

Easily disposed of
No value
Used
Abused
Tossed to the side

Playing dress up
6-inch heels
Short dress
Revealing all of you

All To do it over again the next day
And the next—and the next—and the next

How do you sell a human life and sleep well at night?
Her entire life she was told your beautiful
any man would be happy to have you
she was molded to be a Servant
To rely on looks and use her body as a shared cost

Early in life her mother and aunts thought her to
plan to be a bride before she even could drive
living in a fantasy world Worshiping materialistic things
She was thought to be polite always hold your
head up high with grace make him notice you

Be the baddest in the room

What a mistake

Her Life shouldn't be easily disposed of
Manipulated into thinking that you
could put a price tag on her

Her mother died in an abandoned
apartment building on the east side
Her aunt was hung in a crack house
Her family structure crumbled

She never really knew her father but was shipped
off to him because he was next of kin
The system felt it was best to be reconnected with family
She had to pick up her life and move to an unfamiliar city

She took a two-hour plane ride with a stranger
who told her everything is going to be alright
this is what's best for you
The stranger introduced her to her
estranged father and brothers

The first time she was raped she was 12
By her older brother
She told her father after she was raped again
by her other brother. Her dad smiled and said now you're ready

She felt she had no choice
She put on the attire that was given to her by
her mother six-inch stiletto heels a short spandex dress
face full of make-up and headed out to work the streets

This went on for what seemed like forever
No one asked her name, her age
One day she got tried and refused to work
They found her body burned
in the middle of a parking lot late at night
Selling her a dream of what a beautiful life could be cost her life
That's what the system would do

Broken pieces of a shattered heart

The shattered pieces of her heart lay scattered around her, as she sat in the corner, trying to make sense of what had just happened. She had been playing games with men, jumping from one relationship to the next, hoping to find the love she craved but never truly finding it.

As she sat there, lost in thought, she realized that her actions had led to the destruction of not only her own heart but the heart of the man who had loved her. She had pushed him away, played games with him, and never truly appreciated the love he had for her.

But now it was too late. He was gone, and she was left with only the broken pieces of a shattered heart.

As she looked around, she saw the glass that had been swept up by the pale of men who had come to clean up the mess. But she knew that no amount of cleaning could fix what was broken inside of her.

She thought back to the last time she had seen him, the last time she had pushed him away. She knew now that she had been wrong, that she had made a mistake, and that it was too late to fix it.

But she couldn't help but wonder what could have been, what a healthy relationship could have looked like if she had only given him a chance.

As she sat there lost in thought, she realized that her fear of being alone had led her down this path, that she had been searching for love in all the wrong places.

But now she knew that the only way to heal her shattered heart was to learn to love herself, to find peace within herself, and to be comfortable with being alone.

And as she looked out the window, she knew that the road ahead would not be easy, but she was ready to take the first step towards healing and finding true love, even if it meant starting over from broken pieces.

She made a promise to herself that she would no longer jump in and out of relationships, using them as a temporary escape from her loneliness. She realized that it was time to face her fear of being alone and learn to enjoy her own company.

Days turned into weeks, and weeks into months. She began to focus on self-improvement, pursuing her passions and hobbies that had been long neglected. She found solace in reading, painting, and spending time with close friends who supported her journey toward self-discovery.

As time passed, she couldn't help but reflect on the good man she had pushed away. She realized the pain she had caused him and the missed opportunity for a loving relationship. She knew she couldn't change the past, but she hoped that he had found the happiness and love he deserved.

One day, while attending a local art gallery, she met someone new. His name was Daniel, and he had a warmth and kindness about him that drew her in. They struck up a conversation about the paintings on display, and as they talked, she felt a connection she hadn't felt in a long time.

As they continued to see each other, she took things slow, letting their relationship develop naturally. Daniel was patient and understanding, and he encouraged her to be her authentic self. She no longer felt the need to play games or hide behind a facade.

Together, they built a healthy and loving relationship based on trust and communication. They learned from each other's past experiences and vowed never to hurt each other as they had been hurt before.

As for the man from her past, she had heard that he had moved on and found happiness as well. She was glad to hear it, for she knew that they had both played their parts in the broken pieces of their past relationship.

In the end, she had found the strength to pick up the shattered pieces of her heart and put them back together, not through the pursuit of others, but through self-love and personal growth. And as she held Daniel's hand, she realized that true love was not a game to be won but a bond to be nurtured and cherished, and she was finally ready to embrace it.

Broken pieces of a shattered heart

Broken pieces of a shattered heart
sitting in the corner
glass swept up
by the pale of men
that left them behind
oh no but I'm fine

I told him I wasn't ready
I continued to cancel dates
show up late I'll play this game

She hasn't had a chance to heal
jumping in and out of relationships
before she got over the next
the last one or the one before

Why? She doesn't like being alone
she needs to be held loved
jumping from body to body is her new sport

People deal with relationships differently
some abandon relationships all together
but for her she loves her peace
and search for love anyway she can get it
some people are afraid of being alone

She stops and thinks of what a healthy relationship
could be could have been trying to find you in them
I guess now, I'm locked up in this cage
my freedom taken away still full of rage
sorry I didn't get to say my farewell or goodbye

I know your mother was hurt that wasn't a good thing
you didn't have any children but so sad
no one to carry on your legacy

to be completely honest I tried it wasn't love
it was the chase for me I wanted to win

Sad just a game there was no end
I didn't plan this once you decided to leave for good
I saw it in your eyes this time I couldn't lose you again
not to her I don't know what came over me
everything went black when I snapped
out of it I was in handcuffs I heard sirens

Welp, I guess I did win in the end
you played your game, and I played mine
who is the blame? I blamed you for all the others before
the one's that tore me in half you were a good man I couldn't see
past the pain your life is now destroyed now you are at rest
I awaken from my sleep I never gave him my number
just a thought of going through the pain no rest
all I heard was these beautiful lies before he even
spoke looking into his beautiful eyes

Inside Out

My life flashed before my eyes the day my father died. I remember the day he beat me until I was black and blue. My eyes were swollen, and the blood was rushing from my skull. I screamed for help knowing that my mother was close by, but she never came to save me why would she, she is the one that antagonized the beating. She lied to my father and demanded that he beat me and gave him a stick to hit me with.

I woke up on the ICU I overheard the detective talking saying my lifeless body was found discarded in the alley, beaten, beyond recognition. I went through life trying to figure out the why? Why did she hate her loving baby girl? I don't want to hate her. I wish I could love her, but I don't know how. How do you love when you never received love? What is it anyway? I hear the word repeatedly said to me, but the meaning is dead.

Is love a need or a want? I believed it's a joke. I felt pain in rage from Love, I was done.

Only if I was a better child better daughter, I'm sorry do you love me now.

Wait that's not the way to love.

Looking outside of myself, I found solace in the darkest corners of my soul. The trauma I endured left scars not just on my body, but also on my heart and mind. It was a constant struggle to understand the concept of love when all I had ever known was pain and betrayal.

As I lay in the hospital bed, recovering from the vicious attack that had left me battered and bruised, I couldn't help but reflect on my life. I had spent years trying to please my mother, seeking her approval, and longing for her love. But no matter how hard I tried, it was never enough.

The detective's words about my lifeless body being found in that alley echoed in my mind. It was a stark reminder of how little my mother cared for me. She had not only allowed the abuse to happen but had actively encouraged it. I couldn't fathom why a mother would do such a thing to her own child.

In the weeks that followed, I delved deep into self-reflection. I realized that my search for love had led me down a path of self-destruction. I had been seeking validation from others, hoping that their love would fill the void within me. But I had never learned to love myself.

I began therapy to heal both physically and emotionally. My therapist helped me see that love wasn't about being a better child or daughter, as I had believed for so long. Love was not a bargaining chip or a reward for good behavior. It was a fundamental human need, a source of warmth, connection, and understanding.

I started the arduous journey of self-love, and it was far from easy. I learned to forgive myself for the perceived shortcomings and mistakes. I discovered that love wasn't just an external force; it was something that needed to grow from within. It was a deep, unconditional acceptance of oneself, flaws, and all.

With time and healing, I reached a point where I could look at my mother without anger or resentment. I saw her as a deeply troubled woman who had never learned to love herself either. Our paths had diverged, and I chose not to perpetuate the cycle of abuse and neglect.

I didn't need her love anymore because I had found it within myself. I learned that love wasn't a joke; it was a powerful force that could heal, transform, and bring light to even the darkest of places. I vowed to use the love I had discovered within me to build a better life, one filled with compassion, empathy, and genuine connections with others.

As I continued my journey, I realized that looking outside of myself for love had been a futile endeavor. True love had always resided within me, waiting to be discovered and nurtured. And now, with a heart full of self-love, I was ready to face the world and share that love with others, one step at a time.

With each passing day, I felt myself growing stronger, not just physically, but emotionally and spiritually as well. My therapy sessions were a lifeline, helping me navigate the labyrinth of my past and uncover the layers of pain and trauma that had accumulated over the years. It was a slow and painful process, but I was determined to heal and break free from the chains of my past.

One of the most profound lessons I learned during therapy was the importance of setting boundaries. I realized that I had spent so much of my life trying to please others and seeking their validation that I had neglected my own needs and well-being. It was time to put myself first and protect my newfound self-love.

As I began to set boundaries, I faced resistance from some people in my life, including my mother. She couldn't understand the changes I was making, and she lashed out in anger and frustration. But I held firm, knowing that my well-being was worth the discomfort of confronting her.

Over time, our relationship transformed. While it would never be a typical mother-daughter bond, it became a more distant yet peaceful coexistence. My mother's actions still puzzled me, but I no longer allowed them to control my emotions or define my self-worth. I also began to connect with other survivors of abuse, both online and through support groups. Sharing our stories and journeys of healing provided a sense of camaraderie and understanding that I had never experienced before. We lifted each other up, and together, we found strength in our vulnerability.

One day, as I was walking through the park, I came across a group of children playing. Their laughter and innocence touched something deep within me. I realized that the love I had discovered within myself was not just meant for me; it was meant to be shared with others. I decided to volunteer at a local children's shelter, where I could offer support and love to children who had experienced their own traumas. It was a challenging but rewarding experience, and it gave me a sense of purpose that I had never felt before. Through my interactions with these children, I learned that love was not a joke; it was a precious gift that had the power to heal and transform lives.

As the years passed, my life continued to evolve. I pursued my education and found a career in counseling, specializing in trauma and abuse survivors. I used my own experiences to connect with my clients and offer them hope and guidance on their own healing journeys.

Looking outside of myself had led me to a profound realization: love was not just an abstract concept or a distant ideal. It was a force that could be harnessed and channeled to bring about positive change in the world. My journey had taken me from the darkest corners of my soul to a place of light, love, and purpose. And in that transformation, I had found my true self.

My work as a counselor was deeply fulfilling. I felt a sense of purpose in helping others on their healing journeys, just as I had once been helped on mine. It was a way of giving back the love and support that I had found when I needed it the most.

I continued to volunteer at the children's shelter, becoming a consistent presence in the lives of those young souls who had endured their own hardships. I shared with them the importance of setting boundaries, self-acceptance, and the power of resilience. Seeing them grow and heal brought me immeasurable joy.

Over time, I also began to facilitate support groups for survivors of abuse, providing a safe space where they could share their stories, connect with others, and find strength in their vulnerability. These groups became a source of healing and empowerment, not just for the participants but for me as well.

As the years passed, my mother's health declined, and she found herself in a vulnerable position. The anger and resentment that had once consumed me had faded, replaced by a profound sense of compassion. I realized that she had been a victim of her own past, just as I had been. While her actions were inexcusable, I understood that she had never learned to love herself, and that had led her down a destructive path.

I visited her in the nursing home where she now resided, and we had conversations that we had never been able to have before. I didn't condone her actions, but I forgave her for my sake, not hers. In that forgiveness, I found closure and a sense of peace that I had never thought possible.

My journey had come full circle. I had looked outside of myself, seeking love, and understanding, only to discover that the greatest source of love resided within me. Through my experiences, I had learned that love was not a joke, but a transformative force that could heal and bring light to even the darkest of places.

I continued my work as a counselor, mentor, and advocate, sharing my story and my message of hope with those who needed it. Looking back on my life, I realized that the pain and trauma I had endured had led me to a place of strength, resilience, and a profound understanding of the human spirit.

In the end, my journey was not just about healing myself; it was about using my experiences to make a difference in the lives of others. And as I continued to look outside of myself, I found that the world was filled with opportunities to share love, offer support, and be a beacon of hope for those who needed it most.

Looking outside of myself

In the shadows of my past, a story unfolds,
Of a life where love was lost, and darkness took hold.
My father's rage, a storm that never ceased,
Leaving scars upon my soul, my heart, and inner peace.

The day he beat me, till I was black and blue,
My eyes swollen, my spirit shattered, a nightmare come true.
My mother's betrayal, a wound so deep and sore,
She handed him a weapon; she fed my pain even more.

In the ICU, I awoke from the abyss,
Lifeless body found discarded, a tragic twist.
The detective's words, a bitter truth to bear,
Beaten beyond recognition, in that alley's cold despair.

I searched for answers, for the reasons why,
Why did she despise me, her own flesh and blood,
oh my? I longed to love her, to heal the wounds of old,
But love, an elusive concept, in my heart, it felt so cold.

Is love a need, a want, or just a cruel joke?
It left me in pain and rage, a heavy yoke.
I questioned my worth, as a child, as a daughter,
Apologizing for existence, seeking love in troubled water.

But then I learned, love wasn't earned or begged,
It wasn't a game or a puzzle to be wedged. It dwelled within,
waiting to be set free, A self-love that blossomed,
like a flower from a seed.

In my journey of healing, I found a new way,
To love myself fiercely, in the light of the day.
To let go of the past, to forgive, not forget,
To find strength in vulnerability, and to heal every regret.

Love's not a joke, it's a force to renew,
To mend broken hearts, to create something true.
I've turned my pain into purpose, my anger into grace,
And in loving myself, I've found my rightful place.

What separates us as people?

In today's society, there are numerous factors that have the potential to separate us as people, leading to division and discord within our country. These divisions can often be detrimental to the unity and progress of a nation. When viewed through a third-person perspective, it becomes evident that many of these factors cloud our views of one another and contribute to harmful judgments. Recognizing the importance of getting to know individuals for who they truly are becomes essential in bridging these divides and strengthening the bonds that hold society together.

Culture is one of the most significant dividers among people. Different cultural backgrounds can lead to misunderstandings, stereotypes, and prejudice. People often judge others based on their cultural practices, traditions, and values, rather than taking the time to understand and appreciate the richness of diverse cultures.

Religion is another divisive factor. Beliefs and faith systems vary widely, leading to religious discrimination and intolerance. Preconceived notions and judgments based on religion can hinder the potential for cooperation and understanding among individuals of different faiths.

Politics is perhaps one of the most polarizing factors today. People often align themselves with political ideologies, and these affiliations can lead to strong biases and hostilities toward those with opposing views. Political polarization can hinder constructive dialogue and compromise, which are essential for a healthy democratic society.

Sex and gender identity can also create divides. Gender stereotypes and biases can lead to discrimination and unequal opportunities for individuals based on their gender. These divisions can weaken society by excluding or marginalizing certain groups.

Family values and upbringing play a significant role in shaping one's perspectives and beliefs. Differences in family values can lead to misunderstandings and judgments about others' lifestyles and choices. It is essential to recognize that everyone's upbringing is unique and should not be a basis for judgment.

Social status and class distinctions can create barriers between people. Economic disparities can lead to inequalities in opportunities and access to resources, which can breed resentment and divisions within society.

Titles and education levels can be used as markers of social hierarchy, leading to judgments about intelligence or competence based on one's professional or academic achievements. This can undermine cooperation and collaboration among individuals from diverse backgrounds.

Appearance and age are often used as superficial indicators of a person's worth or capabilities. Stereotyping based on physical appearance or age can lead to discrimination and missed opportunities for valuable interactions and contributions.

Money and wealth disparities can create deep divides in society. Economic inequality can lead to social unrest and resentment, which can have negative consequences for a nation's stability and progress.

Ideological differences, whether related to politics, social issues, or philosophical beliefs, can lead to divisive debates and even hostility. People often cling to their ideologies, making it challenging to find common ground and engage in constructive dialogue.

Amidst these divisions, there is a growing realization that the path forward lies in transcending these barriers and embracing the values of empathy, tolerance, and open-mindedness. By taking a step back and viewing society from a third-person perspective, one can begin to understand the damage that these divisions cause to the fabric of our nation.

As individuals, it is imperative to recognize that culture, religion, politics, sex, family values, status, class, titles, education, appearance, age, money, and ideology are just facets of our complex identities. They do not define the entirety of who we are as human beings. When we allow these divisions to cloud our judgment and hinder our ability to connect with one another, we weaken ourselves as a society.

Getting to know individuals for who they truly are is a vital step in breaking down these barriers. It means engaging in meaningful conversations, listening to diverse perspectives, and learning from one another's experiences. It means looking beyond stereotypes and preconceived notions to discover the common humanity that binds us all.

When we make the effort to understand the intricacies of someone's culture, we can appreciate the beauty and diversity it brings to our world. When we respect different religious beliefs, we create space for spiritual growth and mutual respect. When we engage in constructive political discourse, we can find common ground and work towards shared goals. When we embrace gender diversity, we empower individuals to be their authentic selves. When we acknowledge the impact of upbringing on our values, we foster empathy and compassion. When we address economic disparities, we promote a fairer and more just society. When we value education and experience, we tap into a wealth of knowledge and expertise. When we celebrate diversity in appearance and age, we recognize the richness of human experiences. When we address economic inequality, we ensure that everyone has a fair shot at success. When we engage in open-minded ideological discussions, we can find innovative solutions to complex problems.

This journey towards understanding and unity is not without its challenges. Breaking down the barriers of culture, religion, politics, and the many other factors that divide us requires patience, humility, and a willingness to learn. It may be uncomfortable at times, as it involves confronting our own biases and prejudices. However, it is a journey worth embarking on, as it can lead to a more harmonious and prosperous society.

When we engage in meaningful conversations about culture, we discover the richness of traditions, cuisines, and art forms that can enrich our lives. We learn to appreciate the beauty in our differences and find common ground in our shared human experiences.

Respecting different religious beliefs allows us to foster an environment where people of all faiths can coexist peacefully. It encourages spiritual growth and creates opportunities for interfaith dialogue, fostering a greater sense of community and understanding.

Engaging in constructive political discourse means acknowledging that diverse perspectives can lead to innovative solutions. It means focusing on shared goals and values rather than perpetuating divisiveness. It is through compromise and collaboration that we can build a more stable and equitable society.

Embracing gender diversity empowers individuals to express their true selves and contributes to a more inclusive society. It opens doors for people of all genders to pursue their dreams and ambitions without fear of discrimination.

Recognizing the impact of upbringing on our values allows us to approach others with empathy and compassion. It means understanding that everyone's life experiences have shaped their beliefs and behaviors.

Addressing economic disparities is essential for building a fairer society where opportunities are not limited by one's financial situation.

Ensuring access to education and healthcare for all can pave the way for a more prosperous nation.

Valuing education and experience means tapping into the collective knowledge and expertise of our society. It promotes lifelong learning and encourages individuals to reach their full potential.

Celebrating diversity in appearance and age fosters a more inclusive and accepting society. It reminds us that beauty comes in all forms and that wisdom can be found in people of all ages.

Addressing economic inequality requires policies and initiatives aimed at creating a level playing field. It ensures that everyone, regardless of their economic background, has a fair chance to succeed.

Engaging in open-minded ideological discussions means being open to new ideas and perspectives. It encourages critical thinking and innovation, leading to better solutions for the challenges we face.

In conclusion, while the factors that divide us as a people are numerous and deeply ingrained, the journey towards unity and understanding is one worth pursuing. By embracing empathy, tolerance, and open-mindedness, we can begin to break down the barriers that separate us and build a stronger, more inclusive society. It is through these efforts that we can create a brighter future where diversity is celebrated, and unity prevails.

Divided

In a world divided, torn apart, they see,
By walls of prejudice, that cloud their glee.
A third person's gaze unveils the strife,
The things that sever, the bonds of life.

Culture stands as a formidable wall,
Yet beneath the surface, humanity's call.
Embrace the customs, the dances, the song,
In unity, they all can belong.

Religion's differences, they often fight,
But beneath faith's veil, there's a guiding light.
Tolerance, respect, let hearts unfurl,
For love's the essence of every creed and swirl.

Politics, the arena of heated debates,
Where differences clash, and anger awaits.
Seek common ground, compromise, and mend,
For in unity, democracy shall ascend.

Sex, a divisive line, they often draw,
Yet love knows no bounds, transcending the law.
Celebrate the spectrum of gender and race,
In diversity, they find their rightful place.

Family values, shaped by upbringing's hand,
But beneath the surface, they understand.
Each story unique, each heart's desire,
For love and acceptance, let them all aspire.

Status and class, they may define,
Yet beneath the labels, a shared sunshine.
Bridge the gaps, with compassion in sight,
For humanity's worth, knows no social height.
Titles and education, markers they bear,
But wisdom's path, each heart may share.

Let knowledge unite, let ignorance depart,
For unity starts with an open heart.
Appearance and age, they often judge,
Yet deeper stories, beneath the surface nudge.

In wrinkles and scars, and colors that blend,
In acceptance and love, they all shall mend.
Money, a powerful force, can divide,
Yet shared prosperity, on hope they ride.

Equal opportunity, a dream they chase,
For unity shines in an equal embrace.
Ideology, the source of many a clash,
Yet open minds can break the impasse.

In dialogue and reason, they shall prevail,
For unity's strength is a common sail.
In the end, it's clear to see,
That what divides them can also set them free.
Through empathy, understanding, and love's sweet art,
They'll bridge the gaps and mend each heart.

Trigger Warning

You were 5'2", 90 pounds, and never smiled, terrified of making the wrong moves because if you moved the wrong way, you would get punched and kicked or put out on the street just for looking the wrong way.

You never knew why she was upset or when your next beating was going to happen, you tried to prepare for it every day, but your mother would catch you off guard and just punch you in the face, chase you down the street or lock you out that day.

One day, the abuse became too much to bear. You couldn't take it anymore. You knew that if you stayed, you might not survive the next beating. You knew you had to leave. But leaving was easier said than done. You didn't have any money, job, or place to go. You felt trapped, like there was no way out.

But you had to try. You waited until your abuser was out of the house, then quickly packed a small bag with some clothes and essentials. You took a deep breath and walked out the door, never looking back.

As you walked down the street, you felt a mix of fear and relief. You didn't know where you were going, but you knew that you had to keep moving forward. You wandered for hours, trying to find a safe place to rest. You were tired, hungry, and scared.

But then, you saw a sign that read "Domestic Violence Shelter." You hesitated at first, but then gathered up the courage to walk in. The staff welcomed you with open arms, offering you a warm meal and a safe place to sleep.

For the first time in a long time, you felt like you were going to be okay. You started to attend therapy sessions and support groups, and slowly but surely, you began to heal. It wasn't easy, but with the help of the shelter staff and the other survivors, you found the strength to move on and start a new life.

Years later, you looked back on that day with a mix of gratitude and sadness. You were grateful for the shelter that gave you a chance to start over, but sad that so many others were still trapped in abusive relationships. You made a promise to yourself to do whatever you could to help others who were going through what you went through.

And so, you became an advocate for survivors of domestic violence, working tirelessly to raise awareness and provide resources to those who needed them. You never forgot where you came from, but you were determined to make sure that no one else had to go through what you did.

With each passing day, you became more resilient and determined to create a brighter future for yourself. You attended workshops at the shelter to gain new skills and build your self-esteem. Slowly but steadily, you started rebuilding your life.

One day, while attending a support group meeting at the shelter, you met Sarah, another survivor of domestic violence. Her story was eerily similar to yours, and you could see the fear and desperation in her eyes. You felt an instant connection with her and knew that you couldn't just stand by and watch her suffer.

You offered Sarah a shoulder to lean on, sharing your own experiences and letting her know that there was hope for a better life. You helped her navigate the resources available at the shelter, and together, you began the journey toward healing and independence.

As time passed, both of you continued to support each other, and your bond grew stronger. You found employment and secured a safe place to live, and eventually, you moved out of the shelter, knowing that you were now strong enough to stand on your own.

But you didn't stop there. You and Sarah decided to channel your experiences into something positive. Together, you founded an organization dedicated to helping survivors of domestic violence. You worked tirelessly to raise awareness about the issue, organize fundraisers, and collaborate with other support organizations in your community.

Your advocacy work started to gain traction, and more survivors found solace and support through your organization. You provided them with the resources, encouragement, and hope they needed to break free from their abusive situations.

Over the years, your organization expanded its reach, offering educational programs on healthy relationships, legal assistance, and counseling services. You became a powerful voice in your community, advocating for policy changes to protect survivors and hold abusers accountable.

Through your unwavering dedication and the support of your organization, you helped countless individuals break free from the cycle of abuse and find their own paths to healing and independence. You had turned your painful past into a source of strength and hope for others, and in doing so, you had transformed the lives of many.

The journey from a life of fear and abuse to one of empowerment and advocacy was not easy, but you knew it was worth every moment of struggle. You had not only survived but thrived, and you were determined to ensure that others could do the same.

Trigger Warning

You were 5'2", a wisp of a frame,
Living in shadows, carrying blame.
Eyes downcast, afraid to meet,
The wrath that struck swift, without retreat.

Bruises told stories your voice could not,
A childhood lost, innocence caught.
Each day began with a silent prayer,
For peace, for safety, for love somewhere.

Her rage was sudden, her fury blind,
A mother's love you'd never find.
A punch, a slap, a door slammed tight,
You ran through darkness, fleeing the night.

But one day, fear turned into resolve,
A quiet strength began to evolve.
With nothing but hope in a bag by your side,
You stepped into the unknown, terrified.

The road was long, the nights were cold,
Each step a story, a courage untold.
Until a shelter's light pierced through,
A door opened wide, welcoming you.

Hands reached out, offering care,
A warm meal, a bed, someone aware.
Therapy sessions, voices that healed,
A community built on truths revealed.

Years passed, and scars began to fade,
You found your power, no longer afraid.
A survivor transformed, with a heart so strong,
Turning pain into purpose all along.

You met others like you, bound by despair,
And showed them the strength in learning to care.
Together, you rose, breaking the chains,
Building a future from past remains.

Now your voice echoes, fierce and clear,
A light of hope for all who hear.
You fight for the silenced, the broken, the bruised,
Creating a world where none are abused.

Trigger warning: the pain was real,
But through the hurt, you learned to heal.
From ashes, you rose, with fire to give,
Teaching the world what it means to live.

Natural Women

In a world filled with the beauty of nature, there lived a remarkable woman. She embodied the essence of natural beauty, with curves that flowed like the gentle sway of the wind-blown trees and a magnetic presence that drew all eyes toward her.

Her hips had a natural grace, swaying seductively as she moved, and there was a playful bounce in her step whenever she bent over to pick up her pen. Her lips were soft and spoke the truth with a sincerity that brought life to any conversation. She was a real queen, prioritizing her home and understanding her own worth.

This extraordinary woman looked like a dream come true, a vision of beauty that others aspired to emulate. People admired her, wanting to walk, talk, and even think like her, for she had set the standard of natural beauty.

She was far from average; she was a living legend, a woman who would be remembered for generations to come. Many tried to replicate her, but she remained the original natural woman, an embodiment of grace and elegance.

Her personality was as vast as the ocean, soothing the souls of those lucky enough to know her. She was a place one could always call home, a sanctuary of warmth and love. She excelled in every aspect of life, effortlessly balancing cooking, cleaning, running a business, and raising children. You'd want her on your team, for she was a force to be reckoned with.

This natural woman knew exactly what she wanted in life and never doubted her own worth. She supported others in their journeys, never seeking competition, always recognizing genuine talent, and graciously sharing her space with them.

She possessed an unparalleled discernment, listening not just to respond, but to truly understand. Her wisdom ran deep, and she never let the weight of her past trauma or pain define her. She never played games with others and was as solid as the bedrock beneath her feet.

Never take her for granted, for you would never find another quite like her, this natural woman who was the birth canal of life itself, creating nations and shaping destinies.

In her, all the power and beauty of nature converged to birth a nation, some of whom would go on to rule the world. She was all of that, the inner essence of every woman, reflected in the world around her.

She was the embodiment of a Natural Woman, a living testament to the power of beauty, strength, and grace, forever nurturing life and bringing joy to those lucky enough to know her.

A true embodiment of a natural woman. Sarah's journey towards bringing life into the world was a testament to her strength, grace, and love. Conception marked the beginning of this remarkable journey. Sarah and her partner, John, had dreamed of starting a family for years. They rejoiced when they discovered the joyful news that Sarah was pregnant. It was the spark that ignited their shared dream of parenthood.

As the days turned into weeks, Sarah began to experience the changes that come with the first trimester. Morning sickness tested her resilience, but she met it with determination and a sense of purpose. The natural woman in her recognized the importance of nurturing the life growing within her, and she embraced this new chapter with open arms.

Throughout the second trimester, Sarah's belly grew round and full. She marveled at the tiny kicks and flutters that signaled the presence of her baby. She nurtured herself with nutritious meals and gentle exercises, knowing that her well-being directly impacted the life inside her. Her partner, John, showered her with love and support, understanding the significance of this journey they were on together.

The third trimester brought with it new challenges. Sarah's body bore the weight of impending motherhood, and she faced moments of discomfort and fatigue. But her determination never wavered. With grace and resilience, she embraced her changing body, finding beauty in every stretch mark and curve. The natural woman within her was a beacon of strength and love.

As the days grew shorter, the moment of truth approached. Sarah's body prepared for the miracle of birth. The baby's arrival became imminent, and Sarah's excitement mixed with nervous anticipation. She knew that the birth canal would be the gateway to bringing her child into the world. The natural woman within her understood the importance of this sacred passage, and she faced it with courage.

The day finally arrived when Sarah felt the first contractions. John rushed her to the hospital, where the natural woman's strength shone brightest. With each contraction, she pushed with all her might, channeling the power of generations of mothers before her. And then, in a moment of pure magic, the cries of their newborn baby filled the room, a testament to Sarah's determination and the love that had brought them here.

Bringing their baby home was a momentous occasion. Sarah cradled her child in her arms, feeling an overwhelming sense of gratitude and awe. The natural woman within her knew that this was just the beginning of a lifelong journey of nurturing, teaching, and loving their child.

From those first hesitant steps to the momentous first day of school, Sarah and John stood by their child's side, nurturing their growth and helping them navigate the world. They celebrated every milestone, from the first solid foods to the first day of school, with pride and love.

Sarah, a true natural woman, had not only brought life into the world but also nurtured it with unwavering love and grace. She was a beacon of strength and wisdom, a living testament to the beauty and power of motherhood. Her journey had been a remarkable one, filled with challenges and triumphs, and she embraced it all with the heart of a true natural woman.

Natural Women

The natural shape of her hips that sway seductively
when she moves left, right, and right again.
The bounce in her bottom when she squats
or bend over to pick up her pen
The softness of her lips that speaks life
into any being a truth talker

A real Queen she takes care of home first
and knows her worth a beauty she's a best friend
She looks like what others dream or even pay for
They all want to look like her, talk like her,
walk like her, she is the standard of a natural beauty

There is nothing average about her
she is one for the history books never forgotten
there are many replicas of her,
but she is the original natural woman

Her big personality soothes many souls
she is a place that you would always want to call home
She could cook, clean, run a business and raise children.
You will want her on your team

She knows exactly what she wants.
She never questions her worth
she allows others to shine in their own time
never in competition. She recognizes real,
and share a space while also giving others grace

She's a woman of great discernment.
She listens to understand, and not necessarily to respond.
She doesn't live in her trauma, hurt, or pain
and never tries to run game.
Never take her for granted because you will
never find another one quite like her natural woman

She is the canal where life is formed, creating nation.
She is every woman in natural form, she births a nation,
some whom rule the world, imagine that
She is all of that, she is the inner you I see in me
She is a woman in every essence of the word

She is friend through thick & thin until the very end
She is a mother that teaches & leads by example
She is a sister to many women with no blood relation
She is a lover even through I've been scored so much pain
She is a teacher of life's struggles
I teach the truth not just my point of view
She is a walking testament
life has taught me so many hard lessons
She is a believer in the most high & because of him
She is amazing She is many things and still have room for growth...

Natural Woman

Unexpressive

It was easy for me to walk away before it ended, pretended as though I didn't hurt or feel pain. I told myself I didn't care to make it easier for my heart to let go, moving on was my gift and my curse. I found myself alone again because I couldn't face the drama, I don't argue I told myself, it was his issue, he could debate with himself, I was over this relationship.

I never knew how to properly communicate my feelings to anyone, it was difficult expressing how I felt, the words would get all scrambled up in my head and it was way too much. I would rather just leave and bury another relationship.

My heart felt heavy tears starting to form, I could not want or allow him or anyone to see me cry. I was not weak, my mind was racing and now I was debating if I should stay and face this head on or walk away, maybe I should write a note and he'll understand.

I can't marry this man, why did he propose? Everything was going great, but I knew it was a mistake to let him in. I found the ring and a note with his plans: he set a date when all his family and friends would attend, I didn't want to embarrass this man by refusing his hand in front of all of the people he loves. So, instead of breaking his heart I would walk away, he'll understand

As I walked away, I couldn't shake the feeling of regret that washed over me. I knew that leaving was the easier option, but it wasn't the right one. I needed to face my fear of communication and confront him with my feelings, no matter how difficult it was.

I turned around and walked back to the door, took a deep breath, and opened it. I found him sitting on the couch, his face twisted in confusion as he looked up at me.

"I'm sorry," I said, my voice trembling. "I'm sorry for pretending like everything was okay when it wasn't. I'm sorry for not communicating my feelings properly and for hurting you in the process. I don't want to walk away from us. I want to work through our problems together."

He looked at me for a long moment before standing up and wrapping me in a tight hug. "I'm sorry too," he said. "I should have noticed that something was wrong and talked to you about it. Let's work through this together."

As we sat down to talk, I realized that communication wasn't as scary as I thought it was. It was the key to a healthy relationship and a happier life. And even though it was hard, it was worth it.

Over the following weeks, we began the journey of truly understanding each other. We attended couples counseling to improve our communication skills and gain a deeper insight into each other's feelings and needs. It was challenging, but it was also incredibly rewarding.

As we delved into the complexities of our emotions and worked through the issues that had been festering beneath the surface, our bond grew stronger. We learned to express ourselves openly and honestly, without fear of judgment. Our relationship transformed into a safe space where vulnerability was embraced, not shunned.

With time, the doubts and fears that had once clouded our love began to dissipate. We both realized that the proposal had been a well-intentioned but misguided attempt to hold onto something we cherished. Our love for each other was real, but it needed to evolve beyond societal expectations and pressures.

• • •

Together, we decided to postpone the wedding plans and focus on nurturing our connection. We took trips together, embarked on new adventures, and rediscovered the joy of simply being in each other's company. It wasn't about the grand gestures; it was about the little moments of laughter and understanding that we shared.

Our friends and family may not have understood our decision, but it didn't matter.

We were writing our own story, one where communication, trust, and unconditional love were the cornerstones.

Over time, we did reach a point where we were both ready to commit to a lifelong partnership, but it was on our terms. We had learned the importance of expressing our feelings, facing challenges head-on, and supporting each other through thick and thin.

The day we exchanged vows in an intimate ceremony, surrounded by the people who truly mattered, was a testament to our growth and determination. It was a celebration of our love, not a show for the world. We had overcome our inability to communicate and had emerged stronger, more connected, and deeply in love.

As we danced together under the moonlit sky, I couldn't help but reflect on the journey that had brought us to this point. Our love had been tested, but it had also been strengthened. It was no longer unexpressive; it was a love that spoke volumes in the silence of our hearts.

Our story was no longer about walking away but about walking together, hand in hand, into the future, ready to face whatever challenges life might throw our way. We had learned that love wasn't just about the grand gestures; it was about the courage to stay, to communicate, and to grow together.

In the years that followed, our love continued to flourish and deepen. We had learned that true love was not about the perfection of a relationship, but the commitment to work through imperfections together. Our shared experiences had taught us the value of open and honest communication, and we made it a point to practice it daily.

We found joy in the simplicity of life, cherishing every moment, whether it was cooking dinner together, taking long walks in the park, or cuddling on the couch with a good book. These were the moments that truly mattered, the moments where our love was palpable, and our hearts felt at peace.

As we pursued our individual passions and dreams, we remained each other's biggest supporters. We celebrated each other's successes and comforted one another during setbacks. We had become not only partners but also best friends, relying on each other for strength and guidance.

Over time, we realized that the wedding we had postponed had taken on a new meaning. It was no longer about societal expectations or impressing others; it was about declaring our love and commitment in a way that felt authentic to us. So, on a beautiful, sunny day surrounded by the serenity of nature, we decided to have a small, intimate wedding with only our closest friends and family.

Our vows were a testament to our journey, a promise to always communicate, to face life's challenges together, and to continue growing and evolving as individuals and as a couple. As we exchanged rings and sealed our commitment with a kiss, it felt like the perfect beginning to the rest of our lives together.

Marriage brought its own set of challenges, but our foundation of trust, communication, and unwavering love carried us through. We knew that no matter what obstacles came our way, we would tackle them as a team, supporting and uplifting each other.

• • •

Our story, which had once been marked by an unexpressive fear of communication, had transformed into a beautiful narrative of love's enduring power. It was a reminder that love could conquer all obstacles, heal old wounds, and bring two souls together in a way that was profound and everlasting.

As we looked into each other's eyes, we knew that we had chosen the right path—our own path. Our love, once buried beneath unspoken words and fears, had blossomed into a love story for the ages, a love story where communication was not just a skill but a declaration of our love for each other, every day, in every way.

In the years that followed our wedding, our commitment to communication became the cornerstone of our relationship. We made a conscious effort to share our thoughts, feelings, and dreams with each other, no matter how big or small. It wasn't always easy; old habits die hard, and there were moments when fear or insecurity crept in. But we had learned that confronting those fears together was far better than letting them fester in silence.

We found that the more we communicated, the stronger our connection grew. Our bond deepened as we shared our fears, joys, and vulnerabilities. We discovered that true intimacy was not just about physical closeness but also about emotional closeness, and we cherished every moment of it.

Life continued to present us with challenges, as it often does. We faced career changes, health issues, and the ebb and flow of life's ups and downs. But through it all, we were each other's unwavering support system. We leaned on one another in times of trouble and celebrated together in times of joy.

Our love story was a testament to the power of growth and evolution in a relationship. We recognized that we were not the same people we were when we first met, and that was a beautiful thing. We encouraged each other's personal growth and respected the changes that time brought. Instead of fearing change, we embraced it as an opportunity to learn and adapt together.

Children came into our lives, and we navigated the joys and challenges of parenthood as a united front. We instilled in them the importance of open and honest communication, teaching them that expressing themselves was a strength, not a weakness.

As the years passed, our love continued to flourish. We celebrated anniversaries, overcame obstacles, and grew older together. Our vows, spoken on that momentous day, remained a guiding light in our lives, a constant reminder of our commitment to one another.

Our love story was not one of perfection, but of perseverance. It was a story of two souls who had learned the value of communication and had built a love that was unbreakable. Our journey had transformed our once-fearful hearts into courageous ones, capable of facing any challenge that life threw our way.

As we looked at each other, still deeply in love after all these years, we knew that our love story was not just a tale for us to cherish but also a testament to the enduring power of love and communication, a light of hope for others embarking on their own journeys of love and growth.

Unexpressive

I carried silence like a shield,
Words unspoken, feelings concealed.
It was easier to walk away,
To bury pain and not betray.

I told myself I didn't care,
Avoided drama, too much to bear.
I let love falter, left it behind,
An endless pattern, a fractured mind.

My heart was heavy, my tears held back,
Afraid to crumble, afraid to crack.
To share my thoughts felt too immense,
A maze of words, a tangled defense.

I ran from love, I fled from trust,
Building walls from fear and dust.
When faced with vows, a binding plan,
I chose escape, I turned and ran.

But as I walked, regret took hold,
A whisper of courage, quiet yet bold.
I turned around, I faced my dread,
And spoke the words I'd always fled.

"I'm sorry," I said, my voice unsure,
For years of silence I could endure.
But this time, I chose to stay,
To break the chains and find a way.

Together we sat, unraveling pain,
Each truth spoken, each feeling gained.
We learned to speak, to truly hear,
To shed the weight of unspoken fear.

Through struggles shared, our bond took root,
A love rebuilt, both raw and acute.
Communication, once feared and strained,
Became the bridge where love remained.

No grand gestures, no public show,
Just quiet moments where love could grow.
A touch, a laugh, a simple word,
A love rebuilt, deeply heard.

In time, our hearts began to mend,
A love transformed, no need to pretend.
For silence taught us what we missed,
That love must speak, that love persists.

And as we danced beneath the sky,
Our hearts unguarded, no need to lie,
We knew that love, once repressed,
Could blossom fully when expressed.

The Power of Connection

As I shared my story, I discovered the incredible power of human connection. I found others who resonated with my experiences, and we exchanged our tales with empathy and understanding. This bond fueled my desire to continue sharing, to reach even more hearts and minds. As humans, we crave connection. We yearn for relationships and bonds that make us feel seen, heard, and understood. And when we find those connections, the impact can be profound.

Throughout my own journey, I have discovered just how powerful human connection can be. As I opened up and shared my story, I found others who had gone through similar experiences. We connected on a level that was deeper than words. It was as if we could feel each other's pain, joy, and hope without even having to say a word.

In those moments of connection, I realized that I was not alone. Others had faced similar challenges, and they too had found the strength to overcome them. This sense of camaraderie gave me a sense of comfort and reassurance. It helped me see that the path I was on was not unique, and that there were others who understood what I was going through.

But it wasn't just the comfort of knowing I wasn't alone that made these connections so powerful. It was the way that they motivated me to keep going. As I heard the stories of others, I was inspired by their resilience and determination. I saw that they had faced difficult times and had come out stronger on the other side. And that gave me hope that I could do the same.

These connections also helped me to see the world in a new light. As I met people from different backgrounds and with different experiences, I gained a broader perspective on life. I learned about different cultures, beliefs, and ways of living. And in doing so, I realized that there was so much more to life than the narrow view that I had held before.

This broadening of perspective also made me more empathetic. As I heard the struggles of others, I could relate to their pain and suffering. And even when I couldn't understand their experiences fully, I could still feel their emotions. This empathy helped me to connect with others on a deeper level, to see their humanity, and to care for them as fellow human beings.

The power of human connection is not just limited to the emotional benefits that it brings. It can also have a tangible impact on our lives. Through my connections, I have been able to find new opportunities, gain new insights, and even receive practical support. From job opportunities to mentoring, these connections have helped me to grow and thrive in ways that I never would have been able to on my own.

So, if you're feeling alone or struggling on your journey, I encourage you to seek out connections with others. It may be scary to open up and be vulnerable, but the rewards are well worth it. You may find a sense of comfort, inspiration, and empathy that you never knew was possible. And who knows? You may even find that your connections lead you to a whole new world of possibilities.

As I continued to foster these connections and share my story, I realized that there was a ripple effect at play. The people I connected with were also inspired to share their own experiences, creating a web of support, and understanding that extended far beyond my initial circle. It was a beautiful and organic process that showcased the incredible capacity of human connection to heal and uplift.

One day, as Tim was attending a local support group for individuals facing similar challenges, Tim met Sarah, a woman who had battled a life-threatening illness. Her story was one of sheer determination and unwavering hope. They instantly connected on a profound level, sharing their vulnerabilities and triumphs. Sarah and Tim became fast friends, and our connection went beyond our shared experiences; it was based on mutual respect and a deep understanding of each other's journeys.

As Sarah and Tim continued to support each other, their combined strength seemed to multiply. They decided to take our stories and experiences to a wider audience, aiming to inspire even more people. Together, they began speaking at local events, sharing our tales of resilience and the power of human connection. The message resonated with those who heard them, and soon they were invited to speak at larger conferences and even featured in local media.

The response was overwhelming. They received messages from people all over the world who had been touched by our stories and the connections they had formed. They shared their own experiences, and in turn, connected with them, creating a global network of support and empathy.

One of the most heartwarming moments came when a young girl named Emily reached out. Emily had been struggling with a rare medical condition, and she felt isolated and scared. After hearing our stories, she felt a glimmer of hope and a newfound sense of belonging. They visited Emily in the hospital, and the moment we walked into her room, the power of connection was palpable. They saw the spark of resilience in her eyes, and it was a reminder that no matter how dire the circumstances, human connection could help people find the strength to carry on.

The journey continued, and we soon founded a nonprofit organization dedicated to connecting individuals facing adversity and providing them with a platform to share their stories. Through their work, they witnessed countless lives transformed, not just by our experiences but by the connections they made with others who understood and cared.

The power of human connection had become a driving force in our lives, guiding us to places we never thought possible. It had shown us that when we open our hearts and connect with others, we not only find solace and strength, but we also have the capacity to inspire and uplift those around us.

In the end, our stories were no longer just our own; they had become the connection of hope for many. And as we continued to embrace the power of connection, we were reminded that together, we could change the world, one heart and one connection at a time.

As Sarah and I embarked on this incredible journey of connecting with people and making a positive impact on their lives, we realized that our mission had the potential to go beyond our wildest dreams. The nonprofit organization we had founded, which we called "Connection of Hearts," was growing rapidly. We began collaborating with other like-minded individuals who were passionate about spreading the message of hope through the power of human connection.

One of our most significant collaborations was with David, a talented filmmaker who had been deeply moved by our story. He approached us with an idea to create a documentary that would capture the essence of our journey and the stories of the people we had connected with. David's vision was to use the medium of film to reach even more hearts and minds across the globe.

With David's expertise and the combined efforts of our expanding network, we set out to create the documentary. We traveled far and wide, meeting individuals from all walks of life, each with their own unique story of resilience and the profound impact of connection. From the bustling streets of New York City to remote villages in Africa, we discovered that the universal human desire for connection transcended cultural and geographical boundaries.

• • •

The making of the documentary was a labor of love, and it was during this process that we met Maria, a talented composer who crafted a moving soundtrack that beautifully complemented the stories we were sharing. Maria's music resonated with the emotions of our journey, adding depth and poignancy to the film.

As the documentary neared completion, we received an invitation to showcase it at an international film festival. The response was overwhelming, and the screening was met with standing ovations and tears of the connection the connection inspiration. Our message of the transformative power of human connection was touching the hearts of people from all corners of the world.

The momentum continued to build, and soon we were invited to speak at the United Nations about the role of connection in promoting global empathy and understanding. Our message was clear: when we connect on a human level, we break down barriers, foster compassion, and create a world where everyone feels seen, heard, and valued.

The impact of our work was tangible. We received letters, emails, and messages from countless individuals who had been moved by our stories and the stories of those we had connected with. People were reaching out to support one another, forming their own communities of connection, and finding hope in the midst of adversity.

But perhaps the most significant testament to the power of connection was Emily, the young girl we had met in the hospital. Over time, her health improved, and she became a symbol of resilience and strength in her own right. She joined us on stage during one of our presentations, sharing her story with grace and confidence. It was a powerful reminder that the ripples of connection we had initiated were continuing to spread, touching, and transforming lives in ways we could have never imagined.

Our journey, which had begun with a simple realization of the power of human connection, had evolved into a global movement. We had discovered that the most extraordinary transformations often begin with the simplest of connections. And as we looked out at the world we were helping to shape, we were reminded that together, we could indeed change the world, one heart and one connection at a time.

The Power of Connection

There is a force, unseen yet true,
A thread that binds both me and you.
It speaks through silence, bridges divides,
A path where understanding abides.

When stories are shared, hearts intertwine,
Your pain reflects in the depths of mine.
In the space where words and feelings meet,
A sacred bond is born, complete.

Proper communication, a delicate art,
Reveals the truths buried deep in the heart.
Each word a seed, each pause a breath,
A language of love that conquers death.

To speak with care, to listen with grace,
Heals the fractures we're scared to face.
For in the echo of an honest voice,
We find the strength to make a choice.

Connection is the salve for scars,
A lantern that lights our inner wars.
It whispers, "You are not alone,"
A melody of hope in the unknown.

Through love, the fractured soul can mend,
A power that helps the broken transcend.
Love sees the wounds, yet loves them still,
A force that bends but does not kill.

Empathy blooms where love takes root,
A shared humanity, the sweetest fruit.
In your struggles, I see my own,
A bond unspoken, deeply sown.

Together we rise, stronger than fear,
Our voices a chorus, tender and clear.
Through connection, the world expands,
New perspectives, uncharted lands.

It teaches us that every soul,
Is part of a greater, unified whole.
Love and communication unlock the door,
To a life that offers so much more.

For healing isn't found in solitude,
But in the warmth of a shared interlude.
It's in the glance that says, "I see you,"
In the embrace that makes us anew.

So let us cherish this sacred art,
To speak with kindness, to love with heart.
For in connection, we truly heal,
A bond eternal, vibrant, and real.

Journey to Self-Love

I thirst for love that I never had before I dreamt of it long for it until I came to the realization that I had it all along once I found my true self, I knew what true love was.

As I embraced my true self, I began to see the world through a different lens. I realized that the love I had been searching for all this time was within me all along. It was the love that I had denied myself for so long, the love that I had kept hidden away for fear of rejection and judgment.

But now, I knew that I deserved to love and be loved in return. I opened my heart and allowed myself to be vulnerable, to show my true self to others. And in doing so, I found the love that I had always longed for.

I found people who accepted me for who I was, who loved me unconditionally, flaws and all. They saw the beauty in my imperfections and celebrated them. They lifted me up when I was down, supported me through the tough times, and cheered me on as I pursued my dreams.

Through this journey of self-discovery, I learned that true love isn't about finding someone else to complete us. It's about loving ourselves first and foremost, and then sharing that love with others. It's about being authentic, vulnerable, and open-hearted, and attracting the people who resonate with our true selves.

Now, as I look back on my search for love, I realize that it was all worth it. It led me to the most important love of all, the love that resides within me. And that love has given me the courage to live my life fully, to pursue my passions, and to connect with others in a meaningful way.

With newfound self-love, my life began to blossom in ways I could never have imagined. I embarked on a journey of self-discovery and personal growth that took me to places I had only dreamed of.

I started by nurturing my passions and interests, rediscovering the things that truly made my heart sing. I took up cooking again, a hobby I had abandoned for years, and it brought me immense joy. I joined a local writing group and found solace in the beauty of spoken word, learning to appreciate the world around me in a whole new light.

But it wasn't just about pursuing hobbies; it was about setting goals and working toward them. I decided to go back to school to pursue a degree in a field that had always fascinated me. The process was challenging, but the love I had for myself, and my newfound confidence pushed me forward. I met incredible people along the way who supported my journey and believed in me.

As my self-love grew, so did my relationships with others. I attracted friends who celebrated my authenticity and encouraged me to continue on my path of self-discovery. I was no longer afraid to express my thoughts, feelings, and desires, and this openness strengthened my connections with others.

In the mystery of romantic relationships, my newfound self-love transformed the way I approached love. I was no longer willing to settle for anything less than a deep and meaningful connection. I understood that I deserved a partner who embraced my true self, someone who shared in my growth and celebrated our journey together.

Eventually, I found that special someone who matched my energy and love. Together, we embarked on a journey of mutual growth and self-discovery, supporting each other every step of the way. Our love was built on a foundation of self-love, trust, and respect.

• • •

Through it all, I continued to remind myself that self-love was an ongoing journey, not a destination. There were still moments of self-doubt and insecurities, but I now had the tools to navigate them with grace and compassion. I learned to forgive myself for past mistakes and to appreciate the lessons they had taught me.

My journey to self-love had not only transformed my life but also inspired those around me. I shared my story with others, encouraging them to embark on their own journeys of self-discovery and self-love. Together, we created a community of support and empowerment, where we celebrated each other's victories and lifted each other up in times of need.

Looking back, I realized that the search for love had led me to the most important love of all – the love for myself. It had allowed me to uncover my true potential, to live a life filled with purpose and passion, and to form deep and meaningful connections with others. It was a journey well worth taking, and I knew that it would continue to guide me on the path to a fulfilling and love-filled life.

Journey to Self-Love

I thirsted for love, a well run dry,
A yearning that echoed in every sigh.
I chased it far, through shadow and light,
Believing the answer lay just out of sight.

I dreamt of affection, tender and true,
A love that would heal, a life born anew.
But the mirror whispered a quiet refrain,
"The love you seek begins with your name."

In the stillness, I turned within,
To the parts of myself I'd buried in sin.
The flaws, the scars, the stories untold,
The pieces of me both tender and bold.

As I embraced my reflection whole,
I felt the warmth of a mending soul.
This love I'd denied, so long suppressed,
Rose like the dawn, a heart at rest.

I learned to be vulnerable, to show my face,
To occupy fully my rightful space.
No longer hiding, no longer afraid,
I walked through life, unmasked, unplayed.

And as I opened my heart to see,
Others responded with clarity.
They loved me flawed, they loved me whole,
Their kindness ignited my weary soul.

Self-love became my steady guide,
A compass that lit the path inside.
I set bold goals, I followed my dreams,
My life took on a radiant gleam.

Passions once lost I claimed anew,
A canvas of joy in every hue.
I cooked, I wrote, I spoke, I dared to explore,
Finding purpose behind each door.
In friendship's arms, I found a home,
With souls who cheered me as I'd grown.

Their laughter lifted, their words inspired,
Their presence fueled my inner fire.
And love, that mystery, deep and wide,
No longer a place where fears could hide.

I sought a bond of meaning and grace,
A partner who'd cherish my truest face.
Together we built, together we grew,
A love that was honest, vibrant, and true.

No pretense, no settling, no shadows to flee,
Just two hearts aligned, wild and free.
Yet through it all, one truth remained,
That self-love's journey can't be contained.

It rhythmically flows, it learns, it grows,
A lifelong dance only the seeker knows.
There are days of doubt, moments of fear,
But love whispers softly, "I'm always near."

Forgiving myself, I move with grace,
Each step forward, a sacred embrace.
Now I share my story, a gift, a spark,
To light the way for those in the dark.

Together we rise, a collective tide,
Empowered by the love we hold inside.
For the journey to self-love is worth the stride,
A radiant truth where the heart can abide.
It's the love that fuels, the love that sustains,
A journey of joy through life's endless plains.

Exploring Connections

I wanted to explore more connections which led me to start digging through old documents in my family's attic. I had always been interested in learning more about my ancestors, but I had never had the time or opportunity to really dive into their history. As I rummaged through dusty boxes and faded photo albums, I began to uncover some truly fascinating information.

One document in particular caught my eye. It was an old diary belonging to my great-great-grandmother, who had lived in the late 1800s. As I flipped through the pages, I was transported back in time, reading about her daily life and the struggles she faced as a woman in that era. But what intrigued me the most were her references to a mysterious group of women she called the "Sisters of the Kitchen."

At first, I thought it might be some kind of secret society or religious cult, but as I continued to read, I realized that it was something far more intriguing. The "Sisters of the Kitchen," it seemed, were a group of women who were great. They were highly respected in their community and were sought after for their wisdom and expertise.

As I delved deeper into my research, I began to uncover more and more connections between the women in my family and this ancient tradition of the "Sisters of the Kitchen." I discovered that my great-grandmother had also been a food healer, as had her mother before her. And as I started to explore my own interest in natural food remedies, I realized that this was more than just a hobby - it was a part of my family's legacy.

Inspired by my ancestors, I began to study the "Sisters of the Kitchen," more seriously, taking courses and attending workshops. And as I learned more about the healing power of plants, I felt a deep connection to the women who had come before me, passing down their knowledge and wisdom through the generations.

Now, years later, I have started my own business as an the "Sisters of the Kitchen," following in the footsteps of my ancestor. And though I may never know all the secrets of this ancient tradition, I am grateful for the connection it has given me to my family and to the natural world around me.

My journey into the world of the "Sisters of the Kitchen" continued to unfold as I delved deeper into the practices and wisdom of this ancient tradition. I traveled to remote villages, seeking out elders and healers who still held the knowledge passed down through generations. It was during one of these journeys that I met an elderly woman named Eliza, who claimed to be a direct descendant of the original "Sisters of the Kitchen."

Eliza's eyes sparkled with wisdom as she shared stories of her ancestors and the powerful healing remedies they had mastered. She explained that the "Sisters of the Kitchen" were not just cooks or herbalists; they were the keepers of sacred knowledge, bridging the gap between food and medicine. Their understanding of the healing properties of herbs, spices, and whole foods was unparalleled, and they used their skills to help their communities thrive.

Under Eliza's guidance, I began to learn the ancient art of food healing. She taught me how to identify and harvest medicinal plants, create potent herbal concoctions, and prepare nourishing meals that could heal the body and spirit. It was a transformative experience, and I felt a profound sense of connection to my ancestors as I absorbed their wisdom.

As I continued to study and practice, word of my skills as a food healer spread throughout the community. People came to me seeking remedies for various ailments, from digestive issues to stress and anxiety. It was immensely fulfilling to see the positive impact I could have on their lives, just as my ancestors had done for generations.

I also discovered that the "Sisters of the Kitchen" had a broader purpose beyond healing. They had been advocates for women's empowerment, challenging the societal norms of their time and promoting the idea that women could be the caretakers of their families' health and well-being. Inspired by this, I began to offer workshops and classes to empower other women to embrace their roles as healers and nurturers in their own homes.

My business as a food healer flourished, and I became known not only for my healing remedies but also for preserving and sharing the ancient traditions of the "Sisters of the Kitchen." I compiled their recipes, remedies, and stories into a book, ensuring that their wisdom would continue to be passed down to future generations.

In my own small way, I had become a link in the chain of this remarkable tradition, bridging the past with the present. I often thought about my great-great-grandmother and how she must be looking down on me with pride, knowing that her diary had ignited this passion within me. The connections I had sought in my family's attic had not only deepened my understanding of my heritage but had also given me a profound purpose in life.

Exploring Connections

In the attic's hush, beneath the dust,
I found a link to the past I trust.
Old boxes, worn, with secrets to tell,
Echoed prayers where ancestors' dwell.

A diary lay, its pages worn thin,
A great-great-grandmother's life within.
Her struggles, her joys, her wisdom untamed,
And "Sisters of the Kitchen" quietly named.

At first, a mystery cloaked in lore,
But the words revealed something more.
Not a cult, not a hidden rite,
But women of wisdom, a guiding light.

Healers with hands that knew the earth,
Turning plants and spices to healing worth.
Nurturers, teachers, with love as their art,
Restoring bodies and mending hearts.

I traced the thread through time's embrace,
Found the roots of their enduring grace.
My great-grandmother, her mother too,
Had carried this knowledge, ancient and true.

The call was clear; it echoed deep,
A legacy awake from its centuries' sleep.
I learned the craft, the healing lore,
Studied plants, remedies, and more.

Eliza came, a sage so wise,
Her words like stars in ancient skies.
She showed me how food could heal and bind,
A sacred dance of soul and mind.

Through her, I found not just my role,
But the threads that wove a collective soul.
Women empowered, with voices bold,
Breaking the norms of a world too cold.
Now I stand where they once stood,
In kitchens that hum with something good.

Healing hands, a nurturing art,
A mission carried with all my heart.
Workshops, remedies, stories I share,
Teaching others the power of care.

For connection is not just blood or bone,
It's the ties we weave, the seeds we've sown.
As I teach, as I heal, as I grow,
The love of my ancestors starts to show.

A legacy carried, a purpose renewed,
In the wisdom of women, timeless and true.
So here I stand, a link in the chain,
Their whispers alive in my heart and brain.
Exploring connections, bridging the years,
A journey of love, through joy and tears.

Second Chance

As I lay there, unable to move or speak, I felt a sense of despair wash over me. I was not ready to leave this world yet. There were still so many things I wanted to do, so many people I wanted to meet, and so many experiences I wanted to have.

But then, something miraculous happened. I felt a surge of energy coursing through my veins, and suddenly, I was able to move again. With a burst of strength, I lifted myself out of the grave and stood up, looking around in amazement at the people gathered around me.

They were staring at me in shock and disbelief, but I didn't care. All I could think about was the second chance I had been given. From that moment on, I vowed to live my life to the fullest, to never take a single moment for granted, and to always remember the lesson that had been taught to me by the eclectic symmetry of the ocean waves and clear sky's great times.

I walked away from the graveyard that day with a newfound sense of purpose and a renewed determination to make the most of every opportunity that came my way. And as I looked up at the blue sky above me, I knew that I had been given a second chance for a reason - to make a difference in the world and to live a life that was truly worth living.

In the days that followed, I embarked on a journey of self-discovery and personal growth. I sought out new experiences, challenged myself to confront my fears, and embraced every opportunity that came my way. The world seemed brighter, more vibrant, and filled with endless possibilities.

One of the first things I did was reconnect with the people who mattered most in my life. I reached out to family and friends, sharing my near-death experience and the profound impact it had on me. My relationships deepened, and I cherished every moment spent with loved ones, making sure to express my gratitude for their presence in my life.

I also decided to pursue some of my long-held dreams. I took up painting, something I had always been curious about but never had the courage to try. The act of putting colors on canvas became a therapeutic outlet for my emotions, allowing me to express myself in ways I had never imagined.

As I painted, I found myself drawn to the imagery of the ocean waves and the clear, expansive sky that had played such a significant role in my rebirth. I created vibrant, abstract pieces that captured the essence of those moments, and my art began to gain recognition in local galleries.

But it wasn't just about my own personal growth. My second chance at life had given me a deep sense of empathy for others who might be going through difficult times. I started volunteering at a local shelter, offering a helping hand to those who needed it most. Through these experiences, I forged connections with people from all walks of life, and I learned to appreciate the eclectic symmetry of humanity itself.

Over the years, I shared my story of resurrection with others, using it as a source of inspiration for those who felt stuck or overwhelmed by life's challenges. I realized that my experience had a ripple effect, encouraging others to seize the day and make the most of their time on this Earth.

As the years passed, my art and my advocacy for living life to the fullest became intertwined. I organized art exhibitions that also raised awareness and funds for causes I deeply cared about, creating a powerful synergy between my passion and my purpose.

Looking back, I couldn't help but feel grateful for the second chance I had been granted. I had emerged from the depths of despair and the confines of a grave, reborn with a newfound appreciation for life's beauty and complexity. The eclectic symmetry of the ocean waves and the clear sky's great times had become my guiding forces, reminding me each day to live with purpose, creativity, and love, and to help others do the same.

The electric symmetry of the ocean waves clear sky's great times it was all a blur

I was buried my whole life
Conflicted restricted out of touch
The feeling that I was missing so much rhythmically
contractile consisting of 100 beats per minute

Able to reproduce times two
bringing in new life
while I'm watching mine flash by
my mind is racing I'm praying
but no one hears me

I feel submerged by the clumps of dirt
that's placed on top of me
this can't be the end
I have so many unfinished things
The light is calling me

but I don't want to go
there're so many untold stories
and I can't let go
I'm trying to hold on
and be strong to the end

conflicted restricted out of touch
the feelings that I was missing so much
I need I need you I need you
please don't allow this to be the end
it's not the time for my demise

I feel my fingertips tingling
I'm still alive my eyes pop open
but I cannot move
I cannot breathe
I hear somebody saying it's time

I hear the click clacks
The rolling of the chains
Lowering down my body in a grave
People chanting
from ashes-to-ashes dust to dust

We lay our loved one to rest
no, she did her best
I live my life without fear or regret
But this is not the time for me to be at rest

The Great Divide

Once upon a time, in a vibrant and resilient black community, there lay a hidden wound, a scar that refused to heal. Despite the bonds of shared history, culture, and struggle, this community found itself divided, ununited, torn apart by inner conflicts and prejudices. Stop the fighting, they whispered to each other. Too much rage, too many tears, and a constant living in fear. It was as if they had forgotten the battles their ancestors had fought side by side, the strength they had drawn from unity, the pride they once took in their heritage.

Watch your back, they cautioned one another. All the attacks, the name-calling, the harassment, the shaming, and the blame. They were a community plagued by internal strife; a never-ending cycle of negativity that only served to weaken their collective spirit.

As they lay in their beds at night, contemplating their lives, they couldn't help but acknowledge that the challenges they faced were partly of their own making. Black lives, black families, their people, all yearning for equality, but often tearing each other down with judgments and prejudice.

"I don't like her," they whispered with side-eyes and stares. "Her hair, the way she looks, she's too this or too that." They questioned qualifications, compared degrees, and forgot the shared struggles that had brought them to this point.

The pain ran deep, for some even wished death upon their own people. They had forgotten the greatness from which they descended, the strength and resilience of their ancestors. They had lost the love that once bound them together, the pride they once took in being black.

But buried deep within the hearts of many was a yearning for change, a longing to return to the days when they marched alongside leaders like King and Malcolm, when they cherished each other as black men and women. They remembered when they were strong, respectful, and giving, when they truly acted as a village, a united community.

They realized that the path to justice and peace lay in rekindling that spirit of togetherness. "We must stand together," they said, "for a greater purpose." They understood that the future of their youth, the betterment of mankind, depended on their ability to overcome their differences and embrace their shared history, culture, and potential.

So, they chose to inspire, educate, lead, empower, embrace, love, support, and give hope. They decided to stay woke, to dream and focus on a brighter future. They understood that they were worth it, that their unity was their strength, and that together, they could reclaim the greatness that was their birthright.

And as they looked forward, they knew that the road ahead would not be easy, but it was a journey they were willing to undertake, for the sake of their community, their people, and the generations to come. They were determined to become once again, standing in purpose, and inspiring others to do the same.

• • •

We are divided, ununited, stop the fighting, too much rage to stop the pain, to many tears living in fear. Watch your backs, all the attacks, it's a shame, calling names. Harassing, shaming, blaming, complaining, rage submerged in envy continuing to search for the why. As I lay here and think about our lives, black lives, black families, my people, no equality, we are partly the reason for most of our demise sitting there judging each other. I don't like her side eyes stares, her hair, the way she looks, she's too fat, too tall, too skinny, too short, too light, too dark, what qualifies her to be in charge? I have a Master's degree, I'm much better than she is, all the put downs, hatred, and lies overlooking not lending a helping hand to our fellow man, putting others on a pedestal forgetting what we've been through, no togetherness, degrading our women, our queens what's wrong with this the pain, some wished death on my name. We are descendants from greatness, I'm sitting here restless, relentless, what happened to the Love when the days were fine? When we were proud to be black? We marched like King for what was right and put up a fight. Malcom knew what was right when we cherished black man and women, when we were strong, respectful, giving a helping hand, one community, a village of great women, are those days really gone? Do you feel me? It hurts me deep because I can't trust us, listen there will be no justice or peace until we as a people get back to us. Inspire, educate, lead, empower, embrace, love, support, give, hope, stay woke, dream, focus, we have to be the Greater influence don't allow this society to ruin us. We must stand together for a much greater purpose... get over our differences... it's about the future of our youth ... the betterment of mankind... wake-up, wake up, wake up. Inspire, educate, lead, empower, embrace, love, support, give, hope, stay woke, dream, focus, become once again, standing in purpose we are all worth it...

We are divided
ununited
stop the fighting
too much rage
stop the pain
to many tears
living in fear.

Watch your back
all the attacks
it's a shame
calling names.
Harassing
shaming
blaming
complaining
rage submerged in envy
continuing to search for the why.

As they reflected on the challenges and pain inflicted by their own community, they couldn't help but acknowledge the dark side that had emerged within them. They had been labeled, branded, abused, owned, used, turned, separated, and mistreated. The very people who shared their skin color had caused them immense hurt.

In their lifetimes, they had encountered mistreatment, disrespect, abuse, curses, and betrayal at the hands of their own race. The pain they felt ran deep, for they had never known what hate truly felt like until they faced the betrayal, envy, jealousy, disregard, lies, backstabbing, mistrust, and misleading actions that came from within their own community.

They had been taught that the outsiders were the ones to fear, the ones who were racist, who disregarded and put them down. But they realized that while racism existed outside their community, the nightmares, psychopaths, predators, rapists, and child molesters were not just strangers—they were sometimes their own mothers, fathers, sisters, and coworkers.

The realization hit them hard: it was not always an external threat they faced, but sometimes the very people who looked like them, who shared their heritage and history. They had turned on each other, disregarded one another, harmed, lied, and betrayed one another.

Yet, amidst all the pain and suffering, they held on to a powerful truth: they never gave up on their own people. They still loved their community, and they were determined to stand up for them, to be the change that was so desperately needed.

One voice among them knew that to change the narrative, to shift the stigma that had plagued them for so long, it only took one. One person among them was determined to alter the perception, to change how they thought and felt about their own people.

This one individual understood that to transform their community, they had to change how they loved, connected, treated, cared for, and stood up for one another. They recognized the importance of building trust within their own ranks, of breaking the cycle of nightmares, fears, and tears.

The time had come for them to take control of their own narrative, to change the stigma about their community. They were ready to put an end to the internal battles, the mistrust, and the pain. They were ready to redefine their identity, their unity, and their future.

And so, with unwavering determination, they stood up and declared, "It is time for us to change us. To control the narrative, change the stigma about us. No more nightmares, no more fears, no more tears. It's time to build trust in us, for we are worth it, and we are the architects of our own destiny."

With their declaration echoing through their community, a transformation began to take root. The one who had spoken out was not alone in their desire for change. Others joined, one by one, until a collective force for unity and healing emerged.

They understood that healing required self-awareness, open dialogue, and a commitment to change. They organized community gatherings, open forums, and healing circles where they could share their experiences, acknowledge their pain, and seek reconciliation. They started talking about their struggles with envy, jealousy, and mistrust, acknowledging that these were the scars of a deeply divided community.

The stories that emerged were painful, but they were necessary. People spoke of their own experiences with betrayal and the moments when they had betrayed others. It was a process of confronting their own actions and taking responsibility for them, not as individuals but as a collective.

It wasn't easy. Emotions ran high, and tears were shed as they confronted their demons. But through this process, they began to see the humanity in one another once again. They recognized that their community was not defined solely by their past actions, but by their capacity to change and grow.

As they worked through their pain, they also focused on education and empowerment. They created mentorship programs for the youth and offered opportunities for personal and professional development within their community. They knew that by uplifting each other, they could break the cycle of self-destructive behavior.

But perhaps the most powerful change was in how they began to view themselves and their community. They no longer saw themselves as victims of their circumstances but as architects of their own destiny. They understood that their shared history, culture, and resilience were sources of strength, not division.

Slowly but surely, the community began to rebuild the trust that had been eroded over the years. They celebrated each other's successes, offered support during challenging times, and stood together in solidarity. They no longer allowed internal conflicts to overshadow their shared identity.

The transformation wasn't instant, and there were setbacks along the way. But they were resolute in their commitment to change the narrative about their community. They knew that by coming together, they could overcome the pain and division that had plagued them for too long.

As time passed, the story of their community became one of resilience, redemption, and unity. They had faced their demons, confronted their past, and emerged stronger, more united, and determined to shape a brighter future for themselves and generations to come.

And so, the tale of a black community that had once faced challenges within their own race evolved into a story of hope, healing, and the power of unity. They had rewritten their narrative and, in doing so, had reclaimed their place as a beacon of strength and inspiration for all.

The great divide

As I lay here and think about our lives black
lives black families
we are partly the reason for most of our demise
sitting there judging each other all the put downs

hatred and lies
overlooking
not lending A helping hand to our fellow man

putting others on a pedestal
forgetting what we've been through

no togetherness
degrading or women are queens

what's wrong with this
the pain
we are descendants from greatness
I'm sitting here restless relentless
what happened to the Love
when the days were fine
when we were proud to be black

we marched for what was right
put up a fight
cherished black men and women
when we were strong
respectful giving a helping hand
those days really gone

do you feel me
it hurts me deep
because I can't trust us
listen I am we
there will be no justice or peace
until we as a people get back to we

Ancestors

Our ancestors are remembered
tragically being in slaved,
raped, hung, and put in graves,
leaving their motherland on ships,
bound with chains,
marching trying to make a change,
teaching the truth, and
his own people turned and killed him too.

We are still held down by social norms,
not being accepted by the color of our skin
shot because they were in fear.
We have so many hashtags' names,
but they still won't give. I refuse to live in fear.

Fear of the what if the maybes the why not
I don't wanna be remembered by tragedy
I want to be remembered, by the way,
I made people feel not for what I gave or
what I did I want to stand my truth.
I want you to believe in me like I believe in you.

How do you want to be remembered
still shackled and chains bound by
our colors no one remembering your name
all the great work love you poured.

Let's change and stop keeping score.
No one is the prize. We are all equal.
Let's stop the divide. Be true to who we are
stop putting up a guard allow the real to rain true
I believe in you

Throughout history, our ancestors
endured tragic experiences:
enslaved, raped, and buried in graves
far from their homeland.

They were shackled on ships,
marched in chains, all in the pursuit of change
and truth, only to be betrayed and killed by their own.
Today, we still Struggle with societal norms
that oppress us based on the color of our skin,
leading to senseless shootings driven by fear.

Despite countless hashtags bearing the names
of those lost, justice remains elusive.
I refuse to be remembered solely by tragedy;
instead, I aspire to be remembered for the impact I made
on people's lives, for the emotions I evoked,
and for standing in my truth.
I want you to believe in me like I believe in you.

PART THREE

I Got a Story to Tail

using Tail as a verb

In the Dark

I always had this great feeling about him like he was the truth. Just the thought of him put a smile on my face. It all started back in 2013 sitting around board tried of the regular dating seen I decided to create a profile and join this dating site not thinking I would ever actually meet anyone just passing the time.

I got a few likes had a few in-depth conversations but nothing to intense. No one really grasp my attention that long. Until this one day I received a pleasant greeting which got my undivided attention.

We chatted for a few months he asked me to meet in person I declined of course. It was never my intention to meet anyone in person and I stuck to my guns for a long time, but he was persistent. I was extremely nervous, but I agreed to meet up with him.

He was at the House of Blues that night I picked up a stranger. We drove to the beach and talked for a while.

As the sun began to set, he suggested we take a walk along the beach. At first, I hesitated. It was getting dark, and I didn't know him well enough to trust him completely. But something about him made me feel safe, and I agreed.

As we walked, we talked about everything and anything. It was like we had known each other for years. The moon was high in the sky by the time we made it back to the car, and I realized we had been walking for hours.

He offered to drive me home, and I accepted. As we drove, we talked some more, and I found myself becoming more and more comfortable with him. It was like we had an instant connection.

When he pulled up in front of my house, I realized that I didn't want the night to end. I invited him in for a drink, and he accepted.

As we sat in my living room, sipping wine and talking, the lights suddenly went out. It was pitch black, and I could barely see my own hand in front of my face. I felt a wave of panic wash over me.

But he remained calm. He lit a candle and held it up, illuminating the room just enough for us to see each other's faces. And in that moment, I knew that he was the one.

We spent the rest of the night talking, laughing, and getting to know each other even better. And from that day on, we were inseparable.

Years later, as I looked back on that night, I realized that sometimes, the best things in life happen in the dark.

Our relationship blossomed in unexpected ways. We explored the world together, from hiking in remote mountain ranges to strolling through bustling city streets. Every adventure brought us closer, and we learned to rely on each other's strengths during the challenges we faced.

Over time, our connection deepened, and we decided to move in together. Our home became a sanctuary of love and shared dreams. We painted the walls in vibrant colors and filled the rooms with our favorite books, artwork, and memories of our adventures.

As the years passed, we faced both joys and challenges together. We celebrated each other's successes and provided support during tough times. Our love grew stronger with every passing day, and we knew that we were meant to be together.

One evening, as we sat on our favorite spot on the beach, the same place where we had our first date, he turned to me and said, "You know, I never expected to meet someone like you online. But that chance encounter in the dark changed my life forever."

Tears welled up in my eyes as I smiled and replied, "It changed mine too. I'm so grateful we took that leap of faith."

He took my hand and, with the sound of the waves crashing in the background, he asked me a question that I had been longing to hear: "Will you marry me?"

I nodded, overcome with happiness, and he slipped a beautiful ring onto my finger.

We sealed our commitment with a kiss, feeling the warmth of the moonlight surrounding us. Our wedding was a celebration of love, shared with friends and family who had witnessed the beautiful journey that had brought us together. The ceremony was held on the same beach where we had shared our first walk, and our vows were spoken under a canopy of twinkling stars.

As I looked into his eyes during our wedding, I realized that love could truly be found in the most unexpected places and moments. The darkness that had initially made me hesitant had ultimately led me to the love of my life, and I couldn't have been happier.

In the years that followed, we continued to embrace life's adventures together, knowing that no matter what challenges lay ahead, we would face them with love, laughter, and the unwavering belief that the best things in life often happened in the dark.

In the Dark

It began with a greeting, a simple call,
An online message, nothing at all.
Passing the time, I wasn't prepared,
For the spark of connection that we soon shared.

His words were light, his tone sincere,
A presence felt, though not yet near.
Months of talking, a persistent plea,
"Let's meet," he said, "come walk with me."

I hesitated, afraid to fall,
But his patience chipped away it all.
The night we met, beneath the blues,
A stranger became someone I'd choose.

We drove to the shore, the waves our song,
Hours passed as we walked along.
The sun gave way to the moonlit tide,
In the dark, I felt peace inside.

Back at home, the power failed,
The room felt black, the air seemed veiled.
Yet he lit a candle, soft and bright,
And his calm presence eased my fright.

In that flicker, I saw his soul,
A depth of kindness, my heart made whole.
Laughter echoed through the night,
In the dark, love took its flight.

From that moment, our journey began,
Side by side, woman and man.
We traveled far, through highs and lows,
Building a love that forever grows.

Our home became a sacred space,
Filled with memories time couldn't erase.
The walls told stories, the rooms held dreams,
A life together, stitched at the seams.

On the beach where we first had walked,
He turned to me, and softly talked.
"You changed my world, in the darkest of hours,
You brought me light, love's rarest power."

With waves as witness, stars as guide,
He asked if I'd stay forever by his side.
A ring, a promise, a life to start,
In the dark, he claimed my heart.

Our vows were made under a starry dome,
On the beach that had first felt like home.
The crashing waves, the moon's soft glow,
The perfect setting for love to show.

Years have passed, yet the truth remains,
In the dark, I found love that sustains.
For sometimes life's greatest treasures lie,
In moments unseen by the naked eye.

Through every shadow, through every spark,
We remember the magic born in the dark.
A lesson in love for all to see we greet each other
I'm happy you choose me our love grows

with each passing day laying the foundation
brick by brick no secrets no lie open communication
supporting each other's dreams

Kinda Sorta

He was sort of kind of wrong, I was sort of kind of right; now, I'm sitting here singing this same old tired ass song. Where did I go wrong thinking, believing, hoping, and praying that he was the one. Listening to my friends, "girl give him a chance," "let him in," so eventually I gave in and wasted two years of my time, but it was a lesson there somewhere...

I conversed myself to settle even to the point that I could help in the effort to mold him into a better representation of himself... not realizing that he himself was lost and not willing to transform and reach his full potential of the man he could and should be... but at the end this wasn't working for me not where I wanted to be. I needed out... questioning love.

I was making a statement but not feeling love, I uttered the word but when I spoke, I choked, I can't continue to pretend I'm not feeling it. This charade has to end ... false representation of self this is too much to endure, my heart must stay pure, I can't become bitter because of this façade. Contemplating on how to end this without being a little shady putting myself first remembering my worth.

Just the uttering of the phrase "I love you" to him made me cringe ... can't be fake, had to walk away, fake love, I couldn't make love, I had to wake love, no mistake love, or just in case the love falls away, love is some mistake and that's not me, I have to be true to my soul take control love.

As I walked away from the relationship, I couldn't help but feel a sense of relief. It was like a weight had been lifted off my shoulders. Sure, it was difficult to end things, but I knew it was the right decision for me. I couldn't keep pretending to be someone I wasn't, and I couldn't keep trying to change him into someone he didn't want to be. It was time for me to focus on myself and my own growth.

In the weeks and months that followed, I spent a lot of time reflecting on the relationship and what I had learned from it. I realized that I had ignored some red flags early on, hoping that things would change. I had also convinced myself that I could fix him, which was not fair to either of us. I had to accept that people can only change if they want to, and I couldn't force anyone to change.

I also learned that love isn't just about saying the words "I love you." It's about showing it through actions and being there for someone through thick and thin. I had been so caught up in the idea of love that I had forgotten what it really meant. But now, I was determined to find real love, the kind that would make my heart sing and my soul soar.

As I moved on with my life, I promised myself that I would never settle again. I would never compromise my values or my worth for the sake of a relationship. I would be true to myself, and I would find someone who loved me for who I am, flaws and all.

And so, I continued to sing my same old tired-ass song, but with a newfound sense of hope and determination. I knew that there was better out there for me, and I was willing to wait for it. I embraced my own worth and decided to focus on self-love and self-improvement.

I spent my time pursuing my passions, reconnecting with friends, and enjoying the simple pleasures of life. I traveled to new places, met interesting people, and allowed myself to grow and evolve without the constraints of a stifling relationship.

As I opened myself up to new experiences, I discovered that life had so much more to offer than I had previously realized. I found joy in the little things – a beautiful sunrise, a heartfelt conversation, a quiet moment of reflection. These small moments reminded me of the beauty of life and the importance of being authentic.

In time, I met someone who shared my values and cherished me for who I was. We built a relationship based on mutual respect, trust, and genuine love. It was a love that didn't need to be forced or molded; it simply flowed naturally.

With this new love, I felt a sense of completeness that I had never experienced before. It was a love that allowed me to be my true self, and I cherished every moment of it. I realized that sometimes, the best kind of love is the one that comes when you least expect it, and when you're ready to accept it as it is.

As I looked back on my past relationship, I no longer felt bitterness or regret. Instead, I felt gratitude for the lessons it had taught me and the person it had helped me become. It had led me to a place of self-discovery, self-worth, and ultimately, true love.

And so, I continued to sing my same old tired-ass song, but with a new melody of hope, authenticity, and genuine love. I had learned that love should never be a facade or a compromise. It should be a beautiful, harmonious symphony that brings joy, peace, and fulfillment to the heart and soul.

Kinda Sorta Wrong v. Right

He was sort of wrong, I was kind of right,
Yet I stayed, tangled in love's dim light.
Singing this tired, old, broken tune,
Believing his love would change too soon.

My friends urged, "Girl, give him a chance,
Let him in, let him romance."
I gave in, wasted two years of my prime,
Hoping there was meaning to this time.

I convinced myself I could shape his core,
Help him be the man he was meant to soar.
But he was lost, unwilling to rise,
A man stuck in his own disguise.

And me? I was trapped in a love untrue,
Choking on words I could not renew.
Each "I love you" felt like a lie,
A bitter taste I could not deny.

This wasn't the love I dreamed to find,
Not the bond that enriches the mind.
I needed out, a way to reclaim,
My worth, my joy, my untainted name.

Fake love, I couldn't make love,
Had to wake love, not forsake love.
No "just in case," no fallback plan,
I needed love that held my hand.

To stay pure, to guard my heart,
I had to end what tore me apart.
Walking away, I found my worth,
Reclaiming my soul, my place on earth.

For love, true love, is not a mask,
Not a burden, not a task.
It's the wind unseen, the silent air,
You feel its truth—it's always there.

So, I let go, no longer pretend,
Choosing myself, I began to mend.
Wrong v. Right, I made my stand,
No fake love, just love that expands.

Love is just like the wind.
You don't always see it or feel it,
but you know it is always there.

Don't

Embrace the unknown, for it may bring the greatest joy and love you have ever known. Don't let fear or societal expectations hold you back from experiencing the fullness of love. Let go of the past and allow yourself to live in the present moment, with an open heart and mind. Don't let trauma define you, but instead, use it as a tool to grow and learn from.

Together, we can create a new way of loving, one that is based on mutual trust, respect, and understanding. So, take my hand, and let's embark on this journey together, with nothing but love and light guiding our way. Don't let this moment pass you by, for it may just be the start of a beautiful and everlasting love story.

A new way to love

As we stood there, hand in hand, embracing the idea of a new way to love, we felt a profound sense of connection. It was as though the universe had conspired to bring us together at this precise moment in time, and we were ready to seize the opportunity it presented.

We decided to let go of the baggage from our pasts, the scars of previous relationships, and the expectations society had placed upon us. Instead, we would create our own path, one built on authenticity, vulnerability, and a deep sense of trust.

Our journey began with small steps. We started by sharing our dreams, fears, and insecurities, laying our hearts bare for one another to see. We learned to listen without judgment, to support without reservation, and to cherish the moments of connection we shared. Each day felt like an adventure, an exploration of our souls as we discovered new facets of ourselves and each other. We embraced the unknown, knowing that it held the potential for growth and love beyond measure.

One evening, under a sky filled with stars, we made a promise to each other. We vowed to always be true to ourselves and to one another, to communicate openly and honestly, and to nurture the love that was blossoming between us. It was a pledge to create a love that was uniquely ours, free from the constraints of tradition or societal norms.

Together, we navigated the challenges that life presented, knowing that we had each other's backs. We faced fears head-on, addressing them with patience and compassion. And as we did, we discovered that love could indeed be a transformative force, healing the wounds of the past and opening our hearts to new possibilities.

Our love story became a testament to the power of embracing change, of letting go of control, and of living in the present moment. It was a reminder that love, in its purest form, was a force that could bring light to even the darkest corners of our souls.

As we continued on our journey, we knew that there would be more challenges ahead, but we faced them with courage and unwavering belief in our love. We had found a new way to love—one that was grounded in authenticity, freedom, and the deep connection we shared.

And in each other's arms, we found a love that was not bound by rules or expectations but was limitless and everlasting. We had embraced change, and it had led us to a love that was beyond our wildest dreams.

Don't

I will be the right one for the one
I was meant to love I am full of light
With each new beginning comes a great new story
A story that songs are written for

Imagine that you found love in me
Let's embark on this journey
Remove all doubts
Exhale all of your fears

Hold me close let me in to share all of me with all of you
Understand that fear is a normal response to the unknown
Allow me to walk in your presence in peace
Learn how to just be free

Free from the idea that we have to love traditionally
Traditional is controlled confusion
Confusion creates chaos
Chaos is a form of trauma

Never Allow your dreams to be shattered
by the trauma that you sustained
Trauma will not fit into our rules
We create our own rules just me and you
Imagine living a life without fear without control
Just loving naturally open to beautiful new beginnings

You can go your entire life believing that you will never find me
But here I'm standing in front of you
the love that you've yearned for
Don't allow me to walk away
Embrace change

Measure your life in Kisses not Tears.
Measure it in Love, not Years.

Journey

We were first introduced back in 1992 you were my muse I was intrigued by every vision of you - It ended before it began, we started over and over until it seemed perfect, I poured in all of me until I created what I thought would be the perfect version of what I needed it to be.

I altered you to conform you into what I needed again and again. I got frustrated at times and quit and believed that would be the end, but I just couldn't give up, so I tried and tried again and again, until I felt like it was perfected, but I continue to criticize myself. I thought this was not going to work so I searched for something else that I thought would give me peace of mind. But I always seem to come back to you, it made me happy, I thought this time I'm going to stick with you.

Used as a tool, I evacuated to my safe place, I found solace in you. I've gotten too comfortable here, not something I was accustomed to, for years I wasn't able to trust that just me was enough.

So, I dibbled and dibbled her and there, but I also found myself going back, so here I was again, starting over yet again but this time I was committed, and focused. I was taking notes, studying, pouring into this yes for real 100 percent.

Believing in my truth, mask off, knowing that the highest was going to guide me through this challenging time. Faith is so divine; I could not believe that I ever doubted me I was ready to start from scratch, I connected back with my very first love.

It was refreshing, pure joy, I was optimistic about the future. The worry and fear had dissipated I was starting over, giving it my best, setting the mode with my favorite tune.

You make me happy; I can tell I really love you Frankie Beverly and Maze I start my routine placing everything exactly where it's needed, all my ingredients are in place oh, I can't wait!

• • •

As I journeyed through my relationship with my muse, I learned that perfection is not always the answer. Sometimes, it's the imperfections that make us who we are. I learned that I needed to embrace the journey, the ups and downs, the failures, and the successes, and use them as tools to grow and become a better version of myself.

I discovered that I had been using my muse as a tool to escape from my fears and insecurities. But as I embraced my truth and removed my mask, I found that my journey became more fulfilling and authentic. I was able to trust myself and believe in my abilities.

With my favorite tune playing in the background, I started over, pouring my heart and soul into my craft. I learned that my first love, the passion for creating something delicious, was still inside me. And with that realization, I found a sense of joy and optimism for the future.

As I tasted the food I had created, I knew that this journey was far from over. But I was ready to take on whatever challenges came my way, knowing that the Most-High would guide me through it all. With my ingredients in place and my heart open, I was ready to continue on this journey, wherever it may lead me.

And so, with a renewed sense of purpose and determination, I continued to explore my culinary passion. Each day was a new adventure, a chance to experiment and create something unique. I embraced the idea that it wasn't about achieving perfection but rather about the joy of the process and the love I poured into every dish.

I started to share my creations with friends and family, inviting them to taste the flavors I had carefully crafted. Their smiles and expressions of delight were a source of immense satisfaction and motivation. It was as if my food had the power to bring people together, to create moments of connection and joy.

As I gained more confidence in my abilities, I decided to take the next step in my culinary journey. I enrolled in cooking classes and sought mentorship from experienced chefs who could help me refine my skills and broaden my culinary horizons. It was a challenging path, but I embraced the opportunity to learn and grow.

With each new technique I mastered and each recipe I perfected; I felt a deep sense of accomplishment. I realized that the journey itself was the reward, and the joy I found in creating and sharing my dishes was immeasurable.

One day, while participating in a local cooking competition, I met a fellow chef named Mia. She was passionate, talented, and shared my love for food. We quickly became friends, bonding over our culinary adventures and dreams. Mia became not only a mentor but also a source of inspiration and camaraderie.

Together, Mia and I embarked on a new venture—we opened our own restaurant. It was a dream come true, a place where we could express our creativity and share our love for food with others. We named it "Journey's Table," as a tribute to the path we had walked to reach this point.

Journey's Table became a gathering place for food lovers, a spot where people could savor the dishes we had poured our hearts into. The restaurant's ambiance was warm and welcoming, and it embodied the idea that life's journey was meant to be celebrated.

As we cooked side by side in the kitchen, Mia and I continued to grow as chefs and as friends. We embraced the imperfections and challenges that came with running a restaurant, knowing that they were an integral part of our journey.

Our restaurant thrived, not just because of the delicious food but also because of the sense of community we had fostered. People came not just for the dishes but for the experience, for the stories we shared and the connections we forged.

Looking back on my journey, I realized that it had been a winding path filled with ups and downs, but it had led me to a place of fulfillment and purpose. It had taught me that the pursuit of passion and authenticity was more important than striving for perfection.

As I stood in the kitchen of Journey's Table, preparing to create another memorable meal, I couldn't help but feel grateful for the journey I had undertaken. It had brought me to this moment, surrounded by the warmth of the kitchen, the aroma of cooking, and the knowledge that I was living my truth and sharing my love with the world.

A Feast of Creation

Your taste, the aroma, a symphony divine,
Succulent texture, where art and love align.
The spices dance, the vegetables sing,
Each moment of creation a sacred offering.

Fresh from the earth, nature's sweet gift,
Transformed by hands, a soul's gentle shift.
I'm blessed to create, it flows from within,
A melody of flavors, a harmony akin.

It's innate, this passion, this culinary fire,
A craft that fulfills, that lifts me higher.
With every slice, with every stir,
I feel the essence of life's grand allure.

The colors vivid, the scents profound,
Each ingredient a story, a treasure found.
Food is more than sustenance; it's love's embrace,
A shared connection, a timeless grace.

So here I stand, in the heart of this art,
Pouring soul into each flavorful part.
For in every dish, there's a world to create,
A testament to life—it's simply innate.

You taste the aroma the succulent texture
all the spices fresh vegetables food
I'm blessed to create it's Innate
A gift passed down from generations before

Hard Life

Life hit hard; I was scared but I got up each time reclaiming my time. I fail again, girl get up, and start again. Refocus on you and not on what they expect of you.

Find your passion, learned lessons, it's my time. Living out my dreams in 3D I put everything else on hold. Hold please.

I'm ready to dedicate this chapter to me, it's time to let go and be free, live life the way it is intended to be without fear, persevere.

I'm ready to walk in my truth in life just do what you need to be happy be free, show the world the real me. My story has changed but the name is the same. No more looking back I am reclaiming my time. I'm on track.

I can feel the wind blowing in my hair as I take each step forward. My heart is racing with excitement and anticipation of what's to come. I'm finally living my life for me, not for anyone else.

As I walk down the street, I see the world with new eyes. The colors are brighter, the sounds are sweeter, and the people seem kinder. I feel like I'm finally living in 3D, as if everything was in black and white before.

I've learned so much from my struggles and failures. Each time I fell, I got up stronger than before. I've refocused on myself and my passions, and I'm finally living out my dreams.

It's time to let go of my fears and worries and be free. I'm ready to walk in my truth and be the real me. I don't care what others expect of me anymore. I'm dedicated to my own happiness and well-being.

As I continue walking down the path of my life, I know there will be more challenges and obstacles to face. But I'm not afraid anymore. I'm on track, and nothing can stop me from living my best life. I'm reclaiming my time, and I'm never looking back.

With every step I take, I feel a renewed sense of purpose and determination. The weight of past hardships and expectations has lifted, and I am free to be the person I was always meant to be. The wind in my hair and the sun on my face are reminders of the limitless possibilities that lie ahead.

I've realized that life is too short to be living it for anyone else. It's a precious gift, and I'm determined to make the most of it. My dreams and passions are no longer on hold; they are my driving force, propelling me forward with every breath I take.

I've learned that failure is not an endpoint but a steppingstone to success. Each time I fell, I gathered the strength to rise again, wiser, and more resilient. Those lessons have become my guiding light, showing me the way to a brighter future.

As I walk, I can't help but smile at the beauty of the world around me. The vibrant colors, the laughter of children playing, and the kindness of strangers all fill my heart with gratitude. Life has become a tapestry of moments, and I am determined to make each one count.

I've shed the shackles of fear and self-doubt, and in their place, I've found a newfound sense of self-assurance. I know who I am, and I'm proud of it. I'm ready to show the world the real me, unapologetically and authentically.

The story of my life has evolved, but my name remains the same. I am the author of my destiny, and I'm writing a chapter filled with courage, resilience, and unwavering determination. There's no looking back; I'm moving forward, reclaiming my time, and embracing the beauty of the journey.

With every step, I'm guided by the belief that life is meant to be lived without fear and with a spirit of perseverance. I'm ready to face whatever challenges come my way, knowing that I have the strength to overcome them. This is my time, and I'm walking proudly in my truth, living life to the fullest, and savoring every moment along the way.

Rock Bottom

We all hit rock bottom at some point in our lives
whether financially, mentally, or physically.
Life can be overwhelming, and many of us
 have faced storms without the right tools
to navigate through them. But remember,
At some point in life, we all hit a wall
A breaking point where we stumble and fall.

Whether it's money, the body, or mind,
We feel like we're losing, left far behind.
Life is heavy, storms come fast,
We try to hold on, but we can't last.
Without the tools to navigate through,
The world feels dim, the light untrue.

But somewhere deep, beneath the pain,
A quiet strength begins to sustain.
The power to love, to shift, to fight,
To change the way we see our light.
It starts small, a single thought,
"I am enough," a lesson taught.

To look at yourself with grace, not blame,
To call yourself by your true name.
Self-love is hard, it's not overnight,
It takes persistence, it takes might.
To heal the wounds, to build the tools,
To break away from the world's cruel rules.

Each step forward feels like a win,
The cracks begin to close within.
Strength replaces the doubt you knew,
And hope feels steady, shining through.
So when you're down, at the edge of despair,
Remember your power is always there.

The storms will pass, the sky will clear,
You'll rise from the bottom—no need to fear.

Precipitating Factors

The fact is his behavior always changed when there was a mention of her name, I could not mask the pain, the rage.

How does one control feelings of outrage, disappointment, heartache. Just the discussion of what was and possibly what could be, brings shame.

It wasn't visible to the naked eye; he painted a picture of happiness which didn't match his overlooked actions.

Emotional roller coaster, fear, anxiety, and stress hit all at once, my head was spinning, heart racing, time ticking, flashes of the past happy and sad.

Was it real? Is it real? Time wasted, feelings change, fear settles, holding back tears, heart racing, it seems as though your entire world has ended. Everything was moving slow, heart heavy, indescribable pain. Let go and move on.

Time is ticking, let go.

As time passed, the pain began to lessen. He slowly realized that holding onto his feelings of outrage, disappointment, and heartache was only hurting himself. He began to take control of his emotions and let go of what could have been. He knew that he couldn't change the past and that holding onto it was only preventing him from moving forward.

With time, he learned to focus on the present and embrace the happiness that life had to offer. He stopped dwelling on what could have been and instead focused on what was happening right in front of him. The emotional roller coaster began to slow down, and he found peace in the present moment.

Looking back, he realized that there were many precipitating factors that had led to his pain. But he also knew that he had the power to control his own emotions and to choose how he responded to difficult situations. He learned that letting go was not a sign of weakness but a sign of strength and resilience.

As he moved forward, he took with him the lessons he had learned and the strength he had gained. He knew that life would continue to throw challenges his way, but he was now better equipped to handle them. He was grateful for the pain he had experienced, for it had taught him to appreciate the beauty and joy of life even more.

With each passing day, he found it easier to control his feelings of outrage, disappointment, and heartache. He realized that these emotions were like heavy burdens that he had been carrying for far too long. It was time to let go of the pain and embrace the possibility of healing and happiness.

He understood that it wasn't always visible to the naked eye how deeply he had been affected by the past. He had masked his pain with a facade of happiness, but he no longer wanted to hide his true feelings. It was time to be honest with himself and those around him.

He started seeking support from friends and loved ones, opening up about his struggles and sharing his emotions. The more he talked about his feelings, the lighter the weight on his heart became. He found solace in the understanding and compassion of those who cared about him.

The emotional roller coaster of fear, anxiety, and stress began to subside. His head stopped spinning, and his heart no longer raced uncontrollably. He realized that the pain of the past was fading, replaced by a sense of hope and optimism for the future.

He asked himself the tough questions: Was it real? Is it real? And he found the strength to accept that the past was what it was. He couldn't change it, but he could choose to let go and move on. The fear that had held him back began to dissipate, and he felt a renewed sense of freedom.

Time continued to tick away, and he embraced the idea of letting go. It wasn't about forgetting or pretending the pain never existed, but about releasing the grip it had on his heart and soul. He was ready to move forward, to live in the present, and to make the most of the time he had.

As he took the first steps towards a new chapter in his life, he did so with a sense of purpose and determination. He knew that the journey ahead wouldn't be without its challenges, but he was no longer defined by the precipitating factors of his past. He was free to create a future filled with happiness, love, and fulfillment.

Precipitating Factors

The fact is, his behavior always shifted,
At the mere mention of her name, I felt
pain I couldn't mask inside,
And an external rage I could never hide.

How does one control what breaks the heart?
Outrage, disappointment tearing me apart.
The weight of what was, and what could be,
A shame that clings, refusing to set me free.

To the world, it wasn't clear or seen,
He painted happiness like a vivid dream.
But actions speak where words fall weak,
A truth overlooked, too painful to speak.
An emotional ride I couldn't dismount,
Fear, anxiety, and stress began to mount.

My head spinning, my heart outpaced,
Flashes of moments I couldn't erase.
Was it real? Is it real? I couldn't decide,
Time wasted, feelings change, fear collides.
Tears held back, my heart grows sore,
The world feels slow, I can't take more.

Indescribable pain, heavy to bear,
Letting go seemed like gasping for air.
But time keeps ticking, demanding release,
Move on, let go, to find some peace.
As time moved, the hurt began to fade,
I saw the cost of the choices I'd made.

Holding the pain was a losing game,
I had to release the blame, the shame.
Control returned, piece by piece,
Replacing anguish with a sense of peace.
The past could no longer dictate my days,
I found my strength in letting it blaze.

No longer trapped by what could have been,
I embraced the present, let life begin.
The roller coaster slowed, my heart found ease,
In the here and now, I learned to breathe.
Looking back, I see the triggers, the weight,
But I've learned to master what seemed like fate.

Letting go wasn't weakness, but my greatest art,
A testament to resilience, to a healing heart.
The pain taught me, as pain often will,
To find the beauty, to climb the hill.
And now, when challenges come my way,
I stand unbroken, ready to stay.

Blame

I was at the point of no return
Giving up letting go of this life ending it all
Questioning why. GOD why? Why were all these things allowed to happen to me I was just a child.

Help me believe. I want to believe.

Standing off a ledge contemplating taking my life. Dreaming of what life would be if you never created me. No pain no suffering

No doubt this motherless child

Help me believe I want to believe that you are real, but I still question the how. How could you allow such things to happen to an innocent child?
Grieving alone and I don't have anywhere to call home can't confide in anyone due to the shame that these ordeals have caused, the pain is too much to bear I'm hurt, sad and scared it feels like no one cares
Help me believe, I want to believe, it kills me inside that I'm questioning The Who? What? When? Why? And how?
I try to bury the pain deep in the back of my mind. But I'm triggered sometimes. The first time I was touched I was just six years old. That's how far back I can remember. It was a man that my mother trusted. A super radical religious man. Who introduced himself as Jesus in the flesh?

Can you believe that shit?

Help me believe, I want to believe
I want to find solace in you
I want to believe that everything I learned about you is true

But how could a mother give her child away to a stranger who claimed to pray? He preyed on single lonely woman and had them believe that he was sent by you, your son, flesh of your flesh

Damn what's next?

Help me believe, I want to believe, why does my mother hate me?

She was my blood, she carried me in her womb for 9 months but had no love for me, she didn't care for me, shattered my dreams, she tried to kill me, she gave me away, lied, and attempted to destroy my name, beat me until I was black and blue, and left me in pain, no doctor visits, put me out on the street with a 3 month old baby, you can't imagine all the pain and trauma, turmoil and pain.

Help me believe, I want to believe, I want to overcome this pain, I'm hurting inside, doubting my existence, am I worthy of this life?

I was forced to pray and call out your name, but I didn't feel your presence. All I felt was pain.

She left me to die, apartment in flames, she saved herself, but I am still alive, why? And that wasn't the first or last time.

Help me believe, I want to believe. Where were you when I needed you the most? In the Bible, it says you see all things, is this true?

Every night for so many years I would have the same recurring dream: I'm being chased, someone is trying to kill me. I reach the end with nowhere to go but down, I'm falling, my life flashes before my eyes, no happy times, I give up but before I die, I always wake up.

Awaken in a cold sweat not looking forward to night fall, can't sleep, no rest.

Is this life a test?

Help me believe, I want to believe

Am I worthy of this life? I'm tired of fighting for what's right.

I questioned myself, wondering if I was born a curse from birth? Was I a bad person in my past life and karma is catching up with me in the present one? How does this work God? Please help me understand, was it all a part of your plan? I'm curious as to why a child had to experience such a horrific life.

Help me to believe, I want to believe.

As I stood on the ledge, tears streaming down my face, I closed my eyes and took a deep breath. In that moment, I heard a whisper in my ear. It was so soft that I almost missed it, but it was there. It said, "I am with you."

I opened my eyes, and as I did, I felt a rush of warmth flow through me. It was like nothing I had ever experienced before. It was as though a light had been turned on inside of me. I felt a sense of peace, and I knew that I was not alone.

Slowly, I stepped away from the ledge and sat down on the

ground. With tears still streaming down my face, I looked up to the sky and whispered, "Thank you."

In that moment, I knew that I could believe. I knew that I was worthy of this life, and that I had a purpose. I didn't know what that purpose was yet, but I knew that it was there.

From that day forward, I began to see the world in a different light. I started to see the beauty in the little things, and I realized that even in the midst of pain and suffering, there is still hope.

I knew that I still had a long road ahead of me, and that there would be many more challenges to face, but I also knew that I was not alone. I had a newfound faith that gave me strength, and I knew that I could overcome anything with that faith by my side.

As I walked away from the ledge that day, I knew that my life would never be the same again. But I also knew that it would be better. I had found a new sense of purpose, and I knew that I could make a difference in this world.

With each step I took, I felt a renewed sense of hope and a deep sense of gratitude. And I knew that with faith, anything is possible.

After I walked away from that ledge, I carried with me a newfound sense of purpose and a belief in the possibility of a better life. The questions about whether I was born under a curse or if I was paying for past life deeds still lingered, but I was no longer consumed by them.

I realized that I didn't need all the answers to find peace and meaning in my life. What mattered was the present and the future I could shape for myself. I had survived the darkest of moments, and that resilience was a testament to my strength and the potential for growth. With each passing day, I began to rebuild my life. I sought therapy to help me process the trauma I had endured, and I surrounded myself with a support network of friends and loved ones who showed me that I was not alone in my journey. They helped me understand that I was indeed worthy of love, happiness, and a fulfilling life.

As I continued to heal, I found solace in nature. I spent time in parks, by the ocean, and under the open sky, marveling at the beauty of the world around me. It was during these moments of quiet reflection that I felt closest to the divine presence I had encountered on that fateful day.

I began to volunteer and help others who had faced adversity, sharing my own story of survival and resilience. It was through this service that I started to understand my purpose—to be a beacon of hope for those who had lost their way, just as I once had.

Over time, the pain and trauma of the past began to lose its grip on me. It was not an easy journey, but I held onto the belief that I could overcome anything with faith by my side. I learned to embrace the beauty in the little things and to appreciate the moments of joy and connection that life had to offer.

As I moved forward, I knew that life would continue to have its challenges, but I also knew that I could face them with strength and resilience. I had discovered that belief in myself and in the possibility of a better future was a powerful force.

And so, with each step I took, I walked away from the darkness of the past and toward a brighter, more hopeful future. I knew that I could make a difference in this world, not in spite of my past, but because of it. My journey was a testament to the power of belief and the strength of the human spirit, and I was determined to use it to bring hope and healing to others.

1977

The 28th day of the sixth month born 5 minutes later
 a child entered the world a pair fraternal.
There was no mention of two one behind the other.
Heartbeat as one a daughter and a son.
Life begins. No one was prepared for two.
There was no plan of a baby girl

Ignored given away wrong last name unaware
of whom her father is, was, could be my mother hated me.
From birth I was a curse in her eyes I would never be enough
I will never amount to anything
were the words that she spoke to me.

It was my mission to prove her wrong
that began to take a toll on my life
fighting a battle that I could never win had to give up
the beatings got worse abuse in every form that you could imagine
My childhood memories go back to early as five years old
shivering cold outside in the rain in pain black and blue
from the punches and kicks in the stomach

That's the first night she made me sleep outside
No dinner for you tonight you'll learn not to roll your eyes
get on your knees and pray and ask God for his word today
Church everyday Christianity, Baptist, Catholic

Prayers forced through trembling lips,
Knees bruised, hands clenched into fists.
"Ask God for his word," she'd say with disdain,
As if faith could wash away the pain.

Church pews became my silent cage,
A place of worship, a mask for rage.
Bibles thumped, hymns filled the air,
Yet no one saw the child in despair.

A daughter unseen, a name misplaced,
A life of longing, a love erased.
Her hate was the fire that burned my soul,
Each word, each slap, a gaping hole.

I tried to please, to win her grace,
But nothing could soften her hardened face.

"You're a curse," she hissed, venomous and cold,
Her words, a weight I couldn't hold.
At five years old, I learned to survive,
To navigate storms just to stay alive.

Outside in the rain, shivering and thin,
Fighting battles I was too young to begin.
No dinner, no warmth, just the endless night,
Alone with the stars, my only light.

I prayed, not for her God, but for a reprieve,
A chance to escape, a reason to believe.
Christianity, Catholicism, Baptist ways,
Rituals and doctrines filled my days.

Yet beneath the cross, I found no peace,
Only chains that refused to release.
Still, I carried on, with a fire inside,
A stubborn will that refused to die.

Her hate may have shaped the start of my story,
But it won't define the chapters of my glory.
For every tear, a strength was born,
From every scar, a resilience sworn.

I am more than her words, more than her scorn,
A child of the storm, rising reborn.
1977—the year life began,
For a daughter unplanned, for a warrior who ran.

From shadows to light, from pain to grace,
I found my power in my own space.
And though her voice still echoes near,
It's no longer a source of fear.
For I've rewritten what she tried to erase,
A story of triumph, a life I embrace.

Happy

Still struggling with letting go of all the pain and heartache of what nots, how, and why

I'm processing the pain, still I will heal, she left this earth without closure and I'm fine with that. I carried this pain for way too long. It's time to let go and free myself of the pass continue to be strong make new memories and carry on.

My future is bright, I'm staying in this fight I shall overcome and show that I won. I'm the prize; no more fear or tears, now, giving up is not an option I decided not to continue to walk in the shadows of tragedy and overcome the pain of my past. No longer will the trauma consume my life, I'm free, happy.

I am grateful for the lessons learned and the strength I have gained. I will use this experience to help others who may be going through similar struggles. I am not defined by my past, but by the person I choose to be today and in the future.

As I move forward, I will focus on the present and the future, setting new goals and pursuing my passions. I will surround myself with positive energy and people who uplift me and continue to grow and evolve as a person.

I am proud of how far I have come, and I know that my journey is far from over. But with each step I take, I am one step closer to the person I want to be and the life I want to live. I am ready to embrace the possibilities that lie ahead, and I am grateful for the strength and resilience that have brought me to this point.

I am grateful for the lessons learned and the strength I have gained. I will use this experience to help others who may be going through similar struggles. I am not defined by my past, but by the person I choose to be today and in the future.

As I move forward, I will focus on the present and the future, setting new goals and pursuing my passions. I will surround myself with positive energy and people who uplift me and continue to grow and evolve as a person.

The pain of the past may never completely disappear, but I have learned that it doesn't have to define me or dictate my future. I can choose to be happy, to find joy in the little things, and to live a life filled with love and purpose.

And so, I step into the bright future ahead with a heart full of hope and a determination to make each day a happy one. No longer will I walk in the shadows of tragedy, for I am free, and I am ready to shine.

In the midst of pain and sorrow, I once dwelled, with questions unanswered, my heart aching, I could tell. But now, I'm shedding the burdens of the past, embracing a future where happiness will last.

Happy

I've carried this weight for far too long,
It's time to release it, to sing a joyful song.
No closure received, but I'm fine with that,
I'll let go of the pain, leave it all in the past.

The future shines brightly, I've found my way,
I'll stay in this fight; I'll win this time.
No more fear, no more tears, I declare,
Giving up is not an option, I'm aware.

I'll walk away from the shadows of tragedy,
The trauma that once held me, no longer my reality.
I'm free now, I'm happy, I'm strong,
In the symphony of life, I'll sing my own song.

Grateful for lessons, for strength I've obtained,
I'll use my experience, others' hearts I'll mend.
I'm not defined by the past, I boldly say,
In the present and future, I'll find my way.

I'll set new goals, pursue passions with zest,
With positivity, I'll be forever blessed.
Surrounding myself with those who uplift and inspire,
I'll keep evolving, reaching higher and higher.

Proud of my journey, though it's not yet complete,
Each step I take brings me closer to a feat.
I'll embrace the possibilities with all my might,
For happiness awaits, shining so bright.

The pain of the past may linger,
it's true, but it won't control me, I'll break through.
I choose happiness, joy in every small thing,
In love and purpose, my heart will sing.

I step into the future with hope in my heart,
Ready to shine, to make a fresh start.
No more shadows, I'm finally free,
In this newfound happiness, I'll forever be.

Hurt

I sat across from the table at the far end diagonal from my father, looking straight-ahead at my mother, surrounded by my siblings, the white walls, brown colored rug, sheer curtains. It was the winter of 1990, I was 13 years old, I weighed approximately 109 pounds, I stood about 5'5, my father had just returned home from his extensive stay in Pelican Bay.

We never really discussed the reasons why he ended up in prison all the time, back-and-forth, everything was a secret back then. This was the first time I really interacted or met my father.

I was able to have dinner with all of my siblings at the table, but the pit of my stomach just felt like something wasn't right. My father was talking, we were laughing, he turned and said, "you look like a strawberry." I could just feel myself getting angry and mad because I knew that that wasn't something right.

So, I replied, "I look like me" and turn my body counterclockwise away from him, so he couldn't see the tears forming in my eyes. The next moment I ended up on the floor, blood everywhere, my nose broken, black eye, my father standing over me. He tossed a couple water on my face and made the statement, "I bet you never roll your eyes at me again."

And that's where it all began.

Growing up were hard trying times but we got by, we learned to settle and hold our heads down low. We prayed and overlooked so many things that we're not ok, we manage to grow and move along. The way times were hard, but we got by. This is the story of so many people's lives, it's time to stand up and change the world, we can no longer stay in here and conform.

I will not be silent, I will not be set aside, I will not be looked over because I have a voice and it's time for me to stand up and speak. Not only for peace but for everyone that's just like me, stop settling stop listening to the norm, stop trying to fit in, I would no longer conform, my head is held high I am reaching to the sky, fulfilling all my dreams with dignity. I do believe that this too shall pass, the storm will never last, I'm going to stay focus on what I believe, and pray for better days that I will pave for me.

After that moment of hurt, I realized that I couldn't continue to live my life in fear and pain. I had to stand up for myself and for others who have gone through similar experiences. It was time to break the cycle of silence and create a better world for everyone.

I made a promise to myself that day that I would never let anyone hurt me again. I started to speak up and speak out against injustice and abuse. It wasn't easy, but it was necessary. I found strength in my voice and my experiences, and I used it to create change.

Years went by, and I continued to advocate for those who couldn't speak for themselves. I became a voice for the voiceless, and I knew that this was my calling in life. It wasn't until much later that I realized that my hurt had led me to my purpose.

Today, I stand proud and confident in who I am. I no longer live in fear, and I use my voice to inspire and uplift others. I know that the road ahead won't always be easy, but I'm ready for whatever challenges may come my way.

Hurt may have been the beginning of my story, but it's not the end. I've turned my pain into power, and I will continue to use it to make the world a better place.

Hurt

I sat at the table, the farthest end,
Diagonally placed, trying to pretend.
The white walls watched, the brown rug lay,
A silent witness to that winter day.
Thirteen years, a fragile frame,
109 pounds, a life untamed.

He sat there too, newly returned,
From Pelican Bay, where stories burned.
Secrets cloaked the reasons why,
Prison gates swung like lullabies.
This was the first time we truly met,
A father, a stranger, a deep-seated threat.

He spoke, we laughed, the air felt tight,
But something within me didn't feel right.
"You look like a strawberry," he said with a grin,
A comment that tore at the walls within.
"I look like me," I shot back fast,
Turning away, tears forming at last.

Before I could process the words or the air,
I was on the floor, pain everywhere.
Blood on my face, my nose broken wide,
A blackened eye, no place to hide.
He stood above, tossed water with scorn,
"I bet you won't roll your eyes anymore."
And that's where it began, the story of pain,
A life of learning to weather the rain.

We prayed, we settled, we bowed our heads,
Ignoring the bruises, the words unsaid.
Growing up, we learned to survive,
To move through days just staying alive.
But silence became a heavy chain,
And I vowed to break free from its reign.

I will not be silent, I will not retreat,
I will stand tall on unshaken feet.
No more settling, no more disguise,
My voice will rise, reach the skies.
The hurt became fuel, the anger a fire,
To push me forward, to lift me higher.
I speak for those who can't break through,
For the little girl I once was too.
This storm, I know, will one day cease,
I pray for better days, I fight for peace.
Hurt taught me strength, gave me a choice,
To change the world, to find my voice.
Today, I walk with my head held high,
No longer afraid, I touch the sky.

My pain has become my guiding light,
A mission of hope in the darkest night.
Hurt was the start, but it's not my end,
It shaped my purpose, my message to send.
For every tear and every scar,
I've turned my wounds into who I am.

Unbreakable

You have displayed incredible resiliency and strength throughout your life. Despite facing challenges and enduring hardships, you refused to be broken or influenced by the negative opinions of others. You held your head high, even when tears filled your eyes, and walked with confidence and determination. The beatings you endured, whether physical or emotional, became a badge of honor, a testament to your unwavering spirit.

Throughout your journey, there were whispers of doubts and casting of shadows upon your aspirations. However, you remained steadfast, your spirit unyielding. Each challenge that came your way was seen as a test, an opportunity to prove yourself and push beyond your limits. You refused to rest, continually pursuing your goals with a burning passion. Deep within your heart, you held the unwavering belief that one day you would accomplish your dreams and ignite your fighting spirit.

The doubters' words became nothing more than echoes in the wind, mere fuel for your ambition and strength. You soared high above their shallow words, defying the odds like a soaring bird. Every goal you set, you chased and conquered, transforming doubt into the driving force behind your success. You built a fortress, strong and true, using the bricks they threw at you to construct a solid foundation.

With each goal achieved, their skepticism began to crumble. You proved them wrong time and time again, displaying an unyielding determination and an unshakeable resolve. No matter what they said or tried to do, you remained true to your own path, forging ahead on your own highway.

Now, you stand tall, radiating pride and grace. You have become a living testament to your enduring strength. Despite the bitterness and negativity that surrounded you, you have shown that you are more than what they ever perceived. Let them try, let them condemn, for you will rise above their attempts to break you, again and again.

All your life, they tried to break you down, but you emerged victorious, wearing the crown of victory. They couldn't break you; they couldn't shake you. You have proven that you are a force to be reckoned with, a shining example of resilience and determination.

Never Broken

Unbreakable

They tried to dim your inner light,
With shadows cast in the dead of night.
But your spirit burned, a blazing flame,
Unyielding strength, they couldn't tame.

Through storms of doubt, you held your ground,
Each cruel word, a hollow sound.
The tears you shed, the pain you bore,
Became the steel within your core.

They struck with malice, sharp and cold,
But in your heart, a story bold.
You rose with courage, fierce and true,
And built a world from what they threw.

The whispers of doubt, the sneers, the jeers,
 Became the anthem of your years. You stood,
you fought, you soared, you flew,
Their shallow words could not undo.
Each bruise became a badge you wore,
Each scar, a key to an unlocked door.

You scaled the heights they said you'd fall,
And proved yourself above it all.
Now here you stand, proud and free,
A testament for all to see.

Unbreakable, a force of grace,
A fighter with an endless pace.
So let them try, let them condemn,
You'll rise above time and again.

Their chains could never hold you down,
For you, my dear, wear victory's crown.
Unyielding, unbroken, you shine like the sun,
A story of triumph, the war you've won.

Misplaced rage

Abuse comes in many different forms: physical, mental, and emotional. The cycle of abuse continues and comes in many different patterns. I was hurt, so I hurt you. You remind me of someone that abuse me, so I abuse you, I need you to stay around, so I hurt you and keep you down.

Passing on this pain of rage it leads to distraction, and the cycle continues, especially if we share a child with someone and we don't know how to keep what we feel to ourselves. We may take our rage out on that child or turn the child against the other parent and that is abuse.

Our children become collateral damage, we don't all have the answers, but it starts with us. Healing will take time and even though we may feel like that person wronged us holding on to all the pain only hurts us; stop hurting yourself and heal.

The misplaced rage that we carry within us can have devastating effects not only on ourselves but also on those around us. It can cause us to act out in ways that are harmful and destructive, and the cycle of abuse can continue on for generations.

But it doesn't have to be this way. Healing is possible, and it starts with recognizing the pain and trauma that we carry within us. It takes time and effort, but the rewards are worth it.

We can learn to manage our emotions and find healthier ways to express our anger and frustration. We can learn to forgive those who have wronged us, not because they deserve it, but because we deserve to be free from the weight of our anger and resentment.

We can break the cycle of abuse and create a better future for ourselves and our children. It all starts with us. We have the power to change our lives and the lives of those around us, and it begins with healing our misplaced rage.

The Weight of Misplaced Rage

The rage we carry is a silent,
A weight unspoken, a pain we've worn.
It brews within, a relentless tide,
Breaking us down from the inside.
It lashes out in moments unplanned,
Hurtful words, an unsteady hand.

We harm ourselves; we harm those near,
Repeating cycles fed by fear.
Generations feel the reverberation,
An endless chain of devastation.
But it doesn't have to stay this way,
We can choose a brighter day.

Healing starts with a simple truth,
Acknowledging the wounds of our youth.
The pain we buried, the scars unseen,
The trauma wrapped in places between.
It's hard to face, this path we tread,

Unraveling the stories in our head.
But in the facing, freedom blooms,
Breaking the cycle that silently cries.
To forgive isn't weakness, it isn't defeat,
It's laying your anger at your own feet.

Not for the sake of those who harmed,
But to free your heart, to feel disarmed.
We learn to manage, to breathe, to pause,
To uncover the roots, the buried cause.
To express our anger without destruction,
To rebuild ourselves through love's instruction.

It takes courage, it takes time,
But each step forward is a climb.
Towards a future not weighed by pain,
Towards a life where joy remains.
The power to change is within our hands,
To shape the world, to rewrite the plans.

For our children, for ourselves, for those who stay,
We can break the chains; there is another way.
So let's confront the rage we bear,
Transform the hurt, repair the tear.
The cycle ends where healing begins,
A legacy of love, where peace wins.

Turning Pain into Purpose

As I reflected on the impact of my story, I understood that the pain I had experienced was not in vain. I had the power to turn my suffering into purpose, using my story to create a positive impact on the lives of others.

As I sat down to reflect on my journey, I realized that the most significant growth came from the pain I had endured. The struggles that I faced had taught me the most profound lessons and had become a catalyst for my personal growth.

It wasn't easy to come to this realization. For a long time, I had been consumed by my pain, unable to see beyond it. I felt trapped, like I was drowning in a sea of hopelessness, and couldn't see a way out.

But one day, something shifted inside me. I realized that I had a choice - I could let my pain define me, or I could use it to fuel my growth and create a positive impact on others. That was the day I decided to turn my pain into purpose.

It wasn't an easy journey, and it took time, effort, and a lot of self-reflection to get there. But as I started to heal, I began to see the power of my story. I realized that by sharing my experiences, I could help others who were going through similar struggles.

I started to write about my journey, sharing my story with anyone who would listen. It wasn't easy to be vulnerable and put myself out there, but the response was overwhelming. People reached out to me, sharing their own struggles, and thanking me for speaking up. They told me that my story had inspired them and given them hope.

It was then that I realized the true power of turning pain into purpose. My experiences had the potential to create a positive impact on others, and that was a powerful motivator. It gave me a sense of purpose, a reason to keep pushing forward, even when the journey was tough.

But turning pain into purpose wasn't just about sharing my story. It was also about acting. I realized that my experiences had given me a unique perspective, and that perspective could be used to create positive change.

I started volunteering with organizations that supported people going through similar struggles, using my own experiences to offer guidance and support. I started speaking out about issues that mattered to me, advocating for change, and using my voice to make a difference.

It wasn't easy, and there were times when I felt like giving up. But every time I thought about the people I was helping, the impact I was making, it gave me the strength to keep going.

Looking back on my journey, I realize that turning pain into purpose has been the most significant transformation in my life. It's given me a sense of meaning and direction, and it's allowed me to create a positive impact on the world.

If you're going through a tough time, I encourage you to consider the power of turning your pain into purpose. Your experiences have the potential to create a positive impact on others, and that's a powerful motivator. So don't be afraid to speak up, to share your story, and to act. You never know who you might be inspiring or whose life you might be changing.

As I continued to embrace my newfound purpose, the path ahead was not always smooth, but it was undeniably transformative. I had become a beacon of hope for those who needed it most, and that responsibility weighed heavily on my shoulders. However, it also gave me the strength to push forward and make a difference in the lives of others.

One of the most significant turning points in my journey came when I decided to start a support group for individuals who had experienced similar hardships. I wanted to create a safe space where people could share their stories, find solace in knowing they were not alone, and discover the strength within themselves to heal and grow.

The support group, initially small and intimate, began to grow as more and more people found comfort in our shared experiences. We exchanged stories, tears, and laughter, forming deep connections that went beyond our pain. It was a reminder that, in the midst of adversity, bonds can be forged that are stronger than steel.

• • •

As our support group flourished, we decided to organize events and workshops to raise awareness about the issues we had faced. We collaborated with local organizations and even held a fundraiser to support causes related to mental health, trauma recovery, and resilience.

One of our proudest achievements was when we partnered with a local school to implement a program focused on teaching emotional resilience and coping strategies to students. It was an opportunity to prevent others from going down the same dark paths we had, a chance to plant seeds of change that could grow into a brighter future.

Through these efforts, we discovered the true extent of the ripple effect our stories could create. Not only were we helping individuals in our support group, but we were also impacting our community as a whole. The pain we had endured had become a catalyst for positive change.

Over time, my journey also led me to connect with professionals and experts in the field of mental health and trauma recovery. I learned from their expertise and integrated their knowledge into our support group's programs. This collaboration allowed us to provide even more comprehensive assistance to those in need.

As the years passed, I watched countless lives transform before my eyes. People who had once felt lost and hopeless now radiated resilience and hope. They, too, began to turn their pain into purpose, paying forward the support they had received.

Reflecting on my journey, I realized that the power of turning pain into purpose was not just about personal healing; it was about creating a ripple effect of healing and positive change in the world. It was about using our stories and experiences to uplift others and build a more compassionate and understanding society.

Today, our support group continues to thrive, and our efforts continue to make a difference. I am grateful for the opportunity to turn my pain into purpose, and I am reminded daily that no matter how dark the past may have been, there is always a way to find light and meaning in the journey ahead.

Turning Pain into Purpose

Pain once held me hostage, bound by its weight,
A constant reminder of a relentless fate.
I carried its trauma, its screams in my soul,
But never realized it could make me whole.
At first, I drowned, unable to see,
That within the hurt lay a path to be free.
I let it consume, define my days,
A fog of despair in endless grays.

But one day, the tide began to turn,
A small, quiet flame within me burned.
I saw a choice—stay broken or rise,
To take my pain and reach for the skies.
It wasn't easy, this path I chose,
To confront the hurt, to face the blows.
Yet step by step, I began to heal,
Revealing a strength I could finally feel.
I started to write, to share my pain,
To let others know they weren't alone in the rain.

My words became bridges, spanning the divide,
Helping others find solace, standing by their side.
The stories poured in, raw and true,
Of struggles endured, of skies once blue.
Their courage gave me the will to fight,
To turn my darkness into light.
But words weren't enough—I had to act,
To transform my pain into a lasting impact.

I volunteered, I spoke, I gave my time,
Turning my journey into something divine.
From a support group that began so small,
To a community where we could all stand tall.
We shared our tears, our laughter, our fears,
Forging bonds stronger than the passing years.

Workshops, events, a program for youth,
Teaching resilience, the power of truth.

We planted seeds in hearts so tender,
A legacy of hope they'd always remember.
The ripple grew, its reach expanded,
Lives transformed, spirits unbranded.
From lost and broken to hopeful and whole,
We found our purpose, regained control.
Now I see my pain as a gift in disguise,
A bridge to others, a chance to rise.
It's no longer a burden, no longer my cage,
But a connection of strength on life's vast stage.
If you're trapped in darkness, lost and small,
Know your pain has a purpose, a higher call.

It can break you down or help you grow,
The choice is yours—let your light show.
For every scar holds a story untold,
Every tear a lesson worth more than gold.
Turn your pain into purpose, let it ignite,
A brighter world, full of love and light.

The great pretender

Once upon a time, in the bustling heart of the city, there existed a love story that had captivated the hearts of many. Alee and her partner had been the envy of their friends, a couple whose love seemed as timeless as the stars in the night sky. They laughed together, danced together, and whispered sweet nothings to each other under the moonlight. But even the most beautiful stories have an end, and theirs was no exception.

"I left before it ended," Alee would often tell herself. As she sat alone in her cozy apartment, memories of their time together would replay in her mind like a broken record, all the good times etched vividly in her memory. The world they had built together had come crashing down, and they had been forced to stop pretending.

Alee had always been intuitive, sensitive to the subtle shifts in their relationship. She had noticed the differences, the inconsistencies that had started to unravel their perfect love story. Gone were the sweet names and the affectionate gestures. At times, he seemed distant, as though he were someone she no longer recognized, someone who was all too familiar yet strangely distant.

"I will no longer complain," Alee told herself as she wiped away a stray tear. She had sat up many nights, continuously contemplating the state of their relationship. Should she continue to fight to keep this love alive, or was it time to surrender to the reality that it was fading away? She was exhausted from the endless back and forth, the emotional rollercoaster they were riding. It became painfully clear that they were no longer meant to be.

"I wish you well," she whispered to the empty room, her voice tinged with sadness. He was far away from her now, but she couldn't help thinking about what they could have been. She replayed the love they had shared in her mind, wondering if it could ever be repaired. Their dreams had shifted, and so had their paths.

He had appeared to be all in, talking about lifelong plans and confessing his undying love. He made promises and set goals, but it was as if he considered only his own feelings and desires. It was all about what was best for him, and Alee began to realize that their relationship had turned into a tangled mess.

"The love I imagined we shared has all faded away," Alee admitted to herself. Even though he was physically present, she missed what she thought was him. It was all different now; there was no more "us."

"He painted a good picture of himself," Alee reflected. He had been a master of pretense, weaving a tapestry of lies as time went by. Many things had unfolded that had shattered her trust, and she realized the importance of never underestimating anyone's ability to pretend to be present in a relationship.

As Alee looked into the mirror, she saw a changed person, someone who had changed her perception of love and relationships. He had changed his direction, and she had no choice but to change hers.

And so, in the end, their love story had become a tale of the great pretender. It was a chapter in her life that had ended, leaving Alee with a lesson she would carry with her forever. She knew that true love was not built on pretense, but on honesty, trust, and a genuine connection.

As the days turned into weeks and then months, Alee found herself slowly healing from the wounds of the past. She had severed ties with the great pretender, knowing that it was the right decision, however painful it had been. With each passing day, she began to rediscover herself, gaining strength and clarity.

Alee immersed herself in the things that brought her joy, rekindling old hobbies and forging new friendships. She found solace in the company of friends who understood her pain and provided the support she needed during this challenging time. They reminded her that she was not alone and that there was a bright future waiting for her beyond the shadow of the past.

One evening, as she walked through the city streets that had once been the backdrop of her love story, Alee came across an art gallery. She decided to step inside, drawn to the vibrant colors and emotions that the paintings conveyed. As she wandered through the gallery, one particular painting caught her eye. It was a depiction of a phoenix rising from the ashes, its wings outstretched in magnificent glory.

Alee stood before the painting, feeling a connection to the mythical bird. It was a symbol of rebirth and transformation, a reminder that even in the darkest moments, one could find the strength to rise again. The artist had captured the essence of the phoenix's resilience, and Alee found herself moved by the painting's message.

Inspired by what she had seen, Alee began to explore her own talents and creativity. She started writing again, pouring her emotions onto the pages of a journal. She found therapy in her words, a way to process her feelings and heal the wounds that had been inflicted by the great pretender.

Months turned into a year, and Alee had blossomed into a stronger, more self-assured version of herself. She had learned to trust her instincts and recognize the signs of pretense and deceit. Her heart, though scarred, was now guarded by a newfound wisdom that would serve her well in the future.

One day, as she was sipping her coffee at a local café, Alee's eyes met those of a stranger sitting across from her. There was something familiar in the warmth of their gaze, a sense of genuine connection that she hadn't felt in a long time. They struck up a conversation, and as they talked, Alee couldn't help but feel a spark of hope igniting within her.

This new person in her life was nothing like the great pretender. They were open, honest, and kind. They listened to her stories and shared their own. It was a slow and cautious dance, but Alee realized that it was possible to open her heart again, to trust and love once more. As the days passed, Alee and the stranger grew closer, and a genuine connection began to flourish. It wasn't the whirlwind romance she had once experienced, but it was real, and it was based on authenticity and trust.

Alee had learned that true love was not about grand gestures or pretense. It was about being real, vulnerable, and accepting each other's flaws and imperfections. The great pretender had been a painful chapter in her life, but it had also been a valuable lesson in discerning true love from deception.

And so, Alee's story continued, not as a victim of pretense but as a survivor who had emerged stronger and wiser. She had found her phoenix-like strength, and with each new day, she soared higher, leaving behind the ashes of the past and embracing the promise of a brighter future filled with genuine love and authenticity.

The great pretender

I departed before it concluded,
Recollections replaying in my mind,
the moments we once cherished,

We had to cease the charade,
Noticing the disparities and inconsistencies,
No more endearing words, at times,
it all felt the same,
I've decided not to voice my grievances any longer.

Countless nights spent contemplating,
Should I persist in battling to salvage this love?
Man, you know I've given it my all,
but I'm weary of the constant turmoil,
We're no longer meant to be, it's clear.

I extend my well-wishes from a distance,
Reflecting on what might have been,
replaying it incessantly,
Could the love we once shared be rekindled?
Our dreams have shifted, diverging paths we now tread.

He seemed fully committed,
Engaging in discussions about lifelong aspirations,
Confessing his love, crafting plans alone,
Without consideration for my feelings,
He solely pursued what was best for himself,
A tangled mess we found ourselves in.

The love I envisioned has faded into the ether,
Even though he remains physically present,
I yearn for what I believed he was,
But it's all changed, no "us" remains.

He masterfully painted a facade,
A fabrication that unraveled as time passed,
Revealing countless hidden truths,
Never underestimate anyone's capacity to feign,
To feign commitment in a relationship,
 My perspective evolved; his course altered.

The great pretender

After the Pain

In a small, picturesque town nestled between rolling hills and lush meadows, there lived a woman named Eliza. Her life had been marked by a cautious heart, one that had been wounded in the past. She had always held her feelings close, never allowing anyone to enter the sanctuary of her heart.

Eliza's skepticism towards love had deep roots. She had witnessed the crumbling of love stories that began with such promise, only to fall apart before they had a chance to bloom. She believed that her own heart was safer if she kept it locked away, shielded from the potential heartbreak that love could bring.

But life has a way of surprising us, and Eliza's world was about to change. A new chapter was about to be written in her story, one that she could never have fathomed.

One sunny afternoon, as Eliza strolled through the town's charming streets, she happened upon a small cafe tucked away in a quiet corner. The aroma of freshly brewed coffee and warm pastries wafted through the air, inviting her in. She hesitated for a moment, considering whether to enter or not. It was a chance she wasn't sure she wanted to take.

However, something inside her urged her forward, a voice whispering that maybe, just maybe, this could be different. And so, she pushed open the cafe door and stepped inside.

The cafe was cozy, with soft jazz music playing in the background and the gentle hum of conversation filling the air. As Eliza ordered her coffee, her eyes met those of a stranger sitting alone at a corner table. There was something in his gaze, a warmth and kindness that instantly drew her in.

They started talking, their conversation flowing effortlessly, as if they had known each other for years. It was as though they were reading from the same book, sharing stories of their past, their dreams, and their fears. Eliza couldn't help but feel a connection she had never experienced before.

As weeks turned into months, Eliza's cautious heart began to open. She had taken a chance on this stranger, and in return, he had shown her the beauty of love that she had once thought unattainable. Their love was genuine, built on understanding and acceptance, flaws, and all.

However, life had a different plan in store for them. As time passed, they both realized that their paths were diverging, leading them in different directions. The love that had once flourished between them was now faced with the painful decision to end.

Eliza knew that she had to let go, that holding on would only prolong the inevitable and cause more pain. As they parted ways, she held back her tears, her heart aching with the pain of saying goodbye.

Days turned into weeks, and Eliza found herself mourning the love that had been lost. Her heart felt like a river, tears flowing like an endless stream. But as she wiped away the tears and began to heal, she realized that love didn't have to end in bitterness and regret.

She learned that love starts within, a self-love that could never be taken away. It was a lesson she would carry with her as she embarked on a new journey, one filled with brighter and happier days. And although she could never have fathomed welcoming anyone into her heart, she had discovered that taking a chance on love was worth every moment of pain and joy it brought.

As Eliza continued her journey through life, she carried the lessons from her brief but impactful love affair with her. The memories of that connection served as a reminder that love, no matter how fleeting, had the power to transform her and open her heart in ways she never thought possible.

With each passing day, Eliza grew stronger, her heart mending like a fragile porcelain vase that had been carefully glued back together. She found solace in the beauty of the world around her, the picturesque town with its rolling hills and lush meadows offering a soothing backdrop to her healing process.

Eliza rekindled old passions and discovered new interests. She spent time in nature, taking long walks in the meadows and appreciating the simple pleasures of life. The town's community embraced her, providing a sense of belonging that she had longed for.

One sunny morning, as Eliza wandered through the town's market square, she stumbled upon a quaint bookstore with a weathered sign that read "Whispers of the Heart." Intrigued, she entered the cozy shop, the scent of old books filling the air.

The bookstore was a treasure trove of stories, each book waiting to be opened and explored. Eliza found herself drawn to a particularly worn leather-bound volume, its pages filled with handwritten notes and dog-eared corners. It was a collection of love letters, penned by generations of romantics.

As she delved into the letters, she was captivated by the raw and heartfelt emotions expressed within them. Love, in all its forms and complexities, leaped off the pages. Eliza couldn't help but smile as she read about the joys and sorrows, the longing and fulfillment, that love had brought to the lives of those who had written these letters.

Eliza decided to purchase the book, intending to savor the letters and the stories they contained. Little did she know that these letters would become more than just a collection of words on paper; they would become a source of inspiration and a reminder of the beauty and depth of love.

Over time, Eliza found herself reflecting on her own journey and the love she had experienced. She realized that love, in all its forms, was a precious gift that enriched her life and made her a better person. She had learned that love wasn't just about the destination but also about the journey itself—the moments shared, the lessons learned, and the growth that came from opening her heart.

As she continued to explore the town and its surroundings, Eliza began to embrace life with a newfound sense of gratitude and wonder. She knew that love had the power to transform, to heal, and to inspire. And even though her heart had been tested and bruised, it had also been awakened to the possibilities of a future filled with brighter and happier days.

In the picturesque town nestled between rolling hills and lush meadows, Eliza's story continued to unfold. She had discovered that love, no matter how it entered her life, was a force that could shape her destiny, and she was ready to embrace whatever the future held with an open heart and a hopeful spirit.

After the Pain

I never fathomed welcoming anyone into my heart,
For I'd seen love crumble before it could even start.
I couldn't fathom anyone loving me more,
Then the love I hold within, that I've always kept in store.

But I took a chance on you, against my own doubt,
To see if love could truly be what it's all about.
I can't place all the blame solely on your side,
I noticed the signs, the shifting of the tide.

The love was genuine, that much is true,
That's why I fell for you, and you fell for me too.
We understood each other, flaws, and all,
Without judgment or expectation to stand tall.

Yet, letting go completely is a daunting quest,
Knowing that it's time to move on, at best.
No more beautiful new moments, it's bittersweet,
I mourned within, tears like a river's endless fleet.

My body ached with the pain that we chose to defend,
As we made the decision for our love to finally end.
I held my composure as you walked away,
Though the thought of your absence caused my heart to sway.

Our lives were now on divergent tracks,
We grew apart, and I gazed out the window at the cracks.
For what felt like an eternity, I imagined you nearby,
Walking back in, erasing our pain, starting fresh, I feared.

But I had to grieve, no longer needing your crutch,
I picked up the pieces, my heart's wounds I would touch.
Wiping away the tears, I began to see,
That love starts within, and it will set me free.
In time, I'll understand why we had to part ways,
After the pain, I'll find brighter and happier days.

Consumed by Remorse

In a quiet neighborhood, nestled among the comforting shade of ancient trees, lived a woman named Amelia. Her life, once filled with love and laughter, had taken a sudden and unexpected turn. Consumed by remorse, she wandered through her days in a haze of sadness.

Amelia's heartache was like a relentless storm, unceasing and turbulent. It had begun with a single argument, a heated exchange of words that neither she nor her partner had ever intended to utter. Harsh words had cut deeper than any physical wound, leaving both of them emotionally battered.

Days turned into nights, and nights into weeks, with Amelia unable to shake the profound sense of guilt and regret that engulfed her. The relentless throbbing in her chest mirrored the pounding headache that plagued her every waking hour. It was as if her heartache had manifested into a physical ailment, an affliction that seemed impossible to heal.

Tears flowed like a never-ending river, and Amelia felt like she was withering away on the inside. The pain was overwhelming, and she couldn't bear to face her partner, not yet. She needed time, space, and a place where she could begin the arduous journey of healing.

Amelia longed for the days before that fateful argument, when their love had been a source of joy and strength. She wished she could turn back time, erase the hurtful words, and return to the days when he was all hers. Regret consumed her, knowing that she should have chosen a different way to express her feelings.

She understood now that speaking face to face would have been the right way, but it was too late to turn back the clock. Her heart weighed heavily, and she couldn't delay the inevitable parting any longer. The relationship had suffered irreparable damage, and there was no time for goodbyes.

With a heavy heart, Amelia decided to write a letter to her partner. She poured her soul onto the pages, explaining in detail why they had to part ways. In her words, she expressed the hope that they could still be friends, that the bond they had shared might find a new form.

As she penned the final words of her letter, tears stained the paper. Amelia took a deep breath, letting her emotions flow into each word, and sealed the envelope with a heavy heart. She knew that she still wanted him in her life, and the pain of separation was unbearable.

Days passed, and Amelia was consumed by remorse. She questioned her actions, wondering if she should have called or reached out to him once more. Could they give their love another chance, or was it too late? The memories of their time together haunted her, and she missed her friend deeply.

Amelia called and texted, but there was no response. Her partner remained silent, deep in his own feelings, just as she was. The reality of their separation weighed heavily on her, and the thought that this might be the end was almost unbearable.

As time marched on, Amelia realized that she had to give her partner the space he needed to heal. She couldn't force him to respond or change his mind. It was a painful acceptance that consumed her every thought. Still, deep down, she held onto a glimmer of hope, a belief that their paths might cross again when the wounds had mended.

Consumed by remorse, Amelia found herself in a state of perpetual longing and uncertainty. She couldn't escape the pain of her actions, nor the silence that echoed between them. But she couldn't shake the feeling that their story wasn't over, that one day, when the time was right, they might find their way back to each other.

And so, as the days turned into months, Amelia held onto her remorse and her hope, unsure of what the future might bring.

Amelia's life continued, but her heart remained heavy with the weight of regret. As the seasons changed, the quiet neighborhood around her transformed, painting a beautiful backdrop to her internal struggle. The ancient trees that had once seemed comforting now whispered their secrets in the breeze, offering solace and a sense of timelessness.

In her solitude, Amelia found herself reflecting on the choices she had made and the words she had spoken. She couldn't help but wonder if she had let her fear and frustration overshadow the love that had once bound them together. She knew that it was not just her own heart that had been broken but also the heart of the person she had cared for deeply.

Amelia began to seek solace in nature, just as she did when her heartache was at its peak. She took long walks beneath the sheltering trees, her footsteps echoing her inner turmoil. The tranquil surroundings served as a sanctuary where she could sort through her emotions and make sense of her remorse.

As the months passed, she continued to write letters, pouring her feelings onto paper in an attempt to convey the depth of her regret and longing. Yet, she never sent them, for her partner's silence had become a wall that she couldn't penetrate. She respected his need for space and healing, even as it tore at her own heart.

But Amelia's hope endured. She couldn't shake the feeling that their story wasn't over, that the connection they had shared still held significance. She believed that time had the power to heal wounds, to soften the edges of their painful parting.

Amelia found strength in her own growth and self-reflection. She learned that love, even when it faltered, could serve as a catalyst for personal transformation. She recognized the importance of communication and forgiveness, not only toward her partner but also toward herself.

And then, one crisp autumn day, as the leaves turned fiery shades of red and gold, a notification chimed on her phone. It was a message from him. The silence that had weighed on her heart for so long was finally broken.

With trembling hands, Amelia opened the message. It was a simple "Hello," but it carried the weight of countless unspoken words and emotions. She replied, her heart pounding in her chest as they began to converse once more.

Over time, they navigated the difficult terrain of their past and the uncertain path of their future. They took it slow, rebuilding trust and understanding. The process was not without its challenges, but both were committed to facing them together.

As they rekindled their connection, Amelia discovered that remorse, while consuming, could also be a catalyst for growth and healing. It had led her on a journey of self-discovery and transformation, and it had paved the way for a second chance at love.

Their story, marked by turmoil and redemption, unfolded against the backdrop of the changing seasons. As winter turned to spring, Amelia and her partner found themselves in a place of renewed hope and a deeper appreciation for the love they shared.

And in the quiet neighborhood, nestled among the comforting shade of ancient trees, their love story continued, reminding them both that sometimes, even when consumed by remorse, the heart can find its way back to where it truly belongs.

Consumed by remorse

My heart aches and a headache courses.
Tired of these tears that endlessly flow, inside,
I feel like I'm withering, low.
I can't face him right away, not just yet,
Give me some time, some space, a healing outlet.

Consumed by remorse,
If only I could retract those words, of course,
Turn back time to when he was all mine,
To the days when everything seemed fine.
I thought it was time to share how I feel, But the way I did it,
it didn't quite seal. It should've been face to face, I now realize,
My heart's heavy, but there's no time for goodbyes.

Consumed by remorse,
He wasn't prepared to hear it,
the course, time will tell if it'll ever mend and mend,
So, I'll write him a letter to extend,
To explain in detail why we had to part,
And yes, we can still be friends, my heart.
Let me carefully think this through,
I believe I still want him, it's true.

Consumed by remorse,
I can't believe it's over, this bitter course,
What should I do? Should I call him now?
Reach out and vow that I was wrong somehow?
Can we give this another try, my old friend?
I miss you, I wasn't ready for this to end,
Not in this way, I'll swallow my pride, it's clear,
Tomorrow, I'll try again, let go of the fear.

Consumed by remorse,
I'm just not ready yet, that's the source,
This can't be the end, I can't lose my dear friend,

He's not responding to my calls,
I apprehend. I hope he'll understand and heal in time,
But is this truly the end of our climb? It doesn't feel real,
it can't be the closure, He's ignoring my calls,
adding to the exposure.

Consumed by remorse,
I'll grant him the time he needs,
of course, But is it really the end of our story, so stout?
I can't accept that, it's causing me doubt.
He may be in his feelings, deep and true,
But when he's ready, I hope he'll reach out too,
For now, I'll let him heal, that much is clear,
But I can't shake the feeling that he'll reappear.

Consumed by remorse

Pressure

In a world where passion knows no boundaries, there existed a love story that defied all expectations. It was a tale of two souls drawn together by an irresistible force, a force that pushed them closer, like perpendicular lines converging at a singular point.

Their journey began with a chance encounter, their lives intersecting at a time when they both craved a stress reliever, a respite from the demands of the world. As they got closer, it was as if they were running a marathon of emotions, a passionate race to discover what lay ahead.

Their bodies were close in proximity, and from the moment their eyes met, a spark ignited within them. It was a fire that burned with an intensity they had never known before. Their desires flowed like fluids circulating through their veins, rising higher and higher with each stolen glance and tender touch.

The wait had been excruciating, a period of anticipation that had left them both breathless. But finally, the moment arrived, and their temperature began to rise. Their connection was a fiery conflagration, a combustion of emotions that released a reaction so divine it could only be described as pure ecstasy. It was hot enough to warm a room, their bodies pressed against each other in a feverish embrace.

Visibly proportioned and extremely attractive, they were a sight to behold. Their bodies were perfectly in tune with each other, their connection interactive and electric. The strength and vitality they shared sustained them physically, and in each other's arms, they found the power they had been deprived of for so long. Mentally stimulated, they explored the depths of each other's minds, their connection brilliant and intoxicating.

Their love was like parallel lines, perfectly aligned at all the right angles to create a symphony of pleasure. Their chemistry took flight, a whirlwind of sensations and emotions that left them both in awe. The pressure they applied to each other's body and mind was like a sweet torment, a dance of desire that left them both satisfied in ways they had never imagined. Their love was an ecstasy of a unique kind, a passionate journey that seemed to have no end.

Their drive was powerful, yet their touch was gentle, a delicate balance of passion and tenderness. As their desires melded and intertwined, they craved each other more and more, unable to resist the magnetic pull that drew them closer.

They reset and released, breaking free from the constraints of the world around them. Their love flowed through them like a river, a passionate spree that knew no bounds. In their breathless moments, they came up for air, their hearts racing and their bodies trembling with desire. No one could compare to the love they shared, a love that was as unique as it was intense.

In the end, their bond and connection were a testament to the power of love. It was a force that defied logic and reason, a force that brought two souls together in a fervent embrace. They were a perfect pair, two lines that had converged to form a love story that would last a lifetime.

As their love story continued to unfold, the world around them seemed to fade into the background. They were caught in a whirlwind of emotions, their connection growing stronger with each passing day. The passion that had brought them together was a fire that blazed brightly, illuminating their lives in ways they had never imagined.

Their days were marked by stolen moments and stolen glances, a continuous marathon of affection and desire. Their bodies, once close in proximity, now found comfort in each other's arms. The sparks that had ignited between them had grown into a roaring inferno, their desires flowing like a river that had found its natural course.

Their love was visibly proportioned and undeniably attractive, a sight to behold for anyone who crossed their path. They moved through life in perfect harmony, their connection interactive and electric, a dance of two souls deeply in love. The strength and vitality they shared allowed them to conquer any obstacle, both physically and mentally. In each other's presence, they found the power and inspiration they had been deprived of for so long.

Their drive was powerful, yet their touch remained gentle and tender. They couldn't get enough of each other, their cravings growing stronger with each passing moment. Their connection was like a magnetic force, drawing them closer, making it impossible to resist the pull of their desires.

Their bond and connection were a testament to the enduring power of love. It was a force that defied logic and reason, a force that had brought two souls together in a fervent embrace. They were a perfect pair, two lines that had converged to form a love story that would stand the test of time.

And so, in a world where passion knows no boundaries, their love story continued to evolve, a beautiful symphony of desire, affection, and devotion. They cherished each day they spent together, knowing that their love was a force that would carry them through any challenge life may bring, and their journey was a testament to the enduring power of love.

Their love continued to burn brighter with each passing day, their desires like a river that had found its natural course. It was a force that flowed effortlessly between them, binding their hearts and souls in an unbreakable bond.

Their love, visibly proportioned and undeniably attractive, was a beacon of hope for those who witnessed it. As they moved through life, their connection remained interactive and electric, a dance of two souls deeply in love. Together, they found the strength and vitality to conquer any obstacle, whether physical or mental. In each other's presence, they discovered the power and inspiration they had been yearning for.

In moments of intimacy, they continued to reset and release, allowing themselves to be carried away by the currents of their love. Their passion flowed through them like a river in full flood, and as they surfaced in their breathless moments, their hearts raced, and their bodies quivered with desire. No one could ever hope to compare to the unique and intense love they shared.

Their bond and connection served as a constant reminder of the enduring power of love. It defied all logic and reason, bringing two souls together in a fervent embrace. They remained a perfect pair, two lines that had converged to form a love story that would withstand the test of time.

In a world where passion knew no boundaries, their love story continued to evolve, an exquisite symphony of desire, affection, and devotion. They cherished every moment spent together, knowing that their love was an unstoppable force capable of carrying them through any challenge life might throw their way. Their journey was a living testament to the enduring and transformative power of love, a love that would continue to burn brightly, like a guiding star in the night sky.

Their love blazed ever brighter with each passing day, a fierce flame that defied the constraints of time and space. Their desires flowed between them like a river finding its natural course, a force of nature that could not be tamed.

Pressure

Perpendicular force presses on,
A stress reliever, a passion marathon.
Close in proximity, bodies ignite with fire,
Fluids circulating, rising higher and higher.

I've been waiting for this sweet sensation,
Temperature rising, a fiery conflagration.
Combustion releasing, a reaction so divine,
Hot enough to warm a room, your body against mine.

Visibly proportioned, extremely attractive,
In tune with each other, our connection interactive.
The strength and vitality sustain us physically,
Power deprived, mentally stimulated, oh so brilliantly.

Parallel at the right angles to vertical delight,
Aligned at every level, our chemistry takes flight.
Pressure applied to your body and mind,
Satisfied completely, ecstasy of a unique kind.

Powerful drive, gentle to the touch,
Our desires meld, we crave it so much.
Reset and release, we break free,
It flows through us, a passionate spree.

Breathless moments, we come up for air,
No one can compare to the love we share.
Pressure, our bond and connection so rare,
In this fervent embrace, we're a perfect pair.

Over

Dawn and Paul had once been inseparable, their love an unbreakable bond that seemed like it could withstand anything life threw their way. They had shared countless moments of joy and laughter, and their connection had been like a warm, comforting embrace. But as time went on, cracks began to appear in their relationship, and confusion and doubt crept in like unwelcome shadows.

Confusion and delusions had taken root in Down's mind, clouding her vision whenever she closed her eyes. She couldn't help but imagine things, looking beyond Paul's carefully chosen words and struggling to accept the explanations he offered. The relationship had become a source of distress, and she couldn't ignore the mounting confusion that plagued her.

It was clear that Paul's heart was torn between his desires and the obligations that pulled him in different directions. Down couldn't shake the feeling that she wasn't his first choice anymore, and it was a bitter truth to swallow. She listened to her own voice, echoing with the belief that love shouldn't be this complicated. She regretted letting her guard down, and now it seemed nearly impossible to let go of the turmoil that had taken hold of their relationship.

Down had grown tired of being the sole contributor to their love's effort. She saw that Paul's love came with strings attached, people and responsibilities constantly tugging at him from all sides. The weight of it all made her realize that it was time to walk away, to find someone who was more in control of his life and didn't waver in confusion between right and wrong.

But the process of opening her eyes to the painful reality was a challenge in itself. Down despised dishonesty and the selling of empty dreams. She questioned why they were even in this situation, enduring restless nights filled with a yearning for peace, unable to find solace in sleep. The relationship had become riddled with doubts, too many instances of reading between the lines, and mistrust.

It had all led to an atmosphere of bad vibes and ill feelings, leaving Down to declare that Dawn she refused to be anyone's last choice. She had been down that road too many times before and had no intention of revisiting it. She knew her own worth and had much to offer love, loyalty, trust, and respect. She believed that someday, someone would see and appreciate all that she brought to the table.

Down harbored no hard feelings, for she truly understood that Paul's family and friends took precedence in his life, and she had not been part of his initial plan. She now knew where she stood, and it wasn't a matter of making a fuss; their parting was a necessary step. At her age, she was interested in nothing less than consistency, stability, respect, and loyalty—a foundation that could lead to a lasting commitment, not a fleeting, fly-by-night relationship.

She yearned for a connection where honor, respect, and love were the cornerstones. She longed for romantic getaways, sweet words, walks in the park after dark, and dreams of a future together. She questioned when they would start planning for forever.

At the end of the day, despite her desire to stay and continue their journey, Down couldn't deny the empty space that had formed between them. She had never imagined someone taking Paul's place in her heart. She had loved him from the very beginning, and it was heartbreaking to realize that somewhere along the way, he had decided he needed space, leaving her in a lonely place of confusion and heartache.

As the days turned into weeks, Down and Paul continued to grapple with the void that had settled between them. The echoes of their once vibrant love lingered like a distant melody, haunting their thoughts and dreams.

Despite the pain and confusion, Down found strength in her decision to walk away. She knew that her worth was not defined by being someone's last choice, and she held onto the hope that she would find a love that would honor her love, loyalty, trust, and respect. She understood that sometimes, walking away from what no longer served her was the bravest choice she could make.

Paul, on the other hand, was left to ponder the choices he had made. The pull of his obligations and the expectations of those around him had left him torn, and he had allowed confusion to cloud his judgment. He realized that he had taken Down's love for granted, and her absence had left a void he couldn't ignore.

Restless nights were a common occurrence for both of them. Down yearned for peace and closure, while Paul found himself plagued by regrets and what-ifs. Their love had once been a source of joy, and now it had become a well of sorrow.

Despite the pain, Down held no hard feelings. She understood that life could be complicated, and sometimes, circumstances took people in unexpected directions. She knew that love, real love, was built on consistency, stability, respect, and loyalty, and she remained hopeful that one day, she would find a love that matched her desires and values.

Paul, too, was on a journey of self-discovery. He needed to learn how to balance his responsibilities without sacrificing his own happiness. He yearned to find clarity and to make choices that were true to his heart.

In the quiet moments when they were alone with their thoughts, Down and Paul couldn't help but wonder if there would ever be a chance for their paths to cross again. They both cherished the memories of the love they had shared, and a part of them longed for the days when they had been each other's heart.

As time passed, the pain of their separation began to dull, but the love they had once shared remained etched in their hearts. Down and Paul each embarked on their own separate journeys, seeking answers and a sense of fulfillment. Whether their paths would ever intersect again, only time would tell.

For now, they were left with the bittersweet memory of a love that had been both beautiful and painful—a love that had shaped them in ways they could never have predicted. They carried the lessons of their time together, and they remained hopeful that the future held the promise of new beginnings and a love that would endure.

As the days turned into weeks, the void between Down and Paul seemed to grow wider and more insurmountable. Their once vibrant love had faded into a distant memory, replaced by an uncomfortable silence that filled the spaces where laughter and shared dreams once resided.

Down had found the strength to walk away, knowing that she deserved a love that would honor her worth. She believed in love that came with consistency, stability, respect, and loyalty, and she was determined to find it. The decision to leave had been difficult, but she understood that sometimes, letting go was the only way to move forward.

Paul, on the other hand, was left with the weight of his choices. The pull of his obligations had left him conflicted, and the confusion had driven a wedge between them. He now realized the depth of his mistake, as he faced countless restless nights filled with regrets and what-ifs. The love that had once brought them joy had now become a source of sorrow and longing.

Despite the pain, Down held no resentment towards Paul. She knew that life could be unpredictable, and sometimes, circumstances led people down unexpected paths. She carried the hope that one day, she would find a love that matched her desires and values, built on the foundation of respect and loyalty.

Paul, too, embarked on a journey of self-discovery. He understood the need to balance his responsibilities without compromising his own happiness. The quest for clarity and authenticity in his choices became a priority as he navigated the aftermath of their separation.

In the quiet moments of solitude, Down and Paul couldn't help but wonder if their paths would ever cross again. They held on to the cherished memories of their love, and a part of them yearned for the days when they had been each other's heart.

As time continued to pass, the pain of their breakup gradually dulled, but the memory of their love remained etched in their hearts. Down and Paul ventured down separate paths, each seeking answers and a sense of fulfillment. Whether destiny would eventually lead them back together remained uncertain.

For now, they carried the bittersweet lessons of their past, hoping that the future would bring them the promise of new beginnings and a love that could withstand the trials of life. The story of Down and Paul was one of love, loss, and resilience, a testament to the unpredictable nature of relationships and the enduring hope that someday, love would find its way back into their lives.

Over

Confusion delusions when I close my eyes,
I imagine things I can see beyond your well thought out words
refusing to accept the explanation that was given
I'm getting fed up with this relationship is a mess distress...

You can't always have who or want you want
I guess I'm not his first choice...
listen to my voice in my opinion It shouldn't be this hard
I shouldn't have let down my guard so now
it's hard to let go exhale oh NO...

I'm tired of being the only one trying and his so-called love
comes with strings people pulling him every which way
and that's why I can't stay it's time to walk away...
I need someone that is in charge of his life
 not being confused about what's wrong or what's right...

Sometimes opening up your eyes is the most painful
thing that has to be done.
I despise people who lie or try to sell me a dream.
I don't know why we are here, restless nights,
I need peace, I can't sleep. Many things have been
questionable though out this relationship to much
reading between the lines.

Situations bad vibes, ill feelings, lonely times,
I don't want to be anyone's last choice...
I've been that plenty of times before and
I don't want to open that door once more...
know how I feel I always keep it read.
I have a lot to offer love, loyalty, trust, respect that's
a must and someone one day will see it and appreciate
me and what I bring you know what I mean...

But it's no hard feelings I truly understand your family,
and friends come first— I wasn't a part of your plan

I now know where I stand...
It's not a big fuss... this departure is a must...
At this age I'm only Interested in consistency,
stability, respect, and loyalty...

A foundation something leading to forever a courtship
not just a fly by night relationship people is a trip.
Honor respect and love honey I'm home sweet words
romantics get always walks in the park after dark
planning for forever when we will start...

At the end of the day yes of course I want to stay,
but if I do, I'll remain in this empty space
I never dreamed of someone taking your place I
loved you from the start you were my heart...
But somewhere along the way you decided
that you needed space which left me in this lonely place...

Over

Trauma bond

Sharell and David had grown up in the heart of Los Angeles, in neighborhoods where dysfunction was more common than not. Raised in families that were far from conventional, they had both learned to navigate the complexities of life from an early age.

High school graduation had marked their transition into the working world. Without the privilege of a college education, they dove headfirst into the hustle and grind of the inner city. Money problems were a constant companion, and the phrase "living paycheck to paycheck" became a mantra of their lives.

Despite the odds stacked against them, Sharell and David were survivors. They had seen the worst that life could offer, but they clung to the belief that they could make something more of themselves. Their pasts were haunted by toxic relationships, ones that mirrored the dysfunction they had grown up with.

As they entered adulthood, they found themselves repeating the patterns they had sworn to break. Arguments filled with yelling, endless fussing and fighting, days of not speaking to each other—all of it felt like a never-ending cycle. They shared the same space, but it often felt like they were miles apart.

The bond they shared ran deep, but it was also tainted by the trauma they had both experienced. They understood each other's pain in a way that few others could. "I'm here for you," they would say. "I understand you. I love you because we've been through the same trauma."

In life, it was all too easy to find yourself trapped in a miserable situation, one that became increasingly toxic over time. They had convinced themselves that a hug, a kiss, or a half-hearted apology was enough to heal the wounds they inflicted upon each other. They spiraled deeper into the cycle, making excuses not just for each other's behavior but also for their own.

Sharell and David had to confront a painful truth: they needed to heal individually before they could ever hope to heal together. The love they had for each other was genuine, but it was intertwined with the trauma that had bound them for so long.

Recognizing the need for change was the first step towards breaking free from the cycle of toxicity. Sharell and David had to learn to love themselves first, to prioritize their own well-being and happiness. It was a daunting journey, but it was one they knew they had to embark on.

The trauma bond that had kept them tethered for so long was slowly beginning to loosen its grip. With each step they took towards healing and self-love, they inched closer to a healthier, happier future. Walking away from the toxic patterns of their past was a difficult decision, but it was one that held the promise of a brighter tomorrow.

Sharell and David's story was a testament to the resilience of the human spirit. Despite the odds stacked against them, they were determined to break free from the cycle of trauma and toxicity. It was a journey filled with challenges, but it was a journey they were willing to undertake together, with the hope of finding a love that was free from the shadows of their past.

As Sharell and David embarked on their journey toward healing and self-discovery, they knew that breaking free from the cycle of trauma and toxicity would not be easy. It required introspection, self-compassion, and the courage to confront their pasts head-on.

They began by seeking therapy and counseling, individually and together. Talking to professionals helped them understand the deep-seated issues that had contributed to their toxic relationship patterns. Through therapy, they learned healthier ways to communicate, manage their emotions, and set boundaries.

Self-love became a focal point of their healing process. Sharell and David realized that they needed to prioritize their own well-being before they could truly be there for each other. They started practicing self-care, engaging in activities that brought them joy, and nurturing their physical and emotional health.

Breaking the trauma bond was challenging, as they had to reevaluate their roles in each other's lives. They recognized that their connection had been built on shared pain, and they needed to redefine their relationship on healthier terms. It meant letting go of the toxic patterns they had clung to for so long.

Sharell and David also sought support from friends and family who could provide a positive influence and guidance. They surrounded themselves with people who encouraged their personal growth and healing. It was crucial to build a support system that would help them stay on track.

With time, the grip of the trauma bond slowly began to loosen.

They celebrated small victories along the way—moments of clarity, healthier interactions, and a growing sense of self-worth. Each step forward reaffirmed their commitment to change and gave them hope for a brighter future.

Walking away from their toxic past was a difficult decision, but Sharell and David knew it was the only way to break free from the shadows that had haunted them for so long. They understood that their journey towards healing and self-love was ongoing, but they were willing to undertake it together.

Their story became an inspiration to others who had experienced the weight of trauma and toxicity in their relationships. Sharell and David's resilience and determination showed that it was possible to break free from the chains of the past and find a love that was healthy, nurturing, and free from the haunting echoes of their former lives.

As they continued on their path of healing, Sharell and David looked ahead with hope, ready to embrace a future where they could love and support each other in a way that was truly uplifting and transformative. Their love story was no longer defined by the trauma bond; it was becoming a testament to the power of healing, self-discovery, and a love that could withstand even the darkest of pasts.

Sharell and David's journey of healing and self-discovery was progressing steadily. They were gradually breaking free from the toxic patterns that had haunted their relationship for so long. Their bond had grown stronger, and it seemed like they were on the path to a healthier, happier future together.

However, life has a way of throwing unexpected challenges at us, and Sharell and David were no exception. One evening, as David returned home from work, he noticed Sharell seemed distant and preoccupied. He couldn't help but sense that something was amiss.

Over dinner that night, David gently broached the topic, asking Sharell if anything was bothering her. Sharell hesitated for a moment, her eyes filled with uncertainty, but she knew that honesty was essential in their journey of healing.

Tears welled up in Sharell's eyes as she finally confessed that she had made a terrible mistake. She revealed that she had been carrying a secret, a burden that weighed heavily on her conscience. Sharell admitted that she had cheated on David with her supervisor at work during a vulnerable moment when she had doubted their relationship's progress.

David was stunned, his heart sinking at the revelation. He had believed that their shared commitment to healing and their journey towards a healthier love had been making progress. This revelation shattered the trust they had been painstakingly rebuilding. The room filled with silence as they both grappled with the weight of Sharell's confession.

David felt a mixture of emotions—anger, betrayal, and a profound sense of hurt. Sharell, on the other hand, was overwhelmed by guilt and regret for her momentary lapse in judgment. She knew that her actions had jeopardized the progress they had made in healing their relationship.

As the night wore on, Sharell and David faced a daunting crossroads. Their journey towards healing had taken an unexpected and painful turn, challenging the very foundation of their relationship. The trauma bond that had bound them together was now tainted by a new layer of hurt and mistrust.

The coming days would test their resilience like never before. Sharell and David would need to decide whether they could find a way to rebuild the trust that had been shattered or if this was the breaking point of their tumultuous relationship. Their path towards healing, which had shown glimmers of hope, was now clouded by the shadow of infidelity—a formidable obstacle they would need to confront head-on.

In the wake of Sharell's confession, David found himself grappling with a tempest of emotions. Betrayal and hurt surged within him, and he struggled to come to terms with the fact that the progress they had made towards healing had been derailed by her infidelity. Despite the turmoil that had consumed their relationship for years, he had believed in the possibility of a better future for them.

David's first impulse was to confront Sharell's supervisor—the man with whom she had cheated. He couldn't comprehend how someone in a position of authority at her workplace had taken advantage of her vulnerability. Resolute and seething with anger, he needed answers, closure, and a way to understand the extent of the betrayal.

One evening, David tracked down Sharell's supervisor, arranging a meeting outside of her workplace. He knew that this confrontation could either provide clarity or further complicate the situation, but he was determined to face it head-on.

The encounter was tense, with David demanding explanations and accountability. Sharell's supervisor admitted to his actions, expressing remorse for his role in the affair. He confessed that he had taken advantage of Sharell's emotional vulnerability during a period of doubt and confusion in their relationship. He acknowledged that it was a grave error in judgment and that he deeply regretted his actions.

While this revelation provided some insight into Sharell's actions, it did little to assuage David's wounded heart. He was left with the painful realization that both he and Sharell had contributed to the turmoil in their relationship. The toxic patterns of their past still loomed over them, threatening to engulf any progress they had made towards healing.

As the days passed, Sharell and David found themselves at a critical juncture. They were faced with the decision of whether to navigate the turbulent waters of their relationship once more or to accept that the infidelity had dealt a fatal blow.

Their journey towards healing and self-discovery had taken an unexpected detour into a labyrinth of hurt, mistrust, and betrayal. While they had managed to break some of the chains of their traumatic past, the weight of their present circumstances hung heavily upon them.

The future remained uncertain for Sharell and David. Would they find a way to rebuild the trust that had been shattered, or would the infidelity be the final chapter in their tumultuous love story? The answers remained elusive, and the path ahead was fraught with challenges, decisions, and a deep longing for the healing and love they had once hoped to find in each other.

David's encounter with Sharell's supervisor had provided a semblance of closure, but it did little to ease the anguish he felt. The revelation of Sharell's infidelity had inflicted a profound wound on their relationship, and David struggled to see a path towards healing that didn't involve more pain.

In the days that followed, David withdrew emotionally. He found himself consumed by a sense of betrayal and a growing detachment from Sharell. The love they had once shared had been overshadowed by the weight of their past and the recent breach of trust. It became clear to him that continuing the relationship was no longer an option.

David knew that walking away was the only choice that made sense for his well-being. He believed that Sharell needed to confront her own actions and address the issues that had led to her infidelity. He couldn't be the one to guide her through that process, as he was grappling with his own feelings of hurt, anger, and disillusionment.

With a heavy heart, David made the painful decision to end the relationship. He realized that, for both of them, it was essential to take time apart and focus on their individual healing journeys. The toxic patterns that had plagued their relationship needed to be dismantled, and they couldn't achieve that while still entangled with each other.

The breakup was a somber and tearful affair. Sharell, too, understood the gravity of the situation, and she couldn't find the words to justify her actions or change David's decision. They parted ways, each carrying the weight of their shared history, their journey of healing left incomplete.

David gave Sharell the space she needed to confront her actions and work on her own healing. He understood that the streets held their own lessons and challenges, but he believed that Sharell needed to navigate them alone to truly grow and find herself.

As David walked away from the relationship, he carried with him the scars of their tumultuous love story. He had believed in the possibility of a better future for them, but sometimes, love was not enough to heal the deep wounds of the past. Both Sharell and David were left with the challenge of rebuilding their lives separately, with the hope that one day they might find a love that was truly free from the toxic patterns that had haunted their pasts.

Trauma bond

Recognizing the Trauma Bond
there comes a crucial moment
when you must acknowledge
when it's time to step away.

It can be a challenging decision,
especially when you empathize
with another person's struggles.

You might feel an unwarranted responsibility
to remain, but remember, you owe it to yourself.
You must prioritize your well-being,
guard your heart and use your time wisely.

It's imperative not to confuse love with trauma.
At times, they can resemble each other,
masquerading under the same guise.

"I'm here for you," "I understand you,
"I love you" – these sentiments can arise
because you've both endured
similar traumatic experiences.

Life can entangle you in distressing
circumstances that become toxic over time.
Arguments, shouting matches,
days of silence and sharing the same
space can become the norm.
Perhaps you believe that a hug,
a kiss, or a half-hearted apology is sufficient,
but they don't lead to proper healing.

Instead, you find yourselves trapped
in an endless loop, making excuses,
not just for your own behavior
but for theirs as well.

It's a cycle that spirals out of control.
Before anything else, remember to heal.
Love yourself first.
And when the time comes,
don't hesitate to walk away.
Do it today, for the sake of your own well-being.
This is the essence of the trauma bond.

Eye's Wide Shut

Julie had always been a young girl with a plan. Growing up in South Central Los Angeles, she knew the importance of setting goals and working tirelessly to achieve them. She had risen above the challenges of her environment, becoming a remarkable success story. With no children to tie her down and a great job that paid six figures, Julie had created a life that she was proud of.

Her life was like a well-crafted puzzle, each piece fitting perfectly into the next. Julie had always been a focused and determined individual. But sometimes, even the most meticulous plans could be disrupted by unexpected encounters.

One sunny afternoon, Julie crossed paths with Terrence, a man who seemed to embody confidence and charm. He had a flashy demeanor, and no one could quite figure out how he earned his money, but Julie was drawn to him like a moth to a flame. Terrence knew how to make an impression, and he set his sights on Julie.

Their connection was like a whirlwind, a passionate storm that left Julie feeling intoxicated by the idea of their relationship. Late-night phone calls that extended into the early morning hours, deep and meaningful conversations, and plans for a future together—they all seemed to promise a bright and happy life.

But as the saying goes, "The brightest stars cast the darkest shadows." Julie's tunnel vision, fixated on Terrence and his allure, blinded her to the truth that was lurking in the shadows.

Then, one fateful night, the phone rang, shattering the illusion of their perfect love story. It wasn't Terrence's voice on the other end; it was another woman. She revealed that she was pregnant with Terrence's child, and suddenly, Julie's world came crashing down.

The shock and betrayal were almost too much to bear. Julie felt hurt and confused, with no one to turn to for solace. She couldn't understand how she had been so blind to the deception that had been unfolding right before her eyes.

When she had first met Terrence, he had been a single man. Now, he was a plus one, carrying the weight of not one but two children from two different women. Julie's initial instinct was to run away from this tangled mess, but Terrence was quick to offer apologies and reassurances.

He convinced her that she was the one he truly wanted.

For a while, Julie believed his words, and they carried on as a couple. But it wasn't long before she stumbled upon pictures that shattered her heart into a million pieces. Images of Terrence, the other woman, and their children, posing like a happy blended family, painted a picture of deception that was impossible to ignore.

Julie's pain was unimaginable, and she found herself wishing ill upon the other woman's name. Days turned into nights without a word from Terrence, and when he finally did call, he offered explanations that were too little, too late.

The weight of the lies and games had become too much for Julie to bear. She was tired of playing a role in Terrence's elaborate charade. She knew that she deserved better, that she was a queen and not a pawn in his deceitful game.

Julie had always believed in truth and integrity, values that Terrence seemed to have no regard for. She had learned the hard way that a man was nothing without his word, and Terrence had failed that test miserably.

As Julie's eyes opened wide to the harsh reality of her situation, she realized that she had been living a lie. She couldn't continue down this path of deception and heartache. The images of Terrence's deceit were etched into her mind, and she knew that she had to break free from this toxic cycle.

She had misunderstood his lies and games, but now her eyes were wide open. She refused to live in the shadow of his deceit any longer. Her heart may have been filled with sorrow and pain, but she was determined to reclaim her life and her dignity.

Terrence might have played a good game, but Julie was done being a part of it. She had been blinded by his charisma, but now her eyes were wide open, and she could see through all the deception and lies. She was ready to move forward, leaving behind the darkness that had clouded her life.

Julie's story was one of resilience and self-discovery. She had been through a painful experience, but it had opened her eyes to the truth. As she walked away from Terrence and the web of lies he had woven, she carried with her the lessons she had learned and the strength she had gained from facing adversity head-on.

Her eyes were wide open, and she was determined to live a life that was authentic and true to herself. Julie knew that she deserved a love that was built on honesty, trust, and respect, and she was ready to find it, leaving behind the deceitful past that had held her captive for far too long.

Julie's journey of self-discovery continued as she picked up the pieces of her life shattered by Terrence's deceit. With her eyes wide open to the truth, she realized that she deserved a love built on honesty, trust, and respect. Determined to move forward, she embarked on a path of healing and growth.

Julie decided to focus on herself and her own well-being. She sought solace in her work, pouring her energy into her successful career. Her job, which had always been a source of pride, became a sanctuary where she could channel her strength and determination.

As the days turned into weeks and then months, Julie began to rebuild her life. She rekindled connections with friends and family, nurturing the relationships that had been neglected during her tumultuous relationship with Terrence. Their support and love became a source of comfort and strength.

Julie also turned to therapy to help her navigate the emotional scars left by Terrence's betrayal. With the help of a skilled therapist, she delved into the complexities of her past and the reasons she had been vulnerable to deception. Through this process, she learned to forgive herself for her mistakes and make peace with her past.

One of the most significant lessons Julie took away from her experience was the importance of self-love. She learned that before she could truly love someone else, she had to love and value herself. Her journey of self-discovery included practicing self-care, setting boundaries, and prioritizing her own happiness.

Julie's heart, once filled with sorrow and pain, began to heal. She realized that she was a resilient and strong woman who could overcome even the most challenging obstacles. Her self-esteem and self-worth grew stronger with each passing day.

While Julie was on her journey of healing and self-discovery, Terrence's life continued down a path of deceit and empty charm. He played his games with others, leaving a trail of heartache in his wake. But Julie had closed the door on that chapter of her life, and she was determined not to be another victim of his deceit.

As time passed, Julie's heart began to open once more, but this time it was guarded by the wisdom and self-respect she had gained from her experiences. She was no longer the naive young woman who had been blinded by Terrence's charisma. She knew that love should be built on a foundation of trust and authenticity.

Julie's eyes were wide open to the world and to the possibilities that lay ahead. She was ready to embrace a future that was free from the shadows of her deceitful past. Her story had become a testament to the power of self-discovery, resilience, and the unwavering belief that true love could be found when one first learned to love themselves.

Julie's journey of self-discovery had transformed her into a strong and resilient woman who understood the importance of self-love and self-worth. With each passing day, she grew more confident and determined to create a life that was true to herself.

Her career continued to thrive as she channeled her energy and focus into her work. Julie's success became a testament to her unwavering determination and her ability to overcome adversity. She had found solace in her job, and it was a constant source of pride and fulfillment.

Reconnecting with friends and family played a vital role in Julie's healing process. These relationships provided her with the support and love she needed to rebuild her life. She cherished the bonds she had with loved ones, knowing that they were there for her through thick and thin.

Therapy had become an essential part of Julie's journey. With the guidance of her therapist, she explored the complexities of her past and the reasons that had made her vulnerable to deception. Through introspection and self-reflection, she learned to forgive herself for her past mistakes and accept that healing was a process, not a destination.

Self-love became a mantra for Julie. She prioritized her own well-being, practiced self-care, and set healthy boundaries. Her self-esteem and self-worth grew stronger with each passing day, and she realized that she deserved nothing less than a love that was built on trust, authenticity, and mutual respect.

As Julie continued to flourish on her path of self-discovery and healing, she watched from afar as Terrence's life unfolded. His pattern of deceit and empty charm remained unchanged, leaving a trail of heartache and pain for those who crossed his path. But Julie was no longer entangled in his web of lies; she had freed herself from that toxic cycle.

With time, Julie's heart began to open once more, but this time, it was guarded by the wisdom and self-respect she had gained from her experiences. She knew that the future held endless possibilities, and she was determined to embrace it with open arms.

Julie's story had evolved into a testament to the power of resilience and self-discovery. She had faced the darkness of deceit and emerged stronger and wiser. Her unwavering belief in the importance of self-love had transformed her life, reminding her that true love could only be found when she had first learned to love herself.

Julie's transformation into a strong and resilient woman was nothing short of remarkable. She had learned the importance of self-love and self-worth, and these lessons had become the cornerstones of her new life. With each passing day, her confidence and determination grew, allowing her to create a life that was true to herself.

Her career continued to thrive as she channeled her energy into her work. Julie's unwavering determination and ability to overcome adversity were evident in her professional success. Her job not only provided financial security but also served as a source of pride and fulfillment.

Reconnecting with friends and family had played a vital role in Julie's healing process. She leaned on these relationships for support and love, knowing that they were there for her through thick and thin. These bonds became a source of strength and comfort as she continued to rebuild her life.

Eye's Wide Shut

Blindly building on trust us, but to my surprise I wasn't the only one
tunnel vision overpowered by lust or just the idea of your touch

Late night early mornings phone calls to 1 in the morning
beautiful discussions making plans holding hands
future seemed so bright until that one night
the phone rings but it's not who I wanted it to be
shattered dreams of us our plans
it was you and me but now it's 3

When she speaks, she tells me that she's pregnant with your seed
now it's you plus 2 where does that leave me?
hurt and confused no one to talk to
how could I not see? When I first meet you
you were a single man

Now you're a plus 1 carry the 2 you had a daughter
and she has a son my first reaction was to run,
but you apologized and lead me to believe that
 you wanted me we were good for a while until
 I found pictures of you and her plus 1 and the other 1
 posing like you're a happy blended family

Oh, what pain I wished death on her name
I haven't heard from you in 3 days
the phone rings now you're trying to explain
this is way too much for my soul to bare
how can it be repaired images going through?
my mind still pictures of you and her or the worst

I refuse to live a lie, oh! how I despise
how you lead me to believe that I was the only one
while you were out playing like you were a family with her
I'm tired of playing games I'm a queen not a spade
I gave you space never once complained

I see the world differently than most people
I believe in truth in whatever you do
a man is nothing without his word
I guess you didn't get the memo, but I hope you've learned
all my thoughts of you use to be good
now there filled with sorrow and pain

I misunderstood your lies and games left my heart in pain
you played a good game
now you want me to believe you've changed
and forget all the pain give us another chance
you'll be a better man you just lost the best thing
that ever happen to you fool

I was blinded by you now my eyes are
open wide not shut like before
I can see pass all your games and lies

My eyes are WIDE OPEN NOT SHUT LIKE BEFORE...

36 Weeks

In the depths of her solitude, Sarah found herself in the eye of a storm, grappling with a revelation that would forever alter her life. At 20 years old, her dreams were still painted with the hues of youthful ambition, and the weight of responsibility was a burden she never thought she'd have to carry.

The day she held that pregnancy test in her trembling hands, her world quaked with uncertainty. Two pink lines stared back at her, a silent confirmation of a life growing within her. Sarah's bloodstream was now intertwined with the tiny heartbeat of an unborn child, and she had a choice to make—a choice that would alter her path forever.

To carry this child for 36 weeks would be to willingly embark on a journey filled with turmoil, regret, shame, pain, disappointment, sadness, and anger. Society's eyes, she knew, would be watchful and condemning, ready to discuss her choices, casting her aside as a disgrace.

Sarah felt lost and confused. Becoming a mother this way was not part of her carefully crafted life plan. The thought of bringing a child into the world without their consent weighed heavily on her heart. She understood that people would judge her, their eyes casting shadows of scorn and misunderstanding.

But Sarah had always been a silent warrior. Pain had been her companion, lurking in the unspoken corners of her past. She had endured it silently, keeping her struggles hidden from the world. Yet, now, a new chapter was unfolding, and she couldn't bear the weight of her secret any longer.

With each passing day, Sarah realized that she needed to break free from the chains of shame and pain that had bound her for so long. She understood that sharing her story was not just a means of healing herself but also a way to help others who might be silently enduring their own battles.

With unwavering determination, Sarah began to share her journey. She spoke her truth, not seeking forgiveness or understanding but aiming to free herself from the shame that had imprisoned her for far too long. As she shared her story, she discovered a community of individuals who had faced similar challenges.

Sarah's path to healing was arduous, but it was a path she chose to walk with courage and grace. She learned to forgive herself, to release the heavy burden of shame, and to embrace her newfound strength.

Her story became a beacon of hope for others who had experienced similar struggles. Sarah had transformed from a silent sufferer into a resilient survivor. She was no longer defined by her circumstances but by her ability to rise above them.

As Sarah held her newborn child for the first time, she marveled at the precious life she had brought into the world. The connection was undeniable, a testament to the enduring power of love. She had embarked on a new journey, one filled with challenges, but she walked it with her head held high, no longer burdened by the shadows of her past. Sarah was healed from the shame and pain, and her story had become one of triumph and hope.

Sarah's journey continued, marked by a sense of empowerment and a newfound purpose. She had decided to carry her child, embracing the challenges and uncertainties that lay ahead. The weight of society's judgment still loomed, but Sarah was determined to prove that her love and determination could overcome any obstacle.

Her pregnancy was a time of reflection and growth. As she nurtured the life growing within her, Sarah also nurtured her own inner strength. She sought support from friends, family, and a community of individuals who understood the struggles she faced. Their encouragement and empathy served as a source of inspiration on her path to healing.

Sarah's decision to share her story had a profound impact on others. Her courage inspired those who had similarly hidden their pain to step out of the shadows. Together, they formed a network of support and understanding, creating a safe space for open dialogue about life's complexities.

Throughout her pregnancy, Sarah's bond with her unborn child deepened. She realized that this journey, though unexpected, was a testament to the strength of maternal love. As she prepared for motherhood, she also prepared herself to break free from the chains of shame and judgment.

The day arrived when Sarah welcomed her child into the world. It was a moment filled with overwhelming emotions—joy, love, and gratitude. Holding her baby in her arms, Sarah knew that this precious life was her greatest gift. She had chosen to become a mother on her own terms, defying societal expectations and finding strength in vulnerability.

Sarah's journey of healing and self-discovery continued as she navigated the challenges of motherhood. She faced moments of doubt and exhaustion, but her love for her child was unwavering. Each day was a testament to her resilience and the transformation she had undergone.

Years passed, and Sarah's child grew, a testament to the love and courage that had brought them into the world. Sarah's story remained a source of inspiration, not only for those who had walked similar paths but for anyone seeking the strength to overcome adversity and embrace their own truth.

Sarah had walked through the storms of judgment and shame, emerging on the other side as a beacon of hope and resilience. She had learned that, in the depths of uncertainty, one could find strength, love, and the power to rewrite their own narrative. Sarah was proof that, even in the face of adversity, healing and triumph were possible.

As the years passed, Sarah's journey continued to be marked by resilience and determination. Motherhood had brought new challenges and joys into her life. She cherished each moment with her child, a constant reminder of the love and courage that had brought them together.

Sarah remained an advocate for open dialogue and support for individuals facing similar challenges. Her story had become a beacon of hope for many, and she continued to share it, offering a safe space for others to share their experiences. Together, they formed a tight-knit community of understanding and compassion.

The weight of society's judgment had lost its power over Sarah. She had learned to stand tall, unburdened by shame and criticism. Instead, she drew strength from the love she had for her child and the resilience she had discovered within herself.

Through the ups and downs of motherhood, Sarah remained a source of inspiration for her community. Her unwavering commitment to rewriting her own narrative and embracing her truth served as a testament to the strength of the human spirit.

Sarah's child, growing with each passing day, bore witness to their mother's journey of healing and self-discovery. They learned that love, courage, and authenticity were the building blocks of a fulfilled life. Sarah had not only transformed her own story but had also created a legacy of resilience and hope for generations to come.

In the end, Sarah's journey proved that even in the face of adversity, healing and triumph were not just possible; they were achievable through the power of self-love and the unwavering belief in one's own strength. Her life had become a testament to the enduring human spirit, a reminder that every individual had the capacity to overcome obstacles and embrace their own truth.

36 Weeks

A life connection to mine
breathing inside my bloodstream is yours
if I decide to carry you for 36 weeks

I will have to live in turmoil
regret shame pain disappointment
sadness anger disgust and be disgrace
either way I choose I've sinned

they say I'm so confused and lost
at the thought of becoming
a mother this way
how is it a sin when you did not give consent

people judge you without knowing
the how when what and why
of your life story I wasn't built for pain
but I endured it my entire life

I was silent about the pain inside
but now it's time to release be free
share my story to help heal relive
the hidden parts of me and walk in

glory no more shame or pain
I'm healed from it all

Self-forgiveness is like a flowing stream,
From a heart that's willing to redeem,
Letting go of hurt, pain's heavy hold,
Releasing stories, both new and old.

Life's connection, our shared bond so deep,
Heartbeats within us, the promises we keep,
Yours and mine, entwined through time,
A gift to cherish, love's sacred climb.

Yet, I'm too young to bear this weight alone,
It's time to let go, let understanding be known,
I can't hold your hand, I hope you'll see,
My innocence was taken, wounded, and set free.

If I carry you for those 36 long weeks,
Turmoil, grief, my heartache seeks,
Regret, shame, and pain might take their toll,
Disappointment, sadness, anger, my soul may control.

But in any choice, I make, I know I've sinned,
Judged by those who've never been within,
My life's story, the how, when, what, and why,
My silent cries and hidden tears, I can't deny.

I wasn't meant for this suffering, but I endured,
Wounds, scars, in a world of pain, I matured,
Now I'm ready to release, to break the chain,
To reclaim my life, heal, and rise again.

Forgiveness holds the key to my liberation,
Letting go of the past, a new foundation,
Facing the future with hope and grace,
Cherishing the bond, in a different space.

So, I forgive myself, and I forgive him too,
For the pain and the struggles, the burdens we knew,
With love and grace, I sever the tie,
In my heart, in my soul, in this sacred goodbye.

Facing Reality

In the heart of the bustling city, where the towering skyscrapers reached for the sky and the streets were alive with the constant hum of life, there lived a young woman named Maya. She was one of those individuals whose story was hidden beneath a facade that most people couldn't fathom.

Maya had grown up in a neighborhood where opportunities were scarce, and the odds were stacked against her from the very beginning. Poverty was a constant companion, and adversity seemed to be a way of life. But behind her quiet demeanor and the modest clothes she wore, Maya carried a secret strength that had been forged through years of struggle and determination.

As a child, Maya had watched her parents work multiple jobs, day, and night, just to make ends meet. Their unwavering dedication to their family left a lasting impression on her, and she knew she had to strive for something better. Education became her refuge, a path she hoped would lead her out of the shadows of her circumstances.

Every morning, while others were still lost in the comfort of their dreams, Maya would wake up before the sun and study diligently. She devoured books from the local library and sought knowledge wherever she could find it. Her teachers recognized her potential, and they became her mentors, guiding her towards a brighter future.

Despite the challenges she faced, Maya excelled academically. Scholarships and grants became her ticket out of the city of opportunity where so many had failed. She pursued a college education with unwavering determination, determined to escape the cycle of poverty that had entrapped her family for generations.

Maya's journey through higher education was not without its own set of trials. Balancing work and studies, she often found herself exhausted and overwhelmed. But she refused to give up. Her parents' sacrifices and her own dreams fueled her perseverance.

One day, as she walked across the stage in her graduation gown, accepting her diploma with tears of joy in her eyes, Maya knew that she had defied the odds. She had transformed her life, her family's life, and, in some small way, her entire neighborhood.

But Maya's story didn't end there. With her education, she returned to her city of opportunity, not as someone who had failed but as someone who had overcome. She worked tirelessly to create opportunities for others, establishing scholarships for underprivileged students, mentoring young people who faced the same challenges she once did, and advocating for social change.

Maya's tale was a testament to the fact that you could never judge someone by their appearance or their circumstances. Life was indeed a storybook filled with tales that were often hidden from view. It was a reminder that the human spirit was capable of incredible resilience and strength, and that opportunities could arise even in the most unlikely of places.

As Maya continued to write her own story and inspire others to do the same, she proved that with determination, education, and a heart full of compassion, anyone could turn the darkest chapters of their life into a story of triumph and hope.

Maya's journey continued to unfold in the heart of the bustling city, where her unwavering determination and resilience shone like a beacon of hope. She had transcended her humble beginnings and, armed with her education, returned to the place she once called home.

Maya knew that she had to be a catalyst for change in her neighborhood, where the shadows of adversity still lingered. She channeled her energy and resources into creating opportunities for others who were trapped in the cycle of poverty. Scholarships and mentorship programs flourished under her guidance, offering young people a chance to break free from the constraints of their circumstances.

One of Maya's most significant accomplishments was the establishment of a community center in her old neighborhood. It became a safe haven for children and teenagers, a place where they could access educational resources, counseling, and mentorship. Maya's vision was to provide the guidance and support she had once received from her teachers and mentors.

She didn't stop there. Maya was a tireless advocate for social change. She used her voice and her story to raise awareness about the challenges faced by underprivileged communities. Her efforts sparked conversations about access to quality education, economic disparities, and the importance of providing opportunities for all.

Maya's impact extended far beyond her neighborhood. She became a role model for countless individuals who had once felt trapped by their circumstances. Her life served as a living testament to the idea that with unwavering determination and the power of education, one could break free from the chains of poverty and adversity.

As the years passed, Maya's story continued to inspire others. She saw countless young people go on to achieve their dreams, thanks to the opportunities she had helped create. Maya's journey was a reminder that even in the midst of adversity, one person could make a profound difference in the lives of many.

Maya's tale was a testament to the resilience and strength of the human spirit. It was a story of triumph and hope, a reminder that opportunities could arise even in the most unlikely of places. Maya had transformed her own life and the lives of those around her, leaving an indelible mark on her city of opportunity and beyond.

Maya's journey of making a difference in her city was far from over. She recognized that while she had defied the odds and achieved her dreams, many others in her neighborhood were still struggling to break free from the cycle of poverty and adversity. She felt a profound sense of responsibility to help them find their paths to success.

Driven by her unwavering determination and the desire to create lasting change, Maya embarked on a new mission. She decided to leverage her skills and education to develop a solution that could empower people in inner-city communities like hers to access the resources they needed to succeed.

Maya's vision took shape in the form of an innovative app that she named "OpportunityConnect." This app aimed to bridge the gap between individuals in underserved communities and the opportunities that often seemed out of reach. It was designed to provide a user-friendly platform where people could easily access information and connect with resources that could help them overcome the challenges they faced.

The app featured a wide range of resources, from educational scholarships and job training programs to mental health support and community organizations. Maya collaborated with local businesses, non-profit organizations, and educational institutions to ensure that the app provided comprehensive and up-to-date information.

Maya's app quickly gained recognition within her city, and its impact was felt in countless lives. Students who had once felt hopeless about their educational prospects now had access to scholarship opportunities that allowed them to pursue higher education. Job seekers found employment training programs that opened doors to stable careers. Those struggling with mental health issues discovered accessible resources and support networks.

As OpportunityConnect continued to grow, Maya expanded its reach beyond her city, reaching other communities facing similar challenges. Her app became a beacon of hope for underserved populations across the country, providing them with a lifeline to opportunities they had previously only dreamed of.

Maya's story was a testament to her unwavering commitment to creating positive change. She had not only transformed her own life but had also dedicated herself to empowering others. Through her app and advocacy, she proved that with determination, education, and compassion, anyone could become a force for change, turning the darkest chapters of their lives into stories of triumph and hope. Maya's journey continued, fueled by a relentless belief in the power of opportunity and the strength of the human spirit.

Facing Reality

In the heart of the city where dreams and struggles collide,
Lived a young woman named Maya, her strength she'd never hide.
Born into poverty's embrace, where odds were set so high,
She chose a path of courage, aiming for the open sky.
Behind a quiet demeanor, her spirit blazed with might,
Determined to break free from the shadows of the night.
Her parents worked relentlessly, day and night, they toiled.

Their sacrifice ignited in her a passion deeply coiled.
Education was her refuge, a beacon in the dark,
She'd wake before the sunrise, with dreams that left a spark.
Through books and teachers' guidance, she soared academically,
Scholarships were her compass, leading toward a life, emphatically.
But the journey to her diploma, a path not smooth nor plain,
Balancing work and studies, she felt the weight and strain.

Yet Maya never wavered, her spirit never dimmed,
Her parents' sacrifices and her dreams forever primed.
On graduation day, tears of joy flowed from her eyes,
She'd defied the daunting odds, reaching for the skies.
Returning to her old neighborhood, she didn't hesitate,
To build a bridge of opportunities, she simply wouldn't wait.
Scholarships, mentorships, she created them with care,
Helping young souls break free, offering hope in the air.

A community center blossomed, a haven for the young,
Maya's guidance and support like rays of a hopeful sun.
Advocating for change, she raised her powerful voice,
Awareness for the underprivileged, the path she'd always choose.
Maya's story was a testament, that circumstances don't define,
With determination, education, hearts filled with the divine.
Years passed, and her legacy grew, like ripples on a pond,
A beacon of inspiration, her life story truly fond.

Maya proved that one can rise, even from the darkest well,
Turning challenges to triumph, in her city she did excel.
Her journey carried onward, an unwavering belief,
In the power of opportunity, she conquered every grief.
Maya's tale was a reminder, in life's complex weave,
That with a heart full of compassion, anyone could achieve.

Broken pieces of a shattered heart

Donna sat alone in her dimly lit living room, surrounded by the broken pieces of her shattered heart. It seemed like a lifetime of disappointment, a lifetime of trusting the wrong men and being left behind. She gazed at the fragments of her past relationships, scattered like shards of glass on the floor, reflecting the pain she had endured.

"Why bother?" Donna whispered to herself, her voice heavy with bitterness. She had given up on the idea of true love a long time ago, convinced that it was an elusive dream meant for others, but never for her. The men in her life had proven time and time again that they couldn't be trusted that they were only after one thing, and that thing was not her heart.

She had become a master at jumping in and out of relationships, never giving herself a chance to heal from the wounds of the past. It was as if she was addicted to the chaos, the constant drama of love gone wrong. She couldn't stand being alone, couldn't stand the deafening silence that enveloped her when there was no one else around. So, she jumped from body to body, using love as her new sport, even though she knew deep down that it was damaging her.

Donna stopped for a moment and thought about what had brought her to this point. She had been in search of something real, something true, and had convinced herself that she would find it in the arms of the next man. But instead of love, all she found were empty promises and broken dreams. She had tried to find him, the one who would be her peace, in the faces of countless strangers, but she always came up empty-handed.

She had even told the last man she had been seeing that she wasn't ready for a committed relationship, but deep inside, she had hoped that he would be different. She had canceled dates and shown up late, playing a dangerous game of push and pull, testing his patience and his commitment.

People dealt with relationships differently, she knew that. Some abandoned them altogether, preferring to live a life of solitude rather than risking more heartache. But Donna was afraid of being alone. She craved the warmth of another body beside her, the feeling of being wanted and loved. So, she settled, allowed herself to be loved by someone who was never truly willing to commit.

He had wined and dined her, making her feel like she was the only woman in the world. He had planned late-night romances and weekend getaways, making her believe that there was something real between them. But when she had finally gathered the courage to question him about commitment, he had gone silent, leaving her waiting and wondering.

Days turned into weeks, and Donna's phone remained stubbornly silent. She knew in her heart that he was not the one, that he was just another chapter in her long history of failed relationships. And so, without a second thought, she moved on to the next, hoping that maybe this time, she would find what she had been searching for all along.

As Donna continued to navigate the treacherous waters of love, her negativity about relationships deepened. She had come to believe that all men were cheaters, liars, and heartbreakers. It was a belief that had been reinforced by the countless disappointments she had experienced throughout her life. In her mind, love was a game of deception, and she was determined to protect herself from getting hurt again.

She had a cynical view of the world, convinced that people were only out for their own interests, that they couldn't be trusted. Donna had built thick walls around her heart, and she was determined not to let anyone in. Her friends and family had tried to convince her that not all men were the same, that there were good ones out there, but she refused to listen.

One evening, as Donna sat in her dimly lit living room, nursing a glass of wine, her best friend, Lisa, dropped by unexpectedly. Lisa was a beacon of positivity, a stark contrast to Donna's pessimism when it came to love.

"Donna, I've been worried about you," Lisa said gently, taking a seat beside her friend. "You can't keep going on like this. Not all men are cheaters, you know." Donna rolled her eyes, taking a sip of her wine. "Easy for you to say, Lisa. You found your happily ever after, but I've been through too much to believe in fairy tales."

Lisa sighed, her concern evident in her eyes. "I know you've been hurt, Donna, but you can't let your past dictate your future. There are good men out there, men who will treat you with respect and love. But you have to be open to the possibility."

Donna scoffed, her bitterness evident. "I've heard it all before, Lisa. I've tried and looked where it got me—alone and brokenhearted."

Lisa reached out and gently touched Donna's hand. "You deserve love, Donna. You deserve to be happy. But you have to let go of the past and give love a chance."

Donna looked at her friend, tears welling up in her eyes. She had built walls around her heart for so long that she had forgotten what it felt like to hope, to believe in the possibility of finding true love.

"I'm scared, Lisa," Donna admitted, her voice trembling. "I'm scared of getting hurt again."

Lisa smiled warmly. "I know it's scary, but it's also worth it. Take small steps, one day at a time. Start by letting go of the past and opening your heart to the possibility of love. You never know, the next man who comes into your life might just be the one who proves you wrong."

Donna wiped away her tears, feeling a glimmer of hope deep within her. Maybe, just maybe, it was time to let go of her negative beliefs about love and give it another chance. With Lisa by her side, she was willing to take that first step toward a brighter future, one where love was no longer a game of deception but a genuine, beautiful connection waiting to be discovered.

Donna's heart was torn between the darkness of her past and the glimmer of hope that Lisa's words had ignited. She knew that she couldn't continue down the same path of cynicism and distrust forever but breaking free from her pessimistic mindset seemed like an insurmountable task.

Weeks passed, and Donna tried to heed Lisa's advice. She reluctantly agreed to go on a few dates, trying to open herself up to the possibility of love. Yet, with every step she took, she couldn't help but feel the weight of her past mistakes, her past heartaches, pressing down on her like an anchor.

The dates were lackluster, to say the least. Donna's negative beliefs about relationships kept her from fully engaging with the men she met. She scrutinized every word, every gesture, convinced that they were hiding something, just waiting to betray her trust. Her skepticism and paranoia tainted each interaction, and it wasn't long before her suitors sensed her mistrust and withdrew, leaving Donna to confirm her own negative biases.

After yet another disappointing date, Donna met up with Lisa for coffee. She couldn't hide the frustration in her voice as she recounted her latest encounter. "I told you, Lisa," Donna said bitterly. "There's no such thing as love. It's all just a facade, a game. Every man I meet just proves me right."

Lisa's face fell, concern etched across her features. "Donna, you can't give up after just a few dates. Finding love takes time and patience. You can't expect everything to change overnight."

Donna shook her head, her resolve unwavering. "I'm done with this charade. I've been through too much to believe in fairy tales and happy endings."

Over time, Donna's negativity began to affect her friendships as well. She discouraged her friends from believing in love, citing her own experiences as evidence that it was all a mirage. Lisa and the others watched helplessly as Donna retreated further into her shell of cynicism, pushing away anyone who tried to offer support or encouragement.

As the years passed, Donna's bitterness and pessimism became her defining characteristics. She isolated herself from the world, convinced that love was an illusion that had no place in her life. She watched from the sidelines as her friends found happiness and built families, while she remained trapped in a cycle of self-fulfilling prophecies.

And so, Donna continued to exist in a world where love remained a distant dream, forever out of reach. It was a life of solitude, where the echoes of past heartaches drowned out the possibility of a brighter, more hopeful future.

Despite Donna's increasing isolation and bitterness, life moved on for her friends, including Lisa, who found herself deeply in love and on the brink of getting married. Lisa had always held out hope for Donna, believing that someday she would find a way to heal and open her heart to love again. She wanted her dear friend to be a part of her special day, and she asked Donna to be her bridesmaid.

At first, Donna hesitated, knowing that weddings were a celebration of love, something she had grown to despise. She felt torn between her loyalty to her friend and her stubborn cynicism. However, she ultimately agreed, not wanting to let Lisa down on such an important occasion.

As the wedding preparations continued, Donna found herself thrust into a world of romance and joy, a stark contrast to her own beliefs. She watched as Lisa and her fiancé, Mark, planned their dream wedding, their eyes sparkling with love and anticipation. It was a sight that both warmed her heart and filled her with a sense of bitterness she could hardly contain.

In the days leading up to the wedding, Donna couldn't escape the feeling of impending doom. Her negative beliefs about love and relationships resurfaced with a vengeance. She couldn't bear to see her friend walk down the aisle, believing that Lisa was naively walking into a future filled with pain and heartbreak.

On the day of the wedding, Donna's inner turmoil reached its peak.

She was clad in a beautiful bridesmaid dress, but her smile was strained, her heart heavy with doubt. She couldn't let her friend make such a life-altering mistake, at least in her own eyes.

During the ceremony, as Lisa and Mark exchanged their vows, Donna couldn't hold back any longer. In a moment of desperation, she stood up and interrupted the proceedings.

"Stop!" Donna cried out; her voice filled with anguish. "You can't do this, Lisa! Love is a lie! It's all a charade!"

The entire wedding party and guests were stunned into silence, the joyous occasion abruptly shattered by Donna's outburst. Lisa looked at her friend with a mixture of shock and sadness.

"Donna, what are you doing?" Lisa asked, tears welling up in her eyes.

Donna couldn't find the words to explain her actions. She felt overwhelmed by the weight of her own bitterness and the belief that she was trying to save her friend from a life of misery.

Mark, the groom, stepped forward, his voice calm but firm. "Donna, we love each other, and we believe in the power of love. Please, don't stand in the way of our happiness."

Despite her reluctance, Donna realized that she had gone too far. She stepped back, tears streaming down her face, and watched as Lisa and Mark continued with their wedding vows.

The ceremony continued, but the atmosphere was tainted by Donna's outburst. The celebration, once filled with joy and hope, was now marked by a lingering sense of unease. Donna had sabotaged her friend's special day, driven by her own bitterness and inability to believe in love.

In the aftermath of the wedding, Lisa and Mark forgave Donna, understanding that her actions came from a place of pain and fear. However, their friendship was forever changed, and Donna remained trapped in her self-imposed prison of negativity and mistrust. She continued to discourage those around her from believing in love, convinced that her own experiences were proof that true happiness was nothing but an illusion.

In the wake of the disrupted wedding, tension lingered between Donna, Lisa, and Mark. Lisa was disappointed and hurt by Donna's actions on what was supposed to be the happiest day of her life. She had hoped that Donna's presence at the wedding would bring some positivity to her friend's life, but it had only resulted in further turmoil.

Days turned into weeks, and the strained relationship between the three of them showed no signs of improving. Donna's bitterness and negativity seemed to have reached a point of no return, and she couldn't shake the belief that love was a farce.

One evening, when Mark was away on a business trip, Donna received a late-night phone call from Lisa. Tearfully, Lisa confided in Donna about the strain the incident had put on her marriage. She explained how Mark had been distant and preoccupied, and her trust in him had been shaken by the disruption at their wedding.

"Donna, you have to understand the consequences of what you did," Lisa pleaded. "Our marriage is suffering because of it, and I can't help but blame you for it."

Donna felt a pang of guilt and regret wash over her. She had never intended to harm her friend's marriage, but her cynicism and bitterness had driven her to act in a way that had caused pain to those she cared about most.

As the weeks went by, the once-strong bond of friendship between Donna and Lisa continued to unravel. Lisa couldn't shake the suspicion and doubt that Donna's outburst had planted in her mind. It led to a growing rift between the two friends, and eventually, they decided to part ways.

Their friendship, once filled with laughter, shared secrets, and unwavering support, had come to an end. Donna's negative beliefs about love had not only sabotaged her own chances of finding happiness but had also led to the destruction of a cherished friendship.

In the end, Donna remained trapped in her cycle of cynicism and distrust, convinced that love was an illusion, while Lisa and Mark struggled to repair the damage that had been done to their relationship. It was a painful reminder that sometimes, our beliefs and actions can have far-reaching consequences, affecting not only our own lives but the lives of those we care about deeply.

Pick Up the Pieces

Broken pieces of a shattered heart
sitting in the corner glass swept up
by the pale of men that left them behind
oh no but she's fine

Haven't had a chance to heal
jumping in and out of relationships
before she got over the last one or the one before

Why?

She doesn't like being alone
she needs to be held, loved
jumping from bodies to bodies
it's her new sport she knows he's damaging her

She stops and think
of what it could have been
trying to find you in them I guess

She told him she wasn't ready
she continues to cancel dates
or show up late
I'll play this game she thought to herself

People deal with relationship differently
some abandoned relationships all together
but for her she wanted love
and she thought he would be her peace

In search of love anyway she could get it
some are afraid to be alone
she settled and allowed him to love her

He wined and dined her
made her feel like she was the only woman
in the world planned late night romances
weekend trips but was never willing to commit.

She questioned him as too why in a text it's been 3 days
and not a response yet.
Now she's on to the next.

Blame, the shadow that lingers,
casting its dark veil, Upon the fragments of her heart,
Broken pieces of a shattered heart,
Scattered fragments of a love torn apart.
 In her search for love, she plays her part,
Unaware that healing begins within the heart.

Glamorous Life

Summer was a vivacious young woman who believed that life was a never-ending party. With her infectious smile and boundless energy, she seemed to light up every room she entered.

Summer had grown up in a modest neighborhood, and she had always dreamed of something more glamorous. As soon as she turned 18, she packed her bags and left her small town behind, heading for the bright lights of the city. She believed that this was her ticket to the life she had always imagined.

In the city, Summer was like a fish out of water. She found herself swept up in a whirlwind of parties, nightlife, and the allure of the city's glamour. Every night was a new adventure, a new party to attend, and a new crowd to impress. It seemed as though she was living the dream she had always wanted.

However, the more she immersed herself in this lifestyle, the more she lost touch with reality. Summer started making choices that seemed fun at the time but ultimately began to damage her life. She fell in with the wrong crowd, people who cared more about partying and instant gratification than building a future.

As the months passed, Summer's life began to spiral out of control. She found herself entangled in dangerous situations, often struggling to make ends meet. The glamour she had sought was slowly fading away, revealing the harsh reality beneath.

One night, after a particularly wild party, Summer woke up in a strange apartment with no recollection of how she had ended up there. Her head was pounding, and the room was filled with the stale scent of alcohol and regret. She tried to get up but felt a sharp pain in her side. Looking down, she noticed a bruise she couldn't explain.

Terrified and disoriented, Summer managed to make her way to the bathroom. She stared at her reflection in the mirror, and for the first time in a long while, she saw the pain and confusion in her own eyes. She realized that the party lifestyle had taken its toll, and she was no longer the happy and carefree girl she once was.

Tears welled up in Summer's eyes as the gravity of her situation sank in. She knew that she needed help, but she didn't know where to turn. The people she had surrounded herself with were not the ones who would lend a helping hand in her time of need. Summer felt a wetness coming down her leg she looked down and it appeared to be blood. Summer cleaned herself up and went to the emergency room. Summer was examined by the doctor given a prescription and was told to return in a week. Tears rained down Summer's face, she was afraid not knowing what happened to her. She felt like the nurse was interrogating her and she did not have any answers she couldn't remember what happened before she woke up. At that point Summer vowed to never drink again.

As Summer left the hospital, she clutched the prescription tightly in her hand, feeling a mixture of fear, shame, and determination. She knew that something had to change, and she couldn't keep living the reckless lifestyle that had brought her to this point. The doctor's words echoed in her mind, urging her to return for a follow-up and seek help if she ever found herself in a similar situation.

With a newfound sense of responsibility, Summer decided to confront the people she had surrounded herself with. She realized that her so-called friends were not friends at all but had led her down a path of self-destruction. It was time to distance herself from those who had been a negative influence on her life.

Slowly but surely, Summer started to rebuild her life. She enrolled in therapy to address the underlying issues that had driven her to seek solace in the party scene. She reconnected with her family, who had been worried sick about her and were relieved to see her taking steps toward recovery.

Over time, Summer's determination to stay away from alcohol and drugs became a steadfast commitment. She found solace in healthier activities like yoga, painting, and hiking. These pursuits not only helped her stay sober but also allowed her to discover new passions and talents she hadn't known she possessed.

As the months turned into years, Summer's life transformed in ways she could have never imagined during her darkest days. She found herself surrounded by a supportive and loving community, people who genuinely cared about her well-being and happiness. Her infectious smile, once dulled by the effects of her reckless lifestyle, returned with even more radiance.

Summer's story served as an inspiring example of resilience and the power of self-renewal. She had faced her demons head-on, emerging from the depths of despair stronger and wiser than ever before. Through her journey of self-discovery and healing, she learned that life wasn't just about chasing dreams of glamour and excitement but about finding inner peace, self-acceptance, and true happiness.

With a newfound determination, Summer made a difficult decision. She reached out to her family, whom she had drifted away from since moving to the city. She admitted her mistakes and her need for support.

Her family, worried sick about her, welcomed her back with open arms. Summer began the long and challenging journey of rebuilding her life. It wasn't easy, but with the love and support of her family, she managed to break free from the damaging lifestyle that had once consumed her. She realized that life was more than just a never-ending party, and true happiness came from finding balance and meaning in her existence.

Over time, Summer healed both physically and emotionally. She pursued her dreams with a newfound sense of purpose, making the most of the second chance she had been given. She learned that life wasn't about chasing an illusion of glamour; it was about finding genuine connections, inner strength, and the courage to overcome the obstacles that came her way.

Summer's story served as a reminder that even when life takes us down dark and challenging paths, there is always hope for redemption and the opportunity to rebuild a better, brighter future.

Glamorous Life

She danced in the glow of city lights,
A dreamer chasing starry nights.
With laughter that sparkled,
A carefree gleam,
Summer lived her life in color a vivid dream.

From modest roots, she sought the grand,
A world of glitz she commanded it all.
Parties, people, endless nights,
A whirlwind life of dazzling heights.

But glamour fades, and shadows creep,
Beneath the glitter, the wounds ran deep.
Lost in a maze of fleeting pleasure,
Her life became a fragile treasure.

One fateful night, she woke in pain,
Her mirror reflected tears like rain.
The girl she saw, she barely knew,
Her soul now worn; her joy removed.

The city's glow had dimmed its spark,
Leaving her adrift, alone in the dark.
A bruise, a tear, a haunting plight,
The price she paid for endless nights.

But even in despair, hope can ignite,
A flicker of strength, a guiding light.
She vowed to change, to break the chain,
To reclaim herself, to heal the pain.

Therapy sessions, a family's embrace,
She found her footing, her rightful place.
Yoga, painting, trails to climb,
Each step forward a healing rhyme.

Her smile returned, shining bright,
No longer dimmed by the city's night.
Her story told of pain and grace,
of falling, rising, finding her place.

Glamour's allure had lost its sway,
For true joy lit her life each day.
With balance found and peace restored,
She lived a life she now admired and adored.

Let Summer's tale remind us all,
Even in darkness, we can stand tall.
For life's true treasure isn't the shine,
But love, self-worth, and a soul divine.

Breaking the Silence: Rising from Pain to Purpose

As she lay there bleeding, the woman suddenly heard a knock on the door. At first, Kimberly hesitated, afraid of who might be there. But something inside her urged her to get up and see who it was. Slowly, she made her way to the door, still holding her bleeding wrist.

When she opened the door, she saw a police officer standing on the other side. The officer asked if she was okay, and the woman burst into tears, finally releasing all the pain and fear that had been building up inside her.

The officer immediately called for an ambulance and stayed with the woman until it arrived. As she was being taken away on a stretcher, she realized that she was not alone. There were people who cared about her and wanted to help her heal.

In the hospital, the woman received medical attention for her injuries, and a rape kit was performed to collect evidence. The police also began an investigation into the crime, and the perpetrator was eventually caught and brought to justice.

Although the healing process was long and difficult, the woman received support from friends, family, and professionals. Kimberly realized that she was not to blame for what had happened to her and that she deserved justice and compassion.

Eventually, the Kimberly found the strength to speak out about her experience, sharing her story with others who had gone through similar trauma. Kimberly became an advocate for survivors of sexual assault, using her voice to raise awareness and fight for justice.

Although the memory of the rape would always be a part of her, the woman was no longer defined by it. She had taken control of her life and refused to let the trauma define her. Instead, she was a survivor, a fighter, and a voice for those who had been silenced.

• • •

As she lay in the hospital bed, staring at the ceiling, the woman couldn't stop the flood of emotions. Shame, anger, despair—they all swirled together, threatening to drown her. Kimberly couldn't understand why she felt so heavy, so broken. The memories of the night replayed in her mind, each flash more vivid than the last.

The nurse came in quietly, adjusting the IV and checking her vitals.

She gave the woman a soft smile, as if to say, *It's okay. You're safe now.* But the woman wasn't sure if she believed it. She closed her eyes, letting exhaustion take over, but her sleep was restless, haunted by nightmares of what had happened.

• • •

The days turned into weeks. The physical wounds began to heal, but the emotional ones were harder to mend. Kimberly avoided mirrors, afraid of what she might see staring back at her. She didn't want to talk about it, didn't want to relive the shame and guilt she had buried deep. But every time she tried to push it away, it clawed its way back, demanding to be felt.

One afternoon, a counselor visited her room. She introduced herself as Marie, her voice calm and soothing. Marie didn't push for details, didn't force her to talk. Kimberly just sat there, holding space for her to exist in whatever state she was in.

"It wasn't your fault," Marie said softly, breaking the silence. The words hung in the air, heavy and raw. The woman turned her face away, tears streaming down her cheeks. She wanted to believe Marie, but the weight of her own self-blame was crushing.

• • •

Eventually, the Kimberly agreed to attend therapy. The first session was the hardest. Sitting in a circle with other survivors, hearing their stories, felt like reopening her wounds. But as they spoke, she began to see fragments of herself in their words. She wasn't alone in this pain. Slowly, she started to share her own story, her voice shaking with every word. She cried, and for the first time, she didn't feel weak for doing so.

The group became a lifeline, a place where she didn't have to hide her scars or pretend to be okay. With their encouragement, she began to reclaim parts of herself that she thought were lost forever.

• • •

One day, Marie handed her a small journal. "Write," she said simply. "Even if it's just a word, let it out."

The Kimberly began scribbling her thoughts, her anger, her heartbreak. The pages became a refuge, a way to process the chaos inside her mind. She wrote about the pain, yes, but also about the small victories:

the first day she laughed again, the first time she slept through the night, the first time she looked in the mirror and didn't flinch.

• • •

Months turned into years. The scars remained, but they no longer defined her. Kimberly began to speak at events, sharing her story with courage she didn't know she had. She met women who had walked similar paths, and together, they created a network of support, a community where no one had to feel alone.

The woman became an advocate, fighting for justice and resources for survivors of sexual assault. She lobbied for policy changes, collaborated with organizations, and stood as a voice for those who hadn't yet found their own.

• • •

One night, as she stood on stage at a fundraiser, Kimberly looked out at the crowd. Tears filled her eyes, but they weren't tears of pain. They were tears of pride, of gratitude, of strength. She had turned her pain into purpose, her trauma into a bridge for healing.

"It wasn't my fault," she said, her voice steady and firm. "And it's not yours either. Together, we can break the silence. Together, we can heal."

The room erupted into applause, but it wasn't the sound that mattered to her. It was the knowing—the deep, unshakable truth—that she was no longer a victim. She was a survivor, a warrior, and a guide for others to find their light.

Rising from Pain to Purpose

She woke up in pain
dried up blood on her upper lip
It took what seemed like hours
to pick herself up off the floor.
She began to crawl towards the bathroom
grabbed the door handle for support, stood up,
walked to the mirror and didn't recognize herself
her face was black, and blue covered in dried blood

Head pounding, migraine,
she ran bath water and sat in the tub
until the water was cold to ashamed to ask for help
tears fell from her face that's when
she remembered she was raped
flashbacks of how it started

Blaming herself she contemplated suicide
reach for the razor and began to slit her wrist
believing that no one would miss her
so, no one would care

Random thoughts went through her mind
No one who believe he did this to me
I don't matter
I wanted it
I deserved it
I should've been at his home at 3am
I knew what would happen

He rapped me and took me home
I have to be more careful
It's my fault
It's on me
It's my fault

Flash Backs of the Past

A tear drops from Amy's face rolled down the left side of her cheek landed in between her bosom, she snapped out of her trans and realized that the wetness hit the exact scar that healed from the first attempt on her life by the hands of her father.

Amy shed so many tears over the years falling in and out of destructive relationships trying to hold on to the unrealistic fantasy of what one should or even could be.

Waking up to nightmare after nightmare screams of terror irrupt in her small one bedroom apartment the lights flickered. Flashbacks of the miscarriages after he beat her and drugged her across the pavement because he didn't want a child, well not by her. She cursed the day he was born, not again. This just cannot be happening again.

Amy gathered her strength and slowly got out of bed, her body aching from the memories that haunted her. She made her way to the bathroom and looked at herself in the mirror. The reflection staring back at her was a shell of the woman she used to be. The bruises on her face were still visible, and her eyes were filled with fear and sadness.

Amy knew she had to leave, but where would she go? She had no family, no friends, no one to turn to. She had cut herself off from everyone who cared about her, believing that she deserved the abuse she received. But now, she knew she needed to break free from this cycle of violence and pain.

With trembling hands, she dialed the number of a domestic abuse hotline she had seen advertised on TV. A kind voice answered, and she found herself pouring out her story to a stranger on the other end of the line. The woman on the phone listened patiently and offered her resources and advice.

It wasn't going to be easy, but for the first time in a long time, she felt a glimmer of hope. She wiped away the tear that had fallen on her scar, took a deep breath, and decided. She was going to leave and start a new life, one where she was free from the abuse and pain.

As Amy packed her bags, she felt a sense of empowerment she had never felt before. She was taking back control of her life, and nothing would ever make her feel weak and helpless again. She left her old life behind and stepped into a new world, one full of possibilities and hope. She would never forget the tears she had shed, but she would never let them control her again.

With her bags packed and determination in her heart, she walked out of her small apartment, leaving behind the nightmare that had consumed her for so long. The journey ahead was uncertain, but Amy knew it was the only path to healing and freedom.

The kind voice on the other end of the hotline had given her the contact information for a local women's shelter, a place where she could seek refuge and start rebuilding her life. She hailed a cab and nervously gave the address to the driver. As the city passed by outside the window, she couldn't help but feel a mix of fear and anticipation.

Arriving at the shelter, Amy was met by a group of caring individuals who welcomed her with open arms. They provided her with a safe place to stay, counseling, and access to resources that would help her regain her independence. It wasn't an easy journey, and the scars, both physical and emotional, would take time to heal. But she was determined to break free from her past.

Days turned into weeks, and she slowly began to rebuild her sense of self-worth and self-esteem. Amy attended therapy sessions, joined support groups with other survivors, and started working on her education. She discovered talents and interests she had long forgotten, and her confidence grew with each small step forward.

One day, as she looked at herself in the mirror, she saw a transformation taking place. The bruises had faded, and her eyes were no longer filled with fear but with determination and hope. She realized that she was becoming the person she had always wanted to be, strong and independent.

As time went on, she made new friends at the shelter, people who understood her struggles and offered unwavering support. She found a job and started saving money, planning for a future free from the shackles of her past. And, most importantly, she learned to love herself again, realizing that she deserved happiness and respect.

Years passed, and she had built a new life for herself, a life she had once thought was impossible. She had reconnected with her estranged family, who were overjoyed to see her thrive and had regretted not being there when she needed them most. Her scars were still there, a reminder of the pain she had endured, but they no longer defined her.

She became an advocate for survivors of domestic abuse, sharing her story to inspire others to break free from their own cycles of violence. She knew that there were countless individuals out there who, like her, were trapped in abusive relationships, and she was determined to help them find their way to safety and healing.

As Amy looked back on her journey, she couldn't help but shed tears of gratitude. That single tear that had fallen on her scar had been a catalyst for her transformation, a symbol of the strength and resilience that had always been within her. She had emerged from the darkness into the light, a survivor, a warrior, and a symbol of hope for those who still needed to find their way out.

Her advocacy work became her passion and purpose in life. She dedicated herself to raising awareness about domestic abuse and helping survivors find their own path to healing and freedom. Amy spoke at events, worked with organizations, and even wrote a book about her journey, hoping that her story would inspire others to break free from their own nightmares.

Through her efforts, she met other survivors, each with their own unique stories of strength and resilience. They formed a tight-knit community, providing support and understanding to one another. Together, they organized workshops and support groups, creating a safe space for survivors to share their experiences and heal together.

As the years went by, her impact grew. Amy successfully lobbied for changes in legislation to protect survivors and hold abusers accountable. She received awards and recognition for her advocacy work, but the true reward was seeing the lives she had helped transform.

One day, while attending a support group meeting at the shelter that had once saved her, she met a young woman with fear in her eyes and fresh bruises on her face. The woman's story mirrored her own, and she saw herself in the trembling, frightened girl. Without hesitation, she reached out, offering a hand and a glimmer of hope.

"Just take one step," she said, her voice filled with empathy. "It's scary, but there's a whole world of support waiting for you on the other side."

The young woman took that step, just as she had done years ago. Together, they walked through the challenging journey of healing and transformation. And as the tears of fear turned into tears of strength, they knew that they were not alone. They had each other, and they had the unwavering support of a community that understood their pain.

Through her advocacy and the bonds she had formed, she realized that her life had come full circle. Amy had turned her darkest moments into a source of light for others. Her tears of despair had become tears of empowerment, a reminder that even in the darkest of times, there was always a glimmer of hope.

As she continued her work, she looked at herself in the mirror once more. The reflection staring back at her was not just a survivor; she had become a person of hope, a guiding light for those still trapped in their own nightmares. And she knew that as long as she lived, she would continue to fight for a world where no one had to endure the pain and suffering she had once known.

Flash Backs

A tear traced her cheek, a path it did seek,
Landing softly between her bosom's deep,
Awakening from her trance, she gazed in a glance,
At the wetness upon her scar, memories did creep.

So many tears shed, in destructive threads,
Entangled in relationships' unrealistic spreads,
Chasing a fantasy, an elusive reverie,
Of what one should, or could, be instead.

Nightmares invaded, screams pierced unabated,
In her small apartment, terror unaberrated,
Lights flickered, a haunting trigger,
Recalling beatings, miscarriages, life desecrated.

With strength gathered, she rose from her bed,
Aching body, memories that bled,
To the mirror she turned, her reflection discerned,
A shadowed woman, fear, and sadness widespread.

She knew she must flee, but where could she be,
With no family, no friends, no sanctuary,
Isolated she'd been, from those who would defend,
Believing she deserved the pain and cruelty.

With trembling hands, she sought a lifeline,
Dialing the hotline, a beacon so fine,
Pouring out her tale, to a stranger without fail,
Finding solace and resources that would align.

It wouldn't be easy, this journey she'd seize,
But a glimmer of hope stirred, put her heart at ease,
Wiping away the tear, falling on the old scar clear,
She took a breath and decided to break free.

Packing her bags, empowered, she stood tall,
Reclaiming her life, breaking free from the fall,
Leaving behind the abuse, finding her truth,
In a world of new beginnings, she'd stand tall.
The tears she had shed, etched deep within,
A testament to her strength, her resilient skin,
No longer controlled, by the pain of old,
She embraced a future where her freedom would win.

Where I'm From

Jean Birmingham was born in Los Angeles, CA into a world with a history that seemed both distant and oppressive. She was a young black woman, and her roots ran deep, tangled in a complex web of pain, suffering, and resilience. Her ancestors, like so many others, had been beaten, chained, and forced onto boats as slaves. They had endured unimaginable hardships, and their stories had often been erased or distorted. As Jean grew, she couldn't help but wonder, "Why do they hate us? Why do we still live with the trauma and pain, suffering from the 'maybe' or 'could be' of our history?"

But Jean was not content to remain trapped in the shadows of the past. She was determined to make her mark on the world, to break free from the chains of history, and to celebrate her unique identity with her head held high.

From a young age, Jean had a thirst for knowledge. She devoured books, absorbing the stories of her people's struggles and triumphs. She learned about the civil rights movement, the heroes who had fought for justice, and the poets who had used their words to speak truth to power. These stories ignited a fire within her, a burning desire to be a part of the change she longed to see.

As Jean grew older, she found her voice. She began to write poetry and prose that spoke to the depths of her soul. Her words were a powerful weapon against the lies and distortions that had plagued her people's history. She penned verses of strength, resilience, and hope, reminding herself and others of the indomitable spirit that ran through their veins.

Jean's journey was not without its challenges. She faced prejudice and discrimination at every turn, but she refused to be defined by the stereotypes and biases of others. She knew that her identity was a source of strength, a testament to the resilience of her people, and a bridge to a future where change was not just a dream but a reality.

She became actively involved in her community, volunteering her time and talents to uplift those who had been marginalized and oppressed. She organized events that celebrated the rich cultural heritage of her people, reminding them of the beauty and strength that lay within their roots.

But Jean's most powerful message was one of self-acceptance and self-love. She urged her fellow black men and women to embrace their unique identities, to wear their heritage with pride, and to stand tall in the face of adversity. She believed that the wounds of the past could only be healed through unity, empathy, and a deep understanding of one's own worth.

In the end, Jean Birmingham's determination and unwavering belief in change began to ripple through her community. People began to look at their history not as a burden, but as a source of strength. They started to see the power in embracing and celebrating their unique identities, just as Jean had done.

Jean's journey was far from over, but she knew that she was making her mark on the world, one word, one act of kindness, and one soul at a time. She had learned that the power to create change lay within each individual, and that by embracing their unique identities, they could rewrite the narrative of their history and pave the way for a brighter future.

As Jean Birmingham continued her journey, her passion and determination only grew stronger. She knew that creating lasting change required not just words and actions, but a deep connection with the hearts and minds of her community.

She began organizing workshops and discussions within her neighborhood, inviting people to share their own stories and experiences. These gatherings became a safe space for open dialogue, where individuals could express their fears, hopes, and dreams. Through these conversations, Jean realized that the trauma of the past was still very much present in the lives of her fellow community members. Together, they embarked on a healing journey, acknowledging the pain and suffering that had been passed down through generations.

Jean's words and actions continued to inspire others. She collaborated with local artists and musicians to create powerful exhibits and performances that celebrated their cultural heritage. Through these artistic expressions, she encouraged her community to find strength in their uniqueness, to honor their ancestors, and to envision a future where prejudice and discrimination had no place.

One day, while walking through her neighborhood, Jean noticed a group of young children playing in the park. Their laughter and smiles filled the air, but she couldn't help but wonder if they were aware of the history that had brought them to this moment. She decided it was time to educate the younger generation about their roots and the struggles of their ancestors.

Jean started a youth program, where she taught young black girls and boys about the rich history of their people. She emphasized the importance of embracing their unique identities and understanding the sacrifices made by those who came before them. She wanted these children to grow up with a sense of pride and resilience, armed with the knowledge that they too could make a difference in the world.

Through her tireless efforts, Jean Birmingham's influence extended beyond her community. She began to speak at schools and universities, sharing her story and inspiring young minds to believe in the power of change. Her message was simple yet profound: no matter where you come from, no matter the obstacles you face, your identity is a source of strength and a catalyst for change.

As the years went by, Jean's impact on her community and beyond became undeniable. The younger generation she had mentored grew into confident, empowered individuals who carried forward the torch of change. They continued the work of breaking down barriers and celebrating their unique identities, just as Jean had taught them.

Jean Birmingham had indeed made her mark on the world, not through grand gestures or extraordinary feats, but through the unwavering belief in the power of embracing one's unique identity and the determination to create a better future for all. Her legacy lived on in the hearts and actions of those she had touched, a testament to the enduring strength of the human spirit and the capacity for change.

Where I'm From

Palm trees blue skies
some say it never rains here
movie stars flashy cars
Gun shots
people dying before their time
no regard for our lives
we don't matter to some
Family cookouts
in before the streetlights come on
corner liquor stores churches
east side west side
red, blue color lines

educated street smarts
in these parts
grandma past
single parent homes
roles changed
wrong last name

kicked out at an early age
no proper guidance
moment of silence
teenage parent
stressed out

late nights
two jobs
no car
public transportation

no real home
lost trust
alone and confused
which way do I choose
105-405 110 605 210
all of these numbers can get me to where I need to be
in a city of dreams where everybody think they can make it
and be free church houses schoolhouses
group homes we never know where we turn
and when it's gonna go wrong
red flag blue flag
lots of people claim a territory pollution

What's the solution

History

In the depths of darkness, a light does shine,
A spirit resilient, a soul divine.
Born a black girl, with a history untold,
A journey veiled in chains, yet strong and bold.

Our ancestors, heroes, in shadows they dwell,
Their stories obscured, a silenced knell.
But hear me now, with voice unyielding and clear,
Their struggles, their triumphs, forever I revere.

For in our veins, their blood still flows, A design woven,
where strength arose. They faced oppression, yet refused to fall,
Their spirits endure, a strength for us all.

We bear the weight of an unjust past,
The scars of trauma, memories that last.
But let us rise, in unity we stand,
Embracing our heritage, hand in hand.

No longer bound by the chains of despair,
We weave a new narrative, our truth to share.
In the face of hatred, we find our grace,
For love and acceptance will find their place.

With hearts aflame, our uniqueness we embrace,
A kaleidoscope of colors, our souls ablaze.
No longer confined by society's decree,
We celebrate our identity, wild and free.

So, rise, my sisters, and brothers with heads held high,
Unveil your brilliance, let your spirits fly.
The world may judge, with eyes unkind,
But we shall conquer, hearts intertwined.

For we are black girls, and black boys with strength unbound,
Defying the limits, breaking new ground.
Our heritage a symphony, a song so sweet,
A chorus of resilience, forever to repeat.

In unity, we find our power and might,
A beacon of hope, shining through the night.
Embrace your truth, let your voice be heard,
For together we rise, our spirits undeterred.
In the midst of this world's tumultuous sea,
We'll carve our path, our destinies set free.

Our heritage is our strength, our anchor and guide,
With heads held high, our mark on the world, we'll ride.
For we are warriors of change, with hearts so bold,
A legacy of greatness, a story yet untold.
With every step we take, and every dream we chase,
We'll make our mark on this world, with unwavering grace.

In the depths of darkness, a light does shine,
A spirit resilient, a soul divine. Born a black girl,
with a history untold, a journey veiled in chains,
yet strong and bold. Our ancestors, heroes,
in shadows they dwell, their stories obscured,
a silenced knell. But hear me now, with voice
unyielding and clear, their struggles, their triumphs,
forever I revere. For in our veins, their blood still flows,
A design woven, where strength arose.

They faced oppression, yet refused to fall,
their spirits endure, a strength for us all.
We bear the weight of an unjust past,
The scars of trauma, memories that last.

But let us rise, in unity we stand, Embracing
our heritage, hand in hand. No longer bound
by the chains of despair, we weave a new narrative,
our truth to share. In the face of hatred,
we find our grace, for love and acceptance
will find their place.

With hearts aflame,
our uniqueness we embrace, A kaleidoscope of colors,
our souls ablaze. No longer confined by society's decree,
we celebrate our identity, wild and free.
So, rise, my sisters, with heads held high,
unveil your brilliance, let your spirits fly.

The world may judge, with eyes unkind,
but we shall conquer, hearts intertwined.
For we are black girls, with strength unbound,
Defying the limits, breaking new ground.
Our heritage a symphony, a song so sweet,
a chorus of resilience, forever to repeat. In unity,
we find our power and might, A message of hope,
shining through the night.
Embrace your truth, let your voice be heard, f
or together we rise, our spirits undeterred.

Never Compromised

In the vibrant city of New Orleans, there lived a man named Zachariah. He was a striking figure, standing at a proud six feet tall, with chocolate skin that seemed to shimmer in the southern sun. His muscular body exuded athleticism, a testament to his dedication to physical fitness. But there was more to Zachariah than his outward appearance.

Zachariah had it all – a six-figure job as a successful architect, a charming smile that could melt hearts, and a heart of gold that was always ready to help his community. He had a passion for cooking, a skill he had mastered over the years, and he took pride in his ability to whip up delectable dishes. He could also clean like a pro, making sure his home was always in impeccable order. He was, by all accounts, the perfect catch.

However, there was a catch of a different kind when it came to Zachariah's dating life. Despite his many qualities, his relationships rarely lasted more than six months. It wasn't that he couldn't find someone who was interested in him, but rather, he was the one who always seemed to find something wrong.

Zachariah was a workaholic, and his demanding job often consumed his time and energy. He would spend long hours at the office, perfecting architectural designs and overseeing construction projects. While his career was successful, it left little room for nurturing a romantic relationship. His partners would often complain that they felt neglected and unimportant, leading to the inevitable breakup.

Zachariah was also a perfectionist, always striving for excellence in every aspect of his life. This desire for perfection extended to his relationships, and he often found himself hyper-critical of his partners. He would obsess over small flaws and quirks, convinced that they were insurmountable obstacles. He couldn't help but compare his partners to an idealized image of the perfect companion that existed only in his mind.

Despite his challenges in the realm of romance, Zachariah remained deeply committed to helping his community. He volunteered at local shelters, organized charity events, and supported various community initiatives. He believed in the power of giving back and felt a strong connection to his fellow New Orleanians.

Zachariah also had a deep spiritual side. He believed in a higher power, and his faith provided him with a sense of purpose and guidance in his life. It was during moments of reflection and prayer that he often contemplated his dating struggles and the need for change.

One day, as he stood in the kitchen, preparing a mouthwatering Creole dish for a neighborhood potluck, he had an epiphany. He realized that his quest for perfection had blinded him to the beauty of imperfection in relationships. He understood that no one was flawless, including himself, and that love required patience, acceptance, and compromise.

Determined to break the pattern of his past relationships, Zachariah made a conscious effort to prioritize love over work. He started carving out more time for his partners, setting boundaries at the office, and learning to appreciate the unique qualities of the people he dated. He also sought guidance from his faith, finding solace and wisdom in his spiritual journey.

As the seasons changed in New Orleans, so did Zachariah's approach to love. He began to see the beauty in the imperfect moments, the quirks that made each person unique, and the joy of shared experiences. Slowly but surely, his relationships began to flourish, lasting beyond the six-month mark.

Zachariah learned that love was not about finding someone perfect but about embracing imperfections and growing together. He continued to excel in his career, give back to his community, and nurture his faith, but he no longer let those aspects of his life overshadow the most important one – love.

And so, in the heart of the vibrant city of New Orleans, Zachariah found his own love story – a tale of personal growth, acceptance, and the belief that sometimes, in the most unexpected ways, love finds its way into our lives.

As Zachariah embarked on his journey of personal growth and rediscovered the beauty of imperfections, he had no idea that destiny had a surprise waiting for him. It was at one of the charity events he organized for his community that he first laid eyes on her – Anisha, a woman whose presence seemed to radiate strength and confidence.

Anisha, standing at 5'8" with a beautiful caramel skin tone, was a force to be reckoned with. She too had a six-figure job, working as a successful marketing executive for a prominent New Orleans firm. Her determination and focus allowed her to set and achieve ambitious goals, and she owned several thriving businesses of her own. Her articulate nature and eloquent speech showcased her intelligence and charisma.

But what truly captured Zachariah's attention was her unwavering commitment to her community. Anisha was a passionate volunteer, dedicating her free time to helping those in need. She organized fundraisers, donated to charities, and actively participated in various community initiatives. Her heart, like Zachariah's, beat for the vibrant city of New Orleans.

Their paths crossed at an event that was meant to raise funds for a local youth shelter. Zachariah was overseeing the setup, ensuring that everything went off without a hitch. Anisha arrived as a guest, her enthusiasm for the cause evident in her radiant smile and engaging conversations with fellow attendees. She effortlessly mingled with the crowd, leaving an indelible impression on everyone she met.

When Zachariah and Anisha finally crossed paths, their connection was instantaneous. They shared stories of their dedication to their careers, their love for the city, and their passion for making a difference in the lives of others. Anisha's eloquence and charm left Zachariah captivated, and he found himself drawn to her in a way he had never experienced before.

As they spent more time together, Zachariah and Anisha discovered that they were kindred spirits. They both believed in the power of giving back and shared a strong commitment to their faith, which provided them with a sense of purpose and guidance. Their conversations flowed effortlessly, filled with laughter, shared dreams, and a genuine understanding of one another's imperfections.

Anisha was the equal that Zachariah had been searching for all along, not in the sense of perfection, but in the way they complemented each other's strengths and weaknesses. They learned to balance their busy careers with quality time together, understanding that love required effort and compromise. Zachariah, with his newfound perspective on relationships, embraced the quirks and idiosyncrasies that made Anisha unique.

Together, they continued their community work, combining their efforts to make an even greater impact. Their love story became a beacon of hope and inspiration for the people of New Orleans, a testament to the power of love, acceptance, and shared values.

In the vibrant city of New Orleans, where jazz filled the air and the spirit of resilience was palpable, Zachariah and Anisha's love story flourished, proving that sometimes, when you least expect it, love finds its way into your life, not as a pursuit of perfection, but as a celebration of imperfection and growth.

As the seasons changed and the vibrant city of New Orleans

continued to embrace its rich culture, Zachariah and Anisha's love story blossomed in the most beautiful way. They found joy in the simple pleasures of life – long walks along the Mississippi River, savoring beignets at a corner café, and dancing to the soulful tunes of jazz on humid summer nights.

Their shared commitment to their community only grew stronger, as they united their resources and talents to launch a joint initiative called "Harmony in Crescent," a program aimed at providing educational opportunities for underprivileged youth in the city. Their passion for giving back to the community became a source of inspiration for others, and their love story became a symbol of hope and unity.

Zachariah and Anisha's relationship was far from perfect, but it was filled with genuine love, mutual respect, and a deep understanding of each other's ambitions and imperfections. They continued to work hard in their careers, always striving for excellence, but they had learned to prioritize their love above all else. It was a lesson that had taken Zachariah years to understand, but one that he now held close to his heart.

One evening, as they strolled through the French Quarter, Anisha turned to Zachariah with a twinkle in her eye. "You know, Zach," she began, "we've both accomplished so much individually, but together, we're unstoppable. What do you say we take our love and our dreams to the next level?"

Zachariah looked at her, his heart swelling with love and admiration. "What do you have in mind?" he asked, eager to hear her proposal.

"I think it's time we start our own charitable foundation," Anisha replied. "We can use our resources and expertise to make an even greater impact on this city we both adore. Together, we can create a legacy of love and generosity."

Zachariah nodded; his eyes filled with determination. "Anisha, I couldn't agree more. Let's do it. Let's leave a lasting mark on New Orleans, not just as individuals but as a team."

And so, with hearts full of love and a shared vision for a better future, Zachariah and Anisha founded the "Crescent Unity Foundation." It quickly gained recognition for its dedication to empowering the youth of New Orleans and promoting unity in the community. Their love story, once a tale of personal growth and acceptance, had now become a powerful force for change.

In the vibrant city of New Orleans, where the notes of jazz still filled the air and the spirit of resilience continued to thrive, Zachariah and Anisha's love story was a testament to the enduring power of love, the beauty of imperfections, and the boundless potential that could be unlocked when two hearts joined forces for a common purpose.

The Crescent Unity Foundation became a beacon of hope for the youth of New Orleans, offering educational scholarships, mentorship programs, and community outreach initiatives. Zachariah and Anisha poured their hearts and souls into the foundation, using their combined talents and resources to make a profound impact on the lives of countless young individuals.

Their love story continued to inspire others as they balanced their careers, community work, and their life together. Their relationship had grown stronger with each passing day, and they had learned to cherish the moments of imperfection, laughter, and shared dreams that defined their love.

One summer evening, under the starlit sky of New Orleans, Zachariah took Anisha to the same spot where they had first met at the charity event. He had a small velvet box in his pocket, a symbol of his commitment to their journey together. As they gazed at the shimmering lights of the city, he got down on one knee and spoke from the heart.

"Anisha," he began, his voice filled with emotion, "from the moment I met you, my life has been a journey of love and growth. You have shown me the beauty of imperfections and the power of unity. Will you make me the happiest man in the world and continue this incredible journey with me as my wife?"

Tears welled up in Anisha's eyes as she gazed into Zachariah's loving eyes. She nodded, unable to find words to express the overwhelming joy in her heart. Zachariah slipped a stunning ring onto her finger, and they sealed their love with a passionate kiss under the New Orleans night sky.

Their wedding, held in the heart of the French Quarter, was a celebration of love, unity, and their shared commitment to making the world a better place. The entire city rejoiced in their union, for Zachariah and Anisha had become beloved figures in the community, known not only for their individual accomplishments but for their profound impact as a couple.

Together, as husband and wife, they continued to work tirelessly for the betterment of New Orleans and its youth. Their love story had come full circle, from personal growth and self-discovery to a shared journey of love, purpose, and unwavering commitment to their community.

In the vibrant city of New Orleans, where the notes of jazz still filled the air and the spirit of resilience thrived, Zachariah and Anisha's love story remained a shining example of the enduring power of love, the beauty of imperfections, and the boundless potential that could be unlocked when two hearts were united in a common purpose. They were living proof that love, when shared with purpose and dedication, could change lives, and leave an indelible mark on the world.

Never Compromised

In the realm of devastation, beauty found,
A man stood tall; his presence unbound.
Six feet and three inches, a commanding sight,
Broad shoulders, strength exuding in the light.
His skin, dark chocolate, a rich hue,
Perfect eyebrows framed eyes so true.
Honey-kissed lips, a temptation sweet,
Medium built, a figure so complete.
And when he spoke, a sensual allure,
His voice, deep and captivating, for sure.
It stirred a longing, made me feel alive,
Moistening the depths where passions thrive.
Conversations profound, hearts in sync,
Dreams shared, our souls in harmony link.
He was a masterpiece, a human art,
Chiseled chest, biceps, a sculpted part.
A six-pack intact, a testament to grace,
The epitome of strength in his embrace.
His full black lips and his wide nose,
Symbolizing a heritage only he knows.
In reminiscence, I find myself lost,
Images of him, next to me, embossed.
His voice lingers, his touch still felt,
His lips collide with mine; heartstrings melt.
When I close my eyes, he's there beside me,
His essence embracing, no need to hide.
I almost smell him, taste him so nearby,
Yearning to escape, to him, disappear.
His hands on me, an electric fire,
Caressing, igniting every desire.
My tongue massages, his neck relieved,
Aches and stress, by passion retrieved.
In slumber, dreams intertwine our souls,
He falls with me, where desire unfolds.
With dawn's awakening, thoughts of him entwined,

Craving his touch, between my thighs defined.
To be tasted by his tongue, a fervent need,
A hunger awakened, impossible to impede.
In every waking moment, he's on my mind,
Longing for his return, his touch, aligned.
Come home, my love, our souls entwined,
In this devastating beauty, our hearts defined.

Never comparing

I see love through the eyes of my own existence, never comparing love, or mistaking it for a great feeling. Sex and love are not intertwined, they are separate, love is something you do not what you say or something you give in return or exchange. Most think is an emotion, but for me, I see it differently, love comes with so many things, and it's so easy that we complicate it with our miscued traditional desires. There cannot be an obligation to love, love is so much more than what we feel. It's a mixture of things and when we disconnect our feelings from love and understand love more deeply.

Oh, what a great wonderful connection you will have with your true soulmate. Love is the feeling that something will never dissipate because it's real for the first time. It is not that feeling you get when he penetrates your magic box and hits the spot. Oh, I'm in love, oh no! That's not it.

The true meaning of love transcends mere feelings and goes beyond the temporary sensations we often associate with it. Love is not just an emotion or a fleeting moment of passion. It is a profound connection that extends to the very core of our existence.

Love is not something that can be compared or measured. It is unique to each individual and each relationship. It cannot be mistaken for the physical act of sex, as love and sex are separate entities. Love encompasses so much more than what we feel in a given moment. It is a complex mixture of emotions, actions, and intentions. We often complicate love with our societal expectations and desires. We try to define it through traditional norms and obligations.

However, true love cannot be bound by rules or expectations. It is a free and genuine expression that comes from the depths of our being. When we disconnect our feelings from love and delve deeper into its essence, we can discover a profound connection with our true soulmate.

Love is not a fleeting or dying feeling that dissipates over time. It is a constant force that endures through the ups and downs of life. True love is not about what we say or what we give in return. It is not a transaction or an exchange. It is an unconditional and selfless act of caring, nurturing, and supporting another person. It is about accepting them for who they are, flaws and all, and embracing their essence with an open heart.

Love is not limited to romantic relationships alone. It extends to friendships, family bonds, and even our connection with the world around us. Love is the driving force behind acts of kindness, compassion, and empathy. It is the foundation upon which we build harmonious and meaningful relationships.

To truly understand the meaning of love, we must let go of our preconceived notions and open ourselves to its infinite possibilities. Love is an ever-evolving journey that requires patience, understanding, and a willingness to grow together.

So, when I say, "I love you," let it be a declaration of the profound connection we share with another soul. Let it be a promise to nurture, support, and cherish that bond. Let it reflect the true essence of love—a force that transcends feelings and leaves a lasting impact on our lives.

In the midst of our passionate journey, where desires ran wild and love knew no bounds, we found ourselves lost in a world of pure ecstasy. Our souls had become entwined, and our connection grew stronger with each passing moment.

As we explored the depths of our desires, we discovered new facets of one another, each touch and caress igniting a fire that burned brighter than ever before. We had surrendered to the allure of our love, a love that transcended the physical and delved into the depths of our hearts and souls.

Underneath the radiant sun and the gentle caress of the breeze, our bodies moved in harmony, creating a dance of pure elation. It was a dance of passion, a dance of two souls coming together in perfect unison, and we relished every moment of it.

In this sanctuary of desire, the world outside faded into obscurity, and all that mattered was the intoxicating blend of our love. Time itself seemed to stand still as we savored each sensation, each whispered promise of devotion.

With every shared breath, every stolen kiss, we found solace and happiness that had long eluded us. Our journey had led us to this moment of fulfillment, where our dreams had become reality, and our hearts had discovered their true purpose.

My love, as we surrendered to the depths of our passion, we became one in a world of boundless love and desire. We had found the missing piece in our lives, and in each other's arms, we had discovered a love that was truly eternal.

And so, as we continued on our life's journey, we knew that our love would always burn bright, our desires forever entwined, and our happiness everlasting. In each other, we had found our sanctuary, and in our love, we had found our ultimate fulfillment.

As the days turned into weeks, and weeks into months, our love continued to flourish. We reveled in the small moments, the shared smiles, and the silent understanding that bound us together. Our connection had deepened into something profound, an unbreakable bond that left no room for doubt.

Together, we embraced life's challenges and celebrated its triumphs. We knew that love wasn't just about the passionate moments, but also about the support, trust, and companionship we found in each other. Our desires had led us to this beautiful place, a place where love was the guiding force.

We embarked on adventures, explored new horizons, and faced life's obstacles hand in hand. In each other's presence, we found the strength to conquer any adversity, and in each other's arms, we discovered a haven of comfort and security.

Our happiness was no longer an elusive dream; it was a reality we woke up to every day. We knew that we had been on separate journeys before our paths had converged, but we also knew that those journeys had led us to each other, to this sanctuary of love and fulfillment.

With each passing year, our love grew stronger, and our connection more profound. Our desires had brought us together, but it was our unwavering commitment and deep love for one another that sustained us. We were bound by a love that knew no end.

As we looked ahead to the future, we knew that our journey was far from over. Life would continue to throw its challenges our way, but with our love as a guiding light, we were ready to face anything together. Our passion had ignited a love that was eternal, a love that had found its sanctuary in each other's hearts.

And so, hand in hand, we walked into the sunset, knowing that our love story was still being written, with each day bringing new adventures, new desires, and new opportunities to strengthen the bond that had brought us together. Our love was a sanctuary, a refuge from the storms of life, a place where we found our true selves, and a love that would continue to flourish for all eternity.

As we ventured further into the pages of our love story, the years passed like a gentle breeze, carrying us through the various seasons of life. Our bond grew even deeper with time, a testament to the enduring strength of our love.

We built a life together, filled with shared dreams, accomplishments, and cherished memories. Our home was a sanctuary where love and laughter echoed in every corner. Our love was the cornerstone that held our world together, a steady anchor in the ever-changing sea of life.

Through the ups and downs, we faced challenges head-on, knowing that together, we could conquer anything. Our trust in each other was unwavering, our support for one another unending. We had found a sanctuary not only in our love but in the profound connection we shared.

Our adventures continued, from exploring distant lands to simply enjoying quiet moments together. Each experience deepened our appreciation for the journey we were on, and we embraced the beauty of the world with open hearts and open arms.

As we gazed at the horizon, we knew that there were still countless chapters to be written in our love story. We welcomed the unknown with excitement, for we had each other to lean on, and our love remained as strong as ever.

Our passion, the spark that had ignited our love, continued to burn brightly, a reminder of the intense desire that had brought us together. It was a fire that could not be extinguished, a testament to the depth of our connection and the profound love we shared.

And so, hand in hand, we continued to walk through life's journey, knowing that our love was a sanctuary that would shelter us from any storm. Our love story was a testament to the enduring power of love, a beacon of hope for those who believed in the transformative and eternal nature of love. Together, we embraced the adventure of life, with our love as the compass guiding us forward into the unknown, with the promise that our love would continue to flourish for all eternity.

Intoxicating

As we give in to our desires our passion rises,
an intoxicating blend, Our bodies merging,
connections unleashed, a love that knows no end.

Under the sun's warm embrace, our senses come alive,
Your salty skin on my tongue, a taste that makes me thrive.

Caressed by the gentle breeze, our love's flame starts to ignite,
In this moment of pure ecstasy, we're lost in sheer delight.

With every touch, every hold, our connection grows intense,
Filling each other's souls, exploring one another from head to toe.

No rush, no haste, we savor each and every sensation,
Lost in a world where time dissolves, consumed by pure elation.

Our desires are one, in this dance of bodies and souls,
Bound together by love's embrace, fulfilling our deepest roles.

So let the world fade away, as we surrender to this bliss,
Our bodies entwined, our hearts beating in perfect unison.

For in this moment, we find peace in sanctuary divine,
Where desires are met, and love's ecstasy forever connected.

So, my love, let's surrender to this passionate affair,
In the mood of desire, where pleasures we both share.

For you are the flame that ignites my every desire,
In your arms, my love, I find the fulfillment I aspire.
We have connected as one on this life journey dreams
fulfilled happiness eludes

Hidden Truths

In a small, tight-knit town nestled in the heart of the countryside, the Morrison family had always been known for their strong sense of unity and their unwavering dedication to their values. For generations, they had lived by their own set of principles, often at odds with the laws of the land. They believed in a simple, self-sufficient way of life, free from government interference.

However, the youngest member of the Morrison family, Daniel, held a different perspective. From a young age, he had been curious about the world beyond their secluded farm. His insatiable appetite for knowledge led him to dream of a life as a lawyer, a profession that thrived on understanding and interpreting the very laws his family defied.

As Daniel grew older, his passion for justice and the legal system only intensified. Despite his family's disapproval, he pursued his dream with unwavering determination. He left the farm to attend law school, causing a deep rift within the family. They saw his pursuit of a career in law as a betrayal of their core principles, a rejection of their way of life.

Years passed, and Daniel became a successful lawyer, working in a bustling city far from the countryside he had called home. He had built a life far removed from his family's traditions, but he never forgot his roots. He had always held a glimmer of hope that one day, he could bridge the gap between his family's beliefs and his own.

Then, one fateful day, Daniel received a phone call that would change everything. It was his elder brother, Samuel, his voice filled with desperation. The Morrison family had run into serious legal troubles. Their constant defiance of local regulations and their isolated lifestyle had finally caught up with them. Their farm was facing legal challenges that threatened to destroy everything they had worked so hard to maintain.

Reluctantly, Samuel had reached out to Daniel for help, knowing that his younger brother was the only one capable of navigating the complexities of the legal system. Despite the years of estrangement, Daniel could not turn his back on his family in their time of need.

With a heavy heart, Daniel returned to the countryside he had left behind, ready to assist his family in their legal battle. He knew it wouldn't be easy, given the bitterness that had festered between them over the years.

As the legal proceedings unfolded, Daniel worked tirelessly to negotiate on behalf of his family. He tried to find a middle ground, a compromise that would allow them to maintain their way of life while complying with the law. It was a delicate dance, as he had to balance the values he held as a lawyer with the values of his family.

Despite his efforts, the legal battle proved arduous, and the odds were stacked against them. In the end, the family's patriarch, John Morrison, was sentenced to prison for life, with the possibility of parole.

It was a bitter pill for the Morrison family to swallow. Their way of life had clashed with the laws of the land, and now they were paying a heavy price. But in the midst of the turmoil, a glimmer of hope emerged. Daniel's dedication and legal expertise had secured the possibility of parole for his father, a chance for redemption and reconciliation.

As John Morrison began serving his sentence, a profound change took place within the family. They realized the importance of finding common ground between their values and the law of the land. Daniel had become the bridge that connected their two worlds, and his commitment to justice had left a lasting impact on them all.

Over time, the Morrison family started to mend the rift that had torn them apart. They recognized that Daniel's pursuit of a legal career was not a betrayal but an opportunity to bring their beliefs into the legal system and advocate for change from within.

In the end, the Morrison family learned that their love for each other could transcend their differences. They had come to understand that the pursuit of justice and the preservation of their way of life were not mutually exclusive. With Daniel's help, they began the long journey of reconciling their values with the laws of the land, and in doing so, they discovered a newfound sense of unity and purpose as a family.

As the Morrison family continued their journey towards reconciliation and finding common ground, another shocking revelation came to light, threatening to unravel the fragile bonds they had begun to rebuild.

One evening, as the family sat around the dinner table, the atmosphere was tense yet strangely peaceful. The legal battles that had plagued their lives for so long had taken a backseat to their efforts to heal as a family. It was during this moment of tentative calm that Sarah, the family matriarch, broke her long-held silence.

Tears welled up in her eyes as she began to speak, her voice trembling with emotion. She confessed to a dark secret that had haunted her for years. She admitted to a crime that had been committed years ago, a crime that had led to John Morrison's imprisonment.

She revealed that she, not her husband John, had committed the murder for which he had been accused. He took the blame for a crime he didn't commit, believing that she was protecting her husband and their way of life. It was a heavy burden that she had carried in silence, fearing the consequences for her family if the truth were to come to light.

The revelation sent shockwaves through the Morrison family. They couldn't believe what they were hearing. It was a profound moment of reckoning, as the family grappled with the weight of Sarah's confession. John had been wrongfully imprisoned for a crime he hadn't committed, and it was a secret that had torn their family apart.

In the days that followed, Daniel, now an experienced lawyer, embarked on a mission to clear his father's name. He dug deep into the case, gathering evidence and working tirelessly to prove John's innocence. The legal battle that ensued was as arduous as any the family had faced, but this time, it was to right a grave injustice.

With each new revelation, it became clear that Sarah's confession had been truthful. She had taken her punishment for the crime all in the name of protecting her family. It was a heartbreaking sacrifice that had torn their family apart, but it was also a testament to the depth of her love and devotion.

After a long and grueling legal battle, John Morrison's name was finally cleared. He was released from prison, a free man once more. The family's journey towards reconciliation had taken an unexpected turn, as they came to terms with the sacrifices made in the name of love and loyalty.

In the midst of the turmoil, one of the Morrison children, Emily, decided to write a book about their family's incredible journey. She wanted to capture the complexities of their relationships, the clash of values, and the profound love that had ultimately prevailed. The book became a bestseller, shedding light on the Morrison family's story of redemption and the enduring power of love.

As the years passed, the Morrison family continued to rebuild their lives, this time with a renewed sense of unity and purpose. They had learned that forgiveness was a powerful force, capable of healing even the deepest wounds. And in the face of adversity, they had discovered that their love for each other was a bond that could withstand anything life threw their way.

Their story became an inspiration to others, a testament to the resilience of the human spirit and the unbreakable bonds of family. The

Morrison family had faced the darkest of trials and emerged stronger and more united than ever, a living testament to the enduring power of love, sacrifice, and forgiveness.

In the wake of Sarah's confession and the redemption of John Morrison, the Morrison family had become a symbol of resilience and forgiveness. Emily's bestselling book had not only chronicled their journey but had also shed light on a series of murders that had rocked the family's history.

As the Morrison family delved deeper into their past, they discovered a painful truth that had long been buried beneath layers of secrecy and guilt. Several members of the family had been involved in a string of murders, crimes committed out of desperation, fear, or misguided loyalty to their unconventional way of life. These dark secrets had remained hidden for years, casting a shadow over the family's legacy.

Emily's book had not only explored the redemption of her father but also delved into the family's dark history of violence and murder. The revelations were shocking, and the family had to confront the painful truth about their own actions. They realized that the pursuit of their values had led them down a path of darkness, causing harm to others and tearing their own family apart.

As the family members confronted their own roles in the past, they felt a renewed sense of responsibility to make amends for the pain they had caused. They began to seek ways to help the families of their victims find closure and healing. It was a difficult and emotional journey, but it was a necessary step towards redemption and forgiveness.

The Morrison family decided to use their newfound unity and resources to establish a foundation dedicated to assisting the families affected by the crimes committed by their own members. They reached out to the victims' families, offering support, financial assistance, and heartfelt apologies for the pain they had caused.

Through their actions, the Morrison family aimed to bring healing and closure to those who had suffered because of their past actions. They knew that forgiveness was not just a word, but a series of actions taken to right the wrongs of the past.

In the years that followed, the Morrison family's foundation became a beacon of hope for the victims' families, a testament to their commitment to making amends. The family's story, as told in Emily's book, continued to inspire others to confront their own past mistakes and seek redemption.

The Morrison family had come full circle, from a family divided by secrets and guilt to one united by love, forgiveness, and a shared commitment to making the world a better place. They had learned that the power of forgiveness could heal even the deepest wounds and that redemption was possible for those willing to confront their past and take responsibility for their actions.

Their story served as a reminder that it was never too late to make amends, seek forgiveness, and find a path towards redemption, no matter how dark the past may have been.

• • •

As the Morrison family continued their journey towards redemption and reconciliation, they thought that they had faced the darkest chapters of their past. Little did they know that there were more secrets lurking in the shadows, waiting to be unveiled.

One day, as Emily's book gained even more popularity, it caught the attention of a determined and astute detective named Robert Mitchell. Detective Mitchell had a knack for uncovering hidden truths, and he couldn't ignore the disturbing revelations within the Morrison family's story.

He decided to dig deeper into the Morrison family's past, believing that there might be more to their story than what had been revealed in Emily's book. He started by gathering evidence, interviewing witnesses, and re-examining the cases of the unsolved murders from the past.

As Detective Mitchell pieced together the puzzle, he began to uncover a pattern of suspicious circumstances and connections that led him to believe that there were more murders within the Morrison family than had initially been revealed. He couldn't shake the feeling that there were still secrets waiting to be uncovered.

Detective Mitchell confronted the Morrison family with his findings, and it was during the intense interrogation that more shocking revelations came to light. Several other members of the family confessed to their involvement in additional murders, crimes that had been buried in secrecy for years.

The revelations sent shockwaves through the Morrison family, as they realized the extent of the crimes that had been committed in the name of their values and way of life. They were confronted with the painful truth that they had not only torn their own family apart but had also caused immense suffering to others.

As the evidence mounted, Sarah, the matriarch of the family who had previously confessed to a murder, was arrested, and charged with multiple counts of murder. The weight of her actions and the actions of her family had finally caught up with her, and she now faced the consequences of her choices.

The Morrison family, once on a path of redemption and healing, now found themselves facing a new and harrowing chapter in their lives. They had to come to terms with the full extent of their dark past and the role they had played in the crimes committed by their own members.

Elucidate

Elucidate, unravel the tangled threads,
Within this poem's web of pain and dread.
Let me shed light on this tale of woe,
And bring clarity to the depths below.
In a tunnel vision, our lives did roam,
As chaos reigned and spiraled too unknown.
Lost in translation, words in disarray,
Misunderstood, our lines went astray.
Explanations aplenty, but no solace found,
When he discovered her unfaithful ground.
It made no sense, unreasonable to see,
Expectations shattered, what life should be.
Yet her life excluded me, I pondered why,
Did I not measure up? Did I not try?
Was I present, did I truly care,
Did I see her pain and the burdens she'd bear?
Supporting her dreams, our family's embrace,
Engulfed in my career, I failed to trace,
The tears, the fear, the anguish she bore,
Her heart grew cold, as pain cut to the core.
Betrayal's bitter sting, she concealed her truth,
Played games, elusive, I couldn't deduce.
This wasn't the first time, I held on tight,
Believing our bond would conquer the night.
For better or worse, in sickness or health,
Till death do us part, our vow's sacred wealth.
But I didn't sign up for this twisted affair,
She demands my forgiveness, as if it were fair.
She wants me to provide, to give her my time,
To forgive her lies, her transgressions, her crime.
To forget her mistakes, grant her grace's embrace,
While I pay the price as a provider in this chase.
If only I had been there, more present, and near,
Her straying wouldn't have awakened my fear.
She needed my touch, my kisses, my hold,

To feel like a woman, her desires unfold.
Late-night texts, phone rings, and then silence,
No surprises left, her deceit forms alliance.
The child, not mine, yet I'm his only father,
DNA aside, love's bond I won't sever.
She claims DNA doesn't define a true dad,
Walking away deemed cowardly and sad.
But my heart and mind stand disconnected,
Her orchestrated words, I've long rejected.
One betrayal, perhaps forgiveness could find,
But multiple wounds, scars left behind.
And still, no father for her innocent son,
In this web of deceit, truth seems to shun.
So, elucidate, unravel the painful truth,
In this tale of love's distortion, uncouth.
Let clarity guide us through the murky haze,
And bring healing to hearts lost in this maze.

Intoxicating Soul

In the heart of South Africa, where the land stretched out like a canvas of dreams, there lived a goddess named Nefertiti. She was a beacon of beauty, a symbol of love, and a guardian of her people. Her presence was as intoxicating as the sweetest elixir, capable of captivating not just the mind but also the soul.

South Africa was a land of breathtaking landscapes and untold riches. It was a tapestry woven with the golden sands of deserts, the lush greenery of forests, and the crystal-clear waters of rivers that whispered secrets of the ages. The sun kissed the land with a warmth that made the earth bloom in vibrant colors, and the stars adorned the night sky like diamonds scattered across black velvet.

But the true treasures of South Africa lay in its history, a rich tapestry of queens and kings who had ruled with love and devotion for their people. Nefertiti was the latest in this lineage, a queen who had inherited not just a crown but also the immense love of her subjects.

Her beauty was renowned far and wide, her eyes like pools of liquid ebony that pierced the very core of those who beheld them. But Nefertiti was more than just a pretty face; she possessed an almost otherworldly charm that captivated not just the mind but also the soul. Her love was a source of eternal life and fulfillment, a hypothetical substance believed to maintain life indefinitely.

Her people adored her, not just for her stunning beauty, but for the overwhelming allure of her words and affection. She had a way with language that was both rich and evocative, capable of creating an atmosphere of allure and fascination. Her poetic disposition painted a vivid image of a mesmerizing and enchanting individual, often referred to as the "Intoxicating Soul Elixir."

Nefertiti's laughter rang like bells that chimed with joy, a melody that transcended time and echoed through the hearts of her people. Her touch was a potion, a rare magic, that soothed the wounds of past hurts and healed the deepest of scars. Her voice flowed like liquid gold, a river's song that created a soft plateau where her subjects could find solace.

Whenever Nefertiti wrapped her arms around someone, it was like being held in a warm and loving embrace. She filled their spirits to the brim with love and affection, leaving them craving for more of her presence. She wasn't just wine to tease the lip; she was something more, a potent sip that intoxicated the very core of one's being.

In every moment spent with Nefertiti, her people took the chance to savor all that she had to give. They cherished her love as a source of eternal life, and in her presence, they knew they would forever live. She was their goddess, their queen, their Intoxicating Soul Elixir, and she reigned over the land of South Africa with love, grace, and boundless beauty, creating a legacy that would endure through the ages.

Nefertiti was not just a queen of unparalleled beauty and love; she was also a woman of extraordinary intelligence and wealth. Her grace was not limited to her physical beauty alone; it transcended into her intellect and the riches she bestowed upon her kingdom.

As she walked, it seemed as though she floated above the earth. Her steps were so light and graceful that she appeared to glide on air, leaving behind a trail of enchantment wherever she went. People would gather from far and wide just to catch a glimpse of her, to witness the ethereal beauty and poise with which she moved. It was as if the very ground she walked upon was blessed by her presence.

Nefertiti's intelligence was as dazzling as her beauty. She possessed a keen mind that could unravel the most intricate of problems and devise solutions that left her advisors in awe. Her wisdom was sought not only by her people but also by neighboring kingdoms who recognized her as a beacon of knowledge and insight.

The riches of South Africa seemed to flow endlessly under her rule. The land yielded precious gems that sparkled like stars in the night sky, and gold that glimmered like the sun itself. These treasures were not hoarded, but instead, Nefertiti used them to improve the lives of her people. She built grand palaces and temples, created thriving markets, and ensured that her subjects had access to education and healthcare.

Nefertiti's beauty, intelligence, and wealth were matched only by her unwavering love for her people. She ruled with compassion and fairness, always putting their well-being above all else. Her subjects were not just citizens; they were her extended family, and she cared for them as such.

The love between Nefertiti and her people was mutual and boundless. They celebrated her not only for her outer beauty but for the beauty she carried within her heart. She was their protector, their guide, and their inspiration. In her, they found not just a queen but a goddess who graced their lives with love and abundance.

In the heart of South Africa, where the land was abundant, and the history was rich, Nefertiti reigned as the embodiment of beauty, intelligence, wealth, and love. Her legacy would endure through the ages, a testament to the power of a queen who had truly captured the hearts and souls of her people.

Nefertiti's pride in her heritage was as strong as the roots of the ancient baobab trees that dotted the South African landscape. Her lineage traced back to her mother and father, who had ruled as king and queen before her, and their story was one of inspiration and greatness.

Her father, a man with dark, mahogany skin, possessed a regal presence that commanded respect from all who met him. His eyes, the same beautiful shade of light brown as Nefertiti's, were soul-piercing and filled with wisdom. He was a man of great intelligence, fluent in several languages, and he had a remarkable ability to negotiate and form alliances with neighboring kingdoms. Under his rule, the kingdom of South Africa flourished, and the wealth of the land began to shine even brighter.

Nefertiti's mother, equally resplendent in her dark skin, was the embodiment of grace and elegance. Her beauty was a radiant force, captivating those who had the privilege of seeing her. She was as intelligent as her husband, and together they taught their people the art of business and trade, imparting the skills needed for success. The prosperity of their reign was evident in the opulence of their palace, and the clothing they adorned was nothing short of what one would find in a magazine.

Nefertiti grew up in this environment of beauty, intelligence, and prosperity. She learned from her parents not just how to rule a kingdom but also how to lead with compassion and love. They instilled in her a deep sense of responsibility towards her people, and she inherited their ability to speak multiple languages, fostering diplomacy and unity within her realm.

The legacy of her parents was a guiding light for Nefertiti. She carried their teachings and values with her as she ascended to the throne. She understood that her beauty, intelligence, and wealth were gifts meant to be shared for the betterment of her kingdom, and she ruled with the same grace and fairness that her parents had exemplified.

Nefertiti's reign was a continuation of her family's legacy, a legacy that celebrated the richness of South Africa's history and the love and devotion of its rulers for their people. She knew that she was not just a queen but a custodian of a proud heritage, and she wore that responsibility with pride and honor. Her story, intertwined with the stories of her parents and her people, would echo through the ages as a testament to the greatness that could be achieved when beauty, intelligence, wealth, and love were combined in the heart of a compassionate ruler.

Nefertiti's family was not just a source of inspiration for her; it was a testament to the enduring legacy of greatness. She had two sisters and five brothers, each as rich in intelligence, wealth, and love for their people as she was. Together, they formed a formidable family of rulers, spreading their influence and prosperity across different kingdoms.

Her eldest sister, Cleopatra, was known for her stunning beauty, which rivaled Nefertiti's. She ruled a neighboring kingdom, and her palace was renowned for its grandeur and opulence. Cleopatra was not just a queen but a diplomat who forged alliances with neighboring realms, fostering peace and cooperation in the region. Her people adored her for her wisdom and benevolence.

Amina, Nefertiti's second sister, was a fierce warrior queen who ruled a kingdom on the borderlands. Her strength and strategic brilliance were unmatched, and she led her armies with valor and honor. Amina was also a champion of women's rights, ensuring that her female subjects had the same opportunities as men in her kingdom.

Among Nefertiti's brothers, there were those who ruled neighboring kingdoms, each flourishing under their leadership. Osiris was known for his prowess in trade and commerce, turning his kingdom into a hub of economic prosperity. Thutmose, a master architect, built magnificent monuments and temples that stood as a testament to his reign's splendor. Akhenaten, with his philosophical mind, encouraged intellectual pursuits and the arts, creating a kingdom known for its cultural richness. Horus, the youngest of Nefertiti's brothers, was a scholar and philosopher who governed with a gentle and wise hand. His kingdom was a haven for scholars, artists, and thinkers from far and wide. Together, these brothers and sisters formed a network of powerful and benevolent rulers who supported one another in times of need.

Despite their wealth and influence, each of Nefertiti's siblings remained deeply connected to their roots and the love they had for their people. They ruled with the same compassion and dedication instilled in them by their parents. The bond between these siblings was unbreakable, a testament to the values and principles passed down through generations.

Nefertiti was immensely proud of her family's legacy and the way they collectively enriched the lives of their subjects. They were not just rulers; they were stewards of their lands, champions of justice, and protectors of their people. The story of the royal family of South Africa, with its beauty, intelligence, wealth, and love, continued to inspire generations, a beacon of hope and greatness that shone brightly across the African continent.

Three times a year, or more if time allowed, the royal family of South Africa came together for a grand and joyous occasion: the Royal Family Dinner. It was a celebration of their unity, love, and shared commitment to their people.

Each sibling brought their favorite dish from their respective kingdoms, creating a sumptuous feast that showcased the diverse and rich culinary traditions of South Africa. Cleopatra, known for her diplomatic skills, brought dishes that blended flavors from neighboring regions, symbolizing peace, and cooperation. Amina's contribution was hearty and robust, reflecting the strength and resilience of her warrior spirit. Osiris, the master of trade, brought exotic spices and delicacies from distant lands, enriching the meal with a tapestry of flavors. Thutmose, the master architect, contributed not just dishes but also visually stunning presentations, turning the dining table into a work of art. Akhenaten, with his love for intellectual pursuits, often engaged in lively discussions about philosophy, science, and art during the dinner, stimulating the minds of all in attendance. Horus, the scholar, and philosopher shared ancient wisdom and stories that resonated with the hearts of those gathered.

Nefertiti, as the host, welcomed her siblings with open arms, and their presence filled the palace with warmth and love. The dinner table was a sight to behold, adorned with dishes that were a testament to their unity and the rich cultural heritage of their homeland.

Gifts were exchanged during these gatherings, not as a display of wealth, but as tokens of affection and appreciation. The siblings knew that their greatest treasures were the bonds they shared and the love they had for one another. These gifts were a way to express their gratitude for the unwavering support they received from one another.

As the night continued, laughter, music, and dance filled the air. The royal family celebrated not just their shared bloodline but the shared purpose they had in serving their people. They knew that their love and unity were a source of inspiration for their subjects and a testament to the power of a united and compassionate leadership.

The Royal Family Dinner was a cherished tradition that reinforced the ties that bound the family together. It was a reminder that their greatness was not just about individual accomplishments but the collective impact they had on their beloved South Africa. As they toasted to their love, unity, and the bright future of their kingdom, Nefertiti and her siblings knew that their legacy of beauty, intelligence, wealth, and love would continue to shine brightly, illuminating the hearts of their people for generations to come.

With the Royal Family Dinner serving as a symbol of their unity and love, the royal family of South Africa knew that they had a responsibility to pass down their legacy and traditions to the next generation. They were determined to ensure that the values of beauty, intelligence, wealth, and, most importantly, love for their people, would endure for generations to come.

During the gatherings, they often discussed their plans for the future and how to prepare their children for leadership. They believed in nurturing the potential within each young prince and princess, encouraging them to pursue their passions and develop their own strengths. Nefertiti and her siblings understood that true greatness lay in the ability to empower and guide the next generation.

As the years passed, the children of the royal family began to play a more active role in the Royal Family Dinner. They were taught the significance of the event, the importance of unity, and the values that had been the foundation of their family's legacy. The young heirs were eager to learn from their wise parents and aunts and uncles, absorbing the wisdom that had been passed down through the ages.

The tradition of the Royal Family Dinner became not just a celebration of their accomplishments but a platform for mentorship and guidance. The younger generation witnessed the love, respect, and camaraderie that existed among their elders and understood the importance of cooperation and unity in leadership.

As the years went by, the children of Nefertiti and her siblings assumed leadership positions in their respective kingdoms, continuing the family's tradition of benevolent rule. They were well-prepared, having been instilled with the values of compassion, fairness, and the love for their people.

The royal family of South Africa understood that their legacy was not just about the past but also the future. They were committed to nurturing the potential of their children, just as their parents had nurtured theirs. Through the Royal Family Dinner and their continued guidance, they ensured that the flame of their legacy would burn bright, illuminating the hearts and minds of South Africa for generations yet to come.

And so, the story of the royal family of South Africa continued, a legacy of beauty, intelligence, wealth, and most importantly, love, that transcended time and would forever shine as a beacon of hope, inspiration, and greatness.

Intoxicating Soul Elixir

Her beauty fearlessly beholds eyes

Pierce you're core
she wants just to captivate your mind
she will intoxicate your soul
guaranteed to induce love
a hypothetical substance
believed to maintain life indefinitely

Her love is a source of eternal life
and fulfillment. She is an irresistible,
captivating figure
who embodies love and allure,
leaving a lasting impression
on all who encounter her.

Her presence gleams with pure delight,
She weaves her words, a mystic art,
To stir the depths of every heart.
Her laughter rings like bells that chime,
A melody that transcends time,

Her touch, a potion, magic rare,
It soothes the wounds of past hurt
Like liquid gold, her voice will flow,
A river's song, a soft plateau,
She wraps around you, warm and tight,
And fills your spirit to the brim.

She's not just wine to tease the lip,
But something more, a potent sip,
She'll intoxicate your very core,

Her essence leaves you craving more.
So let her in, embrace the trance,
In every moment, take the chance,

To savor all she has to give,
And in her love, you will forever live.

She possesses an almost otherworldly charm
that captivates not just the mind
but also, the soul.
Her presence is described
 as a source of pure delight,
capable of stirring deep emotions
within every heart
the overwhelming allure
of her words and affection

The language she uses is rich
and evocative,
creating an atmosphere
of allure and fascination.
Her poetic disposition
paints a vivid image
of a mesmerizing
and enchanting individual,
refer to her as the
"Intoxicating Soul Elixir."

Self-Doubt

Denise, a young girl of undeniable beauty and intelligence, lived her life in a constant battle with herself. She was a go-getter, always striving to achieve her goals, but behind her success, there was a dark cloud of doubt that followed her wherever she went.

She would look at herself in the mirror each morning, examining her reflection with a critical eye. "Why can't I be as confident as others?" she would often ask herself, her thoughts echoing in the silence of her room. Denise had always felt like an imposter in her own life, as if her accomplishments were merely flukes, and her beauty was nothing more than a facade.

The world around her seemed to be filled with people who radiated self-assuredness, their smiles and laughter masking the insecurities that Denise felt deep within. She couldn't help but compare herself to others, wondering why she couldn't be as self-assured as her friends, her colleagues, or even the strangers she saw on social media.

One day, as Denise scrolled through her social media feed, a message popped up from a stranger. "Hey beautiful," it began, and the conversation quickly escalated. Denise was taken aback by the stranger's persistence. "Don't be rude," he urged when she hesitated to respond promptly.

Denise's heart raced as she realized that this person was trying to manipulate her with flattery and guilt. It was then that she remembered the words of her grandmother, who had always told her, "Knowing your worth is a great start."

Denise decided to take those words to heart. She realized that she needed to value herself more and not let the opinions of others, especially strangers on the internet, define her self-worth. She politely but firmly told the stranger that she was not interested in continuing the conversation and blocked him.

Over time, Denise started to work on her self-esteem and self-doubt. She sought therapy to address the underlying issues that had plagued her for so long. She began to surround herself with supportive friends and family who reminded her of her strengths and accomplishments.

As the days turned into weeks and the weeks into months, Denise's self-esteem gradually improved. She learned to appreciate her own beauty and intelligence, recognizing that they were not just superficial attributes but parts of what made her unique. She stopped comparing herself to others and started celebrating her own achievements, big or small.

Denise's journey towards self-acceptance was not easy, and there were moments when self-doubt still crept in. However, she had found her voice and her inner strength, and she knew that she was on the path to becoming the confident, self-assured woman she had always wanted to be.

In a world filled with unspoken phrases and hidden insecurities, Denise had learned the power of knowing her worth. She had taken the first step in breaking free from the chains of self-doubt and low self-esteem, and she was determined to continue her journey towards self-love and self-acceptance.

As Denise continued on her journey towards self-love and self-acceptance, she encountered both challenges and triumphs. The therapy sessions provided her with a safe space to explore the root causes of her self-doubt and low self-esteem. She discovered that these negative feelings had been deeply ingrained in her from childhood experiences and societal pressures.

With the help of her therapist, Denise learned techniques to challenge her negative thought patterns. She began to replace self-criticism with self-compassion and self-affirmation. Each day, she would stand in front of the mirror and repeat positive affirmations to herself, gradually rebuilding her self-esteem.

Denise also started to engage in activities that brought her joy and a sense of accomplishment. She joined a community theater group, where she discovered her love for acting and found a supportive and encouraging group of friends. Through acting, she learned to step into different roles and embrace her creativity, which boosted her self-confidence.

One sunny afternoon, Denise decided to create an Instagram account dedicated to sharing her journey towards self-acceptance. She shared her experiences, her struggles, and the steps she was taking to overcome her self-doubt. To her surprise, the response was overwhelmingly positive. People from all around the world reached out to express their own struggles and offer words of encouragement.

Denise realized that she was not alone in her journey. Many people, just like her, battled with self-doubt and low self-esteem. They were inspired by her vulnerability and strength, and Denise found a sense of purpose in helping others on their path to self-acceptance.

Over time, Denise's Instagram account grew into a supportive community of individuals who uplifted and empowered each other. She organized virtual workshops and discussions on self-esteem, mental health, and self-love. Through these activities, she not only helped others but also continued to reinforce her newfound self-worth.

As months turned into years, Denise became a beacon of hope for those struggling with self-esteem issues. Her journey had transformed her into a confident and self-assured woman who no longer doubted her worth. She had learned that beauty and intelligence were not the only measures of value. It was the love and acceptance she had for herself that truly mattered.

Denise's story served as a reminder that the path to self-acceptance was a journey, not a destination. It required patience, self-compassion, and a supportive community. She had turned her once unspoken words of doubt into a powerful message of self-love and empowerment, inspiring others to do the same. In the end, Denise realized that she was not just a go-getter in her external achievements but also in her internal transformation, proving that true beauty and strength came from within.

Words Unspoken

In this word of so many pretty faces
Some painted hidden behind fear, anxiety, hurt, anger, and tears.

Self-doubt, low self-esteem, regret and resentment
plastered across social media pages
There are predators waiting.

He drops a DM hey beautiful I came across your page
and wanted to let you know that. The next five minutes hey there

Don't be rude
Answer me I want bite I'm nice
What's behind his persistent?

Knowing your worth is a great start

In this world of unspoken phrases,
Behind painted smiles and guarded gazes,
Lies a truth so deep and raw,
Waiting to be heard, yet never saw.
Self-doubt, low self-esteem, and pain,
Resentment and regret, our silent chains,
Bound to these emotions, we seek escape,
In the vast realm of cyberspace.
A predator waits, ready to pounce,
On vulnerability, ounce by ounce,
With sweet words, he tries to ensnare,
His true intentions, he'll never share.
"Hey beautiful," he starts the game,
Persistence wrapped in a friendly frame,
"Don't be rude," he prods and pleads,
Hoping to fulfill his hidden needs.
But knowing your worth, you must remain strong,
For it's the first step to right the wrong,
Hold your head high and don't be swayed,
By those who wish to see you fray.
For in this world of unspoken words,
It's important to let your voice be heard,
Rise above the fears and tears,
And become the master of your own sphere.

Twin

Max and his twin sister, Mia, were two peas in a luxurious pod. They lived in the bustling city of San Francisco, where the pursuit of extravagance was a way of life. From their lavish penthouse apartment, they had a spectacular view of the city's skyline, a constant reminder of the opulent lifestyle they desired.

Both Max and Mia were driven by a burning desire for expensive things. They craved designer clothes, fancy cars, and the finest jewelry. Their lives were a never-ending chase to acquire the most extravagant possessions, and they would stop at nothing to achieve their goals.

Their days were filled with work, Max at a high-paying corporate job and Mia as a successful fashion designer. Every spare moment was devoted to chasing their dreams of wealth and luxury, even if it meant sacrificing their well-being and relationships.

One evening, as they sat in their penthouse, overlooking the glittering city lights, Max turned to Mia and said, "Mia, we've been chasing after these expensive things for so long, but I can't help but feel like we're missing something important."

Mia glanced at her brother, intrigued. "What do you mean, Max?" Max sighed, "I mean, we're so focused on material success that we've forgotten to live. We're neglecting our mental, emotional, and physical health in the pursuit of these possessions. What's the point of having all these things if we're not truly happy and healthy?"

Mia hesitated for a moment, contemplating Max's words. She realized that her brother was right. They had become slaves to their desires for expensive things, and it was taking a toll on their well-being.

The next day, Max and Mia decided to make a change. They started by setting aside time for self-care, practicing meditation, and spending quality time with each other and their friends. They also began to volunteer at a local charity, helping those less fortunate than themselves.

As the weeks passed, Max and Mia discovered a newfound sense of balance in their lives. They still pursued their dreams of wealth and luxury but with a healthier perspective. They no longer sacrificed their well-being for material possessions.

One day, Mia received an invitation to a high-profile fashion event showcasing her designs. She was excited but realized that the event was on the same day as a charity event she had committed to volunteering for.

Max encouraged her to follow her passion but reminded her of the importance of balance. Mia decided to attend the fashion event but made arrangements for someone else to represent her at the charity event. She knew that both her career and her commitment to helping others could coexist.

At the fashion event, Mia's designs received rave reviews, and she felt a sense of fulfillment she had never experienced before. Meanwhile, Max continued to excel in his corporate job, but he now took regular breaks to appreciate the beauty of the city and the simple joys of life.

Together, Max and Mia embraced a life of balance. They still pursued their love for expensive things, but they did so without losing sight of what truly mattered—their mental, emotional, and physical well-being, and the joy of living life to the fullest.

As they looked out from their penthouse at the city below, they realized that true success was not just about material gain but about maintaining a harmonious balance in life. They whispered the secrets of balance to each other, reminding themselves and those around them that in the pursuit of dreams, it was essential never to forget to live.

• • •

Mia had a secret that she hadn't shared with him yet. Mia had recently become connected with some dangerous individuals who were involved in bank robberies. The allure of easy money was too enticing for her to resist.

One night, she finally confessed to Max. "Max, there's something I haven't told you. I've been connected with some people who have been robbing banks, and they want me to join them. It's a way to get the money we've always dreamed of the fast track to the lifestyle we desire."

Max was taken aback by Mia's revelation. He knew it was a risky and illegal path, but he also understood the immense pressure and temptation his sister was under. After a long, contemplative silence, he said, "Mia, I can't condone illegal activities, and I can't join you in this. We need to find a legal and ethical way to achieve our goals."

Mia was disappointed but understood Max's stance. However, the temptation was too strong for her to resist. She decided to go ahead with the bank robbery plan, with or without Max's involvement. She met with the bank robbers, who had an inside connection to the bank they targeted.

The heist was meticulously planned, and they executed it flawlessly, escaping with a staggering 2.5 million dollars. Mia's adrenaline surged, and she was hooked. She felt invincible, believing that she had finally found the shortcut to the life of luxury she had always coveted.

She approached Max once more, urging him to join her in another bank robbery. Max was skeptical at first, but seeing the euphoria and determination in Mia's eyes, he reluctantly agreed to go along with the plan, hoping he could keep her safe.

This time, however, their luck ran out. Unbeknownst to them, one of the bank robbers was an undercover cop. As they attempted the robbery, the police surrounded the bank. A chaotic and intense standoff ensued.

Mia and Max found themselves cornered, with no way out. Mia was arrested, her dreams of luxury crumbling before her. Max stood by her, hiring the best lawyer money could buy to defend his sister. He was determined to support her, even though he knew this wouldn't stop her from chasing her tail.

As Mia faced the consequences of her actions, Max couldn't help but reflect on the pursuit of material success and its consequences. He knew that true success should never come at the expense of one's moral compass and well-being. Max hoped that Mia would eventually find a way to balance her ambitions and desires with a more ethical and fulfilling path in life.

• • •

The trial for Mia's involvement in the bank robbery was intense and highly publicized. The evidence against her was overwhelming, and the media painted her as a criminal mastermind who had led a double life while chasing her extravagant dreams.

Throughout the trial, Max stood by his sister's side, unwavering in his support. He had hired the best lawyer money could buy, and they presented a strong defense, emphasizing Mia's remorse and her willingness to change. Max knew that Mia's actions were driven by a deep-rooted desire for a better life, but he also recognized that she needed to face the consequences of her choices.

As the trial proceeded, Mia began to realize the gravity of her actions. The courtroom became a place of introspection for her, as she understood the pain and suffering her pursuit of wealth had caused not only to herself but also to her family. She felt a growing sense of shame and guilt.

Despite their efforts, the jury found Mia guilty of her involvement in the bank robbery. She was sentenced to several years in prison. Max was devastated, but he continued to support his sister, visiting her regularly and sending her letters filled with encouragement.

During her time in prison, Mia had plenty of time to reflect on her life choices. She began to attend therapy sessions and participated in various rehabilitation programs. Slowly, she started to understand the importance of balance and self-reflection, just as Max had urged her to do before.

Max also used this time to reevaluate his own life. He realized that his ambition for wealth had blinded him to the simpler joys and relationships that truly mattered. He decided to make changes in his own life, pursuing success with a more ethical and balanced approach.

As the years passed, Mia served her sentence and was eventually released from prison. Max welcomed her back into their lives with open arms, and they both vowed to leave their pursuit of illegal wealth behind them. Instead, they focused on rebuilding their relationship and their lives with a newfound appreciation for what truly mattered.

They channeled their energy into legitimate endeavors, using their skills and talents to make a positive impact on their community. Max's corporate job allowed him to support various charitable causes, while Mia used her fashion design skills to create clothing lines that promoted sustainable and ethical practices.

Together, Max and Mia learned the true meaning of success. It wasn't about the pursuit of material wealth at any cost but about finding balance, living ethically, and nurturing their mental, emotional, and physical well-being. They whispered the secrets of balance to each other and to anyone who would listen, inspiring others to find their own path to a life well-lived.

Max and Mia's journey towards a balanced and fulfilling life continued long after Mia's release from prison. They were determined to make amends for their past mistakes and use their experiences to help others find a better way to live.

Mia, deeply changed by her time in prison and her journey of self-discovery, became an advocate for criminal justice reform. She used her own story as a powerful example of the importance of rehabilitation and second chances. Mia started working with organizations that supported individuals transitioning back into society after incarceration, helping them find stable employment and rebuild their lives.

Max, on the other hand, remained committed to his corporate

career but with a newfound sense of purpose. He used his influence and resources to advocate for ethical business practices within his company and the industry at large. He supported initiatives that promoted employee well-being, sustainability, and social responsibility.

Together, Max and Mia founded a non-profit organization called "Whispers of Balance," inspired by the lessons they had learned on their journey. The organization aimed to provide support and resources to individuals and families struggling with the pressures of modern life, reminding them of the importance of balance in their pursuit of success.

They traveled to schools, community centers, and corporate offices, sharing their story and encouraging others to prioritize mental, emotional, and physical well-being. They emphasized the value of nurturing relationships, caring for the environment, and giving back to the community.

As the years passed, Max and Mia's message began to resonate with people from all walks of life. "Whispers of Balance" grew into a global movement, inspiring countless individuals to reevaluate their priorities and seek a more balanced and meaningful existence.

Max and Mia had come full circle, transforming from individuals driven solely by the pursuit of expensive things to advocates for a balanced and ethical way of life. They found purpose in helping others find their own path to happiness and fulfillment, whispering the secrets of balance to all who were willing to listen, and in doing so, they left a lasting legacy of positive change in their wake.

Twin Whispers: A Journey to Balance

Twin hearts, bound by blood and strife,
Max and Mia, chasing a luxurious life.
City lights gleamed in San Francisco's glow,
A skyline of dreams, yet shadows below.

Designer threads and diamonds' sheen,
The lust for more was their shared routine.
Days of toil, nights of plans,
Reaching for wealth with restless hands.

But from the heights of their penthouse view,
Max saw the truth that pierced him through.
"Mia," he whispered, "what's the gain,
If we're shackled by this endless chain?"
Mia paused, her heart unsure,
The chase for riches, was it the cure?

Yet secrets lingered in her restless mind,
A darker path she'd soon unwind.
A lure of crime, an alluring game,
A heist that promised fortune and fame.
Max stood firm, his conscience clear,
But love for his twin held him near.

The plan unraveled, their luck ran dry,
Sirens wailed beneath the sky.
Behind cold bars, Mia wept,
As dreams of grandeur silently crept.

Years of penance, lessons learned,
The fire of change within her burned.
Max, steadfast, beside her stayed,
Through letters of hope, their guilt allayed.

From opulence chased to purpose found,
They built a life on steadier ground.

"Whispers of Balance," their noble cause,
A call to those in life's harsh jaws.
Now, they roam where shadows fall,
Murmuring truths to one and all.

Success is fleeting, if balance is lost,
A precious truth, no matter the cost.
Mia and Max, their journey clear,
Twins of hope, with whispers sincere.
From city lights to hearts aglow,
They teach the world what they now know.

Tailspin

In the heart of Watts, California, where a woman named Patricia resided, who, to the eyes of her fellow churchgoers, seemed to be the epitome of holiness. She was always dressed in the finest church fashion, and she made sure to generously contribute her tithes and offerings, and then some, to the congregation. To everyone in the church, Patricia was the ideal Christian, but behind closed doors, she was a different person entirely.

Patricia had two children, but she harbored a deep disdain for them, especially for her youngest, Ana. Ana had known nothing but neglect and abuse from her mother since she was a little girl. Patricia's anger and resentment often bubbled to the surface, leading to cruel punishments and physical violence. Ana's earliest memories were of her mother's wrath, as early as seven years old.

Whenever Patricia became upset, which was all too frequent, Ana would be thrown out of their home into the dangerous, dark streets of Watts. She would wander aimlessly, vulnerable, and terrified. The bruises on her body, the black eyes, broken arms, and cuts on her legs were visible evidence of the horrors she endured.

But it didn't stop there. Patricia's cruelty knew no bounds. She even attempted to poison her own daughter, hoping to rid herself of the burden that Ana represented. Despite the evidence of abuse, Ana was repeatedly returned to Patricia's care after a few short months in the foster care system. The court system, influenced by Patricia's façade of religious devotion and the support of the church community, believed that family reunification was in Ana's best interest.

As Ana grew older, she was shuttled back and forth between her mother and her grandmother's house. Patricia would often complain to the courts, demanding that Ana be placed in foster care. She used every tool at her disposal to punish Ana for merely existing, and it seemed that nothing could save the young girl from her mother's torment.

Patricia's cruelty escalated to terrifying levels. She attempted to take Ana's life on several occasions, suffocating her in her sleep, trying to drown her in the bathtub, and even strangling her in fits of rage. Ana's resilience and will to survive were the only things that kept her alive through these harrowing ordeals.

Eventually, Ana had had enough. She began running away, seeking refuge wherever she could find it, no matter how grim the situation. Life on the streets was harsh, and Ana found herself in many horrifying situations, but anything seemed better than the torment of her mother's house.

Ana's life on the streets of Watts was a brutal struggle for survival. She roamed the gritty neighborhood, often sleeping in abandoned buildings or seeking refuge with strangers who offered temporary shelter. She became acquainted with the harsh realities of life, learning to fend for herself in a world where trust was a rare commodity.

Despite the dangers she faced on the streets, Ana knew it was a safer option than enduring her mother Patricia's relentless abuse. The memory of her mother's attempts on her life haunted her every night, and she was haunted by the fear that one day, Patricia might succeed in her sinister intentions.

One particularly cold and rainy night, Ana found herself seeking shelter in an alleyway, huddled under a cardboard box she had fashioned into a makeshift shelter. As the rain poured down and the wind howled, she wondered if there would ever be an end to her suffering. She had seen other children in similar situations, some who had given in to the despair, turning to drugs or crime as an escape from their grim reality. But Ana remained determined to rise above her circumstances.

It was during this dark time that Ana crossed paths with a compassionate stranger named Sarah. Sarah, a social worker with a heart of gold, had been working in Watts for years, trying to make a difference in the lives of at-risk children. She had heard about Ana's story through the grapevine and had been searching for her for months, determined to offer her a lifeline.

One fateful evening, as Sarah was doing her rounds, she spotted Ana shivering in the alley. She approached her cautiously, offering a warm blanket and a hot meal. Ana, initially wary of strangers, felt a glimmer of hope as she looked into Sarah's kind eyes. It was a small act of kindness, but it was enough to begin to melt the walls that Ana had built around her heart.

Over the next few weeks, Sarah continued to visit Ana, bringing her food, clothing, and companionship. She listened to Ana's painful stories and assured her that there were people who cared about her well-being. Sarah was determined to rescue Ana from the clutches of her abusive mother and the unforgiving streets.

Sarah's persistence paid off as she began the process of involving Child Protective Services (CPS). This time, the evidence of Ana's abuse was overwhelming, and Patricia's facade of religious devotion began to crumble under the scrutiny of the law. With the support of her caring social worker and a team of dedicated professionals, Ana was finally placed in a loving foster home where she could begin to heal.

It was a long and challenging journey, but Ana's resilience prevailed. She went on to graduate from high school, excelling in her studies, and eventually pursued a career in social work herself. Ana's past experiences gave her a unique perspective and a burning desire to make a difference in the lives of other children who suffered as she once had.

As for Patricia, justice caught up with her, and she faced the consequences of her actions in the eyes of the law. Her once-thriving church community began to see through her deceit, and her standing among them crumbled. She was left to ponder the true meaning of her faith and the damage her actions had wrought.

Ana's story serves as a reminder that even in the darkest of times, there can be hope, and that the power of kindness and resilience can overcome even the most horrifying of circumstances.

Ana's life took a dramatic turn for the better once she was placed in her loving foster home. The family that welcomed her with open arms provided the warmth, safety, and stability she had never known. Her foster parents, Lisa, and David were patient, nurturing, and dedicated to helping Ana heal from the deep scars left by her traumatic past.

Under their care, Ana began to rebuild her shattered self-esteem and trust in others. Lisa and David enrolled her in therapy to address the emotional trauma she had endured. Through counseling, Ana learned healthy ways to cope with her past and discovered her inner strength. Her dreams of a brighter future began to take shape.

In high school, Ana's determination and resilience shone through. She excelled academically and became involved in extracurricular activities that allowed her to explore her interests and passions. It was during this time that Sarah, the compassionate social worker who had changed her life, continued to mentor Ana. Sarah became a guiding force, encouraging Ana to pursue her dreams of helping other at-risk children.

With Sarah's support and guidance, Ana decided to pursue a career in social work, just like her mentor. She wanted to make a difference in the lives of children who had experienced the same hardships she had endured. Ana's journey from a vulnerable and abused child to a determined and compassionate young woman was an inspiration to everyone who knew her.

As Ana entered college to study social work, she became actively involved in organizations and initiatives that aimed to support vulnerable youth. She used her experiences to connect with the children she helped, offering them empathy, understanding, and hope. Ana's story resonated with many, reminding them that there was always a chance for a better life, no matter how dire their circumstances might be.

While Ana was building her new life, Patricia faced the consequences of her actions. The evidence of her abuse could not be ignored any longer, and she was brought to justice. She was convicted of her crimes and sentenced to serve time in prison. Behind bars, Patricia had ample time to reflect on her actions and the harm she had caused her own child.

The church community that had once embraced Patricia now distanced themselves from her, realizing the depth of her hypocrisy. They began to focus on true faith, compassion, and helping those in need rather than blindly following someone who had used religion as a shield for her heinous actions.

Ana's story became an inspiration not only to those she helped as a social worker but also to her foster family, her mentors, and anyone who heard of her incredible journey from darkness to light. She showed the world that, with the support of caring individuals and the determination to rise above one's circumstances, it was possible to overcome even the most horrifying of beginnings and emerge stronger, wiser, and ready to make a difference in the lives of others.

Ana's college years were a time of growth and transformation. She dove headfirst into her social work studies, driven by the burning desire to make a meaningful impact on the lives of at-risk children, just as Sarah and her foster parents had done for her. Ana's professors recognized her dedication and potential, offering guidance and mentorship as she pursued her dreams.

During her summers and school breaks, Ana interned at various organizations that focused on child welfare and trauma recovery. She witnessed firsthand the struggles and hardships faced by many children, further fueling her determination to advocate for their rights and well-being.

As she graduated with honors and earned her degree in social work, Ana received an opportunity to work at a prominent nonprofit organization dedicated to helping abused and neglected children. Her journey had come full circle, and she was now in a position to effect real change in the lives of those who had experienced similar traumas to her own.

In her role as a social worker, Ana was unwavering in her commitment to her clients. She provided a safe space for them to express their pain and fears, just as Sarah had done for her all those years ago. She offered empathy, understanding, and a sense of hope, proving that healing and recovery were possible, even in the face of unimaginable adversity.

Ana's story continued to inspire others, and her dedication to her work garnered recognition and support from her colleagues and supervisors. She became a leading advocate for child welfare reform in her community, using her voice to push for changes in the system that had failed her as a child.

Meanwhile, Patricia languished in prison, facing the consequences of her actions and the weight of her guilt. She had ample time to reflect on the pain she had inflicted on her own flesh and blood, and the facade of religious devotion that had allowed her to escape justice for so long.

Over the years, Patricia underwent a transformation of her own. She sought counseling and therapy to address the underlying issues that had fueled her abusive behavior. She came to terms with the harm she had caused her children and the damage she had done to her relationship with her faith.

Upon her release from prison, Patricia reached out to Ana, hoping to make amends for the unforgivable sins of her past. Ana, now a strong and confident woman, agreed to meet her mother, but it was on her own terms. She needed to ensure that Patricia had truly changed and was committed to a path of redemption.

Their reunion was a painful but necessary step on both of their journeys towards healing. Patricia expressed genuine remorse for her actions and vowed to spend the rest of her life working to make amends for the pain she had caused her children.

Ana, though scarred by her past, found it in her heart to forgive her mother, recognizing that true redemption was possible for anyone who sought it earnestly. While their relationship would never be the same, they both embarked on separate journeys of healing, reconciliation, and personal growth.

Ana's story continued to inspire those who crossed her path. She proved that even in the darkest of circumstances, one could find the strength to overcome, to thrive, and to make a profound difference in the lives of others. Ana's life was a testament to the power of resilience, forgiveness, and the unwavering belief that, no matter the past, the future could always be shaped for the better.

As Ana tried to Patricia began the challenging process of rebuilding their relationship, they both knew it would not be easy. The wounds of the past ran deep, and trust had been shattered. Ana wished for a glimmer of hope, a shared desire for reconciliation and redemption.

Patricia never remained committed to her path of transformation. She continued to skip therapy and never sought support from a local church group that focused on healing and personal growth. She continued to be hateful towards Ana.

Ana, on the other hand, was thriving in her career as a social worker. Her tireless advocacy for child welfare reform had started to yield results, and she was instrumental in implementing changes that improved the lives of many vulnerable children in her community. Her work was a testament to her unwavering commitment to making the world a better place for those who had suffered as she once had.

Over time, Ana stopped expecting Patricia to changed and moved on with her life. She tried to have an open and honest conversations, addressing the pain and anger that had festered for so long. Patricia did not want to listen to Ana's accounts of her tumultuous childhood and never expressed genuine remorse for the years of abuse and neglect.

Ana, in turn, shared her journey of healing and the profound impact that her foster parents, Lisa and David, had on her life. She spoke of the transformative power of forgiveness and how her work as a social worker was a way to give back and ensure that other children didn't have to endure the same horrors she had faced.

As the years passed, their relationship slowly dissipated. Patricia never made amends with Ana or with her older child, whom she had neglected as well. They realized that they would never be a functional family or have a bound.

Ana's story continued to inspire those around her, proving that the power of resilience, forgiveness, and the unwavering belief in the capacity for change could heal even the deepest wounds. Her dedication to advocating for at-risk children created a lasting legacy, and she remained a beacon of hope for those who had experienced similar traumas.

• • •

Ana's journey was one of survival against all odds, a tale of a young girl's resilience in the face of unspeakable cruelty. She longed for a life where love and care would replace the darkness that had haunted her for so long, but for now, she was determined to escape the clutches of her abusive and neglectful mother, Patricia, no matter the cost.

Holiness

In the shadowed halls of piety, she'd appear,
Patricia, the church's holiness revered,
In finest fashion, tithes and offerings flowed,
But behind those closed doors,
a darkness showed.

Two children bore the weight of her disdain,
Especially Ana, she caused endless pain,
From tender years, the abuse did start,
Ana's shattered world, her broken heart.

When Patricia's anger raged, and darkness fell,
Ana in the night, through Watts would dwell,
Bruises marked her body, wounds did scar,
The horrors Ana faced, both near and far.

But cruelty knew no bounds within this place,
Poisoned dreams, a mother's cold embrace,
Returned to torment, by a court's decree,
Ana's hopes shattered; her spirit never free.

From mother's house to grandmother's care she'd roam,
A pawn in Patricia's relentless syndrome,
But Ana's strength, though tested, never broke,
She bore the pain, her spirit woke.

Strangled, suffocated, drowning's cold embrace,
Ana faced her torment, held an inner grace,
In dark streets she sought refuge and relief,
Away from a mother's torment and her grief.

Her journey was a tale of will and might,
A young girl's fight to emerge from night,
Seeking love and care where shadows cease,
To replace the darkness with a lasting peace.

Ana's resilience, a beacon, shining bright,
Against the darkest hours of Patricia's night,
A longing for a life where love would soar,
Ana's tale, a testament to strength, and more.

Through the shadowed halls of pain and strife,
Ana fought to reclaim her own life,
Patricia's darkness, she'd finally outgrow,
As towards the light, her spirit began to glow.

With every step on the streets of despair,
Ana carried a burden, a weight she'd bear,
But in her heart, a spark of hope remained,
A renewed strength that could not be restrained.

The courtroom battles, the scars she'd wear,
Ana faced each challenge with a steadfast stare,
Her determination, an unyielding flame,
To break free from Patricia's cruel game.

In the heart of Watts, beneath the moon's soft gleam,
Ana's resilience grew like a mighty stream,
She learned that love was not just a dream,
But a force that could mend, like a soothing cream.

As time passed by, Ana's light did shine,
Her courage and grace, like aged wine,
In college halls, her knowledge did grow,
With dreams of a future, a brighter tomorrow.

She chose to study the art of the heart,
To heal wounds of others, to play her part,
Innocence lost, but compassion remained,
Ana's heart, a fortress, love unconstrained.

Patricia, too, faced a reckoning day,
Her heart and soul took a different way,
Seeking redemption for the pain she'd sown,
A chance to change, her past disowned.

In a world where darkness once held sway,
Ana and Patricia found a new day,
Forgiveness, a bridge from past to now,
Their story, a testament, a sacred vow.

In the shadowed halls where Patricia once stood,
A tale of redemption, of hope understood,
Ana's strength, like a guiding warm glow,
Guiding them both towards a brighter tomorrow.

They never spoke after that day for Patricia
Continued her wicked ways
Ana moved on with her life never to look back
She stayed on track with a forgiving heart she left her mark

With hope in her eyes, she broke free form the pain
She learned that life is a never ending game
Make the right moves stay on the right path
You will win in the end.

ENDING FOR

I Got a Story to Tell, Tale, Tail

As we come to the end of *I Got a Story to Tell, Tale, Tail*, I want to take a moment to thank you, the storyteller, for embarking on this journey with me. Every word you've written, every memory you've unearthed, and every emotion you've poured onto the page has brought you one step closer to finding and owning your unique voice. Your story matters.

Remember, the stories we tell shape the legacy we leave behind. They are the bridge between who we are and who we aspire to be. By sharing your truth—whether it's fictional, raw, humorous, or heartfelt—you are giving others the gift of connection and inspiration.

But this is just the beginning. This book was created not only to guide you through the process of storytelling but to encourage you to continue writing your story in the workbook and journal that accompanies this book. These tools are designed to help you dive deeper, refine your voice, and capture your thoughts in an organized and meaningful way.

If you're ready to take your storytelling to the next level, I invite you to join our class with the Creative Love Network. Together, we'll explore the art of storytelling, sharpen your writing skills, and help you discover the power of your own creativity.

So, my friend, keep writing. Keep sharing. Keep creating. The world needs your voice, your vision, and your story. Thank you for trusting me to walk alongside you on this creative journey.

With gratitude and encouragement,
Andrea Lee (Coach A. Lee)
Creative Love Network

Your Story Awaits

The page is blank, yet full of light,
A canvas ready, pure and white.
With every word, your soul takes flight,
Your story's yours—go write, ignite.
A tale of laughter, love, and pain,
Of sunny days and pouring rain.
Each twist and turn, loss and gain,
A legacy born through joy and strain.
The power's yours, within your hand,
To build new worlds or understand.
The truths you've hidden, bold or grand,
Now rise like waves upon the sand.
So thank you, writer, for your start,
For daring to explore your heart.
Your voice, your story, is pure art,
The world awaits the tales you'll chart.
With journal close and workbook near,
Let courage guide you, shed your fear.
The Creative Love Network is here,
To help your voice ring strong and clear.
Your journey's begun; it has no end,
A storyteller, my dear friend.
So take this gift, the time to mend,
And let your words inspire, transcend.

About the Author: Coach A. Lee

Creative Love Network proudly presents Andrea Lee, affectionately known as Coach A. Lee, a dynamic and passionate leader dedicated to inspiring others through the transformative power of storytelling, creativity, and self-love. With over 20 years of experience in social services, A. Lee is a versatile professional who has made her mark as a writer, poet, life coach, chef, and educator.

As the author of several acclaimed books, including the *Power to Change the Way You Love Yourself* series—whose first book, *10 Life-Changing Steps to Self-Love*, won the prestigious **International Impact Book Award**—*Feelings of Love, Courage & Betrayal*, and *Connections Between Us*, A. Lee's work resonates deeply with readers worldwide. She extends her creative reach to young minds with her children's series, *Cooking with Little Chef Lee & The Culinary Kids*, blending her storytelling prowess with her culinary expertise to educate and inspire.

In addition to her literary accomplishments, A. Lee is the President of the Los Angeles Poet Society, where she fosters a love of poetry and creative expression within her community. She is also one of the driving forces behind Creative Love Network, an organization that merges education and entertainment to empower individuals through workshops, performances, and artistic exploration.

A proud mother of four and grandmother, A. Lee's personal journey of overcoming challenges and finding her voice serves as the foundation for her mission to help others embrace their stories and their power. Her work is a testament to resilience, creativity, and the healing magic of self-expression.

In *I Got a Story to Tell, Tale, Tail*, Coach A. Lee combines her passion for writing with her unwavering belief in the power of self-expression, creating a guide that inspires, heals, and empowers storytellers from all walks of life. Through her award-winning books, transformative workshops, and leadership at Creative Love Network, A. Lee continues to make a lasting impact, one story at a time.

About the Publisher: Creative Love Network

Creative Love Network is a Southern California based poetry and live performance organization that utilizes spoken word and the arts as a means to entertain audiences, deliver targeted messages and positively impact communities. The company is rooted in the understanding that words, whether they are spoken, sang, read or heard, have the power to change lives and shape the world.

The Creative Love Network's Four Pillars — foundational company principles and affirmations — are:

Love:

I will love myself and others, and I will do things out of love.

Organize:

I will organize my life, and I will seek order over chaos.

Value:

I will value the whole of me, and I will see the value in others.

Evolve:

I will evolve into a better me, and I will always work to improve as a person.

I believe that when I LOVE, ORGANIZE, VALUE & EVOLVE,
I am doing my part to make the world a better place.

L.O.V.E.

CreativeLoveNetwork.com

www.ingramcontent.com/pod-product-compliance
Lightning Source LLC
Chambersburg PA
CBHW070408310726
48977CB00003B/601